KOMPROMAT

ALSO BY STANLEY JOHNSON

FICTION
Gold Drain
Panther Jones for President
The Urbane Guerilla
The Marburg Virus [republished as *The Virus*]
Tunnel
The Commissioner
The Doomsday Deposit
Dragon River
Icecap [republished as *The Warming*]

MEMOIR
Stanley, I Presume
Stanley, I Resume

KOMPROMAT

STANLEY JOHNSON

A Point Blank Book

First published by Point Blank, an imprint of Oneworld Publications Ltd, 2017

This paperback edition published 2018

Copyright © Stanley Johnson 2017

The moral right of Stanley Johnson to be identified as the Author of this work has been asserted by him in accordance with the Copyright, Designs, and Patents Act 1988

ISBN 978-1-78607-414-0
eISBN 978-1-78607-247-4

Typeset by Hewer Text UK Ltd, Edinburgh
Printed and bound in Great Britain by Clays Ltd, St Ives plc

Oneworld Publications Ltd
10 Bloomsbury Street
London WC1B 3SR
England

Stay up to date with the latest books,
special offers, and exclusive content from
Oneworld with our monthly newsletter

Sign up on our website
oneworld-publications.com

To my grandchildren

KOMPROMAT

AUTHOR'S NOTE

Kompromat is, to use an old-fashioned term, An Entertainment.

Although the book borrows from recent events, it is a very loose borrowing, being self-evidently a work of fiction and satire, and not a work of history – an antidote to the maxim that truth is stranger than fiction. Readers of this novel should not conclude in any way that any living person misbehaved in the manner that some of the characters in the book regrettably seem to have done.

CHAPTER ONE

Jack Varese, winner of the most recent Best Actor Oscar, was late. Very late. Sitting in the front row of the celebrity audience in St Petersburg's famous Mariinsky Theatre, Russia's long-serving president, Igor Popov, muttered to an aide, 'Where the devil is he? We're going to have to start without him.'

Popov glanced across the aisle to where the German chancellor, Helga Brun, stared stony-faced at the empty stage in front of her. Next to her was China's prime minister, Liu Wang-Ji, and next to him in the VIP line-up came India's prime minister, Nawab Singh.

President Popov was about to go up onto the stage himself to explain the delay when there was a sudden commotion in the wings.

The loud speakers burst into life. 'Ladies and Gentlemen, the guest of honour, Jack Varese, has arrived and will address the gathering.'

'So sorry,' the American began. 'We were delayed by headwinds on the way over from New York so we had to refuel in Helsinki. Guess I should have flown Aeroflot after all! Or else Ron Craig here could have brought me in his Boeing. But, hell, I like to fly my own plane!'

Jack beckoned Craig up onto the stage. 'This is a man who wants to help save the world's tigers. So I said to him. "Welcome aboard, Ron. Your help is sorely needed. President Popov needs your help." So that's why we're all here. To support the World Tiger Conservation Action Plan, which President Popov has launched tonight.'

1

Within a few moments Jack had them eating out of his hand. Popov sat back in his chair and relaxed.

This World Tiger Summit had been very much Popov's own initiative. A passionate outdoors man, he liked nothing better than to be photographed bare-chested in field and forest, preferably with a hunting rifle in his hand. Of course, there were some animals he didn't shoot and the fabled Amur tiger was one of them. There were still a good number of these magnificent beasts left in the wild, way out there in the Russian Far East. Some of them indeed were so far to the east that they sometimes crossed the Ussuri River and strayed into Chinese territory. The previous day, in a tête-a-tête with Liu Wang-Ji, Popov had said, 'You may have killed and skinned all your own tigers, Mr President, but kindly keep your hands off ours!'

When it was Popov's turn to speak he kept his remarks short.

'Today, ladies and gentlemen, we are adopting a World Tiger Action Plan. Yes, there are 450 Amur tigers left in Russian Siberia; yes, there are maybe 3,000 tigers in India; yes, there are tigers in Cambodia, Vietnam, Thailand, Myanmar, Bangladesh and so on. But, believe me, those tiger populations will be extinct unless we take action now.'

Later that evening the presidents and prime ministers of the tiger 'range states', whom Popov had personally invited to St Petersburg, gathered for dinner in the glittering splendour of the Winter Palace.

Edward Barnard, MP and Secretary of State for the Environment, found himself, by some quirk of protocol, sitting next to the German chancellor.

Barnard, an outdoor man himself, was full of praise for the way Popov had handled the event. 'I thought he would just look in and out of the meeting, but he put in three full days. He must really care. And he had some kind words for Europe; he acknowledged the help we have given with his tigers' cause.'

Brun laughed. 'Don't believe everything he says. Our people in Moscow tell me that he's absolutely furious. He thinks we've backed Russia into a corner. From Popov's point of view, we've been running after the Ukraine the way a dog runs after a bitch on heat. We've been expanding NATO right up to Russia's border. We've imposed sanctions over Crimea. I admit we have seen one side of President Popov tonight, the rather pleasant side, but I can't help feeling we are going to see another side very soon. Popov is planning something big. Very big. You mark my words.'

The guests all rose to their feet as President Popov stood up to leave the splendid dining-hall to the sound of trumpets.

Jack, very much recovered from the long journey and its various mishaps, worked the room glass in hand, moving from table to table like a politician running for office.

It wasn't long before he took Barnard's hand and shook it warmly. When Barnard introduced himself, Jack commented: 'So you're the leader of the UK delegation. Secretary of State for the Environment. That's a great handle to have.'

'We may not have any tigers. But the British government wants to make it clear we fully approve of President Popov's initiative.'

Jack laughed. 'Maybe that'll distract him and he'll forget about invading the Baltic States.'

Seconds later, President Popov himself stopped at Barnard's table. He was, Barnard guessed, around five eight in height, a trifle less perhaps. Thinning hair, carefully brushed back to cover a bald spot.

Barnard bowed his head instinctively. This was the Russian head of state. Whatever you might feel about the man, you had to respect the office he held.

A lavishly decorated aide hovered at Popov's side. The president had obviously been well-briefed.

'Please thank your government for the support they are giving to the World Tiger Action Plan,' Popov told Barnard. 'We very much appreciate it. I hope one day soon to come to London to show my appreciation in person.'

As the presidential party moved on, Barnard muttered to himself, 'Dream on!' Reaching for another drink, he found it hard to imagine that Popov would be making a state visit to Britain any time soon. Not in the current climate.

The party began to break up. The limousine was waiting to take him back to his hotel. Sinking back into the plush leather seat of the sleek, black 3-litre BMW that the authorities had made available for the VIP guests, Barnard took his phone from his pocket.

Although some of his fellow Cabinet ministers had joshed that his trip to Russia was a mere jolly, there was after all some important news to convey to the authorities back home. He had absolutely no doubt that, in their separate ways, both the Russian president and the German chancellor had hoped that he, as Secretary of State for the Environment, would convey a message to London, and he was delighted to be able to do so.

How things had changed in Russia over the last few years, he thought. In the big cities at least, it was all bling and gizmos. Wi-Fi was everywhere. Even in a moving car twenty miles outside St Petersburg you could pick up a signal, which was more than could be said for some of the outlying areas of London. Barnard began to tap out his message.

Not far away, at the FSB – the Federal Security Service of the Russian Federation – control centre on Cherniavski Street, Fyodor Stephanov, a tall, broad-shouldered man with a scar on his right cheek, picked up Barnard's message almost as soon as it had been sent.

He printed off a flimsy and walked quickly into the next room where his superior took one look at the text.

'Not even encrypted! Not even the lowest level! What do they take us for?'

He handed the flimsy back to the duty officer. 'You'd better get going,' he said. 'Pass the word. And make sure the women know what to do.'

Stephanov rubbed his hands and smiled. 'They know all right.' In due course, he would be well paid for the video he would offer for sale on the now well-developed market for such material. He always welcomed a little freelance action. He was saving up for that Baltic cruise with his new girlfriend.

CHAPTER TWO

Barnard glanced at his watch as he got out of the car at the Kempinski Hotel. 10:30P.M. St Petersburg time. The night was still young. In London it would be two hours earlier.

He paused for a moment to pick up his key from reception – one of the new-fangled plastic card affairs he rather disliked – and headed for the bar.

Ron Craig, the large, sandy-haired American who sat there with a glass of bourbon in front of him, had one of the most famous faces on American television. He hosted a panel show watched by millions. He was also running for president.

'Great to see you, Mr Craig,' Barnard introduced himself. 'I saw you at the dinner, but you were tied up with President Popov and we didn't have time to talk.'

Craig laughed. 'That Popov! He's quite a guy.' He heaved himself out of his chair and slapped Barnard on the back. 'Did you meet Rosie? Rosie's my daughter. She's passionate about wildlife. But she's also my right-hand man, if you see what I mean. Say hello to Rosie.'

Barnard made a gallant little bow in the direction of the slim and lovely young woman sitting in a plush upholstered seat beside her father.

'Oh, I'm so glad to meet you properly, Mr Barnard,' she said. 'I was stuck next to that Chinese gentleman at dinner and I couldn't understand a word.'

'Rosie's flying with us to the Ussuri tomorrow in Jack's plane,' her father added. 'You're coming too, Jack says. That's great. God knows where we're going to land.'

Barnard pulled up a chair. 'I'm just so pleased we were able to fix this up. I've seen tigers in India, I've seen tigers in Bangladesh, but it's been one of my dreams to see a Siberian tiger in the wild. I told the prime minister that I wasn't coming all the way to Russia to a tiger conference, and then passing up the chance to actually get out in the field to see one.'

'It's going to be tough, isn't it? Cold too?' Rosie looked a bit glum.

'Don't you worry,' Craig patted his daughter on the arm. 'They'll have tents and a campfire. It will do you good. Do us all good.'

Craig slapped his tummy. 'I could lose a few pounds, and a hike will help. Actually, it's happening anyway. If you hit the campaign trail in an American presidential election, you've got to work your socks off. We're not over the top yet. The contest may go all the way to the convention, but I'll tell you something: there's no way in hell that *this* train is going to be stopped.'

Barnard was intrigued. More than intrigued. Impressed. In the UK, even now, when he was virtually home and dry, people were reluctant to take Craig's presidential campaign seriously. All that tweeting. All that tub-thumping, the bombast and the rhetoric. They seemed to think the style of the man was wrong. That it wasn't the way presidential candidates ought to behave. And apart from the style, there was the content of the message. 'Build the Wall!' 'Drain the Swamp!' 'Lock her up!' Strong meat indeed. Too strong for tender stomachs.

But with Craig standing proud and manly before him, haloed in a swirl of feral testosterone, Barnard could see how charismatic he might be to a certain type of voter.

How had Craig found the time to come to St Petersburg? Barnard found himself wondering a few minutes later, once the aura of the powerful man had dropped a notch or two. What kind of business did he have with President Popov that was important enough for him to take a break from campaigning at this crucial stage?

Twenty minutes later, Barnard headed for the lift. He felt decidedly woozy. Don't mix the grain and the grape, his father had always told him. Well, he'd had a lot of wine at the dinner, and several large tots of whisky sitting there in the Kempinski Bar. They were heading for the airport early the next morning for the long flight to Russia's Far East. He hoped to hell his head had cleared by then.

Two young and glamorous Russian women dressed to the nines and wafting clouds of expensive perfume drifted across the hotel foyer to join him as he waited for the lift.

Barnard had noticed them earlier, sitting at a neighbouring table in the bar.

'Good evening, ladies,' Barnard said in what he hoped was a debonair manner. 'Going up too? I'm heading for the eighth floor.'

The two Russian women allowed their lips to curve into what – in this dim light – might almost pass for a smile. 'Eighth floor. Yes, that is good floor for us too,' they purred.

'All aboard then,' Barnard hiccoughed as the doors opened. 'Eighth it is!'

CHAPTER THREE

One of the reasons – indeed possibly the principal reason – Jack had bought the Gulfstream 550 was that he liked to fly it himself. It wasn't just a question of keeping up his flying hours, though with the hectic schedule he led that was always a consideration.

What he loved above all was being alone with his thoughts. Okay, his was one of the world's most famous faces. Quite apart from his latest Oscar, he had starred in a score of movies that had been box-office successes. Women threw themselves at him. Over the years the glamour magazines had speculated about the possible outcome of the many 'relationships' with beautiful women that Jack had pursued, but none of them, so far as the Hollywood gossip-mill knew, had come to anything.

The truth of the matter was that Jack liked to keep his private life private. Was he looking for a soulmate? Someone who, like him, believed that the world's wild places needed to be preserved? If he was, he wasn't saying, not even to himself.

On that particular late April morning, as the Gulfstream 550 took off from St Petersburg's Pulkovo Airport, Jack was looking forward to some uninterrupted 'quality time' at the controls. In fact, since the distance, airport to airport, between St Petersburg and Khabarovsk in Russia's Far East was around 4,000 miles, and since the Gulfstream 550 could cruise comfortably at 40,000 feet at around 600 mph, Jack reckoned that he had at least seven hours ahead of him to reflect on the state of Planet Earth.

And they wouldn't have to refuel. The Gulfstream 550 had a range of 6,700 nautical miles. Hell, Jack thought, if the airport at Khabarovsk was closed because of fog or snow storm conditions, as it sometimes was apparently, they would have easily enough fuel to head for Petropavlovsk-Kamchatsky or even Vladivostok.

As it happened, the weather that morning was perfect. Sometimes when flying at 40,000 feet all Jack could see were the clouds below, but the control tower at Pulkovo gave the forecast as they cleared the plane for take-off.

'You've got good weather all the way to Khabarovsk, Mr Varese,' the tower said.

As he taxied to the end of the runway, Jack noted that the Russian presidential plane, an Ilyushin Il-96, and Russia's own equivalent of Air Force One, was still parked on the tarmac, surrounded by armed guards. There was a bowser next to the plane. It looked as though they had just finished refuelling. Was President Popov still in St Petersburg? Was he about to depart? If so, where was he heading? Moscow? Somewhere else? Did the presidential plane have to file a flight plan? And if someone did file a flight plan, would anyone seriously believe them?

Nowadays, Jack reflected, there was no way of telling what was true and what was false. There were facts and there were 'alternative facts'. Take your pick. In fact, he was often amazed at what was reported about himself, always with the 'collaboration' of a mysterious 'friend' or 'close confidante'. Apparently, so Jack had heard, the Russians had whole cities out there somewhere in the tundra inventing stories, which they then leaked to the media, or somehow planted in the Twittersphere. Black could quite literally become white, and sometimes without even any intervening shades of grey.

Before he acquired his own private jet, Jack as an ordinary, if much cosseted, passenger had flown over Russia a good many times. Scudding high over the vast expanses of the former Soviet Union was often by far the quickest route from A to B where, for example, A was London and B was Tokyo. In fact, if you took the polar route between those two cities you could spend a large proportion of your journey time over Russia, staring down at those vast expanses of forest, snow and ice.

The Gulfstream 550 comfortably accommodated eight passengers and four crew. Two hours into the flight, with the plane on autopilot, Jack clicked on the tannoy.

'Hello, everyone. I hope you're all enjoying this as much as I am. We're taking a modified, great circle route to our destination today, which means we're actually going north as well as east. In fact, if you look out now on the port side of the aircraft you can see the Arctic Ocean. Don't all rush at once or you may tip the plane over! Anyone want to come up front? I've got a spare seat here, although I'm afraid you'll have to leave your drinks behind.'

Craig, sitting in the spacious lounge, immediately beckoned to one of the stewards. 'I'd like to go up front for a while. Can you ask Jack if Rosie can come too?'

'I'm sure that won't be a problem, sir, but I'll check.'

Moments later, the steward returned. 'Mr Varese says to go on up.'

Jack was sitting on the left, so Craig took the right-hand seat in the cockpit. He gazed out at white expanses below.

'By God, look at that ice! Stretches as far as the eye can see, doesn't it?'

'Not half as far as it used to,' Jack replied. 'The ice-free area is getting bigger and bigger.'

Craig pricked up his ears. 'Does that mean commercial ships will soon be able to use these waters year round? Heck, that could be terrific business, couldn't it? You could run cargo from Europe to the Far East without going round Africa and half of Asia. What kind of time frame are we talking about? Roll on global warming! Let's make it happen. I reckon there's a deal to be made here. Did you ever read my book, Jack? *The Real Deal.* A bestseller in six continents, if you count Antarctica.'

'I didn't know penguins can read, dad,' Rosie piped up from her seat in the rear of the cockpit.

'My kind of penguins can. Here, Rosie, you take my seat. I want to go finish my drink.' He got up and Rosie joined Jack.

'It's hard to know whether to take your father seriously, isn't it?' Varese said after a short silence.

'My father's always serious,' Rosie replied. 'If he says he's going to do something, he does it.'

'Like doing a deal with the Russians to open up the Arctic with a spot more global warming?'

'Never underestimate my dad,' Rosie said.

Jack was intrigued. Rumour had it that Rosie Craig was one of the key assets in the vast Ron Craig business. Apparently, Craig listened to her as much as he listened to anyone, and whole sectors of Craig's empire were under her direct control. The Craig name was blazoned on hotels and skyscrapers, and Rosie had a decisive say in the management. Craig's media interests were large and constantly expanding as he purchased newspapers and TV stations around the world.

The plane was flying on autopilot, and would continue to do so for the next few hours. There was a theory that planes actually flew better without human intervention. You had pilotless cars and so why not pilotless planes, Jack had thought to himself on more than one occasion.

He took off his headphones and turned to the young woman sitting in the co-pilot's seat. As the spring sunlight glinted through the window, highlighting the streaks in her expensively styled hair, and catching the shine of her lip gloss, he could only think to himself that, Christ, she was beautiful! The full lips, the swept-back blonde hair, the flawless, pure-marble skin. Something Slavic in the cheekbones surely?

'Here, let me take the head-piece from you, Rosie. It'll get in the way,' he said.

The cabin door behind them was shut. The Gulfstream 550 had a battery of mechanisms to bar unauthorized entry into the cockpit. You would have to literally break down the door to get in from the outside.

Rosie knew what was about to happen. She had known it all along. Was it destiny? Karma? Some mystic happening long preordained?

She – and thousands of young women no doubt – had lusted after Jack Varese for years. None of them had got to within a stone's throw of their target. Poor them. Lucky her! Here she was, daughter of one of the richest men in the world, alone, 40,000 feet in the air and right beside her was Jack Varese, probably the world's most famous actor.

It was a script made in heaven. 'Are we allowed to do this, Jack?'

'It's my plane. I have control,' Jack said.

With the plane on auto-pilot and the cabin door locked, he leaned over to kiss her. He had kissed enough women in his time but oddly enough he had never kissed one in the cockpit of his own plane flying high over Russia.

Just at that moment, as though on cue, the cabin alarm rang. An automated voice said, 'You are being followed by an unidentified aircraft.'

Jack quickly sat up straight and put his headphones back on. Rosie did the same. The Gulfstream was fitted with cameras angled all around outside. Jack switched on the display in front of him.

The automated voice said insistently, 'Closing, closing.'

Although all looked normal and he couldn't see anything untoward, Jack felt the first stirrings of alarm. What was happening?

He switched on the intercom. 'Ladies and gentlemen, we seem to have quite a situation here. It appears that we are being followed by someone and that this someone is closing on us fairly fast.'

He turned to face Rosie. 'You need to return to your seat, but could you ask Terry to come up?'

Terry Caruthers was the co-pilot. However much Jack liked flying the plane himself, it made a lot of sense to have a co-pilot on board, particularly on these long flights. As a matter of fact, having a co-pilot was probably a requirement of the US aviation authority, though he hadn't checked this recently.

Moments later Terry slipped into the co-pilot seat. Jack jabbed the screen in front of him with his finger.

'Whatever plane that is, it's about twenty miles behind us right now, but it's going a lot faster than we are.'

The blob on the screen was obvious.

'Course seems to be precisely the same as ours, doesn't it?' Jack said. 'Shall I push up the speed a bit?'

'Why not?' Terry drawled. 'Seems like we have a race on our hands. This should be fun, shouldn't it?'

'Mach 0.85?'

'We can do better than that,' Terry said.

They felt the engine surge. The Gulfstream 550 could cruise comfortably at 600 miles or 0.8 Mach but the specifications clearly indicated that speeds right up to 0.9 Mach or around 700 mph were possible.

'What the hell is that?' Jack turned his head to the right a minute or so later. Flying alongside him, less than a hundred yards away, was the sleek, dark Ilyushin Il-96 that he had noted earlier that day at St Petersburg's Pulkovo airport.

The other plane was close enough for him to see the pilot. 'Jesus Christ!' Varese exclaimed. 'I think it's Popov. What's he playing at?'

'When you're president of Russia, you can break all the rules you like, I guess,' Terry replied. 'You make 'em, you break 'em!'

Jack pressed the zoom switch. The huge grinning face of President Popov suddenly appeared on the screen in front of them.

'You guys oughta get yourselves a faster plane,' the president's voice came over the intercom.

Even though the two planes were still 200 yards apart, they could feel the shockwave of the Ilyushin's afterburners.

Jack grasped the joystick, disconnecting the autopilot. He eased back the throttle.

This was a race he clearly wasn't going to win.

Speaking into the intercom, he said, 'I think President Popov is having some fun with his latest toy, ladies and gentlemen. You had better make sure your seat belts are fastened. If our friend decides to take it up to Mach One, we're likely to experience some buffeting.'

And that was exactly what Popov did. The Ilyushin's precise performance data were not described, not least in any publication that Jack knew of. But it was perfectly obvious that breaking the sound barrier was well within its capabilities.

Over the tannoy, they heard the president's cheerful comment, 'See you when you arrive. I'll make sure the drinks are waiting!'

Jack could imagine the president giving them a mock salute as he roared ahead and away from them.

It took a while for the buffeting to subside.

Terry, who had served ten years with the USAF before taking up a career as a civilian pilot, broke the silence. 'There are people in Washington who will be quite intrigued to hear about what we saw today.'

There was a knock on the door. Craig poked his head into the cockpit.

'You guys all right?' he said cheerily. 'That was quite something, wasn't it?'

CHAPTER FOUR

It was dark when they landed in Khabarovsk after the long flight from St Petersburg. A helicopter waited on the runway to transport them to the camp at the junction of the Amur and Ussuri Rivers.

The accommodation was not luxurious, but the huts that had been built in a clearing in the forest were sturdy and clean.

'This is a research facility, not a tourist site,' the bearded official who greeted them had explained gruffly. 'We are monitoring tiger movements. We also safeguard the tigers. We will leave tomorrow morning at 8:00A.M. Please have your breakfast first.'

Someone banged on Barnard's door as dawn was breaking.

He dressed quickly. Thick trousers and a tough jacket. Strong boots. They might start off in vehicles, but if they were following tiger spore, he reckoned they would probably spend most of the day on foot. At least the Russian *taiga* – those vast birch forests which covered so much of the country out here in the Russian Far East – weren't as thick and impenetrable as, say, some of the rainforests in the Congo or Southeast Asia.

How lucky he was, he thought, to have a job that took him to some of the most far-flung corners of the world. And you couldn't be much more remote than the Ussuri-Amur triangle, that corner of land where China and Russia meet.

What a pity, he thought, that his wife Melissa wasn't with him. They had been married for over twenty years but he still missed her whenever she wasn't there. Oddly enough, one of the last trips they had taken together had actually been to Russia's Far East. They had gone on a trekking holiday on the Kamchatka Peninsula.

They had been lucky then. The rivers were in spate and the great brown bears could be seen feasting on the salmon. The guides carried guns, of course. As any fool knew, you didn't want to get between a bear and its lunch. You didn't want to get in the way of the men with the guns either. Accidents could – and did – happen.

Barnard had slept well. The effect of whatever it was he had consumed that last night in the hotel in St Petersburg had finally worn off. What on earth could it have been?

He must have gone out like a light, as the last thing he remembered was pushing the button in the lift and the heady scent of the two Russian women standing next to him. Maybe he had just had too much to drink, what with all the toasts at the dinner in the Winter Palace, followed by whatever it was he had drunk at the bar in the Kempinski. If Melissa had been there, she might have seen the warning signs.

They breakfasted sitting around the campfire. Steaming mugs of coffee, pickled eggs, slices of thick brown bread.

Halfway through the meal, they heard the thud-thud-thud of the helicopter. It landed in a clearing fifty yards from the campsite. Moments later, President Popov jumped down and strode over.

Clad in battle fatigues, with a hunting cap pushed far back on his head, he held out his hand for the rifle. The gruff ranger had already explained that weapons were always carried with tigers around.

'Good morning, friends. I hope you are not too tired after your journey.' Popov smiled at them as he ostentatiously hefted the weapon. He turned to Jack with a smirk on his face. 'I got into Khabarovsk in time for a good night's sleep before coming over here this morning.'

Three UAZ-469 Patriot Jeeps were waiting for them, engines throbbing quietly. The UAZ-469 had long been the staple off-road vehicle for Russian police and military units. Connoisseurs rated it as sturdier and more reliable than the Land Rover or Land Cruiser.

The vehicles were painted dark green and bore the logo of the Russian Federation's National Park Service.

Popov, still carrying his rifle, got into the lead vehicle. He beckoned to Barnard. 'Come and join me.'

Barnard hadn't realized until then just how good Popov's English was. He knew that Popov was meant to be fluent in German, having served as the head of the KGB's Dresden office in former East Germany, but Barnard – in common with most other observers – was quite unaware of the extent of Popov's proficiency in other languages.

'What we are planning to do this morning,' Popov explained, 'is to collar a tiger. The Park Service here has set up a tiger-monitoring programme. We want to know how many tigers there are, where they live, what they eat, as well as the pattern of their day-to-day movements. This latter point is particularly important. We believe we are losing significant numbers of tigers, as many as twenty a year, because they cross the river into China. And God knows what happens to them there.'

Popov corrected himself. 'Actually we do know. As I mentioned to the Chinese president back in St Petersburg, the Chinese kill and eat them. Or else they grind up their bones into powder and sprinkle it on their soup as an aphrodisiac. Pah! Real men don't need aphrodisiacs.'

As they drove off along the track into the forest, Popov continued, 'Sergei here' – he gestured to the driver – 'found a recent kill yesterday, about twenty kilometres from where we are now. He was tracking a tiger on foot when he came across the carcass of a deer. Quite a large animal actually, probably a Siberian musk deer. The tiger had obviously had a go at the deer, because most of the haunch had been eaten. Sergei reckons there's a good chance the tiger will be coming back for a second helping.'

The driver said something in Russian which Barnard didn't understand. Popov turned to Barnard. 'Looking at the spoor, he thinks it may be a large male.'

After about an hour, they pulled into a clearing in the forest. The four rangers who had been riding in a support vehicle clustered round the president. Then one of them stepped forward and addressed the party.

'My name is Ivan. I'm the head ranger here. Our plan today is to shoot a tiger. Of course, we are not going to kill it. We're going to dart it. We are happy that President Popov himself is here with us this morning. He is a very good shot.'

'He better be,' Craig muttered. 'I'm not sure I could outrun a tiger, not nowadays. Though there was a time when I could do a hundred yards in almost ten seconds!'

Popov laughed. 'We don't doubt it, Ron. And I can do a thousand push-ups!'

The president was in a jovial mood. 'How's the campaign going?'

'They're gagging for me. By the time we get to the convention, it's going to be a coronation, not a contest.' Craig laughed.

Barnard listened to this brief exchange with some interest. It was obvious that there was a strong rapport between Popov and Craig. What was it based on? he wondered. Was it just friendly, good fellowship, mutual camaraderie, or was there something more? He knew that Craig had huge assets in Russia and he imagined that his ambitions were wider still. Why else should he be spending so much time in this country?

However, if Craig had huge assets in Russia, did he have huge liabilities too? Barnard had heard on the grapevine that US banks were a bit wary of Craig, having been burned once or twice before in their dealings with the famous showman-cum-entrepreneur. Some of the key European banks had been similarly reluctant to lend large sums. But the Russians had stepped into the breach in a big way, or so it seemed. Maybe they were trying to hug Craig close, to make sure he didn't do the dirty on them.

It was time to go. Popov stubbed out his cigarette.

Thirty minutes later, as they followed the track deeper into the forest, Craig wasn't feeling quite so light-hearted. The tiger, he knew, is basically one of nature's finest killing machines and he wasn't sure he wanted to be within spitting distance.

Two rangers, armed with rifles, led the way, with Popov half a step behind them. They were followed by the small party of non-Russians: Craig and his daughter Rosie, Jack, and Barnard. Two more rangers, guns at the ready, brought up the rear.

If a tiger was going to hunt them, he or she would attack from any direction. There was no way of telling. The undergrowth was thick, so it would be easy for the hunters to become the hunted.

They proceeded in total silence. Once or twice, a ranger gestured. 'Pugmark,' he would whisper. 'Quite fresh. Less than hour old.'

'Oh ho!' Craig said to himself. 'This is where the fun begins.'

He reached for his daughter's hand and gave it an encouraging squeeze.

If her father was already wishing he was anywhere else but there – preferably back in New York in his glittering 40th-floor penthouse – his daughter was in a very different frame of mind. The smells and sounds of the forest were intoxicating. She cared passionately about wild animals. And to be out in the wilds of Siberia tracking an Amur tiger was one of the most exciting things she had done for a long time. The feeling of pure joy she experienced was all the more acute because she sensed that her hero, Jack Varese, felt just the same way.

When they were less than two hundred feet from the site of the kill, the lead ranger held up a warning hand, motioning for them to stay back while he went ahead to reconnoitre. If the tiger was there, still feasting on the dead deer, he would give a signal. This would be the moment for Popov to move forward with a tranquillizer gun, closely escorted by two armed rangers, while the fourth stayed behind with the VIPs.

Once the tiger had been darted, the VIPs would be allowed to approach. The rangers would examine the unconscious animal and record their findings on their hand-held computers. This was the way biologists built up crucial data on wildlife populations. The animal would be collared and fitted with a transmitting device which not only recorded and reported the animal's vital functions but also communicated with overhead satellites. In theory the precise location of the collared animal could be ascertained from then on.

Given the propensity of the Amur tiger to cross the border into China, the ability to keep track of precisely where the tigers were and where they might be heading was particularly important. The Russian rangers hadn't yet devised a system of ensuring that the tigers stayed on Russian soil, but they were working on it.

The previous generation of radio collars had been cumbersome. However carefully they had been fitted, they could be knocked off, or damaged or destroyed, as a tiger went about its day-to-day business. If you were a killing machine, sometimes you had to jump through the air to seize your prey. You might have to crash through the forest in hot pursuit of a deer or even a wolf. The miniaturization of the radio collar into a small subcutaneous implant that sent radio signals on a 24/7 basis into the stratosphere for retransmission to a terrestrial monitoring system had transformed conservation field science.

President Popov had a pocket full of miniature transmitters and he was determined, once he had fired the dart, to do the 'collaring' as well.

Naturally the photographers were primed. Video footage and stills of the president 'shooting' and 'collaring' a tiger would be transmitted worldwide within minutes of the event. If there was any delay, that would probably be because Popov's people back in

Moscow needed a chance to check that the material to be transmitted conformed to, and indeed promoted, the image they wanted to convey of a young, dynamic, daring, adventurous and scientifically up-to-the-minute world leader.

In the event, things didn't go entirely to plan. When the lead ranger went forward to the scene of the kill, he found – as he thought he would – the tiger with its head buried inside the Siberian musk deer's ribcage. From time to time, the tiger raised its muzzle, dripping with blood, before returning to the task of crunching through half an animal in the shortest possible time.

In retrospect, it wasn't clear whether the tiger saw or heard the ranger. Either way, before the ranger had time to signal to Popov to come forward to take his shot, the tiger, with a growl, backed away from the kill.

The ranger raised his rifle.

'Don't shoot!' Popov uttered a short, sharp command. He didn't want a dead tiger on his hands. This was not the kind of publicity he was seeking. Better a dead ranger!

Popov raised the darting gun and, as he did so, the tiger crashed along the path towards them.

Quite how Craig ended up on the ground with a tranquillizing dart sticking out of his backside – while the tiger escaped into the forest none the worse for wear – was, in the confusion of the moment, never totally clear.

One thing that was clear was that Ronald Craig, showman and businessman, not to say possible or indeed probable presidential candidate, was decidedly unhappy.

'What the fu—!' His voice boomed loud in the silence of the forest, hastening the speed of the tiger's retreat.

He groaned and slumped to the ground as the dart's concentrated load of ketamine took hold.

The rangers, trained to deal with just such an eventuality, moved rapidly into action. They couldn't wait for the effect of the drug to wear off. The risk of damage to the heart and sensory systems was very real. A dose of ketamine that could knock out a tiger would very likely be lethal for a man, even a man as large as Craig.

'Mr President, pass me the yellow vial, please,' said one of the rangers.

Taking the vial from Popov's outstretched hand, the ranger looked down at Craig's now prostrate and motionless body, much as a butcher might examine a large side of beef. He made a rapid calculation. No point in injecting the whole dose. More like half the dose, or even a third. Though hefty, Craig certainly didn't weigh as much as a fully grown male Amur tiger.

The ranger squirted a shot of the liquid into the air, to make sure the plunger was properly loaded and ready to go. He shuddered to think of the fate that might befall him if by some freak accident he injected a fatal air bubble into the bloodstream of a man who was one of President Popov's honoured guests.

Removing the hunting jacket from the comatose man, the ranger rolled up Craig's right shirt sleeve so that the upper arm was exposed. He felt for and found the vein. Then, with quick professionalism, he injected a 200mg dose of Tolazoline.

While the rangers kept guard – God only knew where the tiger had gone, although everyone hoped it had gone as far away as it possibly could – Craig gradually regained consciousness.

'Christ, my ass feels sore,' he complained. 'Did someone Taser me?'

'Not exactly.' Popov helped the American to his feet. 'There was a small mishap. We're going to get you to hospital as soon as we can.'

Khabarovsk General Hospital was surprisingly clean and well equipped. Craig was wheeled straight away into the theatre. Seconds later, he was lying face down on the table.

'This will only take a minute,' the surgeon said. 'The dart's made quite a wound. We're going to have to swab and disinfect just to be on the safe side. Give you an anti-tetanus too. You'd be surprised how many germs there are out there in the forest.'

'No, I wouldn't,' Craig mumbled, still drifting in and out of consciousness. 'I'm a germaphobe. You go right ahead.'

'You won't feel a thing,' the surgeon said, 'but we'll give you a little local anaesthetic as well.'

When President Popov visited Craig in Khabarovsk General Hospital that evening, the American was well on the way to total recovery. Happily, he was also ready to see the funny side of things.

'Shot in the ass by the president of Russia. I'm going to tweet.'

'Actually, I'd rather you didn't,' Popov said. When he switched on the television, Craig took the point at once.

In the few hours that had intervened since that unfortunate event in the forest, Russian news channels had been running a brilliantly concocted story. All over the country, viewers had been enjoying the footage of a crouching, then leaping tiger, followed by shots of a bare-chested President Popov firing a hunting rifle with deadly accuracy.

'*President Popov saves US politician-tycoon's life in Ussuri hunting incident*,' the newsreader proclaimed. The fate of the tiger was not specified, but the video was interspersed with a series of clips of Craig and his glamorous family in full campaign mode.

One Russian commentator went so far as to suggest that Craig would not only be chosen as the Republican candidate in July, 'There is a high probability that he will win the presidency itself in the presidential election this November, particularly since Mrs Caroline Mann, the likely Democratic nominee, is immersed in scandal owing to her misuse of official communications facilities while serving as Secretary of State.'

When the broadcast finished, Craig said, 'I'm impressed. It's almost like they had all that in the can and were just waiting to run it. And thanks for the plug.'

'Our journalists are very professional,' Popov said with a straight face. 'They have very high standards of accuracy and objectivity.'

Craig sighed. 'I wish our media was like that. They're all over the place. They lie through their teeth, most of the time. Distort the news. Actually make things up! It's so sad!'

Before he left, Popov turned to Rosie, who was sitting at her father's bedside. 'Don't worry, Rosie. Your father will be all right.'

Rosie didn't quite know what to say. She wasn't angry with Popov. How could you be angry with a man who was trying to save the world's tigers?

'I'm sure Dad will be fine,' she said. 'It would take more than a dart to put him out of action.'

'Tell me about it,' Popov sighed. He'd been dealing with Ronald Craig in one way or another for the best part of a decade. There were times when even he felt he had met his match.

CHAPTER FIVE

Barnard hadn't expected to find himself having dinner with President Popov that evening, but when the message was brought to him in his hotel room overlooking the Amur River in the heart of Khabarovsk, he responded immediately.

'Please tell the president I will be delighted.'

What a peculiar day it had been, Barnard reflected. It had started with the tiger hunt; it was going to end in a tête-à-tête encounter with one of the most powerful men in the world.

Actually, it wasn't quite a one-on-one. Barnard was already sitting at a corner table in the hotel dining room when Popov entered, accompanied by a slim, dark-haired man around forty years of age.

'Let me introduce you to Yuri,' Popov said without preamble. 'Yuri Yasonov. Yuri's been with me a long time. He speaks English better than I do. Went to Oxford. Very classy!'

Popov was clearly in a good mood, and he'd possibly already had a shot of vodka or two. Shooting Ronald Craig in the backside with a tranquilizing dart might also have had something to do with it, Barnard reflected.

The restaurant manager quickly came over to take their orders, bowing and scraping. It wasn't every day that the Russian President dropped by. Security men hovered by the door. What the hell was going on, Barnard wondered?

The waiter brought over a large jar of caviar. 'No shortage of caviar in this part of the world.' Popov laughed. 'The rivers in

Kamchatka are positively leaping with sturgeon.' He waved his hand at Barnard's empty glass. 'More vodka please for my British friend here.'

Back in London, before he left for St Petersburg – how long ago it seemed! – Barnard had had a security briefing.

'Get alongside Popov, if you can,' the MI6 man had said. 'This is a unique opportunity. You're going to be in a totally informal setting. But watch out. Popov served for years as the head of the KGB in East Germany. Recruiting agents, running agents, that's meat and drink to him. Once a spy-master, always a spy-master. He'll never get that out of his system. He may try to recruit you. A British Cabinet minister would be a big fish to land. Be sure to keep us posted.'

Popov didn't beat about the bush. He was a busy man. He would be flying back to Moscow later that night.

'May I call you Edward? You may call me Igor.'

'Thank you,' Barnard replied. 'But I'd feel more comfortable sticking to Mr President. We British are pretty conscious of this sort of thing, and you are a head of state after all.'

'As you wish.' Popov seemed mildly put out, but he rallied quickly. 'Let me put something to you, Edward. When I've finished, you can say yes, you can say no or you can say maybe. But if I were you, I'd say yes.'

For the next half hour Barnard sat there as Popov outlined his proposal. Of course, he didn't come to the punch line – the money shot, as it were – straight away. He put the whole thing in context.

'Frankly, Edward, Russia at this point in time feels very aggrieved. *I* feel aggrieved. We went along with the break-up of the former Soviet Empire, and what did the West do? It tried to ram NATO down our throat. The European Union wooed Ukraine shamelessly. Did you ever look at the so-called EU–Ukraine Treaty? Garbage. Total garbage. For many Russians, Ukraine is still part of our motherland. Can we just sit there while they fire missiles at us from just across the border? But of course we don't want a war. Not with anyone.' Popov laughed. 'Russia's not rich enough to fight a war with the West. That's right, isn't it, Yuri?'

Yasonov nodded. 'That's right, Mr President.' Over years of working closely with President Popov, he had learned that it was always safer to say 'yes' when Popov was in full flow. You could try to row back later if you had to.

'If we fought a war with the West, we'd be outgunned. That's the reality,' Popov continued. He drummed his fingers on the table to emphasize his next point. 'America is sixteen times richer than we are in terms of GDP. We're just a middle-ranking nation. And yet . . . and yet . . .'

Barnard could see the man's eyes misting over. What the hell was coming next, he wondered? Popov was working himself up towards the climax.

'And yet, this is literally the largest country on earth. Even today in its diminished form, without its satellite states, Russia still covers one-sixth of the earth's surface. You saw yesterday when you flew out here how vast this land is. Do you know there are nine time zones between here and Moscow? And think of the culture, the history, the literature, the music, the art and architecture. How the hell do they think they can treat us the way they do? For God's sake this is Russia, the greatest country on earth! How dare they?'

Popov was overcome by a sudden fit of coughing. 'You take it from here, Yuri,' he spluttered. 'I've got to go anyway. Goodbye, Edward. I'm leaving you in good hands.'

As Popov stood up, the 'doughnut' of security guards closed round him. An armoured car would be outside the hotel to convey him to the airport, Barnard was sure. Back in Moscow, the private lift, which served the president's office in the Kremlin, was connected directly to an underground garage. But out here in the boondocks it was a different matter.

Once Popov had gone, Yasonov took up where he had left off.

'You should know, Mr Barnard, that I am speaking with the authority of the president when I say we believe there is a better way ahead for all of us. And at this particular moment in time, we believe that you personally have a key role to play.'

Barnard frowned and gave a small shake of his head.

Yasonov's voice took on a firmer tone. 'Let me be clear. For the last decade or more, you have been one of the leading lights of the so-called "Eurosceptic wing" of the Conservative Party. As I understand it, you have a lot of support among Conservative MPs. In spite of that, or possibly because of that, the UK prime minister Jeremy Hartley, has given you an important job in the British Cabinet.'

'I don't hold one of the "great offices of state". Being head of DEFRA isn't the same as being foreign secretary, home secretary or chancellor of the exchequer,' Barnard countered a trifle nervously.

'Don't sell yourself short. Gennadiy Tikhonov, our ambassador in London, rates you very highly. As he puts it, you're one of the players. What you do matters. It matters a lot.'

Yasonov paused. 'Please think very carefully before you answer my next question. In all your dealings with Jeremy Hartley, what was the single act, the single decision if you like, that most took you by surprise?'

'Oh, that's easy,' Barnard replied in a more assertive tone. 'Wednesday 23 January 2013. The day Prime Minister Jeremy Hartley promised the country an In-Out Referendum on Europe. He was making a speech at the Bloomberg office in London. I listened to it on the radio. I couldn't believe my ears. Speaking personally, I was over the moon. As Eurosceptics, we all were. We had been hoping for something like that – giving the country a say on the UK's membership in the EU after forty years – but we never imagined we'd actually get it. A lot of us went out and got drunk.'

'Why did the announcement of a referendum take you by surprise?'

'Politically speaking, it was quite unnecessary. The government wasn't under any kind of threat. The prime minister wasn't under any kind of pressure, and so at the time, however delighted I might have been in a personal sense, I simply couldn't imagine why he had done it. Of course, Hartley made it clear later on in his speech that he would fight hard – "heart and soul" I think were the very words he used – to ensure that the UK stayed in the EU, but that wasn't the point. The genie was out of the bottle.'

Yasonov pushed a flash drive across the table and, after a pause, Barnard surreptitiously pocketed it.

CHAPTER SIX

The eighteenth-century Kharitonenko Mansion at 14 Sofiyskaya Naberezhnaya, situated on the bank of the Moskva River directly opposite the Kremlin, serves as the residence of the United Kingdom's ambassador to Russia, properly known as the Russian Federation. It is probably one of the most important buildings in Moscow, not only because of its fine construction and setting, but also because of its beautifully crafted, ornate interior.

A recent major overhaul and refurbishment had, so the UK security services hoped, removed the listening devices installed in the post-war years by successive Kremlin regimes. Unfortunately, the renovations had taken much longer than originally anticipated, the delay being due – in part at least – to fears that as the old bugs were being ripped out, new bugs were being installed, even though the workforce, comprising mainly ethnic minorities from Central Asia, operated at all times under close supervision. These fears were almost certainly justified. All ambassadors were officially warned before they moved in to assume that all their conversations in the residence would be routinely bugged.

They were also advised that the residence's domestic staff – cooks, waiters, chauffeurs and so on – would most likely be in the direct pay of the FSB, the successor to the KGB. Even those not actually on the FSB's payroll were, it was to be assumed, able and willing to report to the Russian security services.

Sir Andrew Boles, KBE, KCVO, the current ambassador, was not a man to be put off by minor inconveniences. He had served in Laos and Angola, as well as having spent a stint at the United Nations in New York.

So when his old friend Edward Barnard, MP, arrived for dinner one evening on his way back from the Russian Far East and the now famous tiger encounter, he greeted him with enthusiasm.

'Great to see you, Edward! It's been far too long. Julia's out somewhere playing bridge, and the staff have a night off, but they've left dinner for us, I'm glad to say. Let's go straight up to the small dining room.'

Boles pointed at the ornate ceilings in the entrance hall and the heavy woodcarvings on the stairs and walls; ideal places for eavesdropping devices of whatever sort.

'Ah, the small dining room! Yes, of course!' Barnard took the point quickly.

The two men kept their conversation to the banal as they climbed the stairs to the first floor.

'Pavel Ivanovich Kharitonenko, the man who built this house, was just a peasant when he started, you know,' Boles explained. 'But he became a great sugar magnate. The offices for his sugar factories were here and he decided to build a family mansion here as well.'

As they climbed the grand staircase, Boles continued, 'This mansion has hosted the British Embassy since 1931. Winston Churchill entertained Stalin here during the War. The Queen stayed here. And Princess Diana too.'

'Ah, Princess Diana. What a wonderful woman. What a tragic end.'

Barnard spoke loudly and clearly. If the FSB logged his visit as they certainly would, they would note the sympathy he had shown for the late Princess of Wales. Nothing wrong with that.

The two men only got down to business when they reached their destination on the second floor. 'Small dining room' was a palpable misnomer, since the term was used to refer to a solid, cube-shaped construction, which sat incongruously in the middle of an otherwise empty reception room. The cube was clad in heavy, green material designed, so Barnard assumed, to foil any penetrating radiation.

The ambassador swiped his card and the door swung open. It was, Barnard thought, a bit like a prison cell, and as sparsely equipped; the furniture consisted of a table, four chairs, a jug of water and some glasses.

The room was well lit, but Barnard was intrigued to notice that there were no plugs or sockets of any kind. You can't plant a bug in a socket, he thought, where there aren't any sockets.

'Do you want me to turn off my phone?' he asked. Barnard knew that phones could be used as 'microphones' by distant listeners.

'On or off, it doesn't matter. You're safe in here. You might as well be buried at the bottom of the ocean. The Americans call this a SCIF – a Sensitive Compartmentalized Information Facility. That's their jargon. We just call it our "safe room". Of course, we've got a much bigger one at the Embassy in Smolenskaya Street. We use that for larger gatherings. This one's just for my own personal use as ambassador.'

If Barnard was intrigued, and possibly slightly alarmed, by the degree of precaution the ambassador seemed to be taking before talking to him, he gave no sign of it. He had known Boles a long time. Even though Boles had entered the diplomatic service while Barnard had gone into politics, the two men had often had occasion to meet, socially as well as professionally.

'I need your help, Andrew,' Barnard began. 'As you probably know, I've been lucky enough to spend some time – almost on a one-to-one basis – with President Popov. I saw him at the Tiger Conference in St Petersburg where, I have to say, he performed brilliantly. I saw him again in the Ussuri forest on the tiger hunt, which ended, rather bizarrely with Popov firing a tranquillizing dart into Ron Craig's backside.'

Boles uttered a short, explosive laugh. 'Yes, we heard about that.'

'Well, while Craig was recovering in hospital, Popov and I had a quiet dinner in the hotel. It wasn't just the two of us because Yuri Yasonov was there.'

'Ah, Yuri Yasonov. The power behind the throne.' Boles commented. 'One of the cleverest young men in Russia.'

'He's forty.'

'I still call that young. I wouldn't mind being forty again.'

They got down to business.

Barnard took the flash drive out of his pocket and laid it on the table in front of them. 'I don't want to be caught with this as I go through airport security, either here in Moscow or in London,' he said. 'So I'm just wondering if you could send it on to me in the diplomatic bag.'

'Something hot then?'

'So hot, I'm not sure how to handle it.'

Boles picked up the flash drive. 'You've taken a look at this already, have you? Was that wise?'

'No, I'm sure it wasn't wise, but I couldn't resist it. I stuck the stick in my laptop in my hotel room in Khabarovsk and ran quickly through the files.'

'What do you think you have?'

'Something pretty explosive, to say the least. There's a cache of emails here, some with scanned documents attached. Most of the emails have either been sent to, or sent from, the Office of the Prime Minister in Number 10 Downing Street. They cover the period from October 2012 to around August 2015.'

'What's so significant?'

'The early part of 2013 was precisely when Jeremy Hartley was preparing his Bloomberg speech on Europe.'

'Well, let's take a look,' Boles said.

For the next hour, in the sanctuary of the safe house on the second floor of the Kharitonenko Mansion, Boles and Barnard ran through the documents on the flash drive.

From time to time, Barnard – who had the advantage of having already reviewed the material at his leisure – permitted himself a comment.

'Remember how long it took for Hartley's Bloomberg speech to materialize. Look, here's a memo – dated November 2012 – from the PM's Private Office to the foreign secretary's Private Office. See what Humphrey Smallwood says, and Humphrey, as we all know, as head of the Private Office, doesn't speak without the authority of the PM: "The PM is not, absolutely not, repeat not, inclined to include any kind of a commitment to holding a referendum in his Europe speech".' Barnard continued: 'So one deadline passes, then another. Then suddenly, at the beginning of January 2013, things change.'

He flipped quickly through a series of emails. 'It's not always clear who is writing to whom about what at this point. But what is clear is that something is going on. There are frequent references to "PM's telecon with our friends", whoever "our friends" are. Even though the language is usually very circumspect, there are a couple of emails here, which, in my humble opinion, are quite conclusive. Look at this one.'

Barnard read out the text as it appeared on the screen in front of them: 'Please note that this email is sent to Fred Malkin, Conservative Party chairman. "PM is prepared to settle for latest proposal, so we will aim to include appropriate reference in Bloomberg speech. Our friends are talking in terms of ten million, possibly twelve million pounds".'

'Good heavens!' Boles was beginning to take in the full implications of the material on the flash drive.

'Look at this,' Barnard went on. 'Here's the penultimate draft of the Bloomberg speech. It's dated 14 January. Still nothing about a referendum. Now here's the scanned version of the *final* draft with some manuscript additions. Can you read the handwriting? See what it says. "*That is why I'm in favour of a referendum*". That's Hartley's own addition to the draft speech. And in his very own hand. The text as delivered contains precisely the words Hartley personally added.'

Barnard flipped through a few more slides, then shut the computer down. The screen in front of them went blank.

'The rest is, as they say, history. Once the Bloomberg speech was made, an irrevocable step had been taken. Fifteen months later – in May 2015 – there would be a general election. The Conservative manifesto commitment on the Referendum was even more explicit, as I recall, than the Bloomberg commitment. It committed the Conservative Party, as it sought support in the country, to call an In-Out Referendum on Britain's continued membership of the European Union by 2017.'

'So, no wriggle room there, then,' Boles commented. 'Let's not beat around the bush. You're suggesting that someone offered the Conservative Party a sordid deal. Ten or twelve million pounds up front in exchange for a Referendum commitment in the manifesto. This is "cash for policy" on a grand scale. Why ever would the PM want to take the risk?'

'Was it such a risk?' Barnard countered. 'I think Hartley calculated the Referendum commitment would help the Conservatives, but he never imagined they would get an overall majority at the next election. If the coalition with the Lib Dems continued, as he presumed it would, when the time came he could rely on them to kill the Referendum idea stone-cold dead. So basically it was money for jam. But then, when the Conservatives, to everyone's surprise, won an overall majority, Hartley was stuck with the Referendum commitment and he had to deliver.'

The two men sat in silence as they thought about what had just been said.

The next day, back in London, Barnard stopped briefly at his office to clear his desk and dictate his letter of resignation:

Dear Prime Minister,

With the referendum on the United Kingdom's membership of the European Union now only weeks away, active campaigning about to begin and with the government and you personally being firmly committed to remain in the EU, I feel I have no alternative but to offer my resignation as Secretary of State for Environment, Food and Rural Affairs.

I know you have granted Cabinet members on the Leave side permission to stay in their jobs and even to campaign actively against the government's policy of staying in Europe, but this is not for me. I am a supporter of the Leave camp, and I do not see how it is possible to ride these two horses at once.

I have much enjoyed serving as a member of the government.

Yours, Edward Barnard

He drove down to his Wiltshire constituency later that day. His mobile phone rang incessantly. Finally, he turned it off altogether.

His wife heard the car as the tyres crunched on the gravel. She came out to greet him.

'What on earth has happened, darling? The press has gone mad trying to get hold of you. Apparently you've resigned.'

Barnard gave her a kiss, then hugged her tight. For years Melissa had been his rock and comfort. He needed her now. More than ever.

'Yes, that is so. I should have done it long ago. In spite of what the prime minister said about me being free to campaign on the Leave side, my hands were tied. Official government policy is to remain but now that I've left office, I can do what I like.'

Barnard carried a large cardboard box from the car into the hall. The box contained personal papers from his office, framed photos of his wife and their two, now grown-up, children, and other small items of sentimental value, such as a porcelain polar bear from a famous Danish pottery, which he'd once been presented with when he addressed a conference in Copenhagen.

'I could do with a cup of tea,' he said. 'It's been a long day.'

CHAPTER SEVEN

The Rt. Hon. Mabel Killick, who had been the United Kingdom's home secretary for the unusually long period of seven years, decided to chair the meeting of the specially convened COBRA Security subcommittee herself. The name COBRA had, as a matter of fact, nothing to do with poisonous snakes. It actually stood, rather prosaically, for Cabinet Office Meeting Room A. Nonetheless, Killick enjoyed the connotation. Though cool, calm and collected for most of the day, the home secretary, if roused, was ready to strike and strike hard.

In summoning the meeting at short notice, Killick had given some firm instructions to Giles Mortimer, her chief aide, as to the cast of characters she expected to see.

'We don't want the full monty,' she warned. 'Keep it down if you can. I'd like to see Jane Porter from 5 and Mark Cooper from 6 if they are available at short notice.'

When Killick spoke about '5' and '6', she was referring to MI5, the government department responsible for counter-intelligence operations (homeland security) and to MI6, Britain's own espionage agency, the UK's equivalent of the CIA. Until recently, MI5 and MI6 were officially non-existent and couldn't be referred to. People who worked for them had cover jobs. If asked what they actually did, they were trained to give non-committal replies. 'Oh, you know, this and that, one thing or another, here and there . . .'

In the last few years the agencies had come in out of the cold. There was no need any longer for the quiet 'Psst!' of recruiters on darkened streets and the whispered enticement: 'Fancy a job as a spy?' They even had websites. With the current wave of cyber-attacks, technically competent graduates were being enticed by attractive salaries and job conditions to join the fray on a new and challenging field of combat, the cyber battlefield.

Mortimer smoothed his dark, bushy beard. In the early days of his career, well-meaning superiors had suggested that it might be a good idea to prune the luxurious growth, or even get rid of it alto-gether. But Mortimer had resisted all such entreaties.

'People with beards are not all terrorists,' he would reply. That was when he was being polite.

Actually, strictly speaking, Mortimer was the home secretary's joint-chief of staff, since he shared the honour with Holly Percy. Together they made a formidable team. They were, so the press surmised, 'fiercely protective' of their boss and she in turn was devoted to them.

'We had better have Sir Oliver Holmes, too, hadn't we?' Percy said.

Sir Oliver Holmes was chief of the Metropolitan Police and therefore the man responsible for investigating, within his area of jurisdiction, crimes of every sort, including cybercrimes. Tall, fit, and good-humoured, Holmes was within a year of retirement. It would be his job to pass incriminating evidence to the Crown Prosecution Service, which would in turn have to decide how best justice could be served.

The home secretary saw Percy's point at once. 'Yes, of course. There may be a criminal investigation; in fact I'd say there's bound to be a criminal investigation. We don't want ministers to get wind of this enquiry and start destroying evidence.'

Of course, both Mortimer and Percy knew which 'ministers' she was referring to.

Mortimer had one last suggestion. 'Why don't we ask Edward Barnard to open the batting, even though he's resigned from the Cabinet? We've had the ambassador's report from Moscow. We have all had a summary of the material on the flash drive. But surely Barnard can give us the flavour of the matter, not to speak of filling us in on his contact with President Popov.'

Killick sniffed derisively. 'I think Barnard's been doing a bit of off-piste skiing. But, yes, I agree it will be useful to have him.'

The special meeting of the COBRA Security sub-committee was set for 11:00A.M. and it began precisely on time.

'Ladies and gentlemen,' Killick began, 'I want to explain why I have called you together this morning. The reason is simple: as the minister responsible for all Home Office business, including security and terrorism, I suspect that we have experienced, and are possibly still experiencing, a major breach of security as far as communications in and out of Number 10 Downing Street are concerned. Of course, that is of great concern to me. It has happened and is possibly still happening on my watch.

'But the issue we have to consider today has even wider implications than any breach of security that may already have occurred. Each of you has in front of you a bound dossier, in which my people have reproduced some of the most important and significant communications from what I am going to from now on refer to as the "Referendum dossier". Each of these volumes is numbered. Please be good enough to leave the bound folders on the table when you leave this room.'

The home secretary permitted herself a little joke. 'I have counted them all out, and I shall count them back in.'

Killick paused to give her next words the emphasis they deserved. 'I cannot stress how essential it is that you should treat this material with the greatest discretion.'

She turned to the commissioner of police, sitting beside her. 'Sir Oliver, perhaps you could take a moment to explain what we are dealing with in legal terms, in other words going beyond the security issues.'

'Thank you, Home Secretary.'

As the highest ranking police officer in the country, Holmes was proud to wear on his epaulettes the insignia of rank – the crown above a Bath star, above crossed tipstaves within a wreath. As much at home on a police horse as he was in a police car, he had placed his cap, with its chequered peak and distinctive silver braids, on the table in front of him when he sat down, and now he pushed it to one side.

'My job, as you know, ladies and gentlemen,' Holmes began, 'is to fight crime whenever and wherever it occurs. It is my duty to tell each and every one of you today that if you were to divulge to a third party information about what you read here today, or about the discussion which will shortly take place, you could be charged with aiding and abetting the commission of a serious crime, or with helping to conceal or cover up that crime, or assisting others to do so. I have absolutely no wish, as I come to the end of my career, to go out with a bang, but I have to remind you that when I took the oath of office on being appointed commissioner of police, I swore that I would discharge my duties – and I quote "without favour or affection, malice or ill will".

'I take that oath very seriously. So I want to tell you all, without beating about the bush, that we will probably be seeking search warrants as we pursue this case and those warrants may very well include the office or premises of the prime minister himself, as well as those of the chancellor of the exchequer and other concerned parties.'

Holmes wondered, as he pressed on, whether he was laying it on a bit thick. Was anyone, he asked himself, really going to rush out of the room to warn the prime minister and Tom Milbourne, the chancellor, to burn any incriminating documents as soon as possible?

Well, yes, he immediately reconsidered, it was precisely what they might very well do, unless he gave them the sternest possible warning.

How far, he wondered, had the stain and stench of corruption actually spread, if corruption was what they were dealing with? Were some of those actually in the room today implicated? He couldn't rule that out. Indeed, at this point in the proceedings he couldn't rule anything out.

'Let me be clear,' Holmes laid it out for them in no uncertain terms. 'If the authenticity of the material in front of you is conclusively established, then frankly we will be confronted with a scandal of massive proportions, a scandal which could – and I believe should – rock the government to its very foundation.'

Holmes looked pointedly at the home secretary. 'I imagine we would need a clean sweep at the highest levels of government, Home Secretary. Others would have to step in.'

'The election lights on Fortinbras,' Barnard murmured to himself. There were some lines from Hamlet he always remembered.

'Good heavens, Commissioner, let's not get ahead of ourselves,' Killick said.

She finally turned to Barnard. Though he was no longer a member of the Cabinet, everyone in the room recognized the central role he had played in the current crisis.

For the next few minutes Barnard summarized, as concisely as he could, the events of the previous few days: the World Tiger Summit in St Petersburg, the trip to the Russian Far East, the dinner in Khabarovsk with President Popov and Yuri Yasonov.

When Barnard had finished, it was MI5's turn.

'From the Russian point of view,' Jane Porter began, 'this must look like a win-win situation. They hand the tape to Barnard, knowing that if it becomes public the prime minister is finished. And if Jeremy Hartley goes down the drain, his cause goes down the drain too. He is committed, politically and personally, to achieving victory for the Remain camp in the referendum. If he is out on his ear and possibly heading for jail, and if these documents become public, the prospects of Remain winning the vote will suddenly look much thinner than they do today. Precisely the objective the Russians are aiming at. They are fed up with the EU. They would like to get rid of it. Brexit is off to a good start.'

'So what do we do?' Killick was beginning to sound impatient. 'Do we just sit on this Referendum dossier and hope it doesn't emerge before the next election? Do we pretend to the PM that we know nothing and suspect nothing?'

Holmes stood up suddenly. He picked up his chequered cap and solemnly placed it on his head.

'There is no way I could be party to that kind of proceeding. With respect, Madam Chair, you have only one possible course of action. And that is to investigate the documents as quickly and as thoroughly as you can. If those documents show, upon examination, that the prime minister has instigated or cooperated in illegal acts, then you have no alternative except to institute proceedings. That is my view now, and it will remain my view to my dying day.'

To say Sir Oliver Holmes stormed out of Room A of the Cabinet office would be an overstatement. But he certainly swept out majestically. The doorman saluted. What was going on in there, he wondered?

In the end, the meeting sided with Holmes. His opinion, so strongly voiced, carried the day, even though he wasn't present.

Killick summed up. 'There will be no minutes of this meeting. I will not be reporting to the PM or anyone else. If the matter comes up, the agreed answer must be that the subcommittee met informally to discuss various logistical questions. That should be quite enough. As to the substance, I take it we are all agreed that there will be an enquiry and I shall hold myself responsible, together with Sir Oliver Holmes, for seeing that such an enquiry is properly carried out and its conclusions are fully ventilated.'

The home secretary then walked briskly out of the room with her two aides.

The others followed her, looking around for their drivers as they emerged into the street.

Barnard, who no longer had a driver, felt a momentary pang. He missed being a minister of the Crown and a member of the Cabinet. He had liked the feeling of being important even if, in reality, he wasn't very important. Who was it who said: 'nothing matters very much and most things don't matter at all'? Whoever it was, was spot on.

When he got home, Melissa had a large drink waiting for him.

'Cheer up, darling. You're the leader now, leader of the Leavers. People are going to expect great things of you. At the moment, the government has everything in its favour. They've got the funding; they've got the BBC; the polls give them a clear lead. What are you going to do, Edward? You haven't got much time to pull the rabbit out of the hat.'

Barnard felt suddenly confident. More confident than he had felt in a long time, even when he was swaggering around with his ministerial red box.

'I'll take the dogs out before I come up,' he said, as he reached for the whisky decanter.

CHAPTER EIGHT

Jang Ling-Go, director of Forestry and Wildlife in China's Heilongjiang Province, was in a foul mood. He had just received an email from his superiors in Beijing which had completely spoilt his morning.

The email read as follows: 'President Liu Wang-Ji returned recently from a trip to St Petersburg where he was attending the World Tiger Summit as the guest of Russian president, Igor Popov. President Popov belittled China's conservation programme as regards Amur tigers, stating that Amur tigers crossing the Ussuri River from Russia into China were being hunted and killed. President Popov, in a separate bilateral meeting with Chinese President Liu Wang-Ji, pointed out that whereas over 450 Amur tigers were now living in Russia, part of Amur-Heilong eco-region, fewer than twenty Amur tigers are to be found on the Chinese side of the Ussuri. Please report urgently on measures taken within your area of responsibility to safeguard Amur tigers, including the fight against poaching and illegal killing of tigers.'

Jang Ling-Go didn't have to read between the lines. The message was clear enough. China's international prestige was at stake. President Liu Wang-Ji clearly felt he had lost face – and in a very public way – and he wanted something done about it.

One of the reasons for the director of forestry's foul mood was that he felt Beijing's criticism was unjust. Yes, President Popov was right to point out that there were far more tigers on the Russian side of the border than on the Chinese side; and yes he was right to say that the Chinese had – in the past – made a habit of killing tigers which came their way, trading their parts on the black market for huge sums of money. But things surely had changed. His department was urging farmers and villagers in the region to protect and not persecute tigers. His department wasn't always successful, of course. He had to admit that.

And this morning's news didn't improve the situation. A report had just come in that a tiger had apparently forded the river and killed livestock at a forest farm on the Chinese side of the border. Pugmarks found at the site of the kill suggested that the culprit was a large, male tiger. The villagers were roused and seeking vengeance.

Jang Ling-Go called to his assistant through the open door. 'Please ask Shao Wei-Lu to come and see me.'

Minutes later, a young Chinese woman entered the room. 'What's the story on the Shengle Farm tiger?' Jang Ling-Go asked. 'Are the rangers tracking it?'

'They are,' the young woman replied. 'As a matter of fact, we know precisely which tiger we are dealing with. It's already in the database. It came over from Russia three days ago, stopped two days ago at Shengle Farm where it killed two goats, and now appears to be heading back to the forest.'

Shao Wei-Lu opened her laptop. They gazed at the screen. 'See that pulsating dot? That's our tiger. He's about ten miles from the river. Hasn't moved for the last several hours. Probably digesting his lunch.'

'Send a message to call off the patrol. Tell the villagers to go back to their homes,' Jang Ling-Go ordered. 'That tiger may have killed a goat or two. I don't care. Our job here is to demonstrate that the Amur tiger is as safe on our side of the border as it is on the Russian side.'

Jang Ling-Go mopped his brow. The last thing he wanted at this point in time was a dead Amur tiger on his hands.

Shao Wei-Lu was still tapping away at her laptop. Jang was amazed at her dexterity. Though he was far from being an expert himself, he recognized that a combination of camera trapping and telemonitoring had transformed wildlife biology. Nowadays, judiciously placed camera traps recorded animal movements whenever the sensors picked up movement, with the findings being transmitted via orbiting satellites in real time to the control centre.

'What are you looking for now?' Jang Ling-Go asked.

'I've just run the ID programme. Correlating the data from the camera traps with the known movements of the tiger, I've discovered that we are indeed dealing with a large male here, just as the rangers suspected. Looking at the record, this particular male – No. 127 in our database – appears to spend most of its time in Russia, but crosses over into China about once a month. The tiger, of course, doesn't know he's crossing into China.'

'Don't be so sure of that,' Jang Ling-Go said. 'The animals I've met have a pretty good idea of where it's safe to go and where it isn't.'

'Hello. This is odd.' Shao Wei-Lu seemed surprised.

'What's the problem?'

'There's an anomaly here,' Shao replied. 'We manage the database in common with our Russian colleagues. It's one of the exemplary areas of Russia–China cooperation. Our Russian colleagues recently reported that President Popov had personally darted a tiger as part of their ongoing field programmes.'

'So?' Jang didn't see what Shao was getting at.

'Did you see the video of the tiger President Popov darted the other day?'

'Of course I did. It was on all the news channels. Khabarovsk is virtually our local station, if you don't mind watching the news in Russian. I still don't see what you're trying to say.'

Shao Wei-Lu took her time. She sensed that her superior was in a tense frame of mind that morning, to say the least.

'Look, sir.' She added the 'sir' as a sign of respect. 'This ID programme is very effective. Every tiger in the world has a different set of stripes. Feed a picture of a tiger into the computer and the computer will tell you if the tiger is already on the database and, if it isn't, it will create a record for that tiger which can be updated as further sightings come in.

'So what did I do?' she continued. 'I'll tell you what I did. The tiger ID programme can work with moving images as well as still photos. A moving image is simply a sequence of still photos run at speed, isn't it? The programme just picks up individual frames. And what do you think the computer told us when I ran the video of the tiger they put out on the news? Shall I run the clip again?'

Shao Wei-Lu clicked on the clip from Russian television's evening news bulletin, which showed President Popov confronting a large tiger, rifle in hand. Then she tapped another key. 'I've just activated the "analyse and identify" programme. Give it a few seconds and it will come up with the answer. This is a worldwide system. We use it for other wild tiger populations, the Royal Bengal tiger, for example, in India and Bangladesh. If the tiger is not already on the database, it will say so. But it is, isn't it? Look. Here comes the answer.'

"*Tiger, large male, approximately seven years old. Already in database since 18.08.2014 as Amur 127.*"

'So do you see why I'm puzzled?' Shao Wei-Lu continued. 'Do you see why I think there's an anomaly here? That tiger wasn't darted by President Popov. It's been in the system since August 2014.' She pressed another key. 'We can see where that animal has been over the last three years. Right up to the time, a day or two ago, it swam across the Ussuri River and entered Chinese territory. So why did President Popov dart that particular animal, since it was already in the system?'

'Maybe the Russians didn't know the animal was already in the system? Surely that could be the explanation?'

'It could be an explanation,' Shao Wei-Lu conceded, 'but I doubt it. Generally the rangers know their animals. They know which ones are already in the system. If they don't know they usually have time to check. They've all got hand-held computers, not much bigger than your mobile phone. As long as they have some kind of a visual reference, they can check the database. Anyway, if Popov had darted the tiger, we'd have a double signal, as the second micro-transmitter begins to function, but there's no such signal. Instead, we see our tiger bound away from the site of the kill, as though he has been startled or surprised. He makes a rapid loop or two.' She tapped the screen to indicate the tiger's movements. 'Then he quietens down and heads for the border, and a couple of days ago he swims across the river.'

'Oh, my lord!' Jang suddenly realized the full implication of what Shao was suggesting. 'You mean Popov never darted the tiger at all? Maybe they realized that tiger had already been collared, so they let it go. Then why all the pictures on TV of the president with his rifle?'

Shao Wei-Lu thought long and hard before replying. She knew she was getting into deep water. Way above her pay-grade.

But she, as a loyal cadre, felt she had a duty to speak.

'I don't think Popov fired the dart at the tiger,' she said slowly. 'That's not what the record shows.'

CHAPTER NINE

Consisting of seven men, the Standing Committee of the Politburo of China's Communist Party is effectively China's ruling body. As usual, the committee met that May morning in Beijing's Zhongnanhai district, the exclusive area next to the Imperial City, which houses not only the president's office and other organs of state, but which also provides residential quarters for China's most senior politicians and officials.

There was a time when Zhongnanhai had been open to the public, but since the Tiananmen Square protests of 1989, security had been greatly increased. Access had been closed to the general public, with numerous plain-clothes military personnel patrolling the area on foot.

If the Standing Committee of the Politburo was a closed grouping in the most literal sense, it was also closed metaphorically. For the most part its members had spent their lives in the service of the party, often in far-flung provinces. The grandest of all were those who had links by blood or by marriage with the Party's now almost mythic heroes, men whose fathers or grandfathers had been on the Long March with Chairman Mao.

President Liu Wang-Ji called the meeting to order.

'Comrades,' he began, 'I thought I would start today's proceedings by reporting on my recent trip to St Petersburg.'

For the next twenty minutes he recounted some of the details of his encounter with other world leaders at the World Tiger Summit, organized and presided over by Russia's president Igor Popov. His assessments were frank and pithy.

'I was intrigued – and I must confess rather alarmed – by the German chancellor and her apparent closeness to President Popov. Of course, she speaks Russian fluently and he speaks German. That helps. I am told that our security services are in the process of making a full assessment of historic and other links between President Popov and Chancellor Brun.'

He nodded across the table in the direction of Zhang Fu-Sheng.

'Is that not so, Comrade Zhang?'

'Yes, that is so, Mr President,' Zhang agreed.

In the official handout entitled 'Composition of the Standing Committee', Zhang's functions were simply listed as Deputy Leader of the Central Leading Group for Comprehensively Deepening Reforms, but within the standing committee itself and the upper echelons of government it was well known that Zhang was responsible for Ministry of State Security. As one of the most powerful and most active Chinese intelligence agencies, the MSS's main objective was to keep track and neutralize 'enemies' of the Communist Party of China.

'Our sources in Berlin,' Zhang continued, 'indicate that Chancellor Brun appears to be distancing herself from some of the previous policies of the EU regarding Ukraine and NATO and so on. Apparently she may soon be pushing the EU and the US to drop the sanctions over Crimea.'

President Liu Wang-Ji took a sip of the sweet green tea served at all meetings of the Standing Committee. Gaily decorated thermoses were conveniently placed on the table for those who wanted a top-up.

'Most interesting,' he said. 'Your mention of the United States, Comrade Zhang, reminds me to report also on Ronald Craig, presently one of the leading Republican candidates for the presidency.'

In the old days, before the Chinese government banned spitting in public places, there would have been strategically placed spittoons in the Standing Committee's meeting room. Veterans could launch a glob of spit with unerring accuracy over a distance of twenty paces. But spittoons had gone from modern China, much as the practice of binding women's feet had gone.

So instead of spitting, Liu limited himself to an expression of mild disgust.

'Pah! I only spoke briefly with Mr Craig but I was alarmed when he told me that he did not necessarily support the One China policy and might even visit Taiwan!'

There was an explosion of dissent around the table. Comrades present made it clear that they had never heard a more disgusting idea in all their lives. Taiwan was part of China and always would be. The day was coming when the lost sheep would return to the fold and the United States would just have to lump it.

Wang Tao-Yu, China's premier and the Politburo's Number Two member in terms of seniority, chipped in:

'If Ronald Craig becomes the official US presidential candidate, and if he wins the election, I fear we are going to have trouble in the South China Sea.'

Of course they all knew what he was talking about. China had recently been boosting its foothold in the Spratly Islands, a disputed scattering of reefs and islands in the South China Sea more than 500 miles from the Chinese mainland. They had been moving sediment from the seabed to create artificial reefs. So far they had constructed port facilities, military buildings and an airstrip on the islands. Recent imagery showed evidence of two more airstrips under construction. Unfortunately, the Japanese had long regarded the Spratly Islands as their sovereign territory. Up till now, the US had looked the other way. With a new president in the White House, things could change and the US might decide to come down firmly on Japan's side, making a confrontation virtually inevitable.

The discussion continued. More tea was drunk. After a while, Liu summed up the feeling of the meeting:

'We all seem to agree, comrades, that a major geopolitical shift could be in the offing. New alliances seem to be in prospect. And there may be new adversaries too. I say let's stick to the old Chinese proverb, "new friends good, old friends better". United Europe has been good for China. Don't let it go down the drain!'

Once again, Liu looked across the table to Zhang.

'Comrade Zhang, please note our conclusions on this point. If President Popov's objective – heaven forbid – is to achieve the break-up of Europe with or without the assistance of the United States, our objective must be to save it. It will not be the first time that China has found itself on the opposite side of the table from Russia, and it will not be the last. I am glad to know that you and your people are already taking steps to avoid any unfortunate outcomes. Please double and redouble your efforts.'

Rounds of applause were very seldomly heard in the standing committee of the Politburo. That was not the way they did things usually. But the applause that greeted Liu's last remark was long and heartfelt. The China–US relationship, ever since Kissinger and Nixon first came to China back in the early 1970s, had been crucially important. But that relationship might be about to change. In that case, the China–EU relationship, which was almost equally important, might need to be seen in a whole new perspective. Not merely an optional extra, but a vital element in the new world order. Provided of course that the EU itself didn't go down the drain. And that surely couldn't be allowed to happen.

Liu had one last point to cover before bringing the meeting to a close.

'Comrade Zhang, please tell us your conclusions in the matter of the Amur tiger.'

Zhang shuffled the papers in front of him. 'The hour is late, comrades, and you have the detailed report from the director of forestry and wildlife of Heilongjiang Province in front of you. We are quite clear that the tiger, which has recently crossed over from

Russia into China and whose movements we are following closely, is indeed the tiger that President Popov claims to have darted. But it was not in fact darted by President Popov. It was already darted, back in 2014, and has been in the database since then.'

'Comrade Zhang, please come to the point.' Liu couldn't stand people who beat about the bush. 'If Popov didn't shoot the tiger, who or what did he shoot?'

'Mr President. Khabarovsk, as you know, is literally on the China–Russia border. We have many intelligence assets there as you can imagine. Our Russian friends are constantly complaining about illegal migrants from China arriving in their frontier regions. Some of those migrants, I can confirm, work as orderlies and nurses in Khabarovsk General Hospital. We know from our sources that the American Ronald Craig was taken to the hospital on the afternoon of 10 May. Apparently he had a wound which needed treatment.'

'What kind of a wound?'

'Nothing important, as we understand. But it needed looking at.'

'What exactly needed looking at?' Liu Wang-Ji persisted.

'The wound was in Mr Craig's backside, I believe. The left buttock to be precise, according to the information we have.'

'Oh dear!' There was a pause and then Liu wiped the tears of laughter from his eyes. He was as ready to enjoy a joke as the next man. The trouble was, being the leader of a nation of almost one and a half billion people was a pretty serious business. Good jokes didn't come along very often.

'You're not telling me that the president of the Russian Federation shot the possibly next president of the United States in the backside with an anaesthetizing dart!'

Zhang was miffed. 'Yes, Mr President. That is indeed what we believe.'

'But why would he do that?'

'That is precisely what we are trying to find out.'

By then, Liu had regained his composure. 'Please keep us posted, Comrade Zhang.'

And with that he brought the meeting to a close.

Later that day, back in his office at the ministry of state security near the Old Summer Palace in Beijing, Zhang Fu-Sheng summoned his senior staff.

He addressed them in sombre tones. He knew quite well from President Liu's not so subtle warning that his job was on the line.

'We need to know several things,' he began, 'and we need to know them now.'

He ticked off the key intelligence requirements, as he saw them, one by one. 'We know from our sources in Moscow and elsewhere that President Popov is determined to achieve, or at least hasten, the break-up of the European Union. We know that he has been following closely the progress of the Referendum campaign in Britain, which still has a few weeks to run, and is determined that the UK should vote to Leave, not to Remain. I can assure you, comrades, that such an eventuality is not, repeat not, in China's interests.

'So what do we do? I am going to invite Comrade Deng Biao-Su, head of our intelligence and analysis bureau, to give us the benefit of his thinking.'

'Thank you, Comrade Zhang.' Deng stood up. 'To take the first point: what is Popov aiming at? In a nutshell, we believe, as Comrade Zhang suggests, that Popov sees the current Referendum campaign in Britain as an unparalleled – and indeed unexpected – opportunity to achieve an almost seismic change in the world's geopolitical arrangements. Indeed, one could argue that not since Genghis Khan led his hordes from Asia into Central Europe in the twelfth century has such an opportunity presented itself. Our sources in the Kremlin have cited numerous instances of President

Popov talking about the "new domino theory", whereby a vote for Brexit in Britain sets off a chain reaction. One event encourages, indeed precipitates, the next.

'A Brexit vote in Britain will be a devastating blow to the European Union, since Britain is such a major player there, and – incidentally – the second largest contributor to the EU budget after Germany. It will also help to ensure Ronald Craig's victory in the forthcoming American presidential election. And both events, taken together, will kick-start a great wave of popularism in Europe – first in France, then, in Italy, then the Netherlands and – who knows – maybe in Germany itself, that bedrock of the European Union where, as I understand it, the strength of the parties opposed to Chancellor Brun is growing day by day. That wave of popularism is based on the idea that the people themselves will and must "take back control". We will see a resurgence of the "Europe of the nations", not the United Europe that the founding fathers like Monnet and Schuman aimed at.'

'And how, specifically, is President Popov seeking to achieve the result he hopes for?' Zhang asked. 'In the first instance, for example, how will he, or can he, help the Leave side to win in the current Referendum campaign? My information is that the Leave side is at the moment far behind in the opinion polls. The UK prime minister, Jeremy Hartley, is deploying all the resources at the government's command to try to ensure that the Remain side wins. How can Popov tip the balance in the other direction?'

Deng thought long and hard before answering that question.

'We believe that Popov has an agent at the highest level in British government circles. It could be none other than the charismatic Edward Barnard, former Secretary of State for the Environment. Precisely when any such recruitment took place we don't know for sure. We suspect it would have occurred very recently, when Barnard was in St Petersburg for the World Tiger Summit. Indeed, I believe Mr Barnard, and our own beloved leader, President Liu Wang-Ji, exchanged some brief words on that occasion.

'We also don't know for sure precisely what instructions and support Barnard would have received but we can be absolutely sure that he will not be playing the game with an empty hand. I need not stress that from China's point of view the collapse of the European Union, kick-started by Britain leaving the EU, will be very damaging indeed. It will certainly dramatically strengthen Russia's influence in the world. Huge swathes of Central Asia and Eastern Europe could come under Russian domination.'

'And would the United States sit idly by while that happened?' Zhang asked.

'Our assessment at this point in time is that the United States will not be much concerned by the break-up of the European Union. They gave lip-service to the idea of a United Europe, but deep down they were never keen on seeing Europe as a rival power-centre in the world. And if Ronald Craig becomes president we might easily see some kind of *de facto* alliance between Russia and the United States. You scratch my back, and I'll scratch yours. And none of this would be good for China.' Deng paused. 'Perhaps I could call on Comrade Li Xiao-Tong at this point, as the head of the counter-intelligence bureau.'

'Of course, go ahead, Comrade Li.'

'Thank you, Chairman.' Li, an athletic-looking young man with black horn-rimmed spectacles, took up the tale:

'We have decided, comrades, that in this case, as so often, attack is the best form of defence. The Russians appear to have recruited an important asset in their efforts to help the Leave campaign win a victory in the forthcoming UK Referendum. We are going to "turn" that asset and use it to our advantage, so as to ensure that the Remain side win the vote, and the threat to the future of the EU is thereby diminished if not entirely removed.'

There was a sharp intake of breath around the table. 'Turning a major asset', in other words, picking up the enemy's agent and making him or her serve your purposes rather than those of the other side, had always been one of the big challenges in the field of espionage and counter-espionage. Thrillers had been written on the topic by men like John Le Carré, Frederick Forsyth and Robert Harris, and these were authors who knew their onions.

'And how are you going to "turn" Mr Edward Barnard?' Zhang intervened. 'As I understand it, the gentleman's not for turning. He's a family man. Loves horses and dogs. Went to a good school. On to Oxford. That kind of thing.'

'Don't worry, comrade. We'll find a way. You just have to pick the right spot to pierce the armour. Even your classic English gentleman has his weak spot if you know where to look.'

Li Xiao-Tong looked around the room. Colleagues from all twelve bureaux of the MSS were present that day. He had known many of them during that first period of training, at the agency's own university: The Institute of International Relations, in Beijing. And then they had met up again learning 'tradecraft' at the Institute of Cadre Management in Suzhou, not far from Shanghai.

'As a matter of fact, comrades,' Li's smile turned into a leer. 'We think we've already found a way.'

CHAPTER TEN

After Barnard resigned from his position as Secretary of State for the Environment in order to devote his energies to the Referendum campaign, Joyce Dugdale, his private secretary, went through the diary.

'What are we going to do about your talk in Xian, China, on May 7th?' she asked. 'The Chinese Embassy has already been on to us. They're going to be very upset if you don't go.'

'Can't Hilary do it?' Hilary Douglas, MP for Taunton and a rising star in the Conservative Party, had already been nominated as his successor as Secretary of State and was expected to take up her post in the Department of the Environment later that day.

'No, Miss Douglas's people have already said that she couldn't do it. She'll barely have had time to put her feet under the desk. Besides, you're in the programme, and down to speak on the first day. Look!'

Dugdale quickly searched for the link. Together they looked at the screen. The headline, as posted by the Chinese Ministry of Foreign Affairs, read:

WORLD ECO FORUM TO MEET IN XIAN.
ZHANG FU-SHENG TO ATTEND

'China's top politician Zhang Fu-Sheng will meet next week with foreign leaders at the Eco Forum Global Annual Conference 2016 in Xian, capital of Shaanxi Province in Central Asia. The leaders include Papua

New Guinea's (PNG) Prime Minister Roger Wolf, Lucas Behrman, President of the National Council of Switzerland; Deputy President of Kenya, Madison Mboyo; and former UK Secretary of State for Environment, Edward Barnard. Zhang Fu-Sheng will formally open the World Eco Forum.'

Dugdale hadn't finished. 'The Embassy is also trying to set up a private meeting between you and Mr Zhang Fu-Sheng. They said Zhang is a member of the Standing Committee of the Politburo. They hinted that he is a big cheese. I'm not an expert but I can tell you that in China a member of the Politburo Standing Committee is a very big cheese indeed.'

Three days later, Barnard took his seat in the huge Xian International Congress Centre with ten minutes to spare. He had been escorted through the VIP entrance and then 'fast-tracked' through security, but even so the formalities took time. With Zhang Fu-Sheng scheduled to do the honours, no one was taking any chances.

There were giant screens behind the podium. In that vast cavernous hall, one man standing before a lectern could seem small and insignificant. Most people, the evidence indicated, like watching the giant screen rather than the tiny man.

Right up front in the VIP row, Barnard watched and listened to Zhang's opening address.

'Ladies and gentlemen,' Zhang began. 'Honoured delegates, honoured guests from overseas, it gives me great pleasure to declare this important congress open.'

As Zhang spoke, the giant image on the screen behind him changed and was replaced by a shot of the audience. To his surprise, Barnard suddenly saw himself in close-up, staring at the stage. Where the hell was that camera, he wondered?

And then he spotted it, mounted on a wire above the stage, able to traverse the whole stage from left to right and back again.

When, for a second time, he saw himself in close-up, he waved discreetly. I could be at a football match, in one of those crowd shots, when people in funny hats or paint on their faces suddenly realize they are being filmed. He had an almost overwhelming temptation to stick out his tongue and waggle his hands behind his head, but he thought better of it. He might not be a minister of the Crown any longer, but he still had to behave.

Listening to Zhang through his headphones, Barnard was impressed by the clarity and conviction with which the man spoke. A year earlier, China had stuck its neck out. It had bonded together with the United States to force through the international agreement on climate change in Paris at the end of 2015. Now that agreement was at serious risk of collapsing even before it had entered into force. Ron Craig, the most likely Republican candidate, had made it clear that he believed global warming to be a 'giant hoax and an attack on American jobs'. Craig had threatened that if he ever became president he would pull the US out of the Paris Agreement and even out of the parent Climate Change Convention, which had been adopted way back in 1992 at the United Nations first Earth Summit in Rio de Janeiro, Brazil.

Barnard was expecting to hear some tough retaliatory language from Zhang, but whatever the Chinese minister might have thought privately, he went out of his way to respect the conventions of diplomacy. Opening speeches are meant to be uplifting, not full of venom.

'China,' he said, 'will always put ecological environmental protection as an important area of opening up to the outside world, and will fulfil international environmental conventions, as well as taking on international obligations. It will continue to participate in global cooperation to combat climate change, and make important contributions to global ecological security.'

When he had finished his speech, Zhang bowed three times to acknowledge the applause and then followed one of the conference ushers to the seat reserved for him in the VIP row. Martial music echoed from the loudspeakers.

As Zhang walked along the front row, Barnard stood up to greet him as he passed. 'Great speech. Fantastic,' he said.

Zhang bowed and walked on. But at the dinner, later that evening, he sought Barnard out and found time for a private word.

'Ah, Mr Barnard, how good of you to come. We are so pleased to have been able to cooperate with the United Kingdom on these environmental issues. We hope that cooperation may continue even in changed circumstances. But of course China will never intervene in the electoral process of another country.'

For a moment Barnard wondered whether Zhang was making a joke at Russia's expense, since Russia's habit of intervening in other countries' elections was fairly well documented. That very day, he had seen a report on CNN about thousands of 'leaked emails', most of them featuring Caroline Mann, the most likely Democratic candidate in the upcoming US election. The consensus was that the leak was most likely to have originated from Russia and that it could severely damage Mann's chances of winning the election.

Zhang lingered for a moment. 'We hope the Annual Xian Environmental Forum will in time come to be seen as an alternative to the World Economic Forum at Davos in Switzerland. That is why it is so important to us that foreign guests such as you attend this event. We want it to be the "go-to" event of the environmental year.'

It was after 11:00P.M. when Barnard finally returned to his hotel room. Within seconds the telephone rang.

'Please forgive me for phoning you so late. My name is Li Xiao-Tong. I am calling you on behalf of senior minister Zhang Fu-Sheng. Minister Zhang would like to invite you to accompany him early tomorrow morning on a special visit to the famous Terracotta army.'

'That's wonderful. I'm down to give my speech at twelve noon. Would we be back in time for that?'

'Yes, of course,' the voice at the other end of the line assured him. 'Great honour to accompany such senior minister. Meet in lobby 6:00 A.M.?'

As he put the phone down, Barnard felt doubly elated. First, it was obvious that Zhang had a message to convey, though what that message was remained a mystery. Second, he was going to have a personal out-of-hours viewing of the Terracotta Army, far from the crowds of tourists who would invade the site as soon as the gates were officially opened.

His wife, Melissa, had been extremely envious when she heard he was going to Xian.

'I long to see the Terracotta Army,' she had said. 'Lucky old you. Do please take some photos.'

Li was already waiting for him when, on the dot of six the next morning, Barnard emerged from the lift into the glittering lobby of the Xian Hilton.

'Minister Zhang is already in the car.' Li ushered him to the door.

The city was stirring as they drove east. Street vendors had already taken up their positions. The tea-houses were opening. Barnard caught a glimpse of the great Buddhist pagoda, towering over the city's ancient walls.

'That's the Great Wild Goose Pagoda,' Zhang told him. 'Built in the seventh century. If you have time, you can climb up to the top. Wonderful view.'

Even at that time of the morning, the road was beginning to fill up. The driver wove his way skilfully around the handcarts and bicycles, overtaking slower vehicles with a blast of the horn and a firm kick at the accelerator. Occasionally, he would swing out into the centre of the road to be confronted by an oncoming bus or truck.

An hour later, they stood together on the huge mound of earth that covered the tomb of China's first emperor. It was like being on top of the Great Pyramid of Cheops, Barnard thought. The Qin emperor had been far more powerful than the Pharaohs of Egypt. Ramses and Akhenaton had ruled a country, but Qin Shi Huang had ruled a continent.

'Has the tomb ever been excavated?' Barnard asked.

'No. And the Chinese government has no plans to do so at the present time. Qin Shi Huang's grave has been undisturbed for over 2,000 years; it can wait a bit longer. Besides,' Zhang added, smiling, 'the place is meant to be booby-trapped with an elaborate system of crossbows lined up to fire automatically at any intruders! And don't forget,' he pointed to the east, 'down there, a mile and a half away, a whole army stood guard.'

'The Terracotta Army?'

'Exactly. Come on, let's walk there. We can pick up the car later.'

Zhang set off at a brisk pace down the steep slope of the pyramid, still talking as he leapt agilely from step to step.

There had obviously been advance warning of Zhang's visit. A small welcoming party was waiting for them.

An elderly man came forward to shake Zhang warmly by the hand. 'This is Professor Wong,' Zhang explained to Barnard. 'He has offered to show us round. I know this place well, I grew up in Xian. I went to university here before going into politics. I have followed the excavations over the years, but still it's good to have an expert.'

For the next hour the professor gave them an expert guided tour.

'Normally,' he explained, 'visitors don't go down into the pits. They have to stay on the viewing platforms. But when we have a high-level honoured guest, we are allowed to make an exception.'

The professor pulled a card from his wallet and showed it to the guard at the entrance. The man nodded and unhooked the rope to let them pass.

'The first pit was discovered in 1974,' the professor explained, 'by some farmers digging in the fields nearby. The second and third pits were discovered in the summer of 1976, about twenty-five metres to the north of the first pit. We believe there may be more pits to excavate, but we are taking our time. So far they have uncovered more than 1,000 life-sized warriors and horses, twenty wooden war chariots and 10,000 bronze weapons. They estimate that when the excavation has finished there will be over 7,000 warriors, as well as some 600 clay horses and a massive quantity of real weaponry.

'Look at the extraordinary detail of these figures,' he continued. 'The man in front, wearing the long robe, is an officer. See how the tips of his shoes turn up, his long cap, the fine and delicate features. What you are looking at is not a stylized representation but the real thing. Look at the general standing just behind him. Of course there are some standard features, the cap adorned with pheasant's feathers, the long coat with its plate of armour, the hand on the sword. But each terracotta figure represents an actual soldier in Emperor Qin's army. Each and every one of them is different. It's almost as though these were real individuals. They were moulded in yellow clay and baked in a kiln over 2,000 years ago, but even now the realism, the subtlety of the carving is frightening. You look at these statues and you think they could almost march away.'

At the end of their tour, the professor led them into the VIP room where a table had been laid for breakfast.

The professor slipped away to take tea in a side-room with Li Xiao-Tong.

Barnard admired the choreography of the whole affair. This is where we get down to business, he thought, now that the softening-up process is over.

Zhang didn't waste words. 'Emperor Quin Shi Huang united China. The Qin Empire ruled for hundreds of years. The warring states came together. China became the greatest country on earth. In Europe you have had a great experiment. After two world wars which began there, the nations have come together in peace. But now you want to throw it away. I have read your speeches, Mr

Barnard, I have watched you on television. But please tell me why? Why are you doing this?'

'We're not trying to destroy Europe,' Barnard protested. 'We're just trying to take back control of our own destiny. For example, I consider myself to be an environmentalist. I care about nature and wildlife. I am as concerned about global warming as China is, and I congratulate you on the efforts you have made. But I think we can make our own laws, in this area as in others.'

When Barnard continued in that vein for several minutes more, Zhang looked increasingly disappointed.

'I am sorry I have not been able to persuade you, Mr Barnard.'

'Well, I'm sorry you felt you had to try.'

Zhang shook his head. 'China wants to work with a United Europe, not twenty-eight different nations which is what we will have if Europe falls apart. Britain may be the first domino to fall, but it will not be the last. Do you know what we say in China in situations like these? "Be careful what you wish for". That's what we say.'

Zhang stood up. The meeting was clearly over. 'Li Xiao-Tong will accompany you back to your hotel, Mr Barnard. My driver is taking me straight to the airport.'

'I'll be heading there myself later today, after I've made my speech.'

'Good luck with that! Thank you for coming.' Zhang was suddenly affable.

Driving back to Xian, Barnard wondered what China's next step would be. The passion with which Zhang had spoken about a United Europe had taken him by surprise. He sounded a bit like Ted Heath, he thought. Poor old Ted. He had a vision but he could never persuade his party to follow him. Not for the long haul, anyway.

As they got out of the car, Li Xiao-Tong came round to hold the door.

'Minister Zhang has asked me to give you this memento to take back to Britain. Please play it on your video recorder when you get home as a souvenir of your visit to Emperor Qin's Tomb and the Terracotta Army. It tells the story from the first excavations to the present day. I am sure your wife will like it too.'

Barnard was genuinely touched. He had given his hosts a hard time. It was clear to him now that they had planned the one-on-one encounter with Minister Zhang down to the last detail. What on earth did they think? That he could change his mind at the drop of a hat?

Still, it was nice of them to give him a video of the Terracotta army. Melissa would be pleased. He'd taken some photos that morning but it would be good to have a proper video.

CHAPTER ELEVEN

The plane from Xian landed as dawn was breaking. As a last gesture of goodwill to a departing minister, the government had laid on a car. Barnard scanned the papers as they sped west along the M4. He frowned. The *Observer*'s 'Poll of Polls' had Leave at ten points behind.

Harriet Marshall, director of the Leave campaign, was already waiting when Barnard's car rolled into the drive of Coleman Court: the splendid Georgian house that Barnard had bought on first being elected for the South Wiltshire constituency.

'*Nǐ hǎo!*' Marshall said. 'The wanderer returns!'

'Hello to you, too!' Barnard smiled at the young woman who held the door open for him and then helped him with his bag. He congratulated himself, not for the first time, on the fact that the Leave campaign had managed to tempt Marshall to join them. The financial inducement had not been impressive – she could have earned a much higher salary in the City.

Marshall was a profound thinker, a high-level chess player, and indeed, by general repute, probably the cleverest woman in years to have made her name in politics. Not as an MP, but as a Special Political Adviser or SPAD.

She was also a superb strategist, with an ability to create – and then capitalize on – opportunities long before most people even realized they existed.

But she was far from easy to work with. In fact, she was notoriously difficult. Marshall made it abundantly clear that she thought most MPs were time-servers, jobsworths, interested in their own career and not much else. Even ministers, from time to time, felt the lash of her tongue. From her point of view, the people who were the 'extremists' were the people who lived in the Westminster 'bubble', who believed – for example – in an immigration policy that guaranteed free movement rights, even for murderers.

Marshall got results. She had seldom been on the losing side. She didn't intend to be on the losing side now.

There was so much to do and so little time to do it.

The government had all the big guns. Tom Milbourne, the chancellor of the exchequer, was firing one broadside after another, using some convenient – and often heavily massaged – treasury statistics. With Brexit, the chancellor argued, the economy would take a severe tumble. The National Health Service, staffed by foreign doctors and nurses, would collapse; crops would go unpicked in East Anglian fields owing to the sudden absence of migrant workers from the countries of Eastern Europe. One million Poles and half a million Romanians would vanish overnight. The country would go to pot.

The Bank of England, though legally independent, joined in the fun, producing economic forecasts or 'scenarios' of the consequences of Brexit, each one more alarming than the last.

This morning, when Marshall had her first meeting with Barnard, now officially chairman of Leave, she showed no sign of being deterred by the size of the challenge they faced if they were to win on 23 June.

'Let's give them a kick in the balls,' Marshall said. 'We'll put out our own analyses proving that their analyses are wrong. We'll say they are offering a diet of fear while we are offering a veritable smorgasbord of hope.'

'Who's going to crunch the numbers for us?' Barnard asked. 'We don't have much money.'

'We don't need much money. We've got amazing technicians – top mathematicians and computer specialists – working on our database. We know precisely who to hit with direct door-to-door canvassing. And we'll get the message out via social media as well: Twitter, Facebook, Instagram, that kind of thing. Did you know that Ron Craig has twenty million followers on Twitter? No wonder he's leading the pack.'

'I've met Ron Craig,' Barnard said. 'Last time I saw him was in a hospital in the Russian Far East. President Popov had shot him in the left buttock with a tranquillizing dart.'

Melissa brought them coffee and stayed with them while Marshall rolled out a large calendar and spread it on the table.

'I've blocked in at least two major speeches a week,' Marshall said. 'Not in London, of course. We're not going to win in London, so there's no point in wasting a lot of time and energy there. And Scotland's not friendly territory. The SNP is likely to outplay the Labour Party there, but both will be voting Remain.'

She got up, fumbling in her pocket for some drawing pins, and fixed a large map of the UK to the wall.

'If we win at all, we're going to win with English votes. People who like fish and chips, fly the flag of St George, go down to the pub for a pint on Sunday morning, and watch Coronation Street on telly.'

'Oh dear,' Barnard murmured. 'I'm not sure I'm going to be much good at winning over that kind of voter.'

'Don't worry,' Marshall returned to her seat. 'We've plenty of rabble-rousers gagging to sign up to our speakers list. I'm told that Harry Stokes, the mayor of London, or former mayor I should say, is ready to join us. That'll be a tremendous coup.'

'Are you sure he's made up his mind?'

'Of course, I'm not sure. I don't suppose he is either. But that won't necessarily prevent him taking the plunge.'

'That is good news.'

Barnard felt suddenly much more cheerful. If Harry Stokes, the charismatic ex-mayor of London, decided to throw in his lot with the

Leavers, that was very good news indeed. The mayor, whose ebullient exterior concealed a razor-sharp mind and a pronounced streak of political cunning, would be a tremendous catch. The best proof of that was the fact that he had won twice in the London mayoral elections. Given that London had voted overwhelmingly for the Labour Party in all recent general (as opposed to Mayoral) elections, this was an incontestable example of Stokes' Heineken effect: the ability to reach parts of the electorate that others couldn't reach.

'Don't get too excited.' Marshall pricked the bubble with surgical skill. 'Even with Stokes leading the charge, it will be an uphill battle.'

She pulled a piece of paper from her pocket. 'Have you looked at the bookies' odds recently? The betting is overwhelming for Remain. Look, Paddy Power is offering 5 – 1 on a Remain victory. The gap's as wide as that.'

While Melissa fixed the coffee, Marshall looked at the calendar.

'We've got fewer than one hundred days left before Thursday, 23 June,' she said. 'And we've got to make sure that every one of them counts. Speeches, rallies, TV appearances. We're going to be flat out.'

'Our job is to change the odds, then?' Barnard said.

'Our job is to win the vote.'

They worked on through the morning, pencilling in potential speakers on the spreadsheet and blocking off key dates on the calendar. At twelve noon, they took a break.

Melissa returned with glasses, tonic water and a bottle of gin. She poured a stiff one for herself, then – glass in hand – cast an eye on the spreadsheet and calendar.

'But how are you going to use Edward?' she asked Marshall. 'I don't see a lot of days blocked off for him? He hasn't given up a Cabinet job to stand idly by on the sidelines while others fight the battles.'

'Don't worry.' Marshall tried to calm her down. 'You won't have to cook your husband three square meals a day. He's going to have his work cut out, I can assure you, if we're going to win this one. Without your husband this whole exercise is doomed to failure. The Leave campaign will go down in defeat. The tide is flowing too strongly against us. And the government will ride that tide. They will throw everything they have at us. They will find ways of using government resources even when the rules say they shouldn't.'

Melissa was following her closely. 'So what do we do? How do we close the gap?'

Marshall ran her hand over her forehand. 'Melissa – may I call you Melissa?'

'Go right ahead.'

'Imagine, Melissa, that you're a contestant on *Mastermind*. Say you've picked Harold Macmillan as your specialist subject and John Humphrys asks you to quote one of Macmillan's most famous remarks. What do you say?'

'That one's easy,' Melissa said. '"You've never had it so good".'

'Quite right, Melissa.' Marshall turned to Barnard. 'And what would your choice be?'

Barnard thought for a moment. Dear old Harold! He'd been up at Oxford in the 1980s, when Macmillan was chancellor of the university. He had seen the old boy one day, all togged up in his chancellor's robes, presiding over the annual Encaenia, Oxford's grand prize-giving ceremony. Some young journalist had asked him – was it Jeremy Paxman? – what he thought was the most difficult thing about being prime minister. 'Events, dear boy, events,' the old man had replied.

That's what Barnard said now. '"Events, dear boy, events". That's the point you're making, isn't it? We need something to happen. Something that changes the odds in our favour.'

'Precisely,' Marshall said. 'And we can't wait for events to happen by themselves. We don't have time for that. We have to make them happen. A tide, taken at the flood, leads on to fortune!'

As she spoke, Marshall looked quickly out of the window as though she was waiting for something. Barnard followed the direction of her glance and saw a huge red bus with the words VOTE LEAVE: TAKE BACK CONTROL emblazoned on its side. The bus paused by the gate, as though to check that it had arrived at the right place, then it turned off the road to pull into the courtyard of Barnard's Georgian manor. Half a dozen young men and women began to disembark.

'What on earth's that?' Barnard exclaimed.

Marshall pushed back her chair. 'That's the Vote Leave Battle Bus,' she said. 'Just starting its first pre-Referendum tour: Wiltshire, Cornwall, Devon, Somerset and Dorset. I'd say people in the South West region are natural Outers, but it's a good place to test the water, sharpen the message. Do we care about the NHS? You bet we do! Look at the side of the bus. What does it say? £350 million a week goes to Brussels. Let's spend that money on the NHS!'

It was the first time Barnard had seen the Battle Bus. 'Good God', he thought, 'this is really going to happen!'

'What about that £350 million figure?' Melissa asked. 'Is that accurate? I thought we got some of it back in the rebate. And are we really going to spend it all on the NHS which is what we seem to be saying? I'll believe that when I see it!'

An icy note crept into Marshall's voice as she replied. 'This is surely the moment to be focussing on the broad picture, not quibbling about the detail.'

Barnard shot his wife a warning glance as though to say: don't upset this young genius. We can't afford to lose her. Not now. Not ever.

'Come on,' he said. 'Let's go outside and meet the team.'

That evening, after dinner, Barnard remembered the video. He found it in his briefcase, where he had put it on leaving Xi'an, and handed it to his wife.

'Pop it in for me, darling, please. I never know which button to press.'

Melissa inserted the disc into the player and they sat down to watch.

Barnard recognized the presenter immediately: Professor Wong, the old man who had shown both him and Minister Yu around the site less than twenty-four hours earlier. The camera followed Wong as he walked along the rows of Terracotta Army images, zooming in from time to time on some significant detail.

The video lasted for fifteen minutes. As the voice of the narrator faded, a message appeared on the screen. A huge headline proclaimed:

'BREAKING NEWS. UK MINISTER FOUND IN COMPROMISING SITUATION.'

'What on earth?' Barnard spluttered into his drink. On the screen he watched the two blonde, Russian women get into the elevator with him in the Kempinski Hotel (he could almost smell the perfume, even now). He saw them enter the room with him, and then cavort on the bed . . .

'I don't think I want to watch this,' Melissa said. 'Please turn it off. I'm going to bed.'

As his wife stormed out of the room, Barnard picked up the phone and dialled a number.

CHAPTER TWELVE

Mark Cooper, the head of Britain's Secret Intelligence Service, otherwise known as MI6, answered on the first ring.

'Oh, hello, Edward. I was expecting to hear from you, though not perhaps quite this late. I hear you had some interesting meetings in Xian with our friend Zhang Fu-Sheng.'

'That's what I wanted to talk to you about.'

'Hang up for a moment. I'll call you back on another line. I have the number. It's come up on my screen.'

I'll bet it has, Barnard thought. He was fairly sure that Cooper, when he called back, would switch through to the CX system, which the MI6 boffins claimed provided state-of-the-art security against electronic eavesdropping.

Moments later, Cooper rang back. 'Ah, that's better.'

The two men didn't need to talk long. They were both professionals.

'We'll send a bike to pick the disk up first thing,' Cooper said, rounding the conversation off. 'Around 7:00A.M. Are you at home? How are the azaleas?'

'Everything in the garden is lovely,' Barnard replied. 'Best time of the year.'

Except everything in the garden wasn't lovely. Barnard knew he faced a grilling. He tried to reconstruct precisely what had happened that evening in St Petersburg. He remembered being in the bar at the Kempinski. He remembered talking to the two Russian women in the lift. But after that?

Just because they were both members of Whites didn't mean that Cooper wouldn't put him on the rack.

Later that day, that was precisely what Cooper did. He wasn't some political appointee. He had worked his way up through the ranks during his career in the Secret Intelligence Service. He'd applied a few thumbscrews in his time. Metaphorically at least.

There were four of them in the interrogation room. Cooper had brought along his deputy, James Armitage, to enjoy the fun. Shirley Wilson, head of SIS's China Desk, had been hurriedly briefed. So had Roger Wales, head of the Russia Desk.

'You've all seen the material, haven't you?' Cooper began. 'But it may be helpful to take another look now. Our technicians downstairs are looking at the original, but we've run off a copy for the purposes of today's proceedings. I can assure you that copy will be destroyed when we're through.'

He turned to Wilson. 'I'm sorry if you found some of the acts and actions depicted on the video to be distasteful and upsetting? I should have sent out a spoiler alert.'

'Why just me, Mark? Are you telling me you chaps can handle that kind of stuff, but I can't?'

Cooper took the point. It had taken MI6 quite a while to put both male and female employees on an equal footing but they had got there in the end. Or hoped they had.

'Point taken. Anyway, well, why don't you kick off, Shirley?'

'Okay, I will.' Wilson turned to Barnard. She didn't particularly like Barnard or the class he came from and she didn't take the trouble to deny it.

'So did you fuck those two Russian tarts, Mr Barnard?'

Of course, Wilson was only following the standard interrogation manual. Throw them off balance, make them angry. You couldn't strike them – not any longer. Not officially anyway. But there were other ways of hitting them where it hurts.

Barnard was beginning to wonder whether he should have

insisted on having a lawyer present. 'Just a friendly chat,' Cooper had promised, 'once we've had a chance to look at what you've given us.'

Before he had a chance to reply to Wilson, Wales chipped in. 'This was classic Kompromat stuff, Mr Barnard. Ministers who go to Russia surely know the drill: don't talk to strange blonde women in hotel lobbies. Don't go upstairs with them. Above all, don't go to bed with them. Why the hell did you do it? Were you drunk?'

'I guess I must have been.' Barnard sounded defeated. Totally defeated. Suddenly his world had been turned upside down. He wondered if Melissa would leave him. 'The truth of the matter,' he continued, 'is that I don't actually remember what happened. I admit I'd drunk a certain amount at the dinner in the Winter Palace. This is Russia, remember. And it was a festive occasion. Drinking is what you do, unless you want to give offence to your hosts. Then we came back to the bar in the Kempinski. Did someone slip something in my drink at some point? Perhaps. I remember being in the lift with the two women. I remember punching the button for the eighth floor. But after that my memory is blank, I'm afraid, totally blank. I admit it looks like it could be me on the bed there, though you can't see my face.'

Cooper let it run on. The way he saw it, Barnard deserved to suffer, for being careless, if for nothing else. But he realized that it was time to call a halt. They'd all had their bit of fun. It wasn't every day you had ministers, or former ministers, in the dock wondering where the next blow was coming from.

'I'm going to get the technicians in here now. I've just heard they've finished their analysis of the video.'

He pressed a buzzer beneath the table and two young men, one bearded, the other clean-shaven, entered the room.

'Gentlemen, don't keep us waiting. Are these tapes fake or not? If they are fake, fabricated or whatever, can we prove it? If the man in question looks like Mr Barnard, talks like Mr Barnard and fucks like

Mr Barnard, can we plausibly say this is not Mr Barnard? If we can't say – and say convincingly – that it's not Mr Barnard, then the tapes can show up anytime, anywhere with devastating effect.'

'I'm sure that my wife could be of some help,' Barnard interjected, in a still small voice. 'When Melissa had calmed down, eventually, she told me that she realized all along it couldn't be me. "Wow, Edward." she said. "I'd love to think you could do all that, but I know you can't!" '

It was a feeble joke but it served to defuse the tension. On the crucial issue, the verdict of the young technicians was clear. The tapes were fake.

James the Beard explained: 'The images of the two Russian ladies are genuine, no doubt about that. The image of Mr Barnard in the lift is genuine, though he is – it must be said – looking a bit worse for wear. The three of them appear to walk seamlessly into the room. But they don't actually enter the room. Mr Barnard enters the room by himself.'

'You're absolutely sure of that?'

'We got in touch with Moscow as soon as those tapes came in to us. Our people there know the Kempinski well, and it's not the first time they've asked our contacts for some CCTV output from the hotel. On this particular occasion, we knew the day Barnard had been there, we knew the time, we knew the hotel floor, and the number of the room: the CCTV clips they sent over to us earlier today tell the whole story. Barnard gets out at the 8th floor, but the two Russian ladies go on up to the 12th floor, the penthouse suite.'

'And?' Cooper pressed him. 'What next?'

'There is no next,' the other young man chipped in. 'Mr Barnard goes to bed alone and wakes up alone. There are no shenanigans of any kind.'

Barnard felt so relieved he could have cried. Disaster had for a time loomed, but now help was at hand. 'So who's the chap in bed with the two Russian ladies, pretending to be me?'

'He's not pretending to be you, Edward, for heaven's sake. He's doing whatever he's doing, then someone takes that image and makes out it's you.' Cooper sounded irritated. Didn't these politicians understand what they were dealing with? They used to say the camera didn't lie. Balderdash. The camera lied all the time. You could scramble the pixels just like you could scramble eggs.

'Well, who is he then anyway?' Barnard persisted. 'I know who was in the penthouse at the Kempinski that evening.'

Cooper raised a warning hand.

'I think we had better leave that question for the time being.'

The meeting went on for another hour. These were Britain's top security officials. They couldn't afford to leave stones unturned or avenues unexplored.

Eventually Cooper summed things up. 'We need to consider how the Chinese acquired that tape. If the tape was made by the Russians officially, as it were, say by the KGB/FSB, then why would they have passed it to the Chinese? Why would they help the Chinese discredit our friend, Edward Barnard, when Edward's actions, namely to help the Leave campaign, appear to be in Russia's interest? Isn't it more probable that the Chinese spy network in Russia – and that is a very substantial network indeed – got hold of the tapes from some freelance source and then spliced it all together with a view to persuading Barnard here to jump ship of his own accord and ditch the Leave campaign? Which by any reckoning could be a fatal blow for that campaign and very good news for China. So they try a little gentle persuasion instead. Does that make sense? It does to me.'

Barnard had had enough. They could speculate as much as they liked. It wouldn't make any difference. Whatever the Chinese thought they might be doing by making that tape, they had picked the wrong man.

If he had been sure, when he was talking to Minister Zhang in Xian that he was on the right path, he was doubly sure now. A line from Shakespeare came to mind. Macbeth, surely? *'Thou marshall'st me the way that I was going.'*

Good old Shakespeare, he thought, as he picked up his notes, you could always rely on the Bard for a pertinent quote.

Cooper walked out with him.

'We're taking another look at the Kempinski,' he said. 'We're trying to track down those two Russian women. Whatever they put in your drink could have been very dangerous. Glad it wasn't polonium, anyway.' Cooper put out his hand. 'By the way, I wanted to tell you we haven't made much progress with that other file you brought back. The home secretary's rather sitting on it. Some of the emails to and from Number 10 seem to be genuine, not fakes, as we supposed. We've got a bit more digging to do.'

'Dig away,' Barnard urged. 'But please let me know when and if you turn something up.'

'Your car's waiting for you in the underground car park,' Cooper said. 'We can't have you leaving through the front door. The opposition keeps very close tabs on the comings and goings here.'

'And who's the opposition in this particular case?'

'Good question. We're still trying to work that one out.'

CHAPTER THIRTEEN

Bud Hollingsworth leaned back in his upholstered chair in the director's private viewing-room at the CIA in Langley, Virginia, with the remote control in his hand.

'All set?' he inquired.

Wilbur Brown, director of the FBI, who had driven out to Langley earlier that afternoon for a meeting with his counterpart, nodded. 'Good to go,' he said.

Hollingsworth pressed the button on the remote.

'I won't tell you how we acquired the footage we are about to see. I'll just say that the FSB is a bit more porous than its predecessor, the KGB, used to be.'

Brown nodded. If Hollingsworth wanted to protect his sources, he had no problem with that. In spite of all the changes in the organization of US security in recent years, the broad lines of demarcation between the CIA and the FBI remained fairly clear. The CIA concentrated on gathering, analyzing and reporting on intelligence from abroad; the FBI devoted itself to counter-intelligence, notably the threats arising on home turf. So how the CIA went about its job in, say, the Russian Far East was, as far as Brown understood the ground rules, their job, not his.

The first couple of minutes of the film showed the Russian president Igor Popov's helicopter landing in a cleared area in the forest. The next shots showed Popov in combat gear moving through the trees.

'The Russians call this the "*taiga*" or boreal forest,' Hollingsworth explained. 'Mile upon mile of pine, spruce, larch and birch. You can see Ronald Craig walking fairly closely behind Popov. Behind Craig, there's that Brit, I believe his name's Barnard. Ed Barnard, or something like that.'

'Yes, I've heard about Barnard,' Brown said. 'Used to be environment minister in the UK government. Met up with both Popov and Craig at Popov's World Tiger Summit. Then they all went off to the Russian Far East to try to see the Amur tigers in the wild. We're not sure quite what Barnard's relationship with the Russians is. Some kind of "useful idiot" I suspect. We're looking into that. So is MI5, I hear.'

The images ran on. 'Who's that coming after Barnard?' Brown asked. 'Is that Craig's daughter, Rosie? Good-looking girl, eh? And who's that with her? That's not Jack Varese, for God's sake, is it? What's he doing out there?'

As they watched the screen, they saw the tiger coming down the path towards the presidential party. Shouting and confusion ensued. The microphone clearly picked up Popov's command. 'Don't shoot.'

It also picked up Craig's anguished yell: 'What the fu—!'

'I'm going to play that again in slow motion,' Hollingsworth said. 'Keep an eye on Popov. What do you see?'

Hollingsworth ran the tape again. When it had finished, the Director of the FBI gave a long, low whistle.

'Popov didn't aim at the tiger at all, did he? He picks up his gun, points it at the tiger, then as the tiger runs off into the forest, he quickly turns, aims and shoots the dart into Craig's backside. Dead shot! Bullseye! Don't tell me that was an accident?'

'It didn't look much like an accident to me,' Hollingsworth agreed.

Hollingsworth paused the tape, freezing the frame. A ranger knelt beside the prostrate form of Ronald Craig. Next to him stood President Popov with a yellow vial in his hand.

Hollingsworth picked up the phone. Minutes later, a tall grey-faced man with thinning hair joined them.

'Thanks for coming in, John. We need some technical advice here.'

John Hulley, one of the CIA's top boffins, nodded. 'Happy to oblige.'

The CIA director ran the film again. When it was over, he asked Hulley a simple question. 'John, you technical people are always talking about the advances in surveillance techniques. Recording devices no thicker than a human hair. That kind of thing.'

'Well, that might be a bit of an exaggeration. But, yes, the new bugging devices are very small indeed. They can be recharged through solar radiation. Look at what they're doing with wildlife monitoring nowadays. Once you've tagged them, you can track high-flying birds, like the Canada geese or Berwick swans, literally for years. The higher they fly, the more solar energy that little transmitter absorbs.'

'Okay, fine, I've got it,' Hollingsworth said. 'But what I want to know is whether you could use a tranquillizing dart to insert one of these new, highly miniaturized transmitters into a human target.'

Hulley thought for a long moment. 'I'd say it would depend what part of the body you were aiming at? The needle needs to go in at least five millimetres. Okay, the buttocks are a promising target. That's why we inject people in the ass. Plenty of flesh for a needle to sink into. But frankly, I'd say that would have been a lucky shot indeed. Remember, the dart Popov fired would have had to carry the narcoleptic dose, enough to render the target insensible for the desired period of time, as well as the bugging device.'

They mulled it over for a while.

'What about the hospital in Khabarovsk?' Brown had a sudden thought. 'As I understand it, they took Craig into the hospital after the incident. If they put him under again there, or even gave him a local anaesthetic when they were tending the wound from the dart, they could have planted the bug, couldn't they?'

Hulley nodded. 'Now you're talking.'

It took a while for the full implications to sink in. At last Hollingsworth spoke. 'If that device is working, then any time Craig goes anywhere or sees anyone, the Russians could be listening in. Is that right?'

Two days later, President Brandon Matlock sat in the Oval Office waiting for the attorney general to arrive. Normally, the White House legal officers would have drafted some language, having cleared it around town through the normal channels. But these weren't normal times.

In any case, as far as President Matlock was concerned, it wasn't just a question of keeping down the number of people who knew what was going on because of security issues. There was an element of retribution involved too. He could never forget that Craig had been the moving spirit behind the 'birthers': that group of bitter and twisted individuals who argued that Matlock hadn't been born in the US and therefore was not eligible, under the Constitution, to be president.

Determined to produce an absolute zinger of an executive order, elegantly drafted as well as legally watertight, the president had called in Joe Silcock. Silcock, an African-American who in his time had graduated top from Harvard Law School and was now the youngest attorney general since Bobby Kennedy, was generally thought to be one of the smartest lawyers in town.

'Let's get some good language here, Joe, shall we?' the president said. 'What about something along the lines of, "The President of the United States hereby desires and commands Ronald C. Craig to attend forthwith the Walter Reed Army Center in Bethesda, Maryland, with a view to submitting his . . ."' The president paused. 'What's the Latin term for "posterior"?'

' "Posterior" *is* the Latin term.'

'Well, try something else. What about "*gluteus maximus*"?'

'The "*gluteus maximus*" is in the buttocks, I believe. Actually, there are two of them, one on each side. I believe Mr Craig was darted on the left side.'

'Well, he'll have to bring them both in, won't he? Would that be "*glutei maximi*"?'

'Why not just put "backside" or even "ass"?'

'You mean as in, "Just get your ass over to Walter Reed"?'

Even though his term still had a few months to run, Silcock could sense that President Matlock was already demob-happy.

'That will do fine, I'm sure,' he said.

The president signed the executive order with a flourish. He handed the pen to the Attorney General.

'Probably the last executive order I'll sign. Hang on to the pen. It might be worth something one day.'

When Silcock had gone, President Matlock picked up the phone. 'Could you get hold of Wilbur Brown, please, at the FBI? Ask him to step over here if he has a moment.'

When Brown arrived, the president said, 'I've signed the executive order. Walter Reed is on standby. You'll do the necessary, won't you?'

Brown replied simply, 'The FBI's mission is to protect the American people and uphold the Constitution of the United States.'

Years ago, President Matlock recalled, US President Richard Nixon – about to resign his great office in disgrace – had asked the then secretary of state, Henry Kissinger, to pray with him in this very room. What a lot of history the place had seen. He hoped he wouldn't leave with a cloud over his head. But what would happen to his legacy, he wondered?

He stood up from his desk and walked over to the window to look out at the rose garden. 'I'm going, Wilbur, but people like you must carry on the good work.'

'We will, sir.' Wilbur Brown, seventh director of the FBI, felt strangely moved. 'We will carry on the good work. Till hell freezes over. Whatever it takes.'

CHAPTER FOURTEEN

Craig had reached Barnard by phone earlier in the week. 'Come over for my speech in Fort Lauderdale,' Craig had urged him. 'I'm sure you need a break and I could use your help.'

Barnard had checked it out with Marshall. Nowadays, he didn't move without Marshall's say-so. He, Barnard, was officially chairman of the Leave campaign but he was under no illusions as to where the power truly lay. It lay with Marshall. No doubt about that. Sometimes he murmured 'Take back control' when Marshall laid down the law – who was to do what and when – but he never kicked up a fuss. When you had a political genius on your side, you didn't quibble.

Marshall had been totally enthusiastic about the proposed trip to Florida.

'Genius!' she exclaimed. 'Just what we need. A bit of international exposure just at the right time. Make sure Craig mentions Brexit in his speech.'

Barnard needn't have had any worries on that score.

Less than three hours after landing in Florida he watched Craig, the presumptive Republican presidential candidate, come to the podium in front of the cheering, flag-waving, trumpet-parping crowds in the Fort Lauderdale stadium.

Craig's rhetorical style, consisting of short, declaratory sentences, was precisely what his audience was looking for.

'Thank you. I am so thrilled to be in Fort Lauderdale today,'

Craig began. 'Florida is my second home. This is such an amazing state, and filled with so many incredible people.

'We are all going to have to work hard together to win the White House on 8 November. Our victory on 8 November will be a victory for the people.

'It won't be a victory for the pundits, the special interests, the failed politicians. It will be a victory for YOU – for your family, for your country.

'It will be a victory for jobs. For security. For prosperity. It will be a victory for American Independence.

'We will reject the failures of the past and create a New American Future where every child – African-American, Hispanic, and all children – can live out their dreams.

'We will bring back our jobs.

'Rebuild our depleted military.

'Take care of our veterans.

'Unleash American energy.

'Restore law and order.

'And we will make government honest once again.'

Towards the end of his speech, Craig turned to Barnard, sitting on the dais behind the lectern:

'Come up here, Ed,' Craig commanded. Then, lowering his voice as though imparting some confidential information, he added, 'This is the man who's helping to set Britain free. He has started this incredible movement. You're all part of this movement. This movement that we talk about so much. That's been written about on the cover of every magazine all over the world. It's a movement that is just sweeping. It's sweeping across our country. It's sweeping frankly across the globe.'

Craig strode over and hoisted Barnard's arm into the air.

For the moment the two of them stood there, arms held high, like the golden arches of McDonalds, as the crowd went wild.

'Let's hear it for Britain!' Craig trumpeted. 'Let's hear it for Ed Barnard and all who are working with him! They're doing it over there. We can do it over here! Look at Brexit! Much smaller example, but it's still something you can look at. People want to take back control of their countries and they want to take back control of their lives and the lives of their family.'

When Craig said that Florida was his second home, he hadn't been exaggerating. He truly loved the enormous jazz-age mansion, set in its own fifteen acres of land on the narrow strip of land between the Atlantic Ocean and Worth Lake. He had owned it for the last thirty years as part of the Craig empire. Most of the property was now part of the Hasta La Vista private club, with 128 luxurious bedrooms, though Craig and his family still had their exclusive family quarters.

They had a late candlelit supper after the rally, looking out over the ocean. Malvina Craig, Ronald's wife, sat – suavely beautiful – at one end of the table. Craig himself sat at the other end, with daughter Rosie on his right, and Barnard on his left.

'So good to see you again, Ed!' Craig gushed. 'That expedition to Russia's Far East was some trip, wasn't it? We got to see a tiger too. You know my backside's still sore. Godammit, I thought Popov was meant to be a crack shot and he ends up by shooting me in the ass! How's the Brexit campaign going, Ed? Are you on course for victory?'

Barnard saw no point in pretending things were better than they were. 'We're not there yet,' he confessed. 'The government's committed itself to Project Fear. The prime minister and the chancellor of the exchequer are stressing the downside if we leave. And we're not getting the groundswell of support we need. Not yet anyway. I think we've got to raise our game, otherwise we're going to be crushed on 23 June – that's our Referendum day.'

'Don't for a moment think we've got it in the bag either on this side of the ocean,' Craig countered 'We've got a long way to go too. I may win the nomination, but I still need to win the election. Never underestimate Caroline Mann. She's tricky as hell. Did you know the FBI has 30,000 of her unauthorized emails? God knows what she was up to. But are they releasing them? Are they hell? They're terrified that releasing the emails will damage her chances. And the press! Vipers, turncoats, hypocrites. Fake news, that's all they're good for. Lock them up, I say. Lock them all up!'

As Craig worked himself up into a lather of righteous indignation, a uniformed butler entered the room. 'Please forgive me interrupting, Mr Craig. There's a posse of federal marshals here.'

'What the devil's going on?' Craig tossed his napkin onto the table and strode to the door.

The two federal marshals waiting outside the door greeted him politely.

Craig recognized both of them at once. If you were a politician, you made a point of getting to know the local gendarmerie. 'Pedro, Jimmy,' he said. 'For God's sake, what's all this about?'

Pedro Gonzales was more than a little anxious. He'd had a run-in or two with Craig in the past and had not come off best. He certainly didn't want to piss the man off. He might be president one day. He turned to the man at his side, Jimmy Redmond.

'Jimmy, you read it out,' he said. 'You read better than me. Unless it's in Spanish. I'm probably better than Jimmy is at reading Spanish.'

'Just get on with it,' Craig snarled.

'Here we go.' Redmond put on his spectacles.

In the brief time at their disposal, President Brandon Matlock and Attorney General Joe Silcock had done a tremendous job. The Executive Order signed by the president looked good and sounded good. It smelt good too, being printed on heavy, crisp parchment. The marshal began to read:

'Whereas it appears to be possible, if not probable, that Ronald C. Craig may unwittingly have been the target of an unauthorized attack by a hypodermic dart or some other intervention while visiting the Russian Far East . . .

'Whereas it is necessary through a clinical examination to establish whether such an attack or intervention has indeed taken place and to take all appropriate measures . . .

'Whereas the implications for national security of the said event need to be fully evaluated . . .

'Now therefore: I, President of the United States, have decided and determined that the said Ronald C. Craig should be immediately brought by federal marshals to the Walter Reed Medical Center, Bethesda, Maryland, and that the said federal marshals are authorized to use all necessary means, including force, toward that end.

'Signed, Brandon Matlock, 44th President of the United States, 18 May 2016'

As Redmond rolled the parchment up, Craig protested, 'I'm not coming. I'll call my lawyers. I'll take you to court. Executive Orders can be challenged in the courts. A federal judge can grant a stay of execution. I know quite a few federal judges and believe me they listen to me.'

Redmond shook his head. 'Don't go there, sir. That's not a good line to take. You had better come along with us. In the state of Florida, resisting arrest is a pretty serious crime. You wouldn't want that on your record. Not when you're running for the highest office in the land. Besides, it's not all bad news. I didn't read you the PS, the postscript as I believe it's called.'

'I didn't think executive orders had PSs.'

'This one does. It says. *PS: I am hereby making available Air Force One to the federal marshals for the discharge of the aforementioned task.*'

'You better go, Dad,' Rosie said. 'No point in fighting this one.'

Craig looked at his daughter. He respected her judgement. She was one of the few people he trusted.

'You think so?'

'Yes, I think so.'

'Who's going to look after Ed Barnard? I wanted to take him to the Everglades tomorrow. Show him some alligators.'

'I'll do that, Dad. I haven't been to the Everglades for months. You go to Washington. There are plenty of alligators there! They just want to give you a check-up. You'll probably be back by tomorrow.'

Gonzales looked at his watch. 'Take-off is in forty-five minutes. We had better get going.'

'Okay, I'm coming. Just put the handcuffs way.'

Air Force One? Craig rather liked the sound of that anyway. Maybe it wouldn't hurt to check the plane out ahead of time. And besides, deep down, he knew it didn't pay to quarrel with Uncle Sam. Not seriously. If you did, you could find yourself in trouble. Of course, once he made it to the top, the very top, it might be a different matter.

CHAPTER FIFTEEN

The Walter Reed National Military Medical Center, in Bethesda, Maryland, colloquially known as Walter Reed, had a proud history of serving US presidents. President Kennedy's body was brought there in November 1963 for the official autopsy after his assassination in Dallas, Texas. President Eisenhower actually died there in 1969. And in July 1985, President Reagan went in to have some polyps removed from his colon. Craig couldn't help feeling, as the helicopter whisked him to the medical center on the short hop from Andrews Airforce base, that, in some obscure way, he was already treading destiny's path. One way or another, Walter Reed loomed large in the life (or death) of most US Presidents.

Bud Hollingsworth was waiting for him at the entrance. 'Thanks for coming in, Ron,' he said.

Craig pointedly ignored the outstretched hand. 'I don't think I had any choice. Do you mind telling me what this is all about?'

'I can't say much. Classified. Need to know.'

Craig exploded. 'If anyone has a need to know, I do.'

Hollingsworth knew he had to give a little. Though – legally speaking – he had been given powers of restraint, even coercion, he preferred not to use them. He had learned long ago that persuasion was often more effective than force.

'We think your personal security may recently have been compromised. In other words, we think you may be bugged. We don't know for sure, but the evidence points that way.'

'You want to examine my backside, do you?'

'We are certainly grateful for your cooperation,' Hollingsworth replied diplomatically. Craig, he knew, had a short fuse. Things had gone well so far. He hoped this wasn't just the calm before a storm.

They gave him the lightest of anaesthetics. Two hours later, Craig was in the recovery room. Hollingsworth hovered by the bedside.

He held out a small metal tray. 'Take a look at this little blighter,' he said. 'It's plastic. Would never show up with a metal detector, but we picked it up with the MRI.'

Craig studied the small round object on the tray. 'Is that still transmitting as we speak? Are they listening in to us?'

'They were, I imagine, but we switched it off as soon as we extracted it,' Hollingsworth replied.

'How did you do that?'

'With tweezers actually. Good, old-fashioned tweezers. Took a bit of probing.'

'I mean, how did you switch it off?'

'We found the switch.'

'Won't they realize you're on to them?'

In this verbal ping-pong, Craig had just delivered a forehand smash.

'Good point,' Hollingsworth acknowledged. 'We weighed that one carefully. We could have left the transmitter in place and used you as a conduit for false information to feed to the other side. A stool pigeon, if you like. Like the spy thrillers. On balance we decided that this way was better. We believe they'll put it down to a technical malfunction. Happens all the time, you know.'

'What about the executive order the federal marshals laid on me? That's public knowledge, isn't it? Executive orders get published in the Federal Register. They'll find out that way, won't they?'

'This one won't be published in the Federal Register, I can assure you. No more than half a dozen copies of the order existed anyway, and by now they've all been destroyed.'

Craig couldn't help admiring the thoroughness of the operation. 'You guys put in a lot of effort to reel me in, didn't you?'

'You were one big barracuda. We couldn't afford to have you running around, talking to all and sundry and the Russians listening in to every word.'

Craig got out of bed and pulled on his trousers. 'Am I free to go?'

'Free as air.'

'Are you going to send me the bill for the hospital?'

'This one's on the house. Do you want to stay here for the rest of the night?'

'Gee, thanks, but no thanks. I own a few hotels in this town. I'm sure one of them will find a bed for me.'

They gave him a police escort into the City. He pulled out his cell phone and started tweeting his twenty million plus followers:

#IN NATION'S CAPITAL BUT ONLY FOR THE DAY. BACK SOON MORE PERMANENTLY. I HOPE TO CONTINUE FIGHTING FOR YOU!!

Craig felt suddenly cheerful. Okay, his backside was a little sore. They probably had to dig around a bit when they pulled out the bug, but he felt fit as a fiddle otherwise.

He looked at his watch. 5:30 A.M. A bit too early to call in the troops for a surprise meeting. Give them a chance to have a pee and brush their teeth. Ronald Craig was nothing if not considerate. So many people weren't considerate, he thought. Sad.

Two hours later, Craig gathered his team together in his private dining room in the Washington Craig International Hotel. Arguably, the Washington Craig had an even better view of the White House, the other side of Lafayette Square, than the Hay Adams Hotel – its near neighbour – did. Craig wasn't bothered either way. He was already within spitting distance of the presidential mansion. That was what counted.

'I'm making no promises, guys,' he began. 'We're not there yet, but I want you to know that I consider you all to be top-quality candidates for my transition team and after that, who knows? If we win in July, which looks pretty darn likely at the moment, and if we win again in November – and we are going to have to work our butts off to make sure that happens – some or all of you are going to be sitting with me over there in the White House.'

He gestured towards the gleaming white-portico structure just a few hundred feet away. God what a beautiful building it was, he thought. From the outside at least; internally, apparently, the accommodation left much to be desired. Still, that could be fixed. Most things could be fixed if you put your mind to it.

'So let me tell you what's up for grabs,' he continued. 'Of course, it'll be a bit of a merry-go-round. Not all of you will find a seat when the music stops. That's just the way it is. But I can tell you now, if things go to plan, I shall be looking for a chief of staff, a chief strategist, a press secretary, a national security adviser, as well as a counsellor and a special adviser. That's just for starters.'

He looked around the room. 'Some of the people who are going to fill key positions in my administration are already in this room. And it goes without saying that my running mate, the vice-presidential candidate, Senator Elmore Singer, is one of those.'

Craig waved across the table to the white-haired gentleman with the black-and-red striped tie who sat exactly opposite him. 'Welcome aboard, Elmore.'

Craig led the round of applause. 'And let me tell you the good news, from Elmore's point of view at least. As vice-president, he's the person I can't fire!'

He paused. Craig had learned early in life that if you wanted to grab your audience's attention, you had to let the tension build. The deliberate pause, mid-sentence or even mid-word, was a basic rhetorical device. Craig knew that from his school days. A guy called Cicero wrote scads about it, he remembered. Not that he had spent too much time on Cicero. He preferred to be out there earning money.

'There's one other person I'm not going to fire, I can tell you. That's my daughter.' Craig leaned forward to talk into the speaker-phone in front of him.

'Are you there, honey? Say hi to Rosie, guys.'

'Hi Rosie!'

'Say it louder, so she can hear you. Rosie's in Florida. Couldn't make it today.'

'Hi, Rosie!' they shouted again.

'Are you there, Rosie?' Craig repeated.

Rosie's voice came through clear, bright and bubbly, like the cherry-blossoms in the Mall.

'I've just appointed you my "Special Adviser", honey. Say "hello" to the guys.'

'Hello, guys. Great to meet you. Just want to say how proud I am to be part of the team.'

The meeting ran on for an hour. Barring last minute upsets (and they couldn't imagine what those might be), Craig would be elected as the presidential candidate at the Republican National Convention to be held in Cleveland, Ohio, that coming July. So now was a time to look ahead, to the election campaign itself and even beyond.

Legally, of course, President Brandon Matlock would discharge the duties of his great office right up to the moment, on Friday, 20 January 2017, when his successor would be officially inaugurated as the 45th President of the United States. But in practice, as everyone in Washington knew, as soon as the result of the November election was known, power and influence would begin to ooze away from the president in the direction of the president-elect, whoever he or she might be. That was just the way things were.

As the meeting broke up, Craig beckoned to his acting national security adviser:

'Can you stay behind for a moment, General?'

As the room emptied, the two men huddled in a corner. They

spoke for twenty minutes. Craig did most of the talking. General Ian Wright, a four-star general, did most of the nodding.

But at one point, the general intervened. 'What about the Logan Act, sir? The one which makes it a crime for an unauthorized person to negotiate with a foreign power?'

Craig looked puzzled. 'Isn't the Logan Act over 200 years old? And surely no one's ever been prosecuted.'

'Just thought I'd raise the issue.'

'Well, thank you, General. My view is don't bother about the Logan Act. Just go right ahead. Every transition team that I'm aware of makes contact with foreign governments. Let's just anticipate the reality.'

Wright still felt uneasy. He sensed he was being pushed further than he wanted to go. On the other hand he liked the idea of occupying that corner office on the first floor of the White House, diagonally opposite the Oval Office itself, with a discreet bronze plaque reading: 'Gen. Ian Wright, National Security Adviser'.

What the hell! The General made up his mind. As Harry S. Truman put it, 'If you can't stand the heat, get out of the kitchen.'

'I'll have a word with Ambassador Reznikov,' Wright said.

'Get him to sign up to my four-point plan. At least get him to check it out with Moscow. That way we can hit the ground running. We might have a deal.'

A deal! That was the magic word. Could the whole of life be boiled down to simple deal-making? Ron Craig obviously thought it could.

'I'll give it a go, sir,' Wright said. 'Count on me.'

Craig gave the general a friendly punch in the chest,

'That's the spirit,' he said. 'Get up and go. That's what we need. That's what this country needs. Get to work, General. There's a lot hanging on this.'

CHAPTER SIXTEEN

Rosie didn't accompany Barnard to the Florida Everglades National Park after all. They had just finished breakfast on the veranda, looking out at the Atlantic, when the 'Craig for President' Campaign HQ sent a text message: 'Your father's about to appear on CBS'.

So they poured themselves another cup of coffee, turned on the television and settled down to watch. Sure enough Craig soon appeared.

'Looks fresh as a daisy, doesn't he?' Rosie commented. She admired her father's stamina. He must have been up most of the night, and they'd already had the team meeting that morning. But it wasn't just Craig's stamina she admired. Her father's ability to surprise, to shake things up, to think the unthinkable, intrigued and fascinated her. But she wasn't starry-eyed. She was ready to take him to task when she felt she had to. And, to be fair, he was usually ready to listen – to her, at least.

Craig seldomly missed a trick. CBS had given him a platform, and by God he was going to use it! After a few minutes' warm-up, he upped the volume to rant about the media. That was his special bugbear, now as always.

Looking straight at the camera, he stormed, 'The dishonest media: they are part of the corrupt system. Thomas Jefferson, Andrew Jackson and Abraham Lincoln and many of our greatest presidents fought with the media and called them out on their lies. When the media lies to people, I will never, ever let them get away with it.'

Seconds later, Rosie's phone rang.

'Did you watch CBS, Rosie?' Craig asked. 'Did you hear what I said about the media, the lying bastards?'

Rosie held the phone away from her ear, until her father's excitement had subsided.

'You were great, Dad. Just great.'

Craig came to the point.

'I've just had a message from Mickey Selkirk. He's invited you to visit him on his ranch in Australia. He's there at the moment. I want you to go. As you know, Selkirk owns newspapers and TV stations all over the world, scores of them in America by the way. He may say he doesn't interfere with editorial policy. Bullshit! He's interfering by *not* interfering. Go and see him. Up close and personal. Bring him round to our point of view. This is a golden opportunity.'

'You think he's ready?'

'He's gagging for it. Why else is he inviting you at this point? Mickey's like me. He's a deal-maker. Now is the best moment. He may never get a better offer. I'm still a dark horse, as far as the election this November is concerned. Caroline Mann is still way ahead in the polls.'

'So you think he's ready to come off the fence and support us? What do *we* have to offer?'

Craig ran through a list of the key points. Then he asked, 'Is Ed still there?'

'Yes, he is. I was about to take him to the Everglades. He wants to see the alligators.'

'Give the Everglades a miss. Take Ed to Australia with you. If Ed wants to see alligators, he can meet Mickey Selkirk. He's the biggest alligator of them all.'

Since returning from Russia, Jack Varese's affair with Rosie, which had begun in Russia's Far East, had blossomed. Jack had a penthouse apartment at the corner of East 70th Street and Fifth Avenue. As it happened, Rosie's own apartment was only a block away but, while Jack was in town, she didn't spend much time there. She spent most of the time in bed with Jack.

'You certainly live up to your reputation,' she said one morning after a strenuous session.

'Glad you think so. I always aim to be of service. Yes, ma'am!'

She found him funny and intelligent, too.

'I'm not going to stay in films for ever,' he told her. 'There are always younger kids on the block, waiting to pounce. I've got my eye on a political career. Remember Ronald Reagan? Arnold Schwarzenegger? Think I might run for Senate in California next time round.'

'So that's why you're interested in me?' Rosie pretended to be upset. 'Because of the politics? Because my dad's riding the crest of the wave?'

'Hell no, I just like being with you.'

The previous weekend, they had popped over to the Bahamas in Jack's Gulfstream 550. After, Rosie had gone back to Hasta La Vista – there was a campaign to run after all – but Jack had stayed on.

When he'd got Rosie's call that morning, he was tickled pink. 'Great! Fantastic. I'll be there in an hour.' You could almost see Florida from the Bahamas. It was that close.

Was he falling for Rosie? Jack wondered, as he put the phone away. He had been to plenty of parties over the years and had dated myriad lovely ladies – hell, what would he do without them? – but he hadn't fallen for someone in a long time. Not properly.

He met Rosie and Barnard that afternoon at Palm Beach International Airport. Rosie gave him a long, passionate kiss.

'So good to see you, darling.'

'You too,' Jack said.

After they had disentangled themselves, Jack turned to greet Barnard. 'Hi, Ed, great to see you again.'

They completed the formalities and then walked out onto the tarmac to board the plane. Terry came out of the cockpit to greet them.

'Welcome on board, folks.'

'I've brought Terry along to do a bit of the flying,' Jack said. 'Australia's a helluva long way away, even with my Gulfstream.' He pointed to the sleek machine sitting on the tarmac at Palm Beach International's Private Aviation Facility with its engines running. 'Besides, it will be fun to chill out with you guys en route.'

They only broke the journey once, and that was in Easter Island, 2,300 miles west of Santiago, Chile. They disembarked while the plane was being refuelled to make a whirlwind visit to the site of the famous *moai*, gigantic stone statues, carved out of tuff, the light, porous rock formed by consolidated volcanic ash.

Standing there, on a wild, windswept headland, with her arm around the man she was pretty sure she loved, and with the *moai* towering hugely above her, Rosie felt suddenly moved. Nobody yet had fathomed the mystery of Easter Island – or *Rapa Nui* as it was known to its earliest inhabitants. A civilization had flourished and then it had collapsed, within a space of years. Did they cut down all the trees in order to make rollers to shift the giant stones around? Did they die out because of some sudden, mysterious illness? Nobody knew for sure.

'We could make a film,' Rosie said. Of course Jack would have the lead role. He looked a bit Polynesian, to be honest. But there might be a part for her too. Something wild and sexy? She hoped Jack wouldn't give up his movie career too soon. He was so darn good. And besides, the 'Craig for President' campaign needed all the allies in Hollywood they could find. Hollywood hadn't been much help to Craig so far, and that was the understatement of the year.

'So glad you've got Jack Varese on board,' her father had joked. 'In every sense!'

'That's gross, Dad,' she'd responded. She could talk to her father like that. No one else could.

Terry flew the next leg, from Easter Island to Kununurra, while Jack and Rosie snatched a few hours' sleep in the plane's master bedroom with its king-size bed. Barnard had some marginally less grand sleeping quarters in the rear of the plane. 'Way to go', he thought. Funny, wasn't it? Spend some time in the States and you start talking like a Yank.

A party of American tourists had just landed as they were about to leave Easter Island. One or two of them recognized Jack. Not surprising, of course, since Jack at this point in his stellar career possessed one of Planet Earth's more famous faces. As the Gulfstream 550 flew on through the southern night, the tweets from Rapa Nui came thick and fast:

 # Guess what! Saw Jack Varese with a new blonde on Easter Island? Who is she?

#Is Jack Varese making a film about the giant statues? And who's the mystery blonde?

Varese had fans all over the world, which meant he had fans in the northernmost reaches of Western Australia. Yes, there too. By the time they landed at Kununurra, right on Western Australia's boundary with the Northern Territory, quite a reception party had gathered. A young aboriginal female reporter from Kimberley TV thrust a microphone in front of Varese as he strode into the airport building from the plane.

'You heading for El Questro, Mr Varese? Are you going to be meeting Nicole Kidman there? She likes to go to El Questro.'

Jack put his arm round Rosie. 'I'm just fine as I am. Can a man hire a helicopter round here?'

He turned to Terry. 'Take a couple of days off, Terry. We'll pick you up on the way back. Why don't you head down to the coast? Catch some barramundi for your dinner!'

One hundred miles west of Kununurra, sitting in the living room of the farmhouse in the Kimberley that his family had owned for the best part of a century, Selkirk watched the TV coverage of Jack's arrival with interest. He could remember a time when there was no

TV at all up in the outback. Jamie Selkirk, Mickey's father, one of the most brilliant newsmen of his generation, had built up the Selkirk TV network station by station. Kimberley TV was one of the first to go on air, way back in the 1950s, in the vast empty spaces of Western Australia's Kimberley region.

'Don't just concentrate on the cities: Sydney, Melbourne, Adelaide and so on,' Jamie had told his son. 'You've got to get out in the outback too. That's where they really need TV. You can't just go down to the shop and buy a paper. There won't be a bloody shop. Not for miles. Probably not at all.'

By the time Mickey took over, Selkirk Media Pty Ltd covered most of Australia. Mickey's mission had been to build on his father's legacy. And he succeeded. Under his leadership, Selkirk Media had changed its name to Selkirk Global. Mickey had opened offices in New York, London, Hong Kong, Jakarta and a score of other cities around the world.

By then, the great Jamie Selkirk had been dead a long time. And now Mickey himself was no longer a young man. In fact, he was over eighty – would you believe it? But his lust for power was as strong as ever.

As he saw it, there were still huge gaps in Selkirk Global's empire. Okay, he had more or less wrapped Australia up, but he couldn't truthfully say the same of the US or the UK. Selkirk Global was just one of the players there. An important player, yes, but not necessarily dominant.

And that went for other parts of the world too. He hadn't cracked Russia, for a start. And they still had a long way to go in China.

He heard the thud-thud of the helicopter coming in to land on the pad. You didn't own and run a million-acre cattle station in the Kimberley without your own helipad and airstrip.

Mickey left his drink on the bar. He called out to his wife, 'Melanie, they're here!'

Melanie Selkirk, a tall blonde, who had once been married to a famous pop-star, and who herself had appeared on the cover of several bestselling albums, hastened to join her husband on the helipad.

Jack, toting his flight bag over his shoulder, climbed out of the cockpit via the pilot's door, then walked round to open the side door for the others.

'Glad to see you found some transport at Kununurra, Jack. Welcome to Lazy-T station.' Selkirk gave the Hollywood movie-star an all-embracing hug. That's what they all did nowadays, he thought. Hug each other. In the old days, you just shook hands. Most often not even that. Just tipped your hat, if you were wearing one, and said 'Gday'mate.' Never mind. Go with the flow. No harm in that.

Selkirk turned to greet Rosie. Christ, he had known her since she was a baby. And look at her now! What a gorgeous creature.

'Rosie, you look wonderful. Melanie, doesn't Rosie look wonderful? Come on in, everyone. Let's have a drink.'

Selkirk gave them all a great beaming smile. This was the moment he had been waiting for. How did that rhyme go? *Will you come into my parlour said the spider to the fly?*

CHAPTER SEVENTEEN

They had drinks before dinner on the homestead's terrace, with its splendid view of the Pentecost River, as it ran through the Lazy-T cattle station on its way to the Indian Ocean.

Selkirk introduced them to the staff, a middle-aged Chinese couple.

'Meet Ching and Fung,' he said. 'They look after the place. They do the cooking too, I'm glad to say. They've been in this country for years. Go over to Broome and you'll find a whole Chinatown. The Chinese ran the pearl-fishing industry there. Bloody hard work that must have been. They didn't have any health and safety regulations then. Lost a lot of divers. Lost your father like that, didn't you, Ching?'

'Grandfather too,' the man, Ching, said.

After drinks, they had dinner by the pool.

Selkirk, overcoming his natural aversion to Limeys, did his best to be polite to Barnard.

'Been to the Kimberley before, Ed?' he asked,

'Been to Perth and Albany but never to the Kimberley. Great time of year, isn't it?' Barnard waved in the direction of the river. 'Can we swim in the river?'

'Course you can, if you don't mind the crocs,' Selkirk replied. 'Mind you, the freshwater crocs aren't as dangerous as the salties. The salties can come quite a way upstream. Fella got taken by a saltie a few days back at Pentecost River crossing and that's a long way inland.

Came too close to the bank in his boat. You think they're asleep on the bank there but they're not. They can spend days watching. Not moving. Then, bang, you're gone. They spin you round and round and drown you, unless you can manage to jab a knife in their eye. Lull you into a false sense of security, that's what they do.'

Was that Selkirk's preferred *modus operandi*, Barnard wondered? Lulling the opposition into a false sense of security, before striking, suddenly and ruthlessly?

When Ching and Fung had cleared the table, Selkirk tapped on the rim of his glass. It was time to get down to business.

'Melanie and I just want to say how much we appreciate the effort you guys have made to get here. I remember when Tony Blair flew out to the Whitsundays back in 1995. "Mickey, I need your support," he said. "Your newspapers. Your TV. We can't do it without you." Well, I gave him that support. We pulled out all the stops. And the Labour Party won with the largest Labour majority ever.

'So you don't need to tell me why you're here,' Selkirk added. 'But let me say one thing. I want to be perfectly clear about this. I can't be bought, but I can possibly be persuaded.'

They all laughed dutifully. When you come to see a king, you first pay homage. Listening to the fella, laughing at his jokes, even when they are shit-awful, is part of the deal.

After that, they got down to business.

Later that evening, sitting with his laptop on the patio outside his room – no mozzies, thank heavens – Barnard skyped Marshall.

'Harriet, is that you? Look at the screen. I can only see the top of your head.'

'I can't see you at all. Turn the camera on.'

When they had sorted out the technicalities, Barnard explained, 'We've done the deal. Nothing in writing, of course. That's not the way Selkirk works but it's in the bag. Rosie Craig said she had the full authority of her father. If they win the election, they'll rip up the regulator, the FCC, the Federal Communications Commission. If they don't abolish it, they'll bring it to heel. Appoint a new commissioner. And as far as Russia's concerned, an incoming Craig administration will press President Popov to allow Selkirk Global to expand throughout the whole of the territory.'

'Why would Popov agree to that?' Marshall asked.

Barnard leaned into the screen. He pressed his right forefinger to the side of his nose. 'President Popov didn't become one of the richest men in Russia just by sitting around scratching his bum.'

'What about the UK?' she asked. 'Did Selkirk have some specific "asks" there too?'

'He certainly did. He wants a post-Brexit government in Britain to dismember the BBC. To break it up, like we broke up British Rail. He believes the tax-payer-funded Beeb totally distorts the market-place in Britain. He wants a level playing field as far as the media are concerned.'

'And what did you say? Did you stick to the script we agreed?'

'Well, I didn't give him what he wanted. I told him that even a radical post-Brexit government in Britain couldn't sacrifice a sacred cow like the BBC, not overnight anyway. But I did point out that the BBC's charter was up for renewal at the end of the year and that having a new Brexit-led government in power in Britain could make quite a difference.'

'I like it.' Marshall's leering face was hugely distorted by the camera angle. 'Did you fill in the details?'

'I didn't need to. Mickey Selkirk may be over eighty but he doesn't miss a trick. He just said, "Good on ya, mate." Then we shook hands on it.'

Before turning in, Barnard Skyped his wife as well. He hadn't spoken to Melissa for days.

'Where are you?' she asked.

When Barnard told her that he was staying at Mickey Selkirk's million-acre cattle station in the Kimberley, Western Australia, Melissa asked, 'What about the mosquitos?'

'The mozzies are fine. I'm sitting here on the terrace outside my room with the doors open.'

They chatted on.

'If you're going to be jetting around the world for the next few days,' Melissa said, 'I think I'll go to visit Fiona and Michael in Ireland. They've got such a lovely place there. So calming.'

Fiona, their daughter, was a marine biologist. Her boyfriend – partner might be the better word, because they seemed quite seriously taken with each other – was a young Irish lawyer called Michael Kennedy, who specialized in Arctic environmental issues.

'The Arctic's done for, Mrs Barnard, unless we act now', is what he'd told her on her last visit.

'Yes, do go to Ireland,' Barnard urged her. 'God's own country, isn't it? Please give my love to Fiona and say hi to Michael too.'

Melissa was about to disconnect, when she suddenly remembered something she had been meaning to say all along.

'And, Edward, I was thinking about that disgusting film. I knew all along the man on the bed wasn't you.'

'You told me that already,' Barnard mildly reminded her. 'You said I wouldn't have been up for the rumpy pumpy, not that kind of rumpy pumpy anyway!'

'Oh, Edward. Don't take things so literally. You're fine in that department, I promise you. Quite fine enough, anyway, so far as I'm concerned. No, there's something else. Do you still have the film?'

'No, I handed it in to MI5.'

'Can you manage to contact them?'

'I could try. Why do you ask?'

'I'm thinking about the boxer shorts.'

'I didn't see any boxer shorts. The man who wasn't me was stark bollock naked as far as I could see.'

' "The Man Who Wasn't Me" could be the title of a film!' Melissa wiped the tears from her eyes.

'Please get on with it.'

Melissa managed to stifle her laughter before continuing. 'Remember when the man who wasn't you pulls the two blondes onto the bed, and one of them sucks his cock and I can't remember what the other does . . . pees on him, I think. Well, just as all that's going on, I'm pretty sure I glimpsed a pair of boxer shorts on the far side of the enormous bed, which the man had obviously taken off in his hurry to get cracking.'

'And I don't wear boxer shorts. Have I got that right?'

'Well, you might wear boxer shorts on rare occasions,' Melissa conceded. 'But not these shorts. They were red, white and blue, sprinkled with silver stars, so they looked like the US flag!'

'Oh, my God!' Barnard exclaimed. 'You may just have said something important, tremendously important. Ring up Jane Porter, head of MI5, on her private number. Tell her everything you've told me. They've got to check that film again.'

Melissa was thrilled. Helping her husband out with his constituency work was one thing, but this was something else again.

'What's Jane Porter's private number?' she asked.

'I'll text it to you,' he said. 'You never know who's listening.'

Sitting at her desk in the FSB's Lubyanka headquarters in Moscow, Galina Aslanova, the tall, strikingly pretty, head of the Special Operations Unit, picked up the phone.

'I need to see the director at once,' she said. 'This is urgent.'

Pavel Golov had been the director of the FSB for the last five years. Aslanova was one of his most important operatives. As soon as he heard that Aslanova wanted to see him urgently, he switched off the television where he had been watching Dynamo playing Spartak (he didn't normally watch TV at work but this was a historic clash).

'Send her in, please.'

Aslanova had recorded both of Barnard's recent Skyped conversations and she brought the flash drive with her.

'Probably best if we see it on the wide screen, Director,' Aslanova suggested.

When the first tape ended, which showed Barnard reporting to Marshall, Golov was enthusiastic in his praise.

'Superb! So it's all going to plan?'

Aslanova agreed. 'You are right, Director. We are quite confident that, as soon as we give the signal, Selkirk Global will – as requested – unleash a mighty barrage of news and comment.'

Golov gazed at Aslanova with undisguised lust.

'Please call me Pavel.' He wondered how long it might be before he could get her into bed.

'Let's look at the second tape, the one where Barnard talks to his wife,' Aslanova continued.

When it had finished, the director of the FSB let out a deep breath.

'Why didn't you tell me about this before? What do you want from me?'

'A search warrant, signed by you.'

Later that day, Aslanova summoned the team she had assigned to Operation Tectonic Plate. Four women. All fiercely loyal to her.

The oldest, Lyudmila Markova, grey-haired and well over sixty, had served in the FSB for over twenty years. If she resented the fact that a much younger woman had been promoted over her as the Head of Special Ops, she gave no sign of it.

They were all curious. They knew that Aslanova had had a sudden unscheduled meeting with the Director.

'What's this all about?' Markova asked.

Aslanova came straight to the point: 'You've all watched the

Skype conversations. We know there's a video out there and we need to find it.'

She told her deputy, 'All the evidence points to some freelance activity in the FSB office in St Petersburg at the time of President Popov's World Tiger Summit. I want you to take the team down to St Petersburg at once. I want you to find that video and bring it back here under lock and key.'

Her voice hardened. 'Get cracking, ladies. Don't let them bullshit you. They're a pretty macho bunch down there in the St Petersburg office. Do whatever you have to do, even if you have to kick them where it hurts.'

CHAPTER EIGHTEEN

Mickey Selkirk ran about 20,000 head of cattle on Lazy-T's million acres; most of them destined for the lucrative beef export markets of Asia.

'They're going to bring in some cows today,' Selkirk told them at breakfast. 'We've been using helis – R22s – for mustering for the last ten years. Much the best way. A lot of cattle men are using helis for mustering nowadays.'

Jack Varese's eyes lit up. 'R22s? I trained on an R22.'

'In that case, we can use you. The heli-musterers normally work in pairs when they're driving cattle. But one of the pilots is off duty.'

Selkirk drove Jack to the airstrip where a pair of small, red, two-seater helicopters were parked. A wiry young man, wearing jeans and cowboy boots, was already waiting.

'We're in luck, Jim,' Selkirk said. 'Ollie's still sick but I've got a volunteer: Jack Varese. Don't know if you ever go to the movies. You might have seen him.'

The young herdsman touched his hat: 'Don't see a lot of movies round here. You flown one of these before?'

Jack nodded. 'Mother's milk.'

'Keep your eye on me when we're in the air,' Jim Jackson said, 'and we'll work it together. I try to anticipate where the cows might play up and give us trouble. You get to know what sort of move will be able to turn them. To guide them, you've got to get right down, almost to ground level. If your engine fails, you don't have any time to react."'

Jack nodded sagely. 'You can't autorotate out of trouble at that height.'

The two little helis took off and headed west. They had been in the air about ten minutes when they saw the first herd of cattle.

Through the headphones, Jack heard Jim Jackson's voice: 'There are about 500 in that herd. We're looking to bring in about a thousand this morning. So we'll fly past this bunch, round up another herd, bring it back here, and drive 'em both in.'

A minute or two later, they saw another large group of cows. As the helis dropped to tree level, the cattle began to stampede.

'Get out behind them and turn them back,' Jim instructed. 'I'll hover here and stop them breaking south. Then we'll drive them all back together.'

Jack got the hang of it quickly. Sometimes he flew so low that he could actually touch the backs of the cows with the helicopters skis, forcing them to turn.

'Watch out for the trees,' Jim shouted into the RT at one point as Jack manoeuvred through the bush.

They brought about a thousand head of cattle back to Lazy-T that morning.

While the herd was still five miles from the station, Selkirk drove Barnard and Melanie in the Land Cruiser out to meet them. Rosie rode one of the station's horses.

The two little red helis kicked up a cloud of dust as they landed beside the parked vehicle.

Selkirk, ever the gracious host, had brought a large flask of tea. 'You guys must be thirsty.'

Jack looked at Rosie, holding her horse by the bridle, her face glowing. 'Don't you just look the part?'

After lunch, Selkirk took them off to the Bungle-Bungles. 'Just wanted to show Jack I can fly a helicopter too.'

Of course, Selkirk was joking, but he was making a point as well. He wasn't going to be out-flown by any young whipper-snapper.

It was a short hop from Lazy-T to the Bungle-Bungles.

Selkirk flew the Bell 206 Jet-Ranger over the famous beehive domes in a figure of eight pattern. As the helicopter banked, Barnard found himself staring into a series of steep-sided abysses, criss-crossing the mountain range, running for miles through the rock. He could even see tall palm trees, which seemed to sprout from the canyon floor.

Later they trekked through one of the canyons. Taking a break in the shade of a huge overhanging rock, Selkirk gave them a little lecture.

'This is one of the finest rock art sites in the area.' He pointed to the rock face. 'The people who lived here were some of the world's earliest inhabitants. The paintings here could be over 20,000 years old. See this figure here? That's an echidna, a kind of anteater. The aboriginal people believe the hills were formed back in the dreamtime, when an echidna was attacked by a "galah", that's a large white and rather noisy bird. The echidna fought for his life. He dug into the ground to escape, that's how the beehives and gorges were formed.'

Listening to Selkirk talk, Barnard felt a surge of admiration. People were too ready to scoff at the man, he thought. Were they just envious of his success? What was it that drove him? Some elemental form of patriotism, perhaps. An urge to show that Australians, too, could rule the world.

They flew over Lake Argyle on the way back. Selkirk gave them a running commentary. 'This is the largest lake in Western Australia. They dammed the Orde River back in the 1970s. Now the Chinese are here in a big way. They've bought twenty-thousand hectares of irrigated land, as well as the old Kununurra sugar mill. A Chinese company has taken over KAI, Kimberley Agricultural Investments. There's a whole Chinese community up here now.'

Selkirk banked to the left. 'Time to head back. I'll get Ching to rustle up some tea.'

Later, back in the staff quarters of the Lazy-T homestead, Ching heard snatches of Australia's most famous song.

'Once a jolly swagman camped by a billabong
Under the shade of a coolibah tree,
He sang as he watched and waited 'til his billy boiled
You'll come a-waltzing Matilda, with me.'

What fools they all were, he thought. Didn't they know that the world had moved on? Who cared about billabongs? What the hell was a billabong anyway?

Thank God, thought Ching, the time was getting closer when Fung and he could return to the land of their ancestors, and to their beloved Wuxi, the prettiest of all China's ancient cities. They had saved a lot of money working for Selkirk. And they had had a useful additional source of income. For the last ten years, he and Fung had served as undercover agents of the Chinese secret service. As Chinese investment in Northern and Western Australia increased, so did China's network of agents. Hu Wong-Fu, the owner of Kununurra's most popular restaurant, Kimberley Asian Cuisine, was his immediate superior.

That very afternoon Hu had sent him a text with a short and simple message. 'Do it tonight!'

Li Xiao-Tong, sitting in his office in the Ministry of State Security, Beijing, reviewed the report he had received an hour earlier. Thank God for the Chinese diaspora, he thought. There seemed to be almost as many Chinese living outside China as inside, and many of those were fiercely loyal to the motherland. Take Ching and Fung, for example. They had never actually lived in China but they still regarded Wuxi as their ancestral home and planned to return one day. What a splendid idea MSS

Agent Hu had had when he proposed recruiting Mickey Selkirk's two live-in staff as part of the MSS network of secret agents in Western Australia.

You could hardly suspect Ching and Fung of being spies just because they innocently popped into town for a Chinese meal on their day off.

What a good job they had just done! He clicked on the recording that accompanied the email and heard Mickey Selkirk's unmistakably Australian accent: '*So you don't need to tell me why you're here. But let me say one thing. I want to be perfectly clear about this. I can't be bought, but I can possibly be persuaded. So let's look at a deal that's good for both sides.*'

If that wasn't a smoking gun, Li didn't know what a smoking gun was.

Good work, Ching, he thought, picking up that whole conversation. Advances in technology made eavesdropping so much easier nowadays. If you were waiting at table, for example, you could just carry your phone around in your pocket with the record button pressed. Or you could hide the phone in some convenient nearby vessel and leave it there for the duration.

He clicked on the photos Ching had sent. How good Rosie looked on a horse, Li thought. Pity Fung hadn't managed to snap a few pics of Rosie in bed with Jack. They'd be worth a bob or two on the black market. You missed a trick there, Ching, he thought.

Or maybe Ching had other plans for this kind of hot stuff. There were plenty of takers out there, he knew. Photos of Jack Varese and Rosie Craig in bed, even if they were just drinking a cup of tea and reading the Sunday papers, would go viral in seconds.

Li made a mental note to ask Agent Fu to have a quiet word with Ching. If he was selling secrets on the side, somebody should be getting a cut.

MSS held the whip-hand there, he reckoned, as far as Ching and Fung were concerned. That little house in Wuxi, reserved for them as long as they kept the reports flowing, might suddenly disappear off the list of homes available for loyal cadre if it came to it.

Ching went to the store room, opened a crate, and removed a small wooden box. The box was locked but small holes had been drilled in the side.

While the rest of the party was still sitting by the fire, Barnard had turned in early. He felt tired. Maybe the jet-lag was getting to him. Jack, he noted, seemed totally impervious to fatigue.

Barnard had left the terrace door to his room open. He could still hear the sound of singing and laughter from the campfire.

As the party broke up, Jack had taken Rosie aside, telling the others, 'You guys mind if Rosie and I pop over to have a night cap with Jim and Ollie?'

'Go ahead, Jack. Take the ute,' Selkirk had said. 'Please tell Ollie I'm looking forward to seeing him tomorrow. If he's fit to drink, he's fit to fly.'

Barnard undressed as soon as he reached his room, putting his pyjamas on and slipping into bed.

He felt the bite almost at once. A short, stinging pain, followed by a burning sensation.

'What on earth's that?' he shouted aloud.

He flung back the bedclothes to see a black spider, about the size of a baby's fist, with a large red spot on its back, scurrying towards the open terrace door.

Barnard didn't panic easily. He knew he needed a dose of anti-venom. Australia had some of the most poisonous spiders in the world. But you had to know which spider had bitten you.

He picked up a shoe. Two thwacks. One dead spider.

'Hello there!' he shouted. 'Can someone give me a hand?'

Selkirk, like Barnard, had turned in early, but Melanie, who had been catching up on her emails in the sitting room, came running.

'I've been bitten by a spider,' Barnard gasped. He was already short of breath as the toxin kicked in.

Melanie took a look at the dead spider. She was puzzled. 'Not sure what that one is. Looks a nasty piece of work. We need to get you to hospital. I'll get Mickey.'

They helped Barnard to the helicopter. Selkirk ran through the pre-take-off checks. He had taken plenty of shortcuts in his life but never when it came to flying planes.

'Oh, heck,' he swore. 'We're out of fuel. Can't believe this. I thought I'd asked Ching to fill it up when we came back from the Bungles.'

It was another five minutes before they were ready, in which time Barnard began to feel like death.

They took the spider with them in an empty marmalade jar. Even dead, the insect looked lethally menacing.

Dr Phillips, in the Accident and Emergency Unit in Kununurra District Hospital, was as puzzled as Melanie had been.

'Just give me a second.' Taking the jar with him, he hurried out of the room.

He returned less than two minutes later, looking strained and worried. 'I showed it to Professor Cohen, our toxicology expert, who happens to be on duty tonight. It's a Sydney funnel-web spider, the deadliest spider in the world. The professor comes from Sydney. That's the good news. We know what we're dealing with.'

'What's the bad news?'

'We don't have any anti-venom here.'

'Why on earth not?'

'There's no call for it. Sydney's the only place in Australia where this particular spider lives, mostly in dark corners and moist basements. That's why it's called "Sydney". It's never been seen in this part of the world. Not until now that is.'

Barnard lay on the bed in the A&E unit while Dr Philips

examined him. Barnard had been bitten on the right leg, below the knee. The whole lower limb was red and swollen.

He prodded Barnard's stomach. 'Any abdominal pain?'

'I feel as though I've been kicked in the stomach by a horse,' Barnard replied.

While the examination continued, Melanie tapped the words 'Sydney funnel-web spider' into the search bar of her Apple iPhone 7.

'*The bite of the Sydney funnel-web spider is usually painful, both due to large fangs and acidic venom. Convulsions may occur. Death may occur within an hour.*'

She checked her watch. It was already an hour since they'd left Lazy-T. Barnard wasn't dead yet and he hadn't even had any convulsions. Always look on the bright side, she thought.

A tall, white-coated man hurried into the room with a vial in his hand. Professor Cohen said, 'Try the Redback spider anti-venom. It's all we've got.'

They gave him one vial of CSL Redback spider anti-venom first, injected intra-muscularly, followed twenty minutes later by another.

'I feel much better already,' Barnard said.

'You look better, too,' the doctor said. 'Do you want to stay overnight?'

When Barnard politely declined, Dr Philips handed Melanie two more vials. 'He won't have a relapse,' he told her. 'But if he does, give him another shot.'

They were back at Lazy-T before midnight. Barnard couldn't believe he had recovered so quickly. At one point he'd thought he was going to die. The wonders of modern medicine.

Selkirk was pleased as punch. He didn't often fly the heli at night nowadays. 'Do you want a drink before you turn in?'

'No, but I think I'll check the bed before I get in it!'

Ching, meanwhile, had heard the helicopter return. He saw Barnard walk back to the house, with no obvious signs of distress.

What the hell had gone wrong? he wondered.

What kind of anti-venom had they given Barnard in the hospital? Mind you, he thought, if the old man hadn't checked the fuel before take-off, they wouldn't have made it to the hospital at all.

Selkirk's Lazy-T ranch had its own satellite dish. Ching tapped out a message on his laptop and pressed Send.

Li Xiao-Tong's computer pinged. A new email had arrived:

'Regret unable to fulfil your order for one portion of prawn curry. Await further instructions.'

'Damn and blast,' Li Xiao-Tong swore under his breath.

He went upstairs to report to the minister for State Security, Zhang Fu-Shen. He was expecting trouble. Zhang made a habit of saying, 'Failure is not an option'.

Zhang's reaction to the news that Edward Barnard was still alive and kicking surprised him.

'Forget about Barnard,' Zhang instructed. 'We have bigger fish to fry. You sent me the recording of Barnard's Skype call with his wife. Well, I listened to it. She says her husband would never have worn US-flag boxer shorts and I believe her. So the video we used to try to trap Barnard was faked.'

Back in his office, Li fired up his laptop and clicked on the file. There was Barnard in the lift with the two girls; there was the fuzzy, long shot of the three of them on the bed, the man with his face obscured in the tangle of thrashing limbs and there – yes! – were the US-flag boxer shorts, still lying where they fell, like a soldier on the field of battle, when Mr X hurried to join in the fun.

He paused the film, and enlarged the frame. Close-up, the US-flag boxer shorts looked rather attractive. Silky and inviting. Barnard might take a different view but he, Li Xiao-Tong, senior official in the Chinese ministry of state security, rather fancied himself wearing Old Glory underwear.

He enlarged the frame still further until the writing on the waist-band of the briefs was clearly legible: 'PUT AMERICA FIRST' it said.

Li racked his brains. Now who on earth would have 'PUT AMERICA FIRST' sown into the waistband of their underpants?

CHAPTER NINETEEN

The specially constituted inter-departmental team had been studying the video film for more than two hours in the basement of MI5's Millbank headquarters overlooking the Thames, and they were feeling the strain. Analysing frame by frame the video Barnard had brought back from China was hard work. The constant stream of messages from 'upstairs' – the director-general's office – asking for a report on progress contributed to the tension.

Joshan Gupta, head of MI5's technical support services, understood the need to come up with an answer quickly. But he was also deeply reluctant to draw conclusions that the evidence didn't support. MI5 and its sister service MI6 had been deeply scarred by the 'dodgy dossier' at the time of the Iraq war, when Britain's intelligence services had been accused of distorting, falsifying or, at the very least, 'sexing up' evidence relating to Saddam Hussain's supposed weapons of mass destruction (WMD). They didn't want to be caught twice in the same trap.

'Let's try to be clear,' Gupta said. 'The Chinese somehow acquire a video which shows the former Secretary of State Edward Barnard in a compromising position. We all accept that Barnard is indeed the man in the lift with the two Russian ladies but we seem collectively to be conceding that the man on the bed is not Mr Barnard. First, there is Barnard's own statement that he does not believe he is involved, even though he was possibly inebriated or even drugged. Second, CCTV evidence from the hotel shows Barnard entering his room alone, and not in the company of the two Russian ladies. Third, according to Mrs Barnard, Mr Barnard does not normally wear boxer shorts and would certainly never have worn US-flag boxer shorts.'

Gupta paused.

'But surely,' he continued, 'it would be going too far to argue that just because Ronald Craig was in the Kempinski Hotel at the same time as the two Russian ladies, the figure on the bed with the said ladies is indeed Mr Craig?'

Jill Hepworth, one of MI6's Russian specialists, was keen to put forward the alternative point of view.

'Let's blow up those boxer shorts again,' she requested.

As the image of the US-flag boxer shorts appeared on the giant screen in the MI5 basement conference room, Hepworth took out a laser pointer.

'Okay,' she continued. 'We can all see the way PUT AMERICA FIRST has been printed on, or perhaps sewn into, the waistband of the boxer shorts. But let's look a little closer. Do you see the embroidered logo on the left leg, the little white "b" inside a black circle? Do you know whose logo that is? Well, I did some research. It's the Bloomingdales logo. And where is Bloomingdales located? In New York? And where does Ronald Craig spend a good deal of his time? The answer's New York. I read he even flies back home to New York to sleep in his own bed when he's on the campaign trail. He could easily send someone over to Bloomingdales from Craig Tower to buy some boxer shorts.'

Gupta was still sceptical. 'With respect, even if we could establish that Mr Craig buys his underwear at Bloomingdales, this would not necessarily prove that he is the man on the bed.'

Lillian Peters, head of the Foreign Office's security team, who was chairing the meeting, was anxious to bring the meeting to a close.

'So what line do you propose we take?' she asked.

'I would say we hold our fire,' Gupta replied. 'This could be another classic case of kompromat, like that of Yuri Skuratov. Let me remind you that a few years back, Yuri Skuratov, Russia's then prosecutor-general, was in the middle of one of the biggest investigations of his career, tracking down high-profile Russian officials accused of taking huge bribes, when a tape surfaced.

'Grainy footage, apparently captured on a concealed camera, showed Skuratov having sex with two prostitutes. Hours after it aired on Russian state television, Skuratov was suspended from his post, despite his protestations. Popov, who at the time was working at the Federal Security Agency, which we now know as the FSB, publicly certified that Skuratov was the man pictured on the videotape. Surprise, surprise! Yeltsin appointed Popov prime minister in the same year.'

Gupta paused and looked around the room. He felt he was beginning to win over the waverers.

'This is very much a part of the way Russia works,' he continued. 'Intelligence agencies collect compromising information on individuals, or they fake such information to use later, when it's to their advantage. The Skuratov affair is a case in point. Those grainy pictures were Skuratov's undoing but they were almost certainly faked.'

Peters pondered her options. There was always a temptation to rush to judgement, but she shuddered to think of the consequences if they got it wrong.

She made up her mind. 'I would propose that we send a holding report up to Dame Jane. We tell her that we are still considering the file.'

Gupta held up his hand.

'Yes, Mr Gupta.'

'I hope I have not seemed too negative. There may still be a chance of reaching a firm conclusion, one way or the other. There are images which are obscure and grainy, as in the Skuratov case, and then there are images where the face and other features have been distorted, as a result of a deliberate act of pixelation. Let's blow up those images again. If they have been deliberately pixelated, we may be able to depixelate them.'

He had their attention. These boffins, Peters thought, often waited till the last moment before coming up with the goods.

Later that day, Dame Jane Porter went to see the home secretary with no officials present. Her two close aides, Mortimer and Percy, knew most of what was going on. But they didn't need to know everything. Not yet anyway.

Mabel Killick ushered her visitor to the sofa in the corner of her large office in the Home Office. She closed the door and pulled up a chair.

'Well, Jane?' Killick was at her most charming. 'How are you getting on? What's the verdict?'

'They're still working on the Kempinski video,' Porter said. 'They hope to depixelate the images.'

'Ah,' the home secretary nodded knowledgeably. 'When do they expect a result?'

'Hard to say. Apparently this is a long and difficult process with no guarantee of success.'

'What about the memory-stick the Russians gave Edward Barnard? How are things going there? Are all those documents fake, too? The Russians seem to be making a habit of it at the moment, don't they? Fake news seems to be all the rage. You just don't know what to believe.'

'I'm not sure, Home Secretary, that the memory-stick documents are in fact fake,' Porter said. 'We've been going through them one by one. Virtually all of them are, or appear to be, genuine documents emanating from the PM's office. The narrative they portray is indeed the narrative that happened: the run-up to the PM's

Bloomberg speech, the PM's manuscript additions to the manifesto, late in the day, indicating his personal commitment to the Referendum. Those are all genuine verifiable documents, though how they got into the hands of the Russians to form the basis of their Brexit dossier, if I may call it that, is still not clear. That, as you can imagine, is a matter of great concern to us. If Number 10 itself is not secure, who and what is?'

'Hold on a moment,' the home secretary said. 'What about the exchanges the prime minister had with Fred Malkin, Conservative Party chairman, about huge cash transfers into Conservative Party funds in exchange for the Referendum commitment? Surely to heaven those documents aren't genuine.'

Porter sighed. 'Things are not looking good. And it wasn't just the promise Jeremy Hartley gave in the Bloomberg speech. The manifesto commitment was even more explicit. Of course, the PM never expected that he would ever have to deliver on that commitment. The Lib Dems would always have vetoed it. But then the Conservatives won an outright majority and the PM was hoisted by his own petard.'

Killick stood up and walked over to the window. She gazed out at traffic on Horseferry Road. She'd had to take many difficult decisions in her long tenure as home secretary, but this was one of the most difficult.

She turned towards her guest and said in the gravest tones, 'We're going to have to pursue this one wherever it leads, even if it leads to the door of the prime minister himself. You'll have to bring the Met in, and the financial boys. What happened to the money you are talking about?'

Her voice trailed off. For a brief moment she put her head in her hands. If the prime minister had to step down, or was forced out, or – thoughts of the Cayman Islands and illicit personal accounts popped unbidden into her head – yes, conceivably, even went to prison, then who on earth would succeed him?

'We must keep this one under the tightest of wraps till we're ready to spring,' she instructed.

Porter looked down at the home secretary's trademark leopard-print kitten heels. Killick was always ready to spring, she thought.

CHAPTER TWENTY

Lyudmila Markova and her fearsome, all-female team flew down to St Petersburg on the afternoon of Thursday, 26 May 2016. A squad car was waiting to take them to their hotel. Next morning, dressed in full riot gear, they headed for FSB St Petersburg headquarters on Cherniavski Street.

At precisely 8:30A.M. they entered the building, flashed their passes at the security desk and belted up the stairs to the second floor.

They caught Fyodor Stephanov hitching his trousers up on the way back from the toilet. Markova slammed him against the wall and rammed her pistol into his gut.

'Take him down, girls,' she ordered.

The dungeons at Cherniavski Street are not as dark and menacing as the dungeons of the KGB's Lubyanka building in Moscow, but they are the next best thing.

'Do you want the rack or the thumbscrew?' Markova asked. She was only half joking.

Two hours later, the FSB SWAT team had all the information it needed. They had all the original footage, as well as a copy of the video that Stephanov, with the connivance of his superiors at the FSB, St Petersburg, had sold on the black market.

'That was a nice little scam you had going, wasn't it?' Markova had taunted him. 'That wasn't the first time you sold kompromat, eh? Make a practice of it, do you? Hit him again, Maria. Kick him in the crotch. Wrench his arms from their sockets. He'll talk soon enough.'

Maria duly obliged, so did the rest of the team. They were glad to take their turn. Just warming up for the day ahead. That was how they saw it. Galina Aslanova had instructed them to take a tough line and that was what they did.

'How did you find out it was me?' Stephanov whimpered as they left.

'You were the bloody duty officer that night, weren't you? You were stupid enough to ring the girls from your duty phone.' Markova spat at him. 'Who else could it be?'

Five hours later, back in Moscow, Aslanova reviewed the material her SWAT team had brought back from St Petersburg.

'Interesting,' she said. 'Very interesting.' She picked up the phone and hesitated for a moment. The FSB director, Pavel Golov, was out of town for the day. Should she wait for him to come back? Or should she go straight to the top?

She made up her mind. This was a matter that couldn't wait. She had known President Popov for years. He had been her boss for a while when he headed the KGB before going on to higher things. Popov had given her a card with his private number.

She had destroyed the card, but she had memorized the number. She dialled it now.

'Mr President, I need to speak to you in person. I will bring the material.'

'What material?'

Aslanova hesitated. 'I'm so sorry, Mr President. I'm not sure this phone is secure.'

Popov laughed. 'Now you're telling me! I'm at the dacha. Come on over. I'll send a car.'

The sprawling countryside estate of Novo Ogaryovo – a huge parkland containing several stately buildings on the banks of the Moscow River – was about fifteen miles from Moscow on the Rublyovo-Uspenskoye highway. If Popov was travelling there by car, rather than by helicopter (his preferred mode of transport), the police would sideline the traffic so that decoy cars could speed the full length of the route to check for problems. Only then would Popov's twelve-car armoured motorcade race through at speeds of up to 150mph.

Aslanova didn't quite receive the full presidential treatment – hers was just a one-car motorcade – but the driver of the BMW switched on the '*migalka*', or the blue flashing light, which entitled him to ignore legally most rules of the road. Galina arrived at the presidential dacha less than an hour after the telephone conversation with the Russian president.

The term 'dacha' was a misnomer. Novo Ogaryovo bore little resemblance to the structures that Muscovites conventionally called 'dachas': modest country retreats which they had built or otherwise acquired in the outlying rural districts for weekend breaks or to escape the searing heat of the summer. There was nothing modest about Novo Ogaryovo. 'Palatial' would have been a better word. There were half a dozen reception rooms and a dozen guest rooms, a stable to house the president's horses and a *manège* where he could practise dressage. There was also a shooting gallery which he used almost daily and an Olympic-sized swimming pool. The whole estate was enclosed by an eight-metre high fence: a world within a world.

Whenever he could, Popov worked at Novo Ogaryovo rather than in the Kremlin. Over the years, many visiting heads of state had been entertained at the dacha. Some had even been invited to stay the night, a signal honour.

Yuri Yasonov came to the door of the dacha to greet Aslanova. They knew each other well, of course. They had both been part of

Popov's inner circle during his time as director of the KGB. Aslanova had stayed on in the KGB, now renamed FSB, when Popov left the director's post for higher things, but Yasonov had moved with his boss to the Kremlin and now served as Popov's key aide.

'Wonderful to see you,' Yasonov said. 'The president's waiting in the den.'

Aslanova had been to the dacha at Novo Ogaryovo before. She had sometimes been summoned at short notice to attend hastily scheduled conferences, which were presided over by Popov with a degree of formality befitting his position. But she had never before ventured into the president's own personal den.

'Galina! Thank you so much for coming. Wonderful to see you!' Popov wasn't usually so effusive. There were occasions when he could be gruff and taciturn. But this wasn't one of them. He pulled Aslanova towards him, enveloping her in a muscular embrace.

'You and your team did a great job in St Petersburg, I heard,' Popov said. 'I hear some of our people down there had been carrying out unauthorized surveillance and selling reports on the black market. But you set him straight. Gave him what for, so I understand. Good show! Now let's see what you've got.'

Aslanova thought she was going to swoon. They sat side- by-side on the sofa, knees touching. God, the man was sexy, she thought.

As the video played on the wide screen in front of them, she managed, somehow, to concentrate on the matter in hand.

'What we got in St Petersburg,' she explained, 'was the raw material and that's what we're seeing now. The first part shows Barnard having a drink in the bar of the Kempinski and then going up in the hotel lift with the two girls. The second part shows the two girls and Mr X playing around on one of the Kempinski's king-size beds.'

Popov whistled. 'And you think you can identify Mr X, do you?'

'I think we can,' Aslanova said. 'In fact, I'm pretty sure we can.'

For the next thirty minutes, the three of them sat, totally absorbed by the degrading spectacle, faithfully recorded by the FSB's concealed cameras.

'Are you sure this is being filmed in the presidential suite at the Kempinski?' Popov asked at one point.

'Yes, we're sure. See all the gold curtains and marble tops? That's the presidential suite all right,' Aslanova replied. 'And the CCTV shows the girls outside the suite, knocking on the door.'

Popov had spent too much of his career as an intelligence officer to be fobbed off with circumstantial evidence, however convincing it might seem.

'What about the man's face? I agree the body seems right in terms of size and shape. But we need to see the face? Most of the time the man's face seemed to be occupied in ways we can't see.'

'We see the hair, don't we?' Galina was sure she had got it right. 'That sunburst of hair, like a halo. No mistaking that, surely?'

Popov let out a great roar of laughter. 'Halo! That's rich. That's the first time anyone has suggested to me that he has a halo round his head!'

Popov was a man who knew how to weigh up the pros and cons. He was used to that.

'I congratulate you, Galina. You deserve a medal and I shall see that you get it. Will you stay for dinner?'

Aslanova didn't just stay for dinner. She stayed the night.

'I don't have any pyjamas,' she protested half-heartedly.

'I don't see why you need pyjamas,' Popov countered. 'I don't.'

To say that Galina Aslanova and Igor Popov slept together that night was, in a strict sense, misleading. They hardly slept at all.

For Aslanova, it was a dream come true. She had admired this man for so long and now here she was, in his bed, in his arms.

Funny, she thought, how when it came to making love, all that macho stuff went right out of the window. It was almost as though he cared for her.

CHAPTER TWENTY-ONE

Harriet Marshall met Edward Barnard at Heathrow on the latter's return from Australia. They drove down to Wiltshire together.

Melissa was still in Ireland, so Marshall, who by now was very much at home in Coleman Court, fixed breakfast while Barnard showered and changed. It had been a long flight.

'You did a great job with Mickey Selkirk,' Marshall said over coffee. 'The great Selkirk machine is primed and ready to go.'

'What are they waiting for?' Barnard asked 'Shouldn't they be moving into action with all guns blazing?'

'We've got to give them some real ammunition. It's not enough to talk about the Greek crisis, or the problems of the Eurozone or "faceless Brussels bureaucrats". What we've been saying about spending money on the NHS is helping. Our slogan "Take Back Control" appears to resonate. But that's not going to swing it.'

'What is?'

'Concerns about immigration. That's what's going to swing it. The fear that we're being overwhelmed by foreigners. The fear that before our very eyes the whole structure of the country is changing and changing fast. Too fast for people to adapt. All the research we've done – and we've *really* researched this – tells us that immigration is the issue which has come to the top of the pile. Of course there's non-EU immigration, as well as immigration from the EU, but in people's minds it's all jumbled up. Our job is to keep it that way. We don't need clarity here. We don't need to break down the statistics. We just need to keep pointing the finger at the EU as the source of the problem. We need to build on that. Ram the message home. That's what's going to get us first past the winning post.'

'I'm not being defeatist,' Barnard said, 'but I wonder what more we can do.'

'Oh, we can do a lot more and we're going to,' Marshall said. 'I'm just waiting for the signal.'

That signal wasn't long in coming. Marshall drove back to her home in north-west London later that morning. She stopped – as she did every day as a matter of routine – at the newsagent on the street corner, which had a bulletin board outside on which locals could display messages of interest, such as 'cleaner required', 'watches repaired', 'reliable mother offers services'.

Some of the messages had been there a long time. The ink had faded; the edges of the cards were curled. But she noticed one recent addition.

'Three-legged black cat found. Call 077238954978.'

Instead of going home, she drove to the other end of the street where, amazingly, she found a working phone box. She dialled a number. Not the number displayed on the card about the three-legged black cat, but a different number. A number she knew by heart.

A recorded voice instructed her to 'Please leave a message'.

'Forty-five minutes,' Marshall said and then replaced the receiver.

Instead of going home, she did a U-turn and headed for Hampstead Heath. Thirty minutes later, she parked the car and strode off across the huge, wild and open expanse which, miraculously, still managed to survive within the confines of the ever-expanding metropolis of modern-day London.

Of course, historically, Hampstead Heath had provided many opportunities for activities which could be generically described as nefarious. Chief of these was espionage. For decades, controllers had been meeting their agents on park benches or beneath ancient oak trees. And they were right to take advantage of the possibilities that the Heath offered, Marshall reflected. Hotel rooms were routinely bugged, telephones were tapped and emails were gathered by the thousand, like standing wheat in front of a combine harvester. If you could find the right spot on the Heath, with a clear field of fire, as it were, you could get a lot of business done without having to wonder how many people were listening in.

The Russians, of course, with their massive so-called 'trade' mission in nearby Highgate, had over the years found Hampstead Heath tremendously handy.

Marshall had already installed herself on an oak bench, inscribed 'In Loving Memory of Lucy Penstock Who So Much Loved This Wonderful Place', when a jowly man in a dark suit, about forty years old, sat down next to her. The man leaned forward to do up his shoelace as though this was simply an unscheduled stop at a convenient location, then he spoke out of the side of his mouth. (There were people who could lip-read at four hundred yards, if they had a good pair of binoculars.)

'Rijksmuseum, Amsterdam. Next Tuesday. Night watch, 5P.M.,' he instructed.

Marshall arrived a few minutes before five at the appointed place. A cluster of tourists stood in front of the huge canvas. That wasn't surprising since Rembrandt van Rijn's 'The Night Watch' was certainly the most famous painting in the Rijksmuseum and probably one of the most famous paintings in the world.

She joined the group of sightseers. If you want to look inconspicuous, merge in with the crowd.

At two minutes past the hour, she felt a light tap on her shoulder. She turned round at once.

'Good heavens, Yuri,' she exclaimed. 'Fancy seeing you here.'

Marshall hadn't just been acting surprised when Yuri Yasonov tapped her on the shoulder. She really was surprised. She had no idea that the 'contact' she was scheduled to meet in Amsterdam would turn out to be a friend from her university days.

Admittedly they weren't close friends then. Marshall came from a modest background. Her father was a planning officer in Yorkshire. Yasonov, by contrast, was stinking rich, the son of an oligarch, who had cleaned up when President Yeltsin sold off Russia's crown jewels – the gas, the oil, the minerals, the forests – to the highest bidder.

Yasonov had gone to Oxford's upper-class Christ Church while Harriet had enrolled at brainier Balliol. But they had both been on the university chess team. Early on in their acquaintance, Yasonov had come to appreciate Marshall's sheer intellectual brilliance. He was a highly competent chess player himself, but Marshall simply wiped the floor with him.

They had also both played a part in the affairs of the Oxford Union. Yasonov had been President of the Union in his last year at Oxford and Marshall had succeeded him. Though the outgoing president normally gets to select the motion to be debated at the Farewell Debate, Marshall had good-humouredly suggested to her friend that a suitable topic would be: 'This House believes that the power of the Russian Federation has increased, is increasing and ought to be diminished'.

Yasonov had gamely agreed and had been delighted when the motion was resoundingly defeated.

'Let's go for a walk,' Yasonov suggested.

They left the Rijksmuseum to stride along the canal. How beautiful Amsterdam was, Marshall thought, as the late evening sun caught the roofs of the tall buildings that lined each side of the waterway. They called it the 'Venice of the North' and they were not far wrong. She watched the sightseeing boats pass under the bridges, cameras at the ready. Instinctively she turned her head to one side. She didn't want her face to appear, by accident or design, on someone's Instagram account. Officially, she wasn't in Amsterdam at all. She was taking a bit of time off in Wales, recharging her batteries before the big push. She certainly didn't want to be photographed in the company of a senior FSB official, especially if said official was chief of staff to the president of the Russian Federation.

They talked as they walked. As they approached the *Stadhous*, the City Hall, Yasonov said, 'Our information is that the British government is throwing everything they have at this one. Jeremy Hartley, the prime minister, has really gone out on a limb. He's convinced he's brought back a winning package from Europe with the so-called "renegotiation". And the chancellor, Tom Milbourne, is pushing Project Fear for all its worth.'

'I don't think it's worth very much,' Marshall countered. 'Scare tactics by the treasury. That's how I see it.'

'I'm afraid our people in the UK see things differently. Our ambassador sent in a report two days ago. He's convinced the Leave campaign is going to lose. Frankly, Popov is rattled. I don't often see him rattled but he is now. You're one of us, otherwise I wouldn't speak like this, but I'm telling you that as far as Popov's key foreign policy objectives go, Brexit is top of the list.'

'Ahead of Ronald Craig winning the US election?' Marshall interjected.

'I stand corrected. Let's give both objectives equal billing.'

'So what does Popov think we can do that we're not already doing?' Marshall was nettled. She'd been working her socks off.

Yasonov paused, picked up a pebble and tossed it into the water.

'That was just a little splash,' he said. 'We've got a much bigger splash in prospect. President Popov is on his way to Berlin as I speak. Tomorrow he's having informal meetings with the chancellor, then on Friday he is going to give a speech in the Bundestag at the invitation of the German government. I need hardly say that this is a great honour.'

'And he's going to make some key announcement in his speech, is that it?' Marshall asked. 'Something we can seize on, ammunition for our big guns as D-Day approaches?'

'Helga Brun is the one who is going to make the big announcement, not Popov. After Popov's speech to the Bundestag, Brun's going to reply. Mark her words carefully. She's going to give you the opening you need. A great wide-open goal. You'll be able to drive a coach and horses through it.'

'I've got to run,' Yasonov said. 'The plane to Berlin leaves in 90 minutes and I want to be on it. I've got to brief Popov at the Russian Embassy tonight.'

He tapped his nose with his finger. 'We're still working on Helga Brun's speech!'

'Don't tell me anything I don't need to know.'

'Why would I do that?' Yasonov smiled. He stepped off the pavement into the road to hail a passing cab.

CHAPTER TWENTY-TWO

German chancellor Helga Brun cradled the tiger cub in her arms. 'She's so sweet, isn't she? I can't believe she's so beautiful.'

She lowered her head and nuzzled the young cub. 'Thank you, Mr President. Germany thanks you from the heart.'

She handed the animal back to President Popov, before stepping up to the microphone.

'Ladies and gentlemen,' Brun began. 'This is a wonderful moment for the Berlin Zoo, the most famous zoo in the world. Today, thanks to the generosity of President Popov and the Russian people, we are the proud possessors of our first Siberian tiger, truly one of the most beautiful animals in the world. A few weeks ago, I was in Moscow, at the World Tiger Summit organized by President Popov, and I learned then about the tremendous efforts which are being made worldwide to protect tigers. I learned in particular about the work that is being done to save the Siberian or Amur tiger. Am I right, Mr President, that there are around 450 such tigers in the wild?'

President Popov, still cuddling the little tiger, smiled. 'Sometimes they cross over into China, but they quickly come back. They know it's safer for them in Russia.'

Brun laughed; the audience laughed. The TV cameras caught the moment and broadcast it to the world. The image of the Russian president standing next to the chancellor of the Federal Republic of Germany, with an extremely photogenic tiger cub in his arms, was one of the defining moments of Popov's visit that summer to Berlin, the nation's capital. The Chinese government, back in the 1970s, had famously presented the Berlin Zoo with a baby panda, but Bao-Bao had recently died (of old age, nothing more sinister), leaving a gaping hole in an animal-loving nation's hearts.

'We must think of a name for our new guest,' Brun continued. 'We should launch a nation-wide consultation. A referendum like our friends, the British, do.'

The audience laughed again. This was the chancellor at her warmest, most human.

'Perhaps they'll decide to name her Helga!' Popov quipped.

Berlin Zoo is situated at the western end of the Tiergarten, the great park which extends all the way to the Brandenburg Gate. On the north-eastern edge of the Tiergarten stands the Federal Chancellery building.

'Let's walk back across the park,' Brun suggested. 'Some exercise will do us good.'

If Brun had deliberately intended to throw her security detail into confusion, she certainly succeeded. The German chancellor and the Russian president set off on foot across the Tiergarten while a phalanx of special agents trotted along behind them at a respectful distance.

'Such a brilliant idea, bringing us that little tiger cub, Igor,' Brun said. 'Not taken from the wild, surely?'

'No, born in Moscow Zoo. Her mother had a litter of five. Too many really. I'm sure she was glad to give one up in the interests of international diplomacy.'

'Her loss is our gain,' Brun said.

Popov took her arm. There was no way anyone could overhear them. 'Quite like old times, isn't it, Mina?'

He used her codename deliberately.

Growing up in East Germany, in the German Democratic

Republic or GDR, at a time when East Germany was still part of the Soviet Empire, Helga Brun – from the KGB's point of view – had obvious potential as a possible agent. She was young; she was pretty; she was phenomenally intelligent. She spoke Russian fluently. She had not only studied the language, she had visited Moscow twice on state-sponsored trips. She had come to Popov's attention when he was head of the KGB office in Dresden and she was one of the youngest ever professors at Leipzig University, where she specialized in modern languages.

Of course, when the Berlin Wall fell at the end of 1989, the whole world changed. It certainly changed for the KGB in Dresden. Popov remembered that December evening so clearly. From a side-balcony of the KGB's mansion on *Angelikastrasse*, he had watched the crowds ransacking the hated Stasi headquarters. Then a bunch of them had broken off to attack the KGB office itself. In what was probably one of the most defining moments of his career, Popov had confronted them unarmed.

'This house is strictly guarded,' he had said in fluent German. 'My soldiers have weapons. And I have given them orders. If anyone enters the compound, they are to open fire.'

Later, of course, the story was much embellished. In some versions, guards were positioned with AK-47s at the windows of the building ready to shoot. Others claimed that Lieutenant-Colonel Popov, as he then was, had brandished a pistol when addressing the crowds. But the key point was through his prompt and successful intervention Popov gained vital time.

Next day, they had destroyed most of the files, communications, lists of contacts, agents' networks etc. They all went up in smoke. But Popov and his colleagues managed to spirit some of them back to Moscow. One of those files was Mina's.

Well, he had protected her back then, Popov thought. Thanks to him, KGB files from the Dresden office never fell into the hands of the government of the newly unified Germany in the way the Stasi files did. Had they done so, the government would certainly have learned about Mina and it would not have taken them long to discover Mina's real identity. If they had, Brun's brilliant career might have taken a very different turn.

'Those were the days weren't they, Mina?' Popov repeated. 'Do you remember when we walked along the banks of the Elbe together?'

'Don't call me Mina. I'm not Mina.'

'You're lucky the Stasi didn't keep a file, too.'

Brun was suddenly indignant. 'I would never have worked for the Stasi. Disgusting bunch!'

She turned to face him. She had loved him then. They were virtually the same age. And there had been this powerful physical attraction. She had once, daringly, asked him, 'Igor, were you born with an erection?'

By this time they were nearing the far end of the Tiergarten. The security detail was closing up on them. The Chancellery building loomed ahead.

'What do you want?' she asked. 'You had better be quick. In another five minutes we'll be surrounded by guards.'

'I'll give you a hug now, for old times' sake.'

He pulled her towards him in a brief embrace.

CHAPTER TWENTY-THREE

Sitting at the back of the Plenary Chamber in the row of seats reserved for high officials, Thomas Hartkopf, state secretary at the German ministry of the interior, watched with interest as President Popov addressed the special session of the Bundestag.

It was a brief but well-judged speech. At a time when NATO and the EU had been testing Russian patience to the limit with their ill-judged sanctions over Crimea and their crude enticements to both Ukraine and Georgia (encouraging them to join NATO, for heaven's sake!) Popov knew full well that at least in Germany many people, including the chancellor, were reluctant to provoke the Russian bear into a counter-attack, since – as recent history of the twentieth century had shown only too clearly – it would be, above all, Germany that paid the price.

So Popov studiously avoided any mention of the European Union and its irritating ambitions. He emphasized instead the historic ties between Russia and Germany.

'Above all,' Popov said, 'let us stress the friendship between our two great countries. Russian-German relations are as old as our nations. The first German tribes appeared on Russian territory in the late-first century. In the late-nineteenth century Germans were the ninth most numerous ethnic group in Russia. But what is important is not just the numbers, but the role played by these people in the development of the country and in Russian-German relations. They were peasants and merchants, intellectuals, military men and politicians.

'As a good neighbour in the West,' Popov continued, 'Germany often symbolized for the Russians culture, technical intellect and entrepreneurial wit. Small wonder that in the past all Europeans were known as Germans in Russia and the Europeans' settlement in Moscow was known as the German Village!'

Popov paused, playing it for laughs. The honourable members duly obliged with a round of applause. What a showman the man was, Hartkopf thought.

There was more to come. 'Nor should we forget Princess Sophia Augusta Frederika of Anhalt-Zerbst, who made a unique contribution to Russian history. Ordinary Russians called her Mother, but she went down in history as Russian empress Catherine the Great.'

He gestured towards the German chancellor: Helga the Great!

By the time he sat down, Popov had them eating out of his hand. It wasn't just his gift of oratory and the sly sense of humour. The claws for the moment were well-concealed, but they were still there.

When it was her turn to speak, Chancellor Brun sensed the mood lightening in the Chamber.

'I thought I would start by talking about football,' she began. 'I know that's a safe subject. Of course, Germany was delighted to win the last World Cup in Brazil in 2014, and we are all looking forward to the next World Cup in Russia in 2018.'

The parliamentarians applauded enthusiastically. President Popov leaned over to the chancellor and in a stage whisper said, 'Maybe it will be a Russia–Germany final.'

Hartkopf's attention began to wander. It always did when people talked about football. Couldn't stand the game.

So he listened with half an ear as Brun moved on from football to welcome President Popov on his historic visit to Berlin. He heard her speak eloquently of the importance of the relationship between Russia and Germany, as Popov himself had. Then she started on about Europe. Funny, wasn't it, how even the best-intentioned people could drone on?

The chancellor finally grabbed his full attention when she started to reflect on current challenges, particularly the war in Syria, the refugee crisis and its impact on Germany.

'Let me be clear about this,' Brun said. 'In the presence of my good friend, Igor Popov, President of the Russian Federation, whom we are honoured to have with us today, I condemn the surge in German attacks on refugee shelters. That is unworthy of our country. I believe that the issue of asylum could become a bigger challenge for the European Union than the Greek debt crisis or the stability of the euro. Indeed, the issue of asylum could be the next major European project, in which we show whether we are really able to take joint action.'

Hartkopf could sense the sudden change of mood in the Bundestag Plenary Chamber. It was as though a door had been left open and an icy blast had entered the room. Basically, he knew, the members were fed up with the asylum issue. Many of them thought that Germany had been far too generous to refugees already. How many more could the country absorb?

As the chancellor spoke, he could see members fidgeting on their well-padded seats. Surely the chancellor was not going to spoil the morning with some ill-judged platitudes about the need for compassion and brotherly love?

Well, on this particular historic occasion, Chancellor Brun eschewed platitudes entirely. She was not a tall woman, but that morning she stood very tall indeed.

She looked straight out into the body of the chamber, raising her voice, just as she would raise people's hopes around the world.

'Today I pledge,' she proclaimed, 'that Germany will play its full part in resolving this crisis. The UN refugee agency has said that the number of people driven from their homes by conflict and crisis has topped fifty million for the first time since World War II. Fifty million! That is unbelievable. This is a situation which cannot be allowed to continue. Germany will welcome those refugees with open arms. We will do what common humanity requires us to do. We already have over one million refugees in Germany. I promise that we will do more, much more. We *can* do it! And I promise we will do whatever we can!'

While the high-ups were being entertained elsewhere, there was a buffet lunch for officials in one of the Bundestag's dining rooms. Hartkopf found himself standing next to a tall, suave Russian.

They had met several times over the last few years, for example at G8 summits. Russia had been expelled or 'disinvited' from the G8 in 2014, but it still participated in the annual Munich Security Conference.

The two men found a quiet corner where they could talk.

'Chancellor Brun went out on a limb this morning, didn't she?' Yasonov commented. 'If this hadn't been a special occasion, I feel some hard words might have been said by some of the members. They weren't keen on the chancellor's open-ended commitment on asylum seekers, were they?'

'Not at all,' Hartkopf agreed. 'I took a look at my boss, Otto Friedrich, the minister of the Interior. He was purple in the face with rage. That pledge on migrants obviously took him by surprise.'

'Do you think Friedrich will make a move? Will he stand against Brun in the elections?' Yasonov asked.

'Your guess is as good as mine,' Hartkopf replied. 'He may not go for it now, but I don't think he'll wait for ever. And he has that Bavarian power base. That always counts for a lot in German politics.'

'If Mrs Brun goes, Friedrich is the chancellor's natural successor, isn't he?'

'A strong candidate, at least,' Hartkopf acknowledged.

They had ordered a selection of pastries to follow the main course. Yasonov passed the plate across. 'Here's something which might help Dr Friedrich on his way.'

Hartkopf was careful to palm the flash drive before helping himself to a thick slice of Black Forest cake.

Later that night, sitting in his study at home, Dr Otto Friedrich examined the dossier in detail. He was staggered. There it all was in black and white. The fact that her name hadn't shown up in the Stasi files the government acquired after the fall of the Berlin Wall didn't necessarily mean that Helga Brun wasn't implicated. It could just mean she was already in a position to suppress the evidence. But the one file she had not been able to suppress was the one Popov had managed to take back to Moscow when the mission of the KGB's Dresden office was disbanded.

So what had 'Mina' done for the Russians?

'*Mein Gott!*' he exclaimed. He had always wondered about the way Brun had come to power, how she had outmanoeuvred Hans Bloch, when Bloch was chairman of the CDU. Deed done, Brun herself became party chairman and subsequently chancellor. The whole game plan was laid out in the documents. An extremely rude word escaped his lips almost involuntarily. It was obvious what had happened. Brun may have been following instructions from Moscow for years!

There was one document he still had to study, and this one was Russian. It was labelled 'Bundestag: Chancellor's speech'.

'Good God!' Friedrich exclaimed again when he opened the file. The full text of the chancellor's speech which he himself had seen in draft. A diagonal bar across each page said SECRET. How had Popov's people got hold of that? Only a handful of Cabinet members in Germany had seen it in advance.

He had been furious that morning when the chancellor gave that pledge on the asylum seekers, cursing her for ad-libbing.

'We *can* do it! And I promise we *will* do what we can!' appeared in bold red type in the document he had up on the screen.

Friedrich picked up the phone. He'd have to report this.

He paused. Who was he going to report it to? To the chancellor? Not likely, given the circumstances. To the minister in charge of security? Well, he was the minister in charge of security. He could hardly report to himself. Who else then?

Another thought occurred to him. People would ask how he came to be in possession of this explosive information. Was he going to admit that a senior Russian official passed a data-stick to his own state secretary concealed in a slice of Black Forest cake?

There were legal issues, too. In the Federal Republic even ministers of the interior needed court orders. At least they were supposed to have them. He could just hear the federal prosecutor asking with a sneer, 'And have you been spying on the chancellor, Dr Friedrich?'

He replaced the phone. Better to wait.

Judging by the latest news bulletins, Brun's newly announced policy of a Germany 'open-to-all-comers' was already receiving a huge thumbs-down from the electorate.

Her star, as Friedrich saw it, was beginning to fade and the effects of today's speech might sink her altogether.

His own political star, on the contrary, was already rising fast.

When the moment came he would be ready. And he would have the top-secret 'Mina' dossier if he needed extra ammunition to fatally wound the political career of the chancellor.

CHAPTER TWENTY-FOUR

Fyodor Stephanov was still feeling sore from the beating Lyudmila Markova and her team from FSB Moscow had given him. Frankly, he thought they had overdone it. Everyone free-lanced a bit nowadays. Given the wages the FSB paid, that wasn't surprising. He hadn't realized that just about everybody had been chasing that 'Golden Shower' video. Still, it was out of his hands now. Moscow could do what they liked with it. And they no doubt would.

Markova had given him a stern warning. 'Don't do it again,' she advised, twisting his neck with a vice-like grip. 'Otherwise you'll be in real trouble.'

He took her seriously. She was one tough lady. But he needed to supplement his income.

One evening a week, after his FSB shift had ended, he worked for an outfit known as the Internet Research Agency at 55 Savushkina Street, St Petersburg.

Number 55 Savushkina was a newly built, four-storey office block, which housed upwards of 400 internet trolls. The trolls worked in rooms of about twenty people, each controlled by three editors, who would check posts and impose fines if they found words had been cut and pasted, or were ideologically deviant.

The trolls took shifts writing mainly in blogs along assigned propaganda lines for LiveJournal and Vkontakte, outlets that had literally hundreds of millions of viewers around the world. Artists, too, were employed to draw political cartoons. Employees worked for twelve hours every other day. A blogger's quota was ten posts per shift, and each post had to have at least 750 characters.

Bloggers employed at the Savushkina Street office earned approximately 40,000 Russian roubles a week. As far as Fyodor Stephanov was concerned, it was money for jam. The time would come, he thought, when he might pack in his job at the FSB entirely and become a full-time troll.

In the short time he at been working there, Stephanov had discovered that he had a remarkable aptitude for the task.

He had already begun his evening shift when a new PRIORITY TASK dropped into his inbox.

'Another one about Ukraine.' He sighed as he opened the message. 'Was there anything new to say about Ukraine?'

But when he read the instructions, he saw that the new task wasn't about Ukraine at all. It was about the German chancellor's speech and the alleged 'flood of refugees' about to invade Europe.

'Use your imagination!' the instruction said. 'Find video footage of refugees climbing barriers to break through border posts; migrants raping defenceless women, setting fire to buildings, and generally running amok.'

The technical support team at Savushkina Street was first rate. You wrote the words; they found the pictures, cutting, splicing and pasting with precision. Take the Charlie Hebdo massacre in Paris, for example. Easy to tie that one to migrants and asylum seekers. Or that lorry in Nice, literally mowing people down on the *Promenade des Anglais*. Who was responsible for that? Terrorists entering France disguised as immigrants! Cue-in shots of dark-bearded men hurling obscenities at the camera.

That particular evening it seemed the trolls were instructed to churn out not just blogs with photos attached, but whole video clips.

Stephanov was given the task of reviewing one such film in its final stages before transmission. The basic commentary was in English since the clip would go out worldwide on RT and other media.

He put his earphones on and listened to the Russian translation:

'Speaking in Berlin, Chancellor Helga Brun defied critics of her refugee policies by insisting there would be no change to her open-door migration stance.

'Commentators say that Germany has been rattled by an axe attack on a train in Würzburg, a mass shooting in Munich, a machete attack in Reutlingen and a suicide bomb in Ansbach – all within a week. The attacks left thirteen dead. Three of the attacks were carried out by asylum seekers and one by a German-Iranian who harboured a hatred of Arabs and Turks.

'Brun reiterated her credo: "We can do it!" ("Wir schaffen das!"). She has repeated the phrase over and over since Germany's migration crisis exploded, when she opened up the German border to tens of thousands of mainly Muslim migrants stranded in Hungary.

'She said: "We decided to fulfil our humanitarian obligations. I did not say it would be easy. I said back then, and I will say it again now, that we can manage our historic task – and this is a historic test in times of globalization – just as we have managed so much already, we can do it. Germany is a strong country".'

When the video had finished, Stephanov removed his earphones. He wasn't a specialist but he doubted whether that clip could have been knocked out in the brief hours that had elapsed since the chancellor delivered her speech to the Bundestag.

That meant that someone somewhere had had advance notice of what Brun was going to say.

Interesting, thought Stephanov. Very interesting.

*   *   *

At the end of May, with less than a month to go before the Referendum vote, the Leave campaign's policy board gathered for a crucial strategy session at Leave's headquarters in Westminster Towers, a new and prestigious Thames-side office block situated immediately opposite the Houses of Parliament.

Barnard, as Leave chairman, opened the meeting:

'Good morning, ladies and gentlemen. I've been out of the country quite a lot recently but Harriet Marshall, our campaign director, has had her finger on the pulse, and so I am going to ask her to bring us up to date with developments.'

Marshall didn't waste time.

'We've got a lot to thank the German chancellor for,' she began. 'All the data we have indicates that, since her speech, the immigration issue has risen right to the top of the pile.'

She glanced at her notes: 'Our polling data shows the Leave campaign has been gaining momentum in recent days, rising from being eight points behind in mid–late April to a dead heat of fifty percent apiece in the current poll of polls.

'According to a Sky News poll, of the twenty-nine percent of Brits who are still undecided on the issue, twenty-eight percent are most concerned about the impact the EU has on immigration levels, whereas just fifteen percent cite the economy as their biggest concern.

'The Office of National Statistics has admitted that it has underestimated European migration by 1.5 million people. Based on Sky's results, the events of this week could see Leave actually pull ahead for the first time.

'You don't need me to tell you, ladies and gentlemen,' Marshall continued, 'that these results are good news for us. Leave campaigners have been focussing on making the public aware of the leading role the European Union has played in driving immigration to Britain into the hundreds of thousands a year, while hampering the British government's ability to reverse that trend.'

Marshall paused to wait for the round of applause to subside. Then she went on, 'Meanwhile the Remain campaign has been plugging on with Project Fear and its usual scare tactics, warning all and sundry of economic doom should the British people dare to opt to leave the European Union at the Referendum on 23 June. I must say I was a bit shocked to hear Alan Sigsworth, governor of the Bank of England, start talking about recession, inflation, and a "sharp" crash in the value of sterling, lower wages and rising house prices in the event of Brexit". You would have thought Armageddon was round the corner. And the Bank of England is meant to be independent. Tom Milbourne himself might have written the script!'

Looking around the table, Marshall couldn't help thinking that the team was shaping up well. She didn't on the whole have much respect for politicians but this bunch seemed ready to put their shoulders to the wheel.

Take Barnard, for example. Some people might regard Barnard as a kind of 'useful idiot'. And yes it was true he was 'useful', but he was by no means an idiot. Look at the way he had built up the relationships with the Craigs. It was Ronald Craig, after all, who invited Barnard to join his daughter, Rosie, on that vital trip to Australia to woo Mickey Selkirk.

Or take Harry Stokes, the ebullient, blond-haired former Mayor of London. Stokes was absolutely living up to the high expectations people had of him, wowing the crowds wherever he went. He could be serious, too, if it was absolutely necessary.

Or take Jack Kellaway, the former minister for social affairs, who was playing a key role. If Barnard had led the way in resigning from the Cabinet, Kellaway had followed suit soon after.

Another one to watch was David Cole, the former journalist, and friend of Jeremy Hartley, who had somehow managed to keep his position as a member of the Cabinet even though he had joined the Leave campaign. You never quite knew what Cole was thinking behind those huge owl-like spectacles.

And then there was that dark horse, Andromeda Ledbury. She had turned in a couple of very competent television appearances recently and seemed game for any and all future challenges. She was a woman, which helped. Marshall didn't on the whole believe in gender balance and that kind of thing but you couldn't ignore it altogether. Not nowadays.

Yes, it was a decent team, Marshall thought. They had begun talking about an 'alternative government' and, frankly, it wasn't such a ludicrous idea.

She decided to wrap up. There was work to do. 'Let's be clear about this,' she said. 'We may be winning the battle of the airwaves. We may have important parts of the print media on our side. But we are not there yet.'

After coffee, they got down to the nitty gritty. The spread-sheets came out. Speeches and broadcasts were planned. The itinerary of the Leave Battle Bus was carefully plotted to ensure that, though it would criss-cross the country between now and 23 June, it would be back in London in time, it was hoped, for a Victory Drive down Whitehall on the morning of 24 June.

Before they left, Marshall had one last word of caution for them.

'We're on the right track,' she said. 'But there's still one thing which could scupper us. What if the EU, at the last minute, agrees after all to the prime minister's demands in this so-called renegotiation? What if they see which way the wind is blowing and suddenly come up with a vastly improved offer?'

'What kind of an offer might that be?' Barnard asked. 'The EU so far has offered the PM nothing. *Nada. Niente.* Zilch!'

'Don't be too sure,' Marshall replied. 'Rabbits and hats come to mind.'

CHAPTER TWENTY-FIVE

Later that morning, the chamber of the House of Commons was already crowded when Edward Barnard arrived. As a minister, he used to sit on the front benches. Since his resignation, he had to take pot luck on the back benches. He squeezed into a seat under the gallery in time to hear the speaker call for order.

'Statement by the prime minister,' the speaker, the Rt. Hon. Eric Foster bellowed.

Jeremy Hartley, already in his sixth year as prime minister, sprang to the despatch box. Tall, tanned and fit-looking, he exuded confidence.

'Mr Speaker,' he began, 'I have here in my hand a letter which I have received this morning from the president of the European Commission in Brussels, Mr Michael O'Rourke, and with your leave I would like to read this to the House this morning.'

'Oh dear!' Barnard reflected. 'I have here in my hand . . .' That's an unfortunate beginning. That's what Neville Chamberlain said when he came back from Munich after his meetings with Hitler, waving a piece of paper in his hand as he stepped off the plane.

But the prime minister was clearly oblivious to the unfortunate historical parallel. He read out O'Rourke's letter with obvious satisfaction:

'*Dear Prime Minister,*' Hartley began. '*After consulting with colleagues, I would like to invite you to visit me in Brussels at your earliest convenience with a view to resolving all outstanding matters of contention that may still exist between the United Kingdom and the other members of the European Union.*

Yours sincerely, Michael O'Rourke.'

The prime minister waved the letter in the air. He didn't exactly say, 'ha, ha, ha and ho, ho, ho!' but that was clearly what he had in mind.

The House broke into a roar of applause. Order papers were waved. Tom Milbourne, the chancellor of the exchequer, leaned forward in his seat to pat the prime minister on the back.

Looking ineffably smug, the prime minster continued, 'Mr Speaker, I would like to inform the House that I have already written back to the president of the commission. He has in turn indicated that, if our discussions today go well, as I am sure they will, he will call an emergency session of the European Council tomorrow, with a view of reaching a full and final agreement, which I will then of course be happy to bring back to the House.'

As the prime minister sat down, Miles Pomfrey, leader of Her Majesty's Opposition, got quickly to his feet.

'Can the prime minister tell the House what new terms the president of the commission is offering?'

Hartley bounced back up once again. This was the Punch and Judy Show which went on year after year. Nobody seemed to tire of it. People called it the cockpit of democracy.

'I am sure the Right Honourable Member for Tower Hamlets would not wish me to reveal our negotiating hand. I can assure him that I will be focussed as always on obtaining the right deal for Britain.'

More 'Hear, Hear!'s. More applause. More waving of order papers. Honourable Members liked a bit of exercise before lunch.

As he sat there in the hallowed chamber of the mother of parliaments, Barnard had a sudden sinking feeling in his stomach. Was Hartley indeed going to pull a rabbit out of the hat at the last moment?

Was he planning to go to Brussels and come back with some new offer to put to the people in the Referendum, an offer which really would prove irresistible to the electorate, instead of the thin gruel he had come up with so far? He corrected himself. 'Pretty thin gruel' was the precise expression that Joshua Cooper, that languid young man with the impeccable three-piece suit, had used to characterize the results of the prime minister's efforts so far.

If there wasn't some new deal in prospect, then what else was the prime minister up to? One thing you could say about Hartley, the man was effortlessly cool and unflappable. Always looked as though he was enjoying himself. Bloody Eton, Barnard thought.

Barnard was not the only person to be alarmed by the goings-on in the House of Commons. George Wiley, editor of the *Sun*, Britain's largest-circulation daily newspaper, had received the clearest possible instructions from Mickey Selkirk about which bloody side to back in the Referendum.

'Of course, you can make up your own mind,' Selkirk had shouted down the phone. 'I'm just telling you that I would hope that under any and all circumstances the *Sun* will support the Leave campaign. Actually, not just support the Leave campaign. I want you guys to lead the Leave campaign. Time we kicked the other buggers in the teeth!'

'What the hell's going on?' Wiley asked, as he watched the prime minister preening himself that morning.

Half the office had gathered round to witness the surprising new developments.

'Hold the front page!' Wiley shouted.

Over in the Leave offices in Westminster Tower, Marshall picked up the phone. There had been no notice on the bulletin board that morning outside the newsagents at the end of her road. But this was an emergency.

'Westminster Bridge. At two this afternoon,' she said.

She knew her handler would be peeved about having to come down to Westminster when, from his point of view at least, a

Hampstead Heath RV was much more convenient. But today, Marshall thought, the circumstances were really special. Things were moving so fast. She couldn't afford to leave the office for too long. If Hartley really did come back from Brussels with a new last-minute deal on offer, then the leave campaign might have to rethink its whole strategy. It would be as well to get started now.

Nikolai Nabokov, whose cover title was first secretary at the Russian Trade Mission in Highgate, London, but whose real rank and title was that of 'Major' in Russia's security and espionage service was indeed cross. He had been looking forward to strolling up to the bookmaker on Highgate Hill.

Nabokov sighed. His jowls quivered. He checked his watch. If he caught the Northern Line to Embankment, then walked along the river to Westminster Bridge, he'd be in plenty of time.

Marshall was already there, standing on the pavement halfway across the bridge, gazing upstream past the Houses of Parliament, like any other tourist.

'I see the river police are out in force today,' Nabokov said.

'Yes, Parliament's in session.'

Codewords correctly exchanged, they stood there for a moment or two, admiring the view.

'You need to get a message to Moscow urgently,' Marshall said. 'If the PM thinks he's done a deal, that means he thinks Germany's on side. So there must be a mix-up somewhere. Germany's meant to be pushing for tougher, not softer, terms where Britain is concerned. That way more people will vote for Leave – out of sheer disgust at the way we're being treated! You had better move fast. We need to stop this one in its tracks.'

Nabokov hurried off. In the train back to Highgate, he checked the Paddy Power app on his mobile to see that, after the PM's remarks in the House of Commons, the odds had already lengthened against a Brexit victory. Amazing, wasn't it, how quickly the market factored in these things. Definitely time to get a bet on.

CHAPTER TWENTY-SIX

Michael O'Rourke, the first Irish President of the European Commission, was all smiles when Prime Minister Hartley entered his office on the 13th Floor of the European Commission's Berlaymont Building in the heart of Brussels.

'Good evening, Prime Minister,' O'Rourke came to the door of his huge office to greet his distinguished guest. They shook hands warmly.

Hartley was accompanied by Sir Luke Threadgold, Britain's ambassador to the EU, more properly known as the UK Permanent Representative.

'Good evening, Sir Luke,' O'Rourke said.

'Good evening, Mr President.'

In Brussels, it was important to get the titles right. These things counted.

Just as they were sitting down, a tall flaxen-haired woman, in her early thirties, came into the room.

Hartley leapt to his feet. 'Hello, Mary.' He gave her a kiss on both cheeks. During the course of the long and painful negotiation that the prime minister had conducted with Britain's European partners in the run-up to the Referendum, Mary Burns had gone out of her way to be helpful. Or at least as helpful as she could be in the circumstances.

As the president of the commission's chef de cabinet, Burns was one of the most important people in Brussels. She organized

O'Rourke's day. Set the agenda. Nothing came into, or left, O'Rourke's office without Burns knowing about it.

'Come and join us, Mary,' O'Rourke said.

While the prime minister sat on the sofa, the others pulled up chairs.

'As you can imagine,' O'Rourke began, 'I have been working very closely with the member states, very closely indeed, to avoid an unfortunate outcome. I admit that at the beginning we could have done more to help the UK. I'm sorry we didn't. We could perhaps have avoided some very long evenings.'

'All-night sessions, as I remember,' Hartley interjected.

They all laughed. Get a joke in early on. That had always been Hartley's policy.

'The good news, Mr Prime Minister,' O'Rourke continued, 'is frankly that there has been a change of mood among the member states in recent days. They are all increasingly concerned that a vote for Brexit in the Referendum may destabilize Europe as a whole. There are so-called populist movements in half a dozen countries – France, the Netherlands, Italy – I needn't name them all. For my own country, Ireland, Brexit will pose a special problem. Are we going to reintroduce border controls between Northern Ireland and the south? I would hope not. Am I making myself clear, Prime Minister?'

Hartley nodded. The Irish, he thought, sometimes took a long time to get to the point but they got there in the end.

'We realize,' O'Rourke continued, 'that the migration issue has always been at the top of the UK's list of demands in the renegotiation.'

'And it still is,' Hartley said. 'The problem is our plea fell on deaf ears. The other Member States hardly moved an inch.'

The president of the commission, noticing that the door to his office was still open, rose from his seat, and walked across the room to close it.

'At the moment, what I am about to say is totally confidential. The president of the European Council has called a special session at 10:00A.M. tomorrow morning. The truth is that the UK is no longer alone in its concern about migration. There are other member states that are now as alarmed as you are.'

He gestured towards the huge television standing next to the EU flag in the corner of his office.

'If I were to turn on that television now, what would I see? I would see riots in German streets, cars burning in France. In Holland, the phenomenal rise of the anti-Muslim party. And it's not just the TV; the newspapers are full of it.'

'And social media, too, Mr President,' Burns reminded her boss.

'So what are you proposing, Mr President?' Hartley asked quietly.

O'Rourke glanced again in the direction of the door, as though to check that it was still closed.

'What the commission is going to propose tomorrow, at the meeting of the European Council, is a solution to the migration question which I am sure will meet your approval. Let me explain. When you put forward your own proposals earlier this year in the context of the "renegotiation", you proposed that the UK should be able to introduce what you called an "emergency brake" on migration.'

'Yes, and you turned us down flat,' Hartley reminded him. 'If you had accommodated us on that, everything would be different today. But you didn't give us the help we needed. Isn't it a bit late in the day to come forward with something now?'

'I'm afraid you have misunderstood me, Mr Prime Minister,' O'Rourke said. 'What the commission is proposing now is an EU-wide solution to the migration problem. Not just a formula to keep the UK happy but a way forward that will work for every member state. To be specific, we are proposing that *any* member state that believes it is under intolerable pressure as a result of migratory movements may introduce an emergency brake. And the key point is that the emergency brake will be able to last just as long as the member state concerned thinks it is necessary.'

'Why didn't you think of this before?' Hartley asked. 'It would have saved a hell of a lot of trouble.'

O'Rourke did his best to soothe the prime minister's ruffled feelings.

'The time wasn't right then. We think the time is right now.'

'I'd like to see the language,' Hartley said.

O'Rourke turned to his chef de cabinet. 'Mary, would you be kind enough to read the text to the gentlemen.'

Burns had a soft, lilting Irish voice, which could lend light and life to even the dullest prose.

Hartley stood up. 'I'll have to consult the Cabinet on this overnight. As you can imagine, the implications are enormous. This could change everything.'

A thought occurred to him. 'Are all the other member states agreed on this? The Council would have to be unanimous, wouldn't it?'

'The decision of the Council would indeed have to be unanimous. And, yes, as far as we know, all the member states are agreed.' O'Rourke reassured him.

'What do you mean, "as far as you know"?' Hartley asked sharply.

'We are still waiting to hear from our German colleagues. The chancellor apparently has been hard to reach. But we do not anticipate any problems.'

CHAPTER TWENTY-SEVEN

Next morning, Hartley arrived in good time at the Justus Lipsius Building on the Brussels Rond Point Schuman, home of the European Council, the place where the EU's key legislative decisions were taken.

Nancy Ginsberg, the BBC's chief political correspondent, thrust a microphone at him as he strode into the huge, red-granite building, accompanied by Sir Luke Threadgold.

'Is a bad deal better than no deal, Prime Minister?' she shouted.

Hartley gave her a jaunty thumbs up. 'It's going to be a good day for Britain. A good day for Europe, too!'

Arne Jacobsen, the Danish prime minister, then serving as the president of the European Council, decided it was time to start. It was already well past 10:00A.M., the official time for kick-off that day.

Sitting at one end of the huge, lozenge-shaped council table, he strained his eyes to see who was present and who was not. Back in the good old days, there had been just the six founding fathers of what was then the European Economic Community. Now there were twenty-eight members of the community's successor in title: the European Union. The Council table had had to be continually expanded to accommodate the arrival of the new member states. In its latest configuration, it seemed to be almost as long as a football pitch.

Jacobsen noted that the president of the commission, Michael O'Rourke, was already in his seat down the far end of the room. Other delegations were making their way to their allotted places at the table. The room was filling up.

Jacobsen turned to Eloise Pomade, the senior official in the council's secretariat, who sat on his immediate right. She had held the job almost a decade, weathering crisis after crisis. Somehow the EU survived them all. But this Brexit business, she reflected, was in a category of its own.

'Is the German delegation here yet?' Jacobsen asked.

'The German delegation is certainly here. I've seen the German ambassador a moment ago. But I don't think Mrs Brun has arrived yet.'

She picked up a pair of opera glasses and scanned the room. 'No, she's not here.'

Jacobsen waited another ten minutes but the chancellor still didn't arrive. In the end, even in the absence of Chancellor Brun, he decided to open the meeting.

'Ladies and gentlemen, welcome. I would like to thank you all for coming here at short notice. Some of you may indeed wonder why you are here at all. You may believe that when, earlier this year, we concluded our renegotiation package with the UK, the European Council had, as it were, said the last word. That was our final offer.

'And of course I completely understand if that is the view you take. Nevertheless, I, too, as chairman of the council, must take my responsibilities seriously. It has not escaped my notice, and it will certainly not have escaped yours, that Europe today is in the midst of great turmoil. I would venture to state that even the continued existence of the European Union is under threat from the rise of anti-EU populist movements. We cannot discount the possibility of what I may call the "domino effect". What happens in Britain next month may affect what happens in France, in the Netherlands, in Germany, and even – if this is not too fanciful – in the United States of America, where as we all know the presidential campaign has already begun.

'That is why I have asked the president of the commission to make one last effort to find a solution to the British problem, a solution which should ensure that the outcome of the Referendum can be seen as a confirmation, not a rejection, of our common European destiny.'

'Hear, hear!'

Hartley banged the table to indicate his approval. The other heads of state or government joined in the applause.

Jacobsen smiled. He was not on the whole an eloquent man. But he had put a bit of effort into that speech and he was pleased by the reaction.

After that, as was usual, the European Commission led off the discussion.

O'Rourke began by acknowledging the efforts of all those present in the room to avert the looming train wreck.

'Frankly,' he confessed, 'if we had known a few months ago what we know today, we would have made this one last effort, as Mr Jacobsen called it, a good deal sooner. And I would say to the British delegation through you, Mr Chairman, that we should have realized right from the start that the way to deal with this problem of excessive migration was not through some special arrangements with the United Kingdom, but on the contrary through a strong and durable European solution. I would like to say now how grateful the commission is to all the member states, and of course to the council secretariat, for the efforts made to move this matter forward to a successful conclusion.'

O'Rourke looked up from his notes to address the chairman at the far end of the table. 'Would it help, Mr Chairman, if I read out the text of our proposal slowly? I am not sure the document under discussion is yet available in all the official languages, so it may be helpful also to be able to listen to the interpreters.'

'Go ahead, Mr President,' Jacobsen instructed.

O' Rourke was a large man with a booming voice. Like so many of his countrymen, he had a way with words.

He could even make the dull, procedural prose which he had in front of him that morning sound more than halfway interesting.

'This is the text the commission is proposing,' he began:

The Council hereby agrees that:

Where any country has experienced an inflow of workers or other migrants of exceptional magnitude over an extended period of time; and where:

- *the size of the inflow affects essential aspects of its social security system; or*
- *leads to serious difficulties in its employment market; or*
- *is putting 'excessive pressure' on public services or the environment,*

that country may unilaterally derogate from the provisions of Chapter Four, Title I, of the Treaty on the Functioning of the Common Market, by imposing restrictions on the inflow of workers and other migrants, with a view to mitigating or eliminating the economic, social and environmental problems thereby caused . . .

O'Rourke paused, looked up from his papers and gazed about the room.

'That's it, Mr Chairman,' he said.

Hartley had, of course, heard the text the previous day. He'd had a chance to study it in detail. He admired its simplicity and the economy of words, so unlike most EU documents. He could live with it. More than that, he was ready to welcome it with open arms.

Best say so straightaway, he thought. That was always the best tactic. Set the tone of the debate. Make his view clear.

'I am very grateful to you, Mr President, as chair of the council,' he said to Jacobsen: 'And of course to the Commission,' here he gestured to O'Rourke, 'for all the hard work the community institutions and the member states have put in, so that we can today find a solution to what up till now has been an intractable problem.

'What is interesting to me,' he continued, 'is that what seemed in the first instance to be a purely British problem turns out in the end to be a European problem and therefore one that is capable of a European solution.

'I can confirm today that the United Kingdom government welcomes the text that the commission has put forward, and sincerely hopes that it may be adopted unanimously by the council this morning.'

The applause that followed Hartley's brief intervention was more than polite. It was heartfelt.

It really was a different ball game now, they all thought, compared to what it had been just a few months ago. Even countries like Poland and Romania, whose workers travelled in tens of thousands each year in search of jobs in the more affluent parts of the European Union, could see the value of agreed language, which in the end permitted them to take their own decisions about what was right for their country. And if this text really did help to stop the imminent disintegration of the EU, it was surely worth swallowing any objections they might have.

One by one, the heads of state and government took the floor to express their views. Some of them made long speeches; some of them made short speeches, but none of them, not one, took exception to the text the commission had circulated.

The prime minister of Hungary, Lazlo Ferenczy, was positively ecstatic, which was not surprising given that his country was busy erecting huge fences, topped with razor-sharp wire, along the length of its eastern border.

'It is high time we took this step,' he urged. 'My country supports the commission's proposal whole-heartedly.'

The president of France, Jacques Petit, was more nuanced. 'France will not object to the text,' he said. 'The circumstances are indeed very special. But we would suggest the addition of one line at the end, namely that member states that decide to introduce unilateral measures to control migration should nevertheless report such measures to the commission.'

Jacobsen decided to give the French president all the help he could. It was in any case, as far as he could see, a fairly harmless proposal. No one was suggesting that the commission should actually forbid or try to subvert these unilateral measures.

'If I hear no objection, I propose we accept the amendment as proposed by the president of France.' He banged his gavel on the table before anyone had a chance to ask for the floor. 'So agreed.'

The last speaker had just finished when there was a sudden commotion at the far end of the room.

'Ah! I see the German chancellor has arrived,' Jacobsen said. 'Shall we break for five minutes to give Mrs Brun the chance to catch up?'

The five-minute break stretched to ten; ten minutes stretched to fifteen. What on earth was happening, Hartley wondered? He was worried. It looked as though there had been a cock-up somewhere along the line.

'I thought the commission had squared this text in advance with the Germans,' he commented acidly to Threadgold.

'I did too,' Threadgold replied. 'The German ambassador definitely gave it his okay.'

'Well, his okay doesn't count unless Brun's on board too,' Hartley snapped. He could see that members of the German delegation were clustered round the chancellor in a corner of the room. The German ambassador, Otto von Wiensdorf, a huge white-haired man who was the *doyen d'âge* among delegates, seemed to be almost shouting at her.

'This is the only solution, chancellor,' he urged. 'We must agree to it, not block it. And it is in Germany's interest also. We too need this emergency brake. We cannot tolerate the present situation. Europe itself is at risk!'

When Jacobsen called the resumed meeting to order, he gave the German chancellor the floor straightway,

'I would like to apologize, chairman, for arriving late at the meeting this morning,' Brun began. 'I have to admit that I only saw the interesting text circulated by the commission as I was leaving Berlin to come to Brussels. I had to take the time necessary to consult colleagues and officials.'

She paused and took a sip of water from the glass in front of her.

'I am sorry to say, chairman, that my government finds the commission's proposal totally unacceptable. This great European Union of ours is founded on four basic freedoms: the freedom of movement of goods, people, services and capital over borders. My government is not prepared to see those freedoms weakened or diminished in any way.

'So I much regret that I cannot give any comfort today to our British colleagues by agreeing that there is a European solution to their problem. We have no need of a European solution, because there is no European problem. Or certainly no problem that basic humanity and common sense cannot resolve. We should be proud of the opportunities the current crisis offers to us to show our compassion. We should not fight against this. So in the name of my country, I say "no". Germany votes against this text.'

Hartley gathered his papers together and headed for the door. If he was lucky, he thought, he might be able to make a quick dash to the airport before the press hammered him.

The driver had the door open as Ginsberg caught up, BBC camera crew in tow.

Ginsberg was live on air and she made the most of it. 'How did that go, Prime Minister?' she called. 'Kicked in the teeth by Brussels again?'

Hartley stared grimly ahead. There were times when it was best to keep your mouth shut. This was one of them.

Harriet Marshall let out a great whoop of joy as she watched the news from Brussels. The morning had played out even better than she had hoped. The danger that the EU would make a 'too good to refuse' offer had been conclusively avoided. Just as important, Britain had been totally humiliated that morning in Brussels by Chancellor Brun's icy remarks as she trashed the olive branch that had been proffered. That would be worth a point or two in the polls.

'We're on our way', thought Marshall. 'Boy, are we on our way!' That evening the bookies, for the first time ever, had the Leave campaign nudging into the lead.

Thomas Hartkopf was also watching the news that lunchtime. He mopped his brow. Wow, it had been a close-run thing! Too many links in the chain. London must have sent a message to Moscow, who had passed it on to Berlin, but he himself had only received that message that very morning, when the chancellor had already left Berlin for Brussels. He couldn't speak to her directly, so he had to go through Ursula Hauptman, the chancellor's long-time trusted assistant.

'Please tell the chancellor,' he had told her, 'that she should not, absolutely not, approve the commission's proposal for a Europe-wide emergency brake on migration. That is the formal position of the German Ministry of the Interior and we are constitutionally responsible for such matters.'

'The chancellor will be very pleased to hear that,' Hauptman said. 'That accords with her deeply held beliefs. I'll patch the message through to her at once. She should be reaching Brussels about now.'

Later that day, Friedrich summoned Hartkopf in a terrific rage. 'I've just been told that the Ministry of the Interior blocked the

170

commission's proposal. Who gave those instructions? I certainly didn't. We should have agreed to the commission's proposal. It is precisely what Europe needs at this time.'

Hartkopf fessed up. 'I did. You were not available and I was the acting officer in charge. It was my responsibility to take a view. I spoke to Hauptman. She was very supportive.'

Friedrich calmed down a little. Hauptman had been so long at the chancellor's side that she was sometimes called the 'alternative president'.

Hartkopf added a further point. 'Besides, I am sure you will agree that by her actions this morning, the chancellor is digging her own political grave a little bit deeper every day.'

It didn't take long for Friedrich to see what Hartkopf was driving at.

CHAPTER TWENTY-EIGHT

It had been a long day. Fyodor Stephanov reckoned that he had written twelve blogs that evening, which was two more than his quota. It was hard work. You had to use your brain, as well as your imagination.

Natasha, his girlfriend, was visiting friends in Moscow and wouldn't be back until the weekend. Stephanov was looking forward to having a quiet beer and watching a spot of television before he turned in.

His three-hour stint finished at midnight. It was less than half a mile from Savushkina Street to his apartment on the eighth floor of a Soviet-style apartment block. Usually it took him about ten or fifteen minutes to cover the distance, allowing time for a cigarette along the way.

Two men, who obviously knew his schedule, were waiting for him in the lobby of the building. He recognized them at once. They were both Chinese. He had dealt with them on several occasions, back in the days when he was hawking kompromat on the black market. They'd even had a Chinese meal together one night. Ling was older than Kong but both were tough-looking customers.

'What are you doing here?' he tossed the stub of his cigarette into a bin.

'We've come to talk to you.'

'What about?'

'Let's go up to your apartment,' Ling said.

They sat round the kitchen table in his flat. Stephanov had some cans of Baltica in the fridge and he passed them round.

'So what's the problem?' he asked.

'The problem is that material you sold us,' Ling told him. 'You said they filmed that English guy with the two ladies. We've had word back that the man on the bed with the girls wasn't the English guy at all. It was someone else. They want to know who it was. They want the footage, the original footage.'

Stephanov swore under his breath. That bloody film! He wished he had never got involved in the first place.

Well, he couldn't give them the film. Markova and her team had bagged everything up and taken it away with them.

'I can't give you the footage. I don't have it. FSB Moscow took it. You'll have to ask them!'

His visitors didn't appreciate the joke. As part of the Chinese Ministry of State Security's extensive network of agents in Russia, they were under great pressure to deliver the goods. When Beijing said 'jump', you jumped.

Ling took a long pull at his beer. Normally they would have resorted to violence, but with Stephanov it was different. He might have been selling kompromat material on the black market, but he was still FSB.

'What *can* you give us?' Ling said. 'Our clients are anxious.'

Stephanov stood up. 'I'll be right back.'

This was the moment, in cinematic terms, when he would have popped out of the room for a moment only to come back with a loaded pistol to turn the table on the intruders.

But Stephanov didn't have his weapon that evening. He had gone straight from the FSB office to Savushkina Street without it. When you're sitting in front of the computer, you didn't need a suspicious bulge in your back pocket.

'I'll come with you,' Kong said. He stood close to Stephanov in the bedroom, while Stephanov rummaged through a chest of drawers.

'Got it!' Stephanov exclaimed as he found what he was looking for.

Back in the kitchen, he spread the US-flag boxer shorts on the table. 'You can have them. For free. Just don't come back.'

Ling fingered the soft, silky material. 'This is good. Very good. These are boxer shorts the man was wearing? You sure of that?'

'I'd stake my life on it,' Stephanov replied. He examined the inscription on the waistband. 'See what it says: "Bloomingdales' finest"!'

'How much you think these US-flag boxer shorts are worth?' Ling asked.

'A lot of money in the right hands,' Stephanov replied. 'There could be DNA, for example.'

When Ling and Kong had gone, Stephanov poured himself another beer. At least they hadn't beaten him up, he thought. Maybe he ought to retire.

With three weeks to go before the Referendum, Barnard took time off for lunch at the Athenaeum Club. He'd been a member for years. He didn't go to the club often, but when he did he usually enjoyed himself. Most of the people who belonged to the Athenaeum were tremendously brainy. The club kept a special book recording the names of club members who had won the Nobel Prize in physics, chemistry, economics or whatever. Barnard was very ready to recognize that he wasn't in that league. He didn't regard himself as an intellectual – he'd read geography at Oxford – but he was capable of contributing to a discussion in the bar or around the members table if he felt he had something to say.

One of the nice things about the Athenaeum was that it had reciprocal arrangements with similar clubs around the world. If you were visiting Sydney, for example, you could dine at the prestigious Union Club, and vice versa.

Barnard found himself sitting at the long members table next to a tall, greying Australian. 'My name's Irwin Jones. I'm Professor of Toxicology at Sydney University,' the man introduced himself.

'And I'm an MP campaigning to take Britain out of the EU,' Barnard replied. 'Does toxicology include the study of spider bites?'

'It certainly does.'

Barnard spent the next few minutes telling the Australian Professor about his recent narrow escape in the Kimberley.

'I had a terrace room at Lazy-T. I guess the spider came in through the open window. They rushed me to Kununurra District Hospital. Took the dead spider, too. Luckily there was a top toxicologist there that night. He took one look at the thing and said it was a Sydney funnel-web spider. *Atrax robustus*. He even gave it the Latin name.'

Jones looked surprised. 'Can you remember the name of the toxicologist? I might give him a call.'

'Professor Cohen, as I recall. I'm going to send him a note. He probably saved my life.'

'Cohen? I know Cohen. Toxicology's a small world. He used to work at Sydney Hospital before moving west. Will you forgive me a moment? I need to use the phone.'

'There's a booth downstairs where you can make a call,' Barnard told him. 'The club doesn't allow mobiles in the public rooms.'

Minutes later, the professor returned. 'I talked to Cohen. Woke him up actually. He remembered you well. Said he gave you the Redback spider anti-venom but basically he didn't expect it to work. The venom of the Sydney funnel-web spider is based on the protein toxin robustoxin. The venom of the Redback spider is based on latrotoxins. Apples and oranges. Said you were lucky to survive. People do survive a bite from the funnel-web spider without anti-venom treatment, but not many, I must say.'

The professor paused. The kedgeree on his plate needed his attention. Then he added quietly, 'You ought to call the police, you know.'

Barnard was puzzled. 'Why would I call the police? I was bitten by a spider. I recovered. End of story.'

'I fear not.' The professor pushed his plate aside. 'Is there somewhere we can talk?'

They took their coffee out on to the terrace, overlooking the garden. London, that June morning, could not have looked lovelier.

'Look, it's quite simple,' Jones explained. 'There are no, repeat no, Sydney funnel-web spiders in Western Australia. That's why the hospital in Kununurra didn't have the specific anti-venom for that sort of spider. They are simply never found up in that part of the country. As a matter of fact, the only place in the world that they are found is in Sydney and the neighbouring area. That's why they're called what they are. And that's why Cohen was so confident about his identification. He comes from Sydney himself. Knows the critters well.

'So if there are no Sydney funnel-web spiders up in the Kimberley,' Jones continued, 'how is that you got bitten by one? Have you got any enemies, Mr Barnard? Someone was trying to kill you up there, that's for sure. If they have tried once and failed, they might try again.'

'Good God!' Barnard exclaimed. 'I see what you're getting at.'

Just at that moment a cloud passed across the sun. Barnard shivered.

Sir Oliver Holmes made space in his diary that very afternoon.

Barnard walked across St James's Park to New Scotland Yard. Deputy Commissioner Cornelia Gosford, a handsome woman of medium height with short, salt-and-pepper hair, was with Holmes when he arrived.

'I've asked my deputy to join us. Cornelia looks after our links with the Three Fs. That's Friendly Foreign Forces, Australia included.'

Barnard, in his long career as a politician, had met Gosford on several occasions. She was bright as a button. Had a doctorate from Cambridge. Probably belonged to the Athenaeum, too. The word on the street was that she was in line to succeed Holmes when he stepped down a few months from now. If she did, she would be the first woman to head the Met. Not that she wouldn't have made it in her own right anyway.

'Delighted to see you again, Deputy Commissioner,' he said.

Barnard told his Kimberley story once more. Holmes didn't interrupt, but once or twice he made notes on a scratch pad.

When Barnard had finished, Holmes looked at his deputy. 'Do you want to come in at this point, Deputy Commissioner?'

Gosford just had a query. 'You said the couple who ran the house at Lazy-T, as opposed to the station hands, were called Ching and Fung. Do you know their full names? Of course, we can find out, but it would be easier if we had the family name. It sounds to me as though there's an MSS cell up there in the Kimberley. A murderous one, too, if your story is anything to go on. Didn't you say Selkirk had to top-up the fuel that night when they were trying to rush you to hospital? Somehow, apparently, Ching had forgotten to fill up the heli. I'll get on to our friends in the Australian Federal Police – the AFP – at once. They'll probably need a search warrant for Lazy-T. Is Mickey Selkirk still there?'

'I think he's back in the States,' Barnard said.

'That's a pity,' Holmes cut in. 'I'm sure the AFP would have wanted Mickey Selkirk to be there when they raid his property. Lots of mileage there in PR terms!'

They all laughed. When Gosford had left the room to set things in motion, Holmes said to Barnard, 'We ought to give you a body-guard, at least until the Referendum's over. We've been assessing the threat to public figures for some time. We think you qualify for protection.'

'Good God!' Barnard protested. 'I'm just a figurehead in this campaign. The Leave side needed a chairman and my name popped out of the hat. The only reason I'm chairman is that I stuck my head above the parapet before the others did.'

'Don't underestimate your influence, Edward,' Holmes said. 'Leave is within spitting distance of winning this fight. That wouldn't have happened without you. As we see it, the Chinese Secret Service first tried to blackmail you, then to kill you. Three strikes and you're out. Whether you like it or not, we're going to keep an eye on you.'

As Holmes showed his guest to the door, he murmured, 'By the way, we've finished our work on that file you brought back from Russia. Our report's with the home secretary. She seems to be sitting on it at the moment. I must say I don't blame her.'

He held the door open. 'I shouldn't be telling you this, but we think most, if not all, of those documents are genuine. Let the chips fall where they may,' he concluded cryptically.

'Do you mean . . . ?' Barnard began.

'I don't mean anything at this moment,' Holmes said. 'We were asked to report on the authenticity or otherwise of the documents we examined. That we have done. It is for others to draw the appropriate conclusions. I'm a policeman, not a politician.'

After leaving New Scotland Yard, Barnard walked back into St James's Park. Girls in summer dresses walked around the lake. Some were sunbathing in bikinis. He sat on a bench and mentally ticked off the names of the waterfowl: Mallard, Shelduck, Wigeon, Gadwall, Teal, Pintail, Shoveler . . .

A hundred yards away, Jerry Goodman, one of the 'watchers' Holmes had put in place that very afternoon, spoke quietly into his radio. 'Not much going on. He's watching the birds in St James's Park. No, I mean the real birds. The birds on the lake. Not the dolly birds. Plenty of those around today too. Out.'

CHAPTER TWENTY-NINE

The Turkish president, Ahmet Ergun, was in a foul mood. He felt betrayed. There were three million Syrian refugees in his country. Turkey had fed them and watered them. Europe might complain about the 'flood' of migrants. That was garbage. Turkey, under his leadership, had made heroic efforts to stem the tide. But he expected a little something in return.

And what had he got? Nothing. Absolutely nothing. Turkey was still out in the cold. They'd been talking for years about Turkey joining the EU and they didn't mean a word of it. Those guys in Brussels looked on the Turks as though they were some kind of barbarians, conveniently forgetting that the Ottomans had ruled half of Europe for over 500 years. Why did the French eat croissants for God's sake?

Sitting in one of the many reception rooms of his enormous new palace in Ankara, the nation's capital, the Turkish president called for more coffee.

'Please bring my wife, too,' he said.

When Nuray came and sat down beside him on the sofa, he said to her, 'Today, I'm going to do it.'

Nuray nodded. 'It is time.'

For decades now she had been her husband's rock and support. She had even chosen to wear the headscarf, sending a message to the nation that had not gone unnoticed.

'It is time,' she repeated. 'For too long we have grovelled to Europe. You should rip up the agreement with the EU about the refugees.

Europe has not kept its side of the bargain. We applied to join the EU in 1987. They told us there are thirty-five chapters to negotiate and most of them haven't even been opened. Be serious, Ergun.'

'I am being serious,' Ergun said. 'I have given the instruction this morning.'

What Ergun did not tell his wife was that the precise timing of his decision, as well as important details relating to scope and method, had been thrashed out in detail on the occasion of President Ergun's recent visit to Moscow. As Turkey sought to distance itself from the EU and to seek allies elsewhere, for example with a new agreement on Turkey-Russia collaboration, there had been one issue where Popov had insisted that urgent action by Turkey would be tremendously helpful.

'Just open the taps, Mr President,' Popov had urged. 'And do it now. That'll make them squeal.'

That afternoon, Ergun flew down from Ankara to Sanliurfa airport in southern Turkey. From there he was escorted to Suruç, Turkey's largest refugee camp. He arrived at around noon and almost at once mounted a makeshift stage to make one of the most important speeches of his career.

As the sun beat pitilessly down, bouncing off the bleached, almost white, soil, Ergun looked out over at the rows of tents and at the crowds of refugees – men, women and children – who now gathered around the podium.

He began on a serious patriotic note. 'Today, I want to say how proud I am of the effort Turkey has made to deal with an unprecedented crisis. We have over three million refugees in our country, more than any other nation in the world. Here in Suruç, we have the largest refugee camp in Turkey. Just over the border in Syria, the fighting is still raging. Refugees are still coming. Day by day, hour by hour, minute by minute.

'As I have said, Turkey is proud to play its part. But we cannot bear this immense burden alone. Europe has not risen to the challenge. But now we have heard the German chancellor say "we can do it". So I say, bravo. At last the world is waking up. Today I am saying to you here in Suruç, and in the many other camps in this country, that you are free to leave. We shall speed you on your way. We shall help you cross over to Lesvos, Kos and Chios. We shall escort you in safe convoys to the Bulgarian border or up the Black Sea coast to Romania.

'My sincerest wish is that you have happy memories of your stay in Turkey!'

With that, a hastily assembled band played some martial music. As the president stepped down from the stage, a fleet of buses rolled up to carry the refugees away to a hopefully brighter future, a scene that was replayed at the fifty other refugee camps scattered throughout Turkey.

In the car heading back to the airport, Ergun commented to his escort for the day, General Aslan Bolat, 'Well, that's a start. Of course, the people in the camps are only the tip of the iceberg. There are at least two million refugees living in the cities as well, without actually being in the camps.'

General Bolat stared straight ahead. The Turkish Army would, he knew, soon confront a critical decision. Did they continue to back the president with his increasing autocratic tendencies or did they do what the Turkish army had historically done at times of crisis: intervene to restore the legacy of Turkey's great founding father, Kemal Atatürk?

'Well, what do you think, General?' Ergun said.

'We must trust in your guidance, Mr President,' he said.

Ergun grunted. 'And in God's too.'

If Suruç camp was some distance from Europe's borders, other refugee camps were much closer. The camp in Edirne, for example, was virtually within spitting distance of the Bulgarian border. Less than an hour after President Ergun had finished his speech in Suruç, the guards at the border post on the Turkish side of the Maritsa River flung the gates open to let a horde of refugees stream across the bridge, overwhelming the guards on the Hungarian side. Refugees who couldn't gain access to the bridge began to ford the river. Chaos reigned.

Possibly the most dramatic scenes, as recorded on the world's televisions, were filmed on the Aegean coastline, where, by some quirk of history, Greek islands such as Lesvos, Kos and Chios were to be found almost within a stone's throw of the Turkish mainland. Not a day passed without lives lost. Rickety boats sank. Even with life jackets, exhausted refugees drowned. And the promised land, when they reached it, was not the Nirvana they hoped for. Selkirk Global News outlets went out of their way to show pictures of sodden refugees being verbally abused by exhausted locals or pushed back into the boats.

Marshall, watching television at home after a long day campaigning, could barely contain her enthusiasm. She shouted to her partner, 'Christine, come and look at this. You won't believe it!'

She turned up the volume as the TV showed a pitched battle between a crowd of migrants and a stern phalanx of policemen, advancing ruthlessly, Perspex shields held in front of them. Rocks were thrown, followed by a sudden burst of gunfire.

'Brilliant!' Marshall clapped her hands. 'Totally brilliant. And that was the BBC. Fox News ran a much longer piece. So did Sky. Just what we needed. That should shift the polls.'

Christine Meadows, an eminent scientist with a sheaf of publications to her name, was beginning to be seriously worried about Harriet. As a researcher, she was used to reaching evidence-based conclusions and one of the conclusions she was coming to was that her partner was, quite frankly, losing it.

'Hold on a moment, darling,' she protested. 'I know we, or rather you, want to win this Referendum but does that mean anything and everything goes?'

Marshall looked at her in surprise. She gestured at the television. 'This stuff is like gold dust for us. This refugee crisis couldn't have come at a better time. First, Chancellor Brun, then President Ergun. Both of them coming in right on cue.'

'I think I'll leave you to it.' Christine went up to her study. She was still trying to finish her latest book. She switched on the computer, found the file, picked away at the keyboard. But still she couldn't concentrate. What on earth had gotten into Harriet? She was working day and night. Kept on popping out to visit the newsagent at the end of the road with some lame excuse about picking up the evening paper.

Given the pressures of the campaign, with Harriet being awake half the night, they had been sleeping in separate rooms in recent weeks. When she came down to breakfast next morning, Harriet had already left. The car had gone, too. She was surprised. Harriet normally took the tube to Westminster, then walked over the bridge to the Leave office in Westminster Tower.

She noticed a crumpled piece of paper on the kitchen table. Maybe she had left her a note.

It wasn't actually a piece of paper. More like one of those cards they stick up in the newsagent. Yes, that was exactly what it was. Another of those notices about a missing three-legged black cat. 'Three-legged black cat found' the notice said. 'Ring 077238954978'.

On a whim, Christine rang the number. There was a strange screeching noise at the other end of the line. Then an automated voice said. 'This number has been disconnected.'

Odd, Christine thought. Very odd indeed. What on earth was going on?

CHAPTER THIRTY

With one week to go before polling day, Barnard took the day off. He spent the morning on farm chores, went for a ride after lunch (his bay mare, Jemima, though getting on in years, was still good for a day's outing with the local hunt), then worked on his papers at the table in the drawing room.

The French windows opened out onto the terrace. In the middle distance, beyond the water meadows, the gentle hills of the Wiltshire Downs glowed in the afternoon sunshine.

What a lucky man he was, Barnard thought. When all this was over, he could spend a bit more time at Coleman Court: dam a chalk stream, make a pond, build a folly. That kind of thing.

His musings were interrupted by his wife, Melissa, carrying a tray of goodies.

'Scones, clotted cream and strawberry jam,' Melissa proclaimed. 'Only seven more days left. Let's celebrate.'

'Let's wait at least till tomorrow before we open the champagne,' Barnard cautioned. 'I may fall flat on my face tonight.'

'I'm sure you won't, darling.'

Truth to tell, Barnard, who was usually as unflappable as they come, was just the tiniest bit nervous about the event in which he would be participating that evening. Not since 1933, when the Oxford Union had considered the motion 'this House will in no circumstances fight for its King and Country' had an occasion been so widely heralded.

Back then, the whole country had awaited the outcome with bated breath, and when the Oxford Union decisively approved the motion, waves of anger and disgust had risen across the land. The *Daily Express* trumpeted: 'DISLOYALTY AT OXFORD: GESTURE TOWARDS THE REDS'. Cambridge University threatened to pull out of the annual boat race. Winston Churchill made a tub-thumping speech calling the result 'That abject, squalid, shameless avowal'.

There was every chance, Barnard thought, that the evening's debate in the Oxford Union, more than eighty years later, would prove equally, if not more, controversial. The Referendum was rapidly descending into a free-for-all knockout contest with Marquess of Queensberry rules suspended for the duration.

Melissa was just clearing the tea things away when she heard the sound of tyres crunching on gravel. She looked up to see a black four-wheel drive Range Rover with tinted windows enter the courtyard. She put the tray down and went outside.

Jerry Goodman, thirty-four years old, ex-Royal Marines and now a member of the Met's Special Security Squad, got out of the vehicle.

'Good evening, Ma'am,' he greeted Melissa.

'Hello, Jerry,' she said. Then, as two other plain-clothes officers emerged from the vehicle, she added, 'Hello, Tom; hello, Anna. Come in and have some tea. We'll be ready in a jiffy.'

She took them into the kitchen and left them there, cradling mugs of tea in their hands, while she went upstairs. Barnard had already put his dinner jacket on.

'The team's here,' she said. Strange, wasn't it, she thought, how quickly they had got used to having 'security' around.

The Barnards had a Range Rover, too. They left in convoy.

'You go first,' Goodman said. 'You may as well head straight for the union. They've got parking spaces for us there.'

'That's something,' Barnard said. 'Last time I made a speech at the union in Oxford, I spent half-an-hour looking for a place to park.'

Barnard studied the order paper while his wife drove. The terms of the motion, he observed, deliberately echoed that famous 'King and Country' debate so many years ago. It stated 'that this House will in no circumstances vote to leave the European Union'.

The motion was due to be proposed by Lord Middlebank of Upper Twaddle. It was to be seconded by none other than Tom Milbourne. The first speech for the opposition was to be made by Andromeda Ledbury, with Barnard himself scheduled to fire the last salvo against the motion before the floor debate and the final vote.

'Do you know what you're going to say tonight?' Melissa asked as they turned off the A34 into Oxford. 'The whole debate's going to be televised apparently. Have you got some notes at least?'

Barnard laughed. 'If I can't make a speech about Europe without notes, after months of campaigning, it's time I headed for the knackers' yard.'

Marshall was waiting for them at the entrance to the Oxford Union building. She ushered Melissa to her seat in the chamber, while Barnard met the other speakers in the anteroom. Lord Middlebank had already arrived. His flowing fair hair had turned a silvery colour with the years, but he was still strikingly handsome.

'Hello, Edward.' Though he proffered his hand there was a frosty edge to his voice. 'I sincerely hope you lose this debate and lose the vote next week. You are doing great damage to the country.'

'I'm sure you'll say so this evening,' Barnard replied. No point having a fight now, he thought. Fisticuffs could come later.

He moved out of range to study the photos displayed on the wall of the anteroom. Back in the day, he'd been a competent performer at the Oxford Union himself, though he had never made it to president. If he had, he too would be hanging on the wall in a silver frame. So many famous names, he thought, as he moved along the row. Gladstone, Wilberforce, Curzon, Asquith, Hogg, Foot, Heseltine, Bhutto, Johnson – what a galaxy!

The photographs were arranged in chronological order. When he came to the 1990s, he paused to peer more closely. Howard R. Marshall, it said. President, Trinity Term, 1995. How odd, he thought. Howard R. Marshall could have been Harriet Marshall's twin, the resemblance was so striking. Did Marshall actually have a twin brother? If so, why had she never mentioned him?

Sitting next to H.R. Marshall was another man whose face was familiar. Y. Yasonov, he read, Treasurer. Good God! This was really too much! If Marshall had a twin brother, she had kept very quiet about it. And why had the name 'Yasonov' not rung a bell with her? Yasonov had been more than Howard Marshall's contemporary at Oxford. He had been a close collaborator. They had apparently both served as officers of the union at precisely the same time. How bizarre!

When he came back to Britain after that tiger-tagging expedition in Russia's Far East, Barnard distinctly remembered telling Marshall that he'd had a private dinner in Khabarovsk with President Popov and his key aide, Yasonov. Popov, as he recalled, had said something about Yasonov having learned his 'classy' English at Oxford. Marshall hadn't picked up on that at all. If Yasonov had been close to her twin brother, surely Marshall would have heard of him, even met him at some May Ball or at a union debate or whatever.

And then the truth struck him. There was only one possible explanation. Howard R. Marshall was actually *Harriet* Marshall. It wasn't a question of there being twins. Howard had actually changed sex. For some reason, known only to him (or her), Howard had become Harriet.

Barnard was still trying to work it all out when the union steward struck the gong. The debate was about to begin. The officers of the union, led by the current president, Arthur Pemberton, filed into the chamber, followed by the speakers. The TV cameras began filming. Louisa Hitchcock, star presenter of the BBC nightly news digest, set the stage for millions of viewers around the world.

'Tonight we come to you from Oxford,' she began, 'from the Oxford Union, one of the world's most famous debating chambers, modelled on the House of Commons. Eighty-three years ago, the Oxford Union held a vitally important debate, a debate which resonated across the continent of Europe. The topic then was: "Should Britain go to war?" The topic today is equally important. Should Britain leave the European Union?'

The cameras panned to the speakers. 'And what a tremendous line-up of speakers we have,' Hitchcock continued. 'On the Remain side we have Lord Middlebank of Upper Twaddle; as well as Tom Milbourne, the chancellor of the exchequer. On the Leave side, we have Andromeda Ledbury, MP, and Edward Barnard, chairman of the Leave campaign. The vote will be taken at the end of the debate. Ladies and gentlemen, fasten your seat belts!'

Lord Middlebank, opening the debate, was in tremendous form. Before his elevation to the peerage, he had spent years in the House of Commons. At a time when good old-fashioned oratory was going out of fashion, Middlebank bucked the trend.

'We shouldn't be having this Referendum at all,' he thundered. 'I fail to understand why such a commitment was included in the Conservative manifesto. I can only conclude that the prime minister totally miscalculated. Maybe he assumed that the Conservatives would not win an overall majority in the election and therefore there would be no need to deliver on the manifesto commitment since it would be vetoed by their coalition partners. If that is the case, ladies and gentlemen, then I put it to you, this is cynicism of the highest order!'

Ledbury, leading for the Leave side, did her best. With speaking engagements up and down the country, she had grown daily in confidence and stature over the weeks of campaigning. She was graceful. She was witty.

'I am delighted to follow Lord Middlebank of Upper Twaddle. I am so sorry. I've got that wrong. I shouldn't have said Upper

Twaddle. I should have said Utter Twaddle!' The young audience loved that. And they warmed to her, too. She was the dark horse – dark filly, really – who had come up fast on the rails in the final furlong. Barnard mentally tipped his hat to her.

Up in the BBC commentary box, Hitchcock commented, 'No one knew very much about Andromeda Ledbury before the start of the campaign but, so far, she hasn't put a foot wrong.'

Milbourne, when it was his turn to speak, seemed strangely hesitant. Maybe he knew that the tide was beginning to turn in favour of Leave. And when he started talking about the dire measures he would be forced to introduce if the country 'voted the wrong way' his audience sensed that he had made a colossal error of judgement.

Once again, Hitchcock summed it up. 'The chancellor has already given us Project Fear. He has told us that the ice caps will melt if we vote to leave Europe. Financial markets will collapse. Granny will starve in the attic. But today, before this Oxford audience, he has gone one step further, promising the country a 'punishment budget', like a punishment beating, if we dare to vote Leave.'

Hitchcock looked straight at the camera. 'Tonight the chancellor, normally so shrewd, may have made a fatal miscalculation.'

Sitting there, waiting his turn to come to the despatch box, Barnard found it hard to concentrate. He simply couldn't put the photo he had seen in the anteroom out of his mind. The photo that showed Harriet (then Howard, of course) Marshall sitting next to Yuri Yasonov. If Harriet/Howard and Yasonov had been friends and colleagues at Oxford, were they still friends now? If so, why hadn't Harriet/Howard ever mentioned it?

He decided to send an urgent message to Goodman. 'Something fishy going on. Keep an eye on Harriet Marshall. Sitting next to my wife, left front.'

Pemberton, Oxford Union President in the Trinity Term of 2016, had a powerful voice which he did not hesitate to use.

Sitting in his high-backed chair in white tie and tails, he boomed,

'I now call upon the Right Honourable Edward Barnard, MP to make the final speech opposing the motion.'

As he stood up, Barnard could see Marshall a few feet away, waving the order paper in front of her face, like a fan. Funny, Barnard thought, it was almost as though she was signalling or something.

Goodman, standing by the door so as to keep an eye on the packed hall, glanced down at his mobile when Barnard's message pinged in. He spotted Marshall immediately, waving the paper. Then he saw her look up at the crowded balcony, turning her head to the right as she did so. What was Marshall looking at, he wondered? Then he saw it. At the far end of the hall, above and behind the balcony, was the old projection box, left over from the days when undergraduates came to the chamber on wet Sunday afternoons, not to debate, but to watch classic films in their original celluloid. The box had to be big enough to hold the projectionist. Some of those old films, like *The Manchurian Candidate*, needed three or four reel changes before the film was over.

The Manchurian Candidate! 'Oh my God', thought Goodman. As he remembered it, the assassin chooses a high vantage point right at the back of the stadium to shoot the candidate at that giant rally in New York.

He quickly pulled out some pocket binoculars to scrutinize the projection block more closely and, as he did so, he saw the barrel of the rifle emerge.

Goodman spoke urgently into his lapel mike. 'Anna, Tom, are you up there? There's a guy with a gun on the balcony. In the old projection box. Take him out!'

Then Goodman hurled himself across the room, just as Barnard walked to the despatch box to begin his speech. You could have handguns, you could have Tasers, but in the end the old-fashioned rugby tackle often worked best. Goodman's shoulder hit Barnard hard, in the ideal spot for a good clean tackle, halfway up the thigh, and Barnard crashed to the floor like a wing three-quarter hurtled into touch by the corner-post. The sound of gunfire erupted in the room. First, a single shot, coming from the projection box, then a brief staccato volley, as both Anna and Tom returned fire.

The gunman's bullet, which would surely have smashed into Barnard had he not been brought low by Goodman's rugby tackle, demolished an antique plaster bust of former prime minister William Gladstone, scattering debris over the despatch box.

Goodman picked Barnard off the floor, slung him over his shoulder, and headed for the door. 'We've got to get you out of here!' he said.

In the BBC commentary box, Hitchcock barely missed a beat. 'Extraordinary scenes here tonight in Oxford,' she said. 'The debate has broken up in confusion. A gunman has tried to assassinate Edward Barnard, leader of the Leave campaign, but that attempt appears to have failed. I have just watched Barnard being rushed from the debating chamber by security officers. As I speak, the search continues for the would-be assassin.'

There was a sudden commotion outside the BBC's makeshift studio on the balcony as a SWAT team rushed past. The camera caught that, too.

'Next time I come to the Oxford Union, I'll bring a flak jacket,' Hitchcock announced, with studied nonchalance.

CHAPTER THIRTY-ONE

The attempt on the life of Edward Barnard made headlines around the world. In the confusion following the exchange of gunfire, the would-be assassin had slipped away, apparently down the fire escape, leaving behind a collapsible, high-powered rifle and a stack of leaflets saying 'KEEP BRITAIN IN EUROPE'.

Back in London the next morning, after the eventful evening in Oxford, Tom Milbourne, de facto leader of the Remain campaign, held an emergency meeting of the core Remain team.

'This attempted murder is already being pinned on us. The "KEEP BRITAIN IN EUROPE" leaflets found on-site don't help,' he told them. 'Of course, we've put out a denial, but that's not enough. Leave is up two points this morning and the trend is against us. For some reason I can't understand, people seem to like Edward Barnard. They don't want Europhile maniacs to take a pot shot at him. I tell you, if they'd taken a vote at the union last night, we would have been absolutely hammered.'

Geraldine Watson, MP for Milton Keynes and deputy leader of Remain, chipped in, 'Maybe it's not all bad news, Tom. I've just received a Google alert. Harriet Marshall, the Leave campaign's wonder-worker, has been taken in for questioning this morning. Everything's very hush-hush. There's some suggestion that Marshall has been in contact with the Russians.'

'What kind of contact?' Milbourne asked sharply. 'I had dinner with the Russian ambassador last week. Great guy. Gave me a

Château Petrus 1957 to celebrate the 60th anniversary of the Treaty of Rome. Sharing a bottle of wine with the Russian ambassador doesn't make me a spy. They'd have to pay me huge sums for that. Or make me editor of the *Evening Standard*!'

He was joking, of course.

Watson was still looking at her phone. 'They got a search warrant. Seized Harriet Marshall's computer.'

'That sounds more interesting,' Milbourne said.

It wasn't exactly the third degree but it wasn't a picnic either.

MI5's top interrogator, a huge Nigerian called Mnogo Abewa, told Marshall, 'You're being held under the Prevention of Terrorism Act. That means we can do pretty much as we like with you without anyone being able to stop us. I could sit on you, for example. I'm twenty stone. I'd just squash you flat. Wouldn't leave a mark.'

Marshall said nothing. Her tradecraft, surely, had been perfect. She had never used her phone to communicate with her 'handler' and never sent an email or a text. What the hell did they have on her?

'Okay, you don't want to talk. That's fine by me,' Abewa said. 'So I'll do the talking. I'll just run through what we have on you.'

He opened the file, took out a document and passed it over.

'See that?' he said. 'That's a photocopy of something we found in your dustbin. I've got the real thing here,' he tapped the file, 'but we'll keep that for court. If I gave it to you now, you might just pop it in your mouth and swallow it, then where would we be?'

Harriet Marshall examined the document. 'Doesn't mean anything to me. Someone's missing a three-legged black cat, apparently. Looks as though they put a notice on a board somewhere.'

Abewa sighed. 'On the morning you picked up the message, you phoned your handler at the Russian trade mission. No, I don't mean you phoned the number on the card: 077238954978. We know that's a fake number. You phoned Nikolai Nabokov's number, the number you know by heart, from the phone box at the end of your road.'

Abewa pushed a button. Marshall heard herself say. 'Forty-five minutes.'

'That could be anyone,' Marshall said.

'How about this then? This is a call you made to Nabokov on your office line. Tut tut.' Abewa shook his head disapprovingly. 'I thought they would have told you not to use the office line and certainly not when you're phoning one of the numbers on our list.'

He punched the button again. This time Marshall heard her own voice even more clearly. 'Westminster Bridge. Two o'clock. This afternoon.'

'We tracked you on the bridge, too, of course. You told us the time and the place, thank you very much. Had our team ready when you got there. Of course, we've known about Nabokov for ages. Have to send him packing now. Back to Moscow. Won't be the first time we've sent the Russkies packing. Won't be the last time either.'

Abewa's own phone pinged. 'Ah, apparently Nabokov's already gone. Flew out this morning on KLM. Rats leaving a sinking ship, eh?'

Half an hour later, they took a break. Abewa looked at his watch. 'Interview interrupted at 10:45A.M.' he said.

Jane Porter who had been watching the interview through the one-way window, was waiting for Abewa outside the room. 'I don't have to tell you,' she said, 'that this is pretty sensitive stuff. What do you think the Russians have been trying to do with Harriet Marshall?'

She made the question seem so innocent, so naive.

'How about trying to influence the result of the Referendum? Will that do for starters?' Abewa replied.

'You're going to have to do better than a newsagent's card dug out of someone's rubbish bin,' Porter said. 'And a casual meeting on Westminster Bridge. Did anyone hear what they actually said?'

Abewa was a Tigger, not an Eeyore. 'Don't worry. We'll get there,' he assured her. 'I'll try my "enhanced interrogation techniques". They usually work.'

'Tell me about Yuri Yasonov,' Abewa asked Harriet when he came back into the interview room. 'You met him at Oxford. When you were Howard, not Harriet. You were friends there. Must have been. You were both officers of the Oxford Union, as I understand. Then, after you left Oxford, you went to Russia for two years. What did you do there? Why didn't you tell Barnard you knew Yasonov? What were you concealing? Did Yasonov himself recruit you? Did you ever meet Igor Popov? Why did you go to Amsterdam? Why did you meet Yasonov in the Rijksmuseum?'

The questions came thick and fast. Marshall blocked them all. Just pushed her pawns forward, keeping her king well-guarded. If you played chess as well as Marshall did, you soon realized that – contrary to expectations – defence was often the best form of attack.

At the end of the morning, Abewa came, crucially, to the attempt on Barnard's life.

'Why were you fanning your face with the order paper, when Barnard got up to speak?' Mnogo asked. 'It wasn't particularly hot, as I understand. I think you were sending a signal. A signal which meant, "When I wave my order paper to fan my face, be sure to shoot the next man who gets up to speak". Isn't that what you were telling him? So what does that make you? A murderer or at least an accessory to murder? This is serious stuff, Harriet. You can't go on stonewalling.'

After a while, Marshall said, 'I'd like to call a lawyer.'

Later that morning, Porter went to see the home secretary.

'We've some pretty clear *prima facie* evidence that Russia has been trying to influence the result of the Referendum,' she said.

Killick sighed. 'I wish the beastly thing was over. Okay, Jane, just summarize the key points. What exactly is Russia doing? It's all very well having stuff in the *Guardian*, but where's the hard evidence?'

'Well, Home Secretary.' Porter chose her words carefully. 'We've been building the case for some time. First, there's the so-called Referendum dossier, the one Barnard brought back from Russia. Did the Russians actually pay good money to the Conservative Party as a whole, or to the PM or Conservative Party chairman in particular, so as to ensure there was a commitment to the Referendum, first in the prime minister's Bloomberg speech, and then in the Conservative manifesto?'

'And what's the answer to that question? Remind me,' Killick asked. 'I read Sir Oliver Holmes' report. Very diplomatically phrased. Couldn't make head or tail of it.'

'I agree, it's complicated. Sir Oliver's people are convinced the documents are genuine in the sense that that they were sent to or from the prime minister's office. On the other hand, there is no evidence that money ever changed hands.'

'No evidence of "cash for Brexit" transactions?'

'None that they can find. But that's not conclusive of course. These City folk are quite adept at covering their tracks.'

Killick obviously didn't want to go further down that route. 'Let's leave that one for the moment. We'll have to revert at some later date, I'm sure. What else do we have?'

'The Russians have helped Leave nobble large chunks of the press and media to ensure that the Leave message gets maximum attention'.

'And the third point?'

'We think the Russians influenced Helga Brun at a crucial moment on the immigration issue. There's some suggestion of a long-standing link between the chancellor and Russian Intelligence.'

Killick groaned. 'I can't believe this. Don't tell me there's more.'

'I'm afraid there is. Though we haven't yet found the man who fired the shot, we suspect there may be some active Russian involvement here, too. Harriet Marshall had a long meeting with a man we assume is her Russian handler on Hampstead Heath the day of the Oxford Union debate. We think they planned the assassination attempt there.'

Killick looked shocked. 'Are you telling me that Harriet Marshall was ready to have her own leader, Edward Barnard, assassinated if that helped the Leave campaign gain another point or two in the polls?'

'That is precisely what I suspect. And I'm suggesting that the key player throughout, on the Leave side at least, has indeed been Harriet Marshall. Our feeling is that's she's been a Russian sleeper ever since she left Oxford. As a matter of fact, we believe she may have actually been recruited while she was an undergraduate there, known as Howard Marshall. She was to be properly trained later – following a sex-change operation – when she worked in Moscow after leaving university. We always focus on Cambridge as a hotbed for Russian spies and seem to forget about Oxford.'

The home secretary, who had been at Oxford herself, commented acidly, 'It's hardly a badge of honour to be recruited by the KGB or FSB.'

She rose and paced the room in her smart animal-print heels. 'It's too late to cancel the referendum,' she said. 'The damage is done. If we go public with what we know, or suspect, the Leave campaign will laugh us out of court. They'll say we've cooked the whole thing up in a last desperate move to discredit them before the vote. They'll throw the book at us. How many authorizations do you have, Jane, for all those wire taps and surveillance operations? Are you sure your hands are clean? And, from what you've told me, I'm not sure your interrogator was playing strictly by the rules.'

Killick made up her mind. And once she had made up her mind, she was hard to sway.

'We may not like it,' she said. 'But we are where we are.'

'What do we do about Harriet?' Porter asked.

'Put her on a plane to Moscow,' the home secretary said. 'And tell her not to come back. Not ever.'

CHAPTER THIRTY-TWO

At 6:00A.M. exactly, on Friday, 24 June 2016, Noel Garnett, the BBC's veteran reporter and commentator, announced that Vote Leave had secured more than half the votes cast. Britain had voted for Brexit.

At 8:15A.M. on that day, the United Kingdom's prime minister, Jeremy Hartley, with his wife Miranda at his side, emerged from the famous black door at Number 10 Downing Street to concede defeat.

He gave a moving and statesmanlike address.

'Good morning, everyone.' Hartley began. 'The country has just taken part in a giant democratic exercise, perhaps the biggest in our history.

'Over thirty-three million people from England, Scotland, Wales, Northern Ireland and Gibraltar have all had their say.

'There can be no doubt about the result.

'I was absolutely clear about my belief that Britain is stronger, safer and better off inside the European Union, and I made clear the referendum was about this and this alone—not the future of any single politician, including myself.

'But the British people have made a very clear decision to take a different path, and I think the country requires fresh leadership to take it in this direction.'

Many people in Britain, and indeed around the world, had stayed up all night. Others had just switched on their television sets or radios. Few doubted the sincerity of the prime minister's feelings. Killick was one of them.

Later that morning, Hartley received an urgent message from the home secretary, a message he could not ignore.

Soon after 1:00p.m., she entered Downing Street by the back door and was shown to the prime minister's study with no officials present.

'I've sat on it as long as I could, prime minister,' Killick said. 'I wanted to be sure I had all the facts. But now I do have the facts, I don't think I can keep quiet any longer.'

'Keep quiet about what?'

'The Referendum dossier, of course,' the home secretary replied. She took him through the evidence step by step.

'Our experts have subjected the dossier to the most rigorous examination. We are convinced that every single document is genuine, and that includes the additions in your own handwriting to the draft of your Bloomberg speech, back in January 2013, when you wrote: "that is why I am in favour of a referendum". I admit we have not been able to trace the £10 million or £12 million paid by persons unknown in exchange for this commitment. But that doesn't mean the transaction never occurred. Wouldn't you agree? The expression "Laundromat" has a whole new meaning nowadays.

'Forget about brown envelopes full of fivers in exchange for putting down a few Parliamentary questions,' Killick continued. 'Some would say that the whole future of our country seems to have been up for sale. As home secretary I am in charge of the police and law enforcement, and I am interested therefore in what precisely went on. Without prejudice, of course.'

The prime minister sighed. 'I give you my word that I never asked anyone for money and I state categorically that no money was ever paid. That was just part of the Brexit dossier. I wanted to make it as convincing as possible and the financial aspect was crucial.

People are always happy to believe the worst where money is involved.'

'Why did you need a dossier at all?' the home secretary asked. 'Please help me out here.'

So Hartley, patiently and without guile, explained the whole scheme.

'Having the commitment in the manifesto to hold a referendum was the first crucial step. But that referendum had to be won, and won convincingly, by Leave. Frankly, at the beginning of this year that simply didn't look likely. Even the pro-Leave members of the Cabinet, like David Cole, were clinging on to their portfolios and the perks of office, instead of getting out on the road and campaigning for Brexit. I thought, "Good grief, we can't just let UKIP run this one". Simon Henley may be a good man to have a drink with. Not bad on telly, I suppose. But UKIP was really a one-man band. I had this feeling of total panic. Here we were with this tremendous opportunity and we were in danger of letting that opportunity slip through our fingers. The Leave campaign needed a leader, and they needed one fast.'

'So you picked Edward Barnard?' Killick was beginning to understand what Hartley was driving at.

'Precisely,' Hartley replied. 'Barnard may not be the sharpest pencil in the box but he has real leadership qualities. I thought, if Barnard takes up the challenge of leading Leave, things will begin to move in the right direction. So I worked up the Referendum dossier, as you call it, and made sure Barnard got to see it. I was absolutely convinced that, once he did, Barnard would resign on the spot from the government. But he would be driven by a sense of honour and duty not to stand on the sidelines. He would say to himself, "I can't let the Referendum be won by trickery and subterfuge by that devious bastard, Jeremy Hartley. If it's going to be won at all, it has to be won fair and square".'

'My God!' the home secretary exclaimed. 'How devious can you get? You made sure the Russians had the dossier and that they in turn gave it to Barnard. Wasn't that collusion?'

'Oh, come on, Mabel. The Russians aren't bogeymen. We shared the same objective: getting the UK out of the EU. And if the EU, post-Brexit, itself disintegrates, is that such a bad thing? For hundreds of years, British foreign policy has aimed at stopping the creation of a single hegemonistic power on the continent of Europe. We fought Spain, we fought France, we fought the Prussians and we fought Hitler. Even today, over there in Brussels, they're talking about a common European defence force to supplement the disastrous Eurozone. Those guns might one day point at us. Can we really let that happen? The sooner the whole thing's dismantled, the better for everyone.'

'What you're basically saying, Prime Minister,' Killick tried to sum up, 'is deep down, you were always a Leaver, not a Remainer even though you stood as a Remainer as far as the electorate is concerned. Your priority, in the so-called renegotiation, was to make sure that you failed, rather than succeeded. "Pretty thin gruel" was precisely what you were hoping for and that was what you got. Of course your brilliant scheme, your wizard wheeze, was almost frustrated when the EU looked as though they had a real plan to deal with migration. Fortunately Helga Brun scuppered that one at the last moment!

'But to make your plan work, you had to stay undercover. If you had actively campaigned for Leave, you would have split the Conservative Party from head to toe. Tom Milbourne, for example, would have challenged you for the leadership on the spot. So now that you've announced your resignation, you're going down with a smile on your face. Mission accomplished!'

'Got it in one,' Hartley said. 'Didn't you hear me humming that little tune, when I walked back into Number 10, after my speech this morning? People tell me the mic picked it up.'

The home secretary was curious. 'What *was* that tune? I thought I recognized it.'

' "The Eton Boating Song",' Hartley replied. ' "*Swing, swing together. Tum-ti-ti, tum-titi-tum!*" '

Moments later, the home secretary left Downing Street by the front door. The cameras flashed.

'Are you going to throw your hat in the ring, Home Secretary?' Ginsberg, the BBC's chief political reporter, called out.

Killick smiled enigmatically and strode on.

CHAPTER THIRTY-THREE

Melissa Barnard let the phone ring for a while. She was listening to *The Archers*. She wanted to hear what had happened to Helen in her domestic abuse storyline. The phone wouldn't be for her anyway. Not at 7:00P.M. All her friends knew she would be listening to the radio at that time. And Edward was out for a ride. As a matter of fact, it was the first time Edward had ridden Jemima since that evening at the Oxford Union when Jerry, the security man, had rugger-tackled him. Almost broke his leg. He had a socking, great bruise on his thigh.

The phone went on ringing. In the end she picked it up. It was the Downing Street switchboard. 'The prime minister's trying to get in touch with Mr Barnard.'

'Well, I'm afraid my husband's out with Jemima. He doesn't have his phone with him.'

'Does Jemima have a phone? We could maybe get a message to him that way.'

'Jemima's his horse.'

Melissa didn't add that sometimes she felt her husband preferred his lovely bay mare, 16.2 hands, to his own dearly beloved wife. She watched him sometimes, sneaking an apple from the basket, when he headed out to the stable. And he talked to Jemima in a low, crooning way. He never talked like that to her.

'Could you possibly tell Mr Barnard that the prime minister would very much like to see him at 3:00P.M. tomorrow? We'll leave his name at the gate, of course.'

'Of course.' What on earth was that about, Melissa thought?

Barnard hadn't the foggiest either. 'Beats me,' he said, when Melissa gave him the message. As far as he was concerned, now that the Referendum was over, he was out to grass.

Still, they watched the news on the BBC later that evening. A removal van was parked at the back entrance to Downing Street; men burdened with packing cases streamed out of the house like warrior ants.

'Tomorrow, Mrs Mabel Killick, Britain's new prime minister, will kiss hands with Her Majesty the Queen and take the oath of office. This is likely to happen around nine in the morning. She will then proceed to Number 10 Downing Street. She will spend her first day constructing her new Cabinet. There will be good news for some, bad news for others. One thing is sure: Mabel Killick will make up her mind what she wants and then she will stick to her decision.'

Barnard arrived at the Downing Street gate in plenty of time for his 3P.M. appointment with the prime minister. The press and TV were out in force, lined up with cameras pointing at the famous door. Who's in? Who's out? That was the story of the hour.

'We don't need to see your passport, Mr Barnard,' the duty-guard said. 'We know you very well. Good luck.'

A line from Coleridge's 'Ancient Mariner' came to him, as he emptied his pockets at security.

'We were the first / that ever burst / into that silent sea.'

The door opened as Barnard approached. He had been to Number 10 often enough in the past but he always wondered just how they managed to open the door at precisely the moment you got there. Some secret sensor, perhaps. Or PC Plod looking through a spyhole. He'd find out one day, no doubt.

Giles Mortimer met him inside. 'Very good of you to come in, Mr Barnard. I hope your leg is better. Let's go straight on up.'

Mortimer had, like his colleague Holly Percy, moved with the new prime minister from the Home Office to Number 10. Barnard followed him upstairs, looking at the photos of former prime ministers on the wall. Mrs Thatcher had already waited more than a quarter of a century for some female company, so a few more days wouldn't matter.

The prime minister was in the Cabinet Room. They shook hands. She motioned to him to take a seat. Barnard noted that her two aides, Mortimer and Percy, were in close attendance.

They spent a couple of moments in polite chit-chat. Then Killick said, 'I suppose you're wondering why you're here? It's quite simple really. You were the chairman of the Leave campaign. You were and are a national figure. I was tremendously struck by the shock and concern that people on all sides showed last month when an attempt was made on your life. People trust you.' She paused and looked straight at him. 'I want you to be chancellor of the exchequer. I'm sure you'll be a great success.'

The news struck him like a thunderbolt. Chancellor of the exchequer! One of the great Offices of state.

'But what about Tom?' he blurted. 'Tom Milbourne?'

'I've just sacked him. He came and left by the back door ten minutes before you got here.' She looked at her aides. 'Short and sweet. Wouldn't you say, Giles?'

'Short, but not exactly sweet, Prime Minister,' Mortimer replied.

Later that evening media news bulletins carried the full list of major appointments, decisions on some minor posts being carried over to the next day.

The most dramatic news was that the new prime minister had dismissed Milbourne, chancellor of the exchequer and leading Remainer, in what had apparently been a brief and ill-tempered exchange. Almost equally dramatic was the news that Milbourne's successor was to be Barnard, former chairman of Leave.

The BBC's Nancy Ginsberg commented, 'The days have passed when chancellors were happy to use matchsticks and not much else to help them with their budgetary calculations. Given the turmoil that the Brexit vote has already brought about in terms of the drastic decline in the value of sterling, not to speak of all the other complications for the economy which may arise, the new chancellor will certainly need to have his wits about him. That said, there is no doubt about Edward Barnard's enormous popular appeal, not merely as a leading Brexiteer, but also as a man who only last month survived a cowardly assassination attempt. Barnard is that unusual character. A man whom people, all kinds of people, seem to trust. Perhaps that is the real reason Mrs Killick has chosen him.'

Apart from Barnard's appointment to the Treasury, the new prime minister had produced another stroke of genius. Harry Stokes, the ebullient and charismatic former Mayor of London, had been offered – and had accepted – the post of foreign secretary.

The news bulletins showed the new foreign secretary leaving Downing Street with a cheerful look as though this was the way he had planned it all along.

'Tremendous opportunity!' he shouted to the waiting crowd. 'Broad sunlit uplands! Best of all possible worlds! Incredible honour!'

Ginsberg was back on air. 'Fenella Gibson has succeeded David Coles at the Ministry of Justice,' she explained. 'And a Department for Exiting the European Union has been created, headed by that pugnacious street-fighter, Sam Berryman, as well as another department, designed to build new trading links with the brave new world out there beyond the EU. That is to be headed by Monica Fall, MP for Blyth.'

Later that day, Barnard moved into his office in the Treasury. He found a note from the former chancellor on the chancellor's desk.

'Good luck, Ed, in your new job,' he read. 'Hope you enjoy sitting at this desk. Should give you a chance to help clear up the mess you have created! Yours ever, Tom'.

CHAPTER THIRTY-FOUR

Sir Andrew Boles, KGB, KCVO, was delighted by his transfer from Moscow to Washington, D.C. With the United Kingdom heading for the door, as far as the European Union was concerned, it was obvious that the UK–US bilateral relationship would be absolutely pivotal.

Killick, the new prime minister, had called him personally.

'Obviously we don't know at the moment which of the US presidential candidates is going to win in November,' she said. 'Caroline Mann has a brilliant track record, but I can't help feeling that Ronald Craig may surprise us all. It could be Brexit all over again.'

'Well, if Craig wins, I'll make it my priority to ensure that you're the first world leader to be invited to the White House.'

World leader! Maybe that was laying it on a bit thick, Boles thought, as he put the phone down. Killick had served a long apprenticeship in the Home Office. She had yet to show her mettle on the international stage.

Two weeks later, Boles was already *en poste* in Washington D.C., as the new British ambassador. Apart from his pleasure at being promoted to this top diplomatic assignment, the move to Washington had contributed massively to domestic harmony. His wife, Julia, had been only too happy to exchange Moscow's stresses and strains for a new life in D.C. The magnificent Lutyens-designed mansion at 3100 Massachusetts Avenue, North-West Washington, D.C. was a consummation devoutly to be wished.

If life in D.C. slows down over the summer (and it does), it resumes with a vengeance in September after Labor Day. Whenever they could, the ambassador and his wife tried to have breakfast together. This was, above all, an opportunity to fine-tune their diaries. The vital relationships in Washington, with senators and congressmen, with key government officials and White House staffers, were formed not so much through official contacts but in the course of much more personal interactions: on the golf course, at exclusive downtown clubs (some didn't even have a name-plate on the door) and, above all, at small intimate dinners at home.

Around 6:00P.M. in the first week of September 2016, the car carrying Barnard on his first official visit to Washington, swept through the imposing wrought-iron gates of the British Embassy. In spite of the residual ache in his injured leg, Barnard did his best to bound up the double staircase, to be greeted at the top by Boles.

'Edward. How good to see you. You're looking well.'

'I'm feeling well,' Barnard said. 'Even though I've just got off a plane.'

Half an hour later, after Barnard had had a quick shower and changed his clothes, the two men sat together on the terrace, pre-dinner drinks in hand.

They hadn't seen each other since Moscow.

'My God, what a summer!' Boles began. 'I can't help wondering whether Killick didn't do some kind of a deal with Hartley. Go quietly or the coppers will be feeling your collar.'

'Let's not go there,' Barnard replied. 'We are where we are.'

He stood up as Julia Boles came to join them on the terrace. The butler served champagne and the evening sun bathed the embassy's vast lawn in a soft golden light.

'We're going to be a very small party tonight,' Boles said. 'We know you're friends with Rosie Craig, so invited her. Her office said she was thrilled. Having you here was obviously a major draw. Big plus for the embassy. Rosie's not just her father's daughter. Apparently he consults her on just about everything.'

'She's bringing Jack Varese, too,' Julia added. 'I gather you were all in Australia together a few weeks back.'

'We were indeed. That was quite an adventure,' Barnard said.

While they waited for Rosie and Jack to arrive, Boles summarized the current political scene:

'Basically, Caroline Mann is in trouble. For some reason best known to himself, Wilbur Brown, who, as you know, is the director of the FBI, with only a few weeks to go before the election, has just announced that the FBI is reviewing some 30,000 of her emails, all of them mailed to or from her private, unauthorized server. This has been a total bombshell as far as her presidential campaign is concerned. Caroline has slumped in the polls.'

'How did the FBI get the emails?' Barnard asked.

'Well, they haven't told us so directly, but the most likely source seems to be WikiLeaks.'

'And how did WikiLeaks get them? From the Russians?'

'Almost certainly.'

'So how did the Russians get them?'

'This is where it gets a bit murky,' the ambassador replied. 'It looks as though some FSB-related units hacked into the Democratic National Committee and then into Caroline Mann's own emails. But all this is still pretty speculative. The odd thing is that apparently the FBI has also got a whole lot of compromising material on the Craig campaign, too. But so far it hasn't announced any plan to release it.'

'No favouritism there then?' Barnard chuckled.

They spent a few moments checking Barnard's schedule for the next day. 'You've got meetings at the Treasury in the morning, then lunch at the IMF,' Boles told him. 'Then drinks here tomorrow evening. Lots of people keen to meet the new chancellor of the exchequer. We'll get you to Dulles in time for the last flight back to Heathrow.'

'Sounds fun,' Barnard said.

'Oh, by the way,' Boles added. 'We left a gap in your schedule after lunch. If you're up for it, you could call in at the FBI. Wilbur Brown is very keen to see you. Nothing to do with finance. That's why we haven't put it on your formal schedule. As far as I understand, it's something to do with that trip you made to the Russian Far East. Something they need to check. He didn't say much on the phone. Just said he would greatly appreciate it if you could spare a moment.'

'Pretty much like a Royal Command, isn't it?' Barnard commented.

'That's what I thought, too,' said Boles. 'You can use my car tomorrow. I won't need it. If you're summoned to the FBI, you may as well arrive in an armour-plated Rolls Royce, don't you think?'

'Sounds good to me,' Barnard agreed. 'I don't want anyone else taking a pot-shot at me.'

Rosie arrived moments later. She gave Barnard a big hug.

'It's so good to see you again,' she said. 'Last time we met you had just been bitten by a deadly poisonous spider and now you're the new secretary of the Treasury.'

Barnard returned the greeting. 'In the UK, I'm called chancellor of the exchequer. Pretty much the same job as your Treasury secretary's, except you guys have a lot more money.'

Rosie turned to her hosts. 'Jack's on his way. He's on the phone to Dad. Dad wants Jack to endorse his candidacy, but Jack's playing hard to get. Says Dad has to change his tune on global warming and promise to stand by the Paris agreement. Just for starters.'

Boles laughed. 'Good luck with that. There's going to be a sigh of relief all round if your father changes tack on that one.'

When Jack finally arrived, they went straight on into dinner in the small, private dining room.

'Rosie was telling us before you arrived that you've been talking to her father about global warming,' Boles said, once they were settled. 'Can you tell us what he said, or is it a secret?'

Jack laughed. 'Nothing's a secret in this town. People know what you've said, before you've said it.'

He was suddenly serious. 'Rosie and Edward will remember the time I flew them from St Petersburg to Khabarovsk earlier this year to look for Siberian tigers in the Russian Far East. I was piloting my Gulfstream 550. Rosie's father was with us on that amazing trip and he came up front to sit in the co-pilot's seat. We were flying a great circle route over the Arctic. That's one of the most magnificent spectacles you will ever see. The Inuits live up there, the polar bears, the seals, the walruses. Makes you want to cry, it's so beautiful.

'There was I, flying the plane, and thinking how global warming was already working a massive change in the Arctic environment. The ice cap is shrinking, year by year. The polar bears are starving because they can't get out on the ice to hunt seals. The oil rigs will soon be sprouting in the ocean where the ice used to be.

'Then I saw Ron looking out the window and I realized that he wasn't seeing what I was seeing. He wasn't looking at a magnificent, pristine environment, now seriously threatened. No, what he saw was a massive opportunity for Craig Shipping. He was thinking that he could cut thousands, literally thousands of miles off a journey from Europe to Asia if he could get rid of the ice in the Arctic Ocean. And he was thinking about the possibilities for Craig Oil if he could do a deal with Russia over exploitation rights. There are billions of barrels of oil up there. Never mind the risk of blow outs or maritime disasters.

'Do you know what Ron Craig's precise words to me were?' he concluded. 'They were "Roll on global warming"!'

'I'm totally with Jack on this one,' Rosie said. 'I'm giving him all the help I can. My father listens to me sometimes.'

'That's the understatement of the year. He listens to you *all* of the time,' Jack countered. 'If he's elected, they'll be giving you your own office in the West Wing, right from the get-go.'

After dinner, Julia showed Rosie around the house. The three men went out on to the terrace.

'I can't tell you how glad I am that you're raising some of these key environmental issues with Craig,' Barnard told Jack.

'Actually, I'm raising them with both candidates,' Jack replied. 'Caroline Mann has got a better track record, that's all. Also,' Jack lowered his voice, 'there are people around Craig who believe any future deal between the US and Russia can't just be limited to sanctions, human rights, weapons or whatever. They want an agreed regime for the Arctic, too, a regime which gives pride of place to Craig Oil and Craig Shipping, not to speak of Craig Hotels.

'Well, I'm all for an agreed Arctic regime,' Jack continued. 'I just want to make sure it has the strictest standards of safety for shipping and a ban on oil wells in the Arctic Ocean and full protection for wildlife and native peoples.'

'Are you sure you ought to be saying all this?' Boles asked.

'Hell,' Jack replied. 'I'm in love with Rosie. I'm not in love with her dad.'

Barnard went to bed that night in a sombre mood. The stakes were suddenly so much higher than he had realized. You could at a stretch sympathize with Russia over the Crimea and even Ukraine. You could argue that Russian intervention on Syria had not been wholly negative. But that didn't mean you had to buy into the whole Popov agenda, including accelerating, not reversing, global warming.

Was it too late to get Craig to change his mind?

CHAPTER THIRTY-FIVE

Wilbur Brown, director of the FBI, strode across the room to greet his visitor.

'Mr Barnard, I really do appreciate you making the time to stop by. When I heard you were coming to Washington, I said to myself, "Here's a golden opportunity to throw some light on something that's been troubling us".'

'Happy to help in any way I can,' Barnard said.

Brown explained the problem. 'Some time back we had word that the Chinese Ministry of State Security believed President Popov deliberately fired a tranquillizing dart into Ronald C. Craig's backside during Craig's visit to the Russian Far East earlier this year. I should add that the Chinese came to that conclusion because the tiger which Popov was theoretically aiming at was already darted and in the system so it wouldn't have made much sense to dart it again. Do you follow me?'

'I do indeed.' Barnard tried to recapture in his mind that amazing morning. The tiger bounding towards them, Popov with his rifle, Craig going down with a dart in his left buttock.

'It was a confusing situation,' Barnard added. 'But, yes, I would say that the Chinese theory is certainly worth exploring. At the time I thought it odd that an expert shot, as Popov apparently is, missed his target. On the other hand, Craig was more or less in the direct line of fire.'

'Well, actually we too thought there might be something in the Chinese theory,' Brown said. 'From our own sources in Russia – I'm not going to say who or where – we tracked some actual footage of the tiger-darting incident, rather than the shots of President Popov heroically confronting the tiger which they showed on Russian TV. We examined the film carefully and we came to the conclusion that there was a very real possibility Ronald Craig had indeed been deliberately targeted by Popov. It wasn't just an accident. If that was the case, then Popov obviously had some ulterior purpose in mind and the most likely scenario, as we assessed it, was that the tiger-darting episode provided the perfect opportunity for the FSB to get something on Ronald Craig, in the most literal sense. There were various possibilities. Craig could have been fitted with a microscopic transmitter right in the forest there. Or he could have been accessed, if that's the right word, when he was taken into the hospital in Khabarovsk after the incident.

'To cut a long story short, the CIA and the FBI together requested an Executive Order from the president addressed to Mr Craig, requiring him to present himself forthwith to the Walter Reed Army Medical Center in Bethesda. Mr Craig duly complied with the order. An examination was made. We found no recording device.'

'Excuse me one minute,' Barnard interrupted. 'I was staying at Hasta La Vista, the Craig place in Florida, when the federal marshals came to whisk Craig away to Walter Reed. Rosie Craig was in touch with her father after the examination. She told me that they actually discovered a small, plastic recording device, concealed somewhere on Ron Craig's body. I'm not sure where.'

Brown smiled. 'Well, that's what we told the doctors to tell Craig when he came round. We thought there was less chance of him kicking up a fuss if he believed he really had been bugged by the Russians. But, no, they didn't actually discover anything. We were disappointed. We really believed they had tagged him and it turned out they hadn't.'

Barnard was puzzled. 'So what's the issue? No recorder, no transmission. All's well that ends well, surely?'

The director of the FBI sighed. 'It's not quite as simple as that. I wish it was. We have reason to believe that our suspicions were right all along. We think the Russians may still be receiving transmissions from a recorder concealed somewhere about Ron Craig's person.'

'Can you give me an example?' Barnard asked.

The Director of the FBI took his time. He examined his finger-nails, fiddled with his phone, pushed a finger in his ear. Then he made up his mind.

'I take it you're cleared for Five Eyes material?' he said. 'What I'm going to tell you is on a Five Eyes basis. Is that clear?'

'Absolutely. I'm a member of Her Majesty's Privy Council, duly and properly authorized to receive secret briefings,' Barnard replied solemnly. Why on earth hadn't someone told him about Five Eyes before he headed for Washington? Maybe chancellors of the exchequer didn't 'need to know'.

'I'll be back in a moment,' Brown said. 'The machine's with my secretary.'

While Brown left the room, Barnard quickly searched for 'Five Eyes' on his iPhone.

Seconds later he read: *'Five Eyes: top-secret intelligence sharing agreement, dating back to 1946, originally between the US and the UK, but subsequently expanded to include Canada, Australia and New Zealand.'*

Thank God for Google, Barnard thought.

Brown came back with the tape deck, placed it on the table and pressed the switch.

'Listen to this,' he said.

Barnard heard Jack's unmistakable tones. 'Christ, Ron,' he was saying, 'you've got to take global warming seriously. It's the key issue of our time.' Then he heard another voice which he also recognized. 'Bullshit, Jack, it's a giant hoax perpetrated by and for the Chinese to make US manufacturing uncompetitive.'

'My God!' Barnard exclaimed. 'How did you get that? I was with Jack last night. He was late at the embassy because he'd been

216

arguing on the phone with Craig about global warming. That's definitely authentic.'

'Do you want to hear a bit more?' Brown asked. He pressed the switch again.

'Who gives a fuck about the polar bears?' they heard Craig say. 'Ten years from now, there's going to be a fleet of Craig super-tankers steaming through the Arctic Ocean. The polar bears will have to go play somewhere else.'

They listened a few more moments. The argument between the two men became increasingly heated. Then Jack said, 'Rosie's not going to like it.' Craig replied, 'I'm the candidate, not Rosie. And Rosie's not going to be president, I am.'

'Do you get my point?' Brown pushed the machine to one side. 'We believe Craig may still be carrying, somewhere on his body, a miniature transmitter. The guys who examined him in Walter Reed did a lousy job.'

'That could be a phone-tap, not a transmission surely.'

'Yes, it could be, but it isn't. After that call with Jack, Craig goes to the toilet. Bigly. Do you want to hear that too?'

Brown had the video ready. As Barnard watched the clips, it all came back to him. There was Popov with the dart gun, with Craig behind him; there he (Barnard) was, followed by Rosie, and there, for Christ's sake, was the tiger! Huge, beautiful, brilliant – and snarling with fury.

The images which followed were blurred and confused until the focus shifted to show a picture of Craig on the ground with a hypodermic dart embedded in his backside.

'Hold it there!' Barnard instructed. 'Now run it again. Look! See that ranger, kneeling beside Craig. Popov is standing next to him. The ranger says to Popov, "Mr President, give me the yellow vial", or something like that. Then he rolls back Craig's sleeve.'

The next clip was of Popov helping Craig to his feet.

Barnard continued to provide a running commentary. 'Craig is holding his right upper arm, where the ranger injected the Tolazoline. My guess is that if you're looking for a secret mini-transmitter, forget about Craig's buttocks. Go for the right upper arm. And check out that ranger. Maybe he's on the books of the FSB.'

'You could be right. You could just possibly be right!' Brown said. 'We should have thought of that and we didn't.'

'What are you going to do now?' Barnard asked. 'Ask Craig to report to Walter Reed again?'

Brown shook his head. 'I don't think the Republican presidential candidate would take kindly to that. He already thinks we're bugging his phone. Are we Five Eyes still?'

'Roger that!' Barnard replied. 'Five Eyes all the way!'

The director of the FBI tapped the side of his nose meaningfully. 'We might just do nothing,' he said. 'For the time being at least.'

CHAPTER THIRTY-SIX

Joshan Gupta, Head of MI5's technical support services, reckoned that he had spent at least one hundred hours on that bloody film.

At first he had assumed that the images of the man on the bed in St Petersburg's Kempinski Hotel, whoever he was, had been simply pixelated and that with persistence it might be possible to de-pixelate them. He had worked evenings and weekends, but still he had made no progress. He finally realized that the images were not only heavily pixelated; they were encrypted as well. If you couldn't crack the code, you couldn't see the images.

Of course, MI5 had its own military-grade versions of most of the photo-encryption and decryption programmes available on the internet. But you were always playing catch-up. Nowadays the most innocuous messages could be sent in code. More than one billion people in 180 countries used end-to-end encryption for everyday communications. Only you and the person you were communicating with knew the content of the message.

In the end, Gupta was forced to report to his superiors in MI5 that he had drawn a blank as far as establishing the identity of the mystery man was concerned.

There the matter rested until one evening, out of the blue, a pop-up message appeared on his screen:

'5 Star Kempinski Hotel, Moika 22, Moscow. No booking fees. Late Check-out until 4P.M. Early Check-in from 11A.M. Free Underground Parking.

Free Wifi, Turn down Service, Room Comfort Menu including Golden Shower, Garage Parking, Kids' Club etc.'

He almost missed it. Golden Shower!

Gupta picked up the phone to talk to his supervisor. 'Mohammed,' he said, 'I think we've got a breakthrough. We're going to need the director to come down here pretty quickly.'

Mohammed Abbas, the ranking officer in Gupta's section, went to fetch the MI5 director and escorted her to Gupta's desk.

Porter was not herself a technical expert, but she was a quick study and ready to grapple with the jargon of cyber warfare, even if she didn't fully understand it.

'This could be a trap, couldn't it?' she asked. 'If you click on this "Golden Shower" link, couldn't you be compromising the integrity of our whole system? Opening the link might allow them to launch a Trojan Horse, a worm or a virus, or some other malware, which could literally close us down.'

Abbas wasn't so sure. 'I don't think that's what they're after. I think they're trying to tell us something.'

Porter looked around the room. It wasn't often that she came down into the bowels of the ship. A hundred people or more were working at their computers. This was where the war on terror was waged. Day after day, hour after hour. There was so much at stake.

'Let's go for it,' she said. 'If the whole thing goes up the spout, it's my head that will roll. Are you okay with that?'

Of course, they were okay with it. They only hoped she'd put it in writing.

Gupta clicked on the link. Seconds later the video began to play. They had all seen it before, of course, but still it didn't make for pleasant viewing. Porter shuddered involuntarily when it came to the 'Golden Shower' scene. What kind of man enjoyed that?

At first, even in the depixelated version, it wasn't easy to distinguish the facial features. The man's hair, a great orange-blond mop, got in the way. But then, suddenly, as the girls moved off the bed and the man came up for air, they had a clear view of his face, looking straight at the camera. He had a nasty scar on his right cheekbone.

Later that day, Porter chaired an inter-departmental meeting. Roger Wales, head of MI6's Russia desk, and Jill Hepworth, one of 6's technical experts, came over the river from Vauxhall Cross to 5's headquarters in Millbank.

'So who is this man on the bed, if it's not Ronald Craig?' Porter asked.

'We're pretty sure we know the answer.' Wales sounded smug. He had good reason to be. MI6 had spent years, and a good deal of taxpayers' money, refining their facial recognition system.

'As we all know,' Wales continued, 'facial recognition systems are still far from perfect. Ideally, we look for 3D methods. These can achieve significantly higher accuracy than their 2D counterparts. In fact, I would say that 3D methods of facial recognition now rival fingerprint recognition. Unfortunately, the video we have just seen can't be analysed in 3D, but the good news is that the facial images we have are clear and usable. We have run them through the database and we have double-checked with our people in Moscow.'

He paused and looked round the room, making the most of the moment. 'We believe with 99.3% certainty,' Wales continued, 'that the man on the bed goes by the name of Fyodor Stephanov, an FSB operative based in the St Petersburg office. We believe that the "Golden Shower" scenario was a freelance operation organized by Stephanov, and possibly some other colleagues in St Petersburg, to generate commercially valuable kompromat material. We further believe that the video we have just seen, with Stephanov as the male lead, was both pixelated and encrypted to disguise Stephanov's identity and then spliced into the genuine footage of Edward Barnard meeting the two Russian ladies in the lift in the Kempinski. The consolidated film was then sold or otherwise made available via the black market to agents of the Chinese Ministry of State Security. The MSS, as we know, then tried to blackmail Edward Barnard.

'For the purposes of the film Stephanov used some obvious props. The US-flag boxer shorts, as we have seen, feature prominently in the film. And the depixelated version of the film shows Stephanov wearing a wig resembling the flamboyant hairstyle of Mr Ronald Craig.

'Even if this started out as a freelance scam in the FSB St Petersburg office, it is clear that Moscow somehow got wind of it. Our people confirm that the FSB office in St Petersburg was raided the other day by an all-female SWAT team from Moscow. Lyudmila Markova, the team leader, was positively identified by one of our agents just as she left the FSB offices on Cherniavski Street followed by four other women, all bearing boxes or cartons of office computers, files and other material.

'We therefore believe,' Wales concluded, 'that Moscow found what it was looking for, namely the original, undoctored, depixelated footage of the "Golden Shower" film.'

Wales turned to the man sitting next to him at the table. 'I'd like to pay tribute, if I may, to our colleague, Joshua Gupta. You will all recall the scepticism Joshua expressed when we first met in this very room to review the film. He argued that just because there was a pair of US-flag boxer shorts on the bed with "PUT AMERICA FIRST" inscribed on the waistband, we shouldn't necessarily conclude that the man involved in that "Golden Shower" scene was Ronald Craig. He was right.'

Gupta accepted the tribute gracefully. 'Those boxer shorts will turn up one day. I expect they'll find a big fluffy hairpiece, too!'

They all laughed, grateful for some light relief.

CHAPTER THIRTY-SEVEN

Chinese President Liu Wang-Ji sat at his desk in Zhongnanhai, the old imperial enclave that lay immediately west of the Forbidden City, waiting for Zhang Fu-Shen, the minister of State Security, to arrive. The two men had known each other a long time. They both belonged to the small group of people who could trace their ancestry back to the men or women who had been with Mao Tse-Tung on the Long March more than seventy years earlier. On the first of October each year, the anniversary of the founding of the Chinese People's Republic, these direct descendants of the Heroes of the Revolution climbed up to the great wide balcony above the Gate of Heavenly Peace to gaze down on the crowds in Tiananmen Square.

'Hello, old friend,' Liu Wang-Ji said when Zhang Fu-Shen arrived. 'Have some tea.'

They sat in armchairs, side by side. Liu poured tea.

Zhang had brought a small parcel with him, wrapped in brown paper with a red ribbon around it tied in a neat bow. He placed it on the ornamental carved-wood table in front of them.

'Please open it, Mr President,' he said. 'My people couldn't find the film, but they found these instead.'

The Chinese president unwrapped the package. 'What are these?' he asked, holding up the silk boxer shorts, emblazoned with the US flag and the embroidered message: 'PUT AMERICA FIRST'.

'They are the proof we need,' Zhang replied.

'Proof of what?'

'Proof that we have been barking up the wrong tree. The DNA evidence was conclusive. No American was involved in the "Golden Shower" episode. Certainly not an American presidential candidate. The boxer shorts belonged to the FSB operative in St Petersburg who set up the whole scam in the first place.'

The president fingered the shorts. He examined the label. 'It says "Bloomingdales' Finest. Made in China". That's something to be proud of anyway, I suppose.'

Liu Wang-Ji lit a cigarette. His doctor had advised him to give up smoking, but to no avail. He might as well have asked a wolf to stop baying at the moon.

'So what do we do now?' Liu asked. 'You don't seem to have made much progress so far. You failed to neutralize Edward Barnard. Britain voted to Leave and now the EU itself seems to be about to break up. Who knows what is going to happen in France, or even Germany? You thought you had a big fish there in the Kempinski Hotel, but you ended up with a minnow. I hope you have something else up your sleeve.'

The Chinese president's voice still sounded friendly enough, but Zhang noticed a steely tone which had not been there before. He realized that his own future was poised on a knife-edge. Liu, in his rise to the highest post in the land, had treated his rivals with extreme ruthlessness. Some of them had met with 'unfortunate accidents'; others had gone to jail in remote provinces. Still others had simply disappeared and their bodies had never been found.

He knew he was sipping his green-leaf tea not in the Hall of Supreme Harmony, but in the Last Chance Saloon.

'Well, yes, I do have a plan,' he said, 'a way to turn the tables.'

'It had better be good,' Liu Wang-Ji observed.

For the next fifteen minutes, the Chinese president listened with increasing interest as Zhang Fu-Shen explained his new scheme in detail.

'Do you remember that meeting of the Politburo Standing

Committee we had back in May, here in Zhongnanhai, when we discussed US–China relations?' Zhang asked.

'Of course, I remember it. I chaired it.'

'Then you will also remember,' Zhang continued, 'that we discussed the famous Amur tiger incident.'

'I certainly do,' Liu replied. 'I dined out on that story for weeks.'

'And do you remember that at that same Politburo meeting I reported that Ronald Craig, the presidential candidate, had been treated in Khabarovsk General Hospital for a buttock wound?'

President Liu smiled. 'I laughed like a drain, as I recall.'

Zhang came to the point. 'The Politburo's instructions to the Ministry of State Security were recorded in the minutes of the May meeting of the Standing Committee. I have brought them with me. Shall I read out the precise words?'

Zhang fished the paper from his pocket. 'Point nine of the minutes reads as follows:

"*The Minister in charge of the Ministry of State Security is hereby instructed to investigate why the president of the Russian Federation, Igor Popov, shot US presidential candidate Ronald C. Craig in the backside with a tranquillizing dart*".'

Zhang laid the paper on the little wooden table next to the US-flag boxer shorts. 'What I am about to say now, Mr President, is for your ears only.'

'Go ahead, Minister Zhang.' Their friendship might have dated back for decades, but business was business. Zhang was going to have to come up with something pretty good or he was for the chop. Literally.

Zhang took his time. He knew this was a make-or-break moment.

'As you know,' he began, 'Khabarovsk is situated on the Russia–China border. There are many ethnic Chinese living and working there. One of the surgeons in Khabarovsk General Hospital is

Professor Gung Ho-Min. Professor Gung is also one of the MSS key agents in Khabarovsk. One day Gung was informed by the hospital authorities that he might be required to attend to a high-level patient who, in the very near future, would be brought into the hospital suffering from a wound to the buttocks. He was instructed, when tending the wound, to insert subcutaneously in the patient's upper right arm a mini radio-transmitter which would be made available to him at the appropriate time.'

'And Professor Gung didn't query these instructions?' Liu asked.

'No, he didn't,' Zhang replied. 'This is Russia, remember. People do what they're told, particularly when, like Professor Gung, they belong to a vulnerable ethnic minority. But in my opinion,' Zhang continued, 'Gung showed particular brilliance and insight. He was able to procure from MSS sources within Khabarovsk one of our own mini radio-transmitters. While the patient was anaesthetized, he inserted the Russian transmitter, as instructed, in the patient's upper right arm, while inserting the Chinese transmitter in the left buttock.'

President Liu whistled. 'Are you saying that Ronald Craig, the man I met in St Petersburg at the World Tiger Conference and who is now quite possibly about to be elected President of the United States, has been bugged both by the Russians and by us? We both have something on him, in the most literal sense!'

'That's exactly what I'm saying,' Zhang replied.

He took out his mobile phone, put it on the table and turned up the volume.

'Listen to this, Mr President. This is a recording of a conversation which took place yesterday in Washington, around 2:30P.M., Eastern Standard Time. The system we have installed sends the actual GPS location of the originating transmission, give or take ten metres on either side. In this particular case we know that the transmission originated at 2650 Wisconsin Avenue, North-West Washington, D.C. That happens to be the address of the Russian Embassy.'

'Hold on a moment,' Liu Wang-Ji protested. 'There's no reason why a presidential candidate shouldn't visit the Russian Embassy. A presidential candidate can call on the Russian ambassador, might even have drink or dinner. Russian officials can talk to American officials in their own homes, too.'

'In theory, that's right,' Zhang agreed. 'The US doesn't have an Official Secrets Act like other countries, but don't forget that the US has the Logan Act which makes it a crime for an unauthorized person to actually negotiate with a foreign power. That's the key issue.

'I ought to explain,' Zhang continued as they settled down to listen to the tape, 'that there seem to be three people in the room at the Russian Embassy. One of them is Ronald Craig himself. The other we believe is Bert Rumbold, Craig's right-hand man and director of strategy for Craig's presidential campaign. The third person is Georgiy Reznikov, the Russian ambassador to the United States, who is hosting the meeting.'

He pressed the 'play' button. 'You'll hear Craig's voice first,' Zhang said.

Given that the mini-radio-transmitter was placed several millimetres below the tough skin of Ronald's Craig's *gluteus maximus*, the clarity of the recording was remarkable.

'*Okay guys,*' they heard Craig say. '*This is what we're offering if I'm elected president. Number one, the US is going to drop the current sanctions against Russia, as regards Crimea and the Ukraine. We would hope that NATO will follow us in this, but even if they don't we will act unilaterally.*

'*Number two: if I'm elected president, the United States will not challenge the deployment by Russia of the ground-based, nuclear-capable 9M729 missiles, even though possession of these missiles is a violation of the terms of the INF. Bert, what the hell does INF stand for?*'

'Now we're going to hear Bert Rumbold,' Zhang commented.

Sitting there in Zhongnanhai, Beijing, seven thousand miles from Washington, they heard a low throaty comment: '*INF means the Intermediate-Range Nuclear Forces Treaty, Ron.*'

'*Thanks so much, Bert. We understand the 9M729s have a range of 620*

*to 3240 miles. Apparently they hit Syria from the Caspian the other day. So if
we agree that their use is compatible with the INF, then Russia can legally hit
every capital in Europe. More to the point, perhaps, Russia will be able to blast
the living daylights out of every city in China.*

'*Let's take China's build-up in the South China Seas. I believe the United
States must be ready to go to war with China over these illegal bases. But it
would be better still if Russia and the US could take a coordinated approach.
We can say to China "Pull back from the Spratlys" or the Russians will whack
Chengdu or Xian or wherever their 9M729 missiles can reach. We could also
put pressure on them to deal with North Korea, tell North Korea to nix their
nuclear testing programme, for example. And if the Chinese don't deal with
North Korea, we will!*'

'Good God,' Liu Wang-Ji exclaimed. 'This is dynamite!'

A new silky, cultivated voice, speaking perfect English, was heard
on the recording:

'*Interesting. Very interesting,*' Reznikov said. '*Let's talk about global
warming, too? As you may know, President Popov believes that Siberia should
blossom like the rose. He believes Russia needs the massive increase of produc-
tivity in Siberia that global warming will make possible. How can a Craig
administration help here?*'

'*We can help bigly,*' they heard Craig reply. '*Global warming's bullshit,
a giant hoax perpetrated by the Chinese to grab American jobs. I'll make sure
we pull out of the Paris Agreement. I'll dismember the EPA – the Environmental
Protection Agency – and revive the American coal industry. Believe you me,
we can warm up Siberia in no time at all. One degree, two degrees, three
degrees, ROCK! We'll rock around the clock tonight! Remember Bill Haley and
his Comets, Ambassador?*'

Sensing that the US Republican presidential candidate was on a
roll, Reznikov quickly interrupted. '*Thank you, gentlemen. This has
been a most productive meeting. I can assure you that President Popov will be
pleased. In view of what I have heard today I am authorized to tell you that
between now and election day, we will make sure that our cache of emails from
the Democratic National Committee, including those from Caroline Mann,*

the Democratic presidential candidate, is deployed to the fullest possible extent. We further undertake to offer Craig Shipping and Craig Oil the most favourable terms possible as far as their operations in the Russian Arctic are concerned.'

Reznikov paused. *'Of course, we will, I hope, have further conversations, many further conversations, when Ron – may I call you Ron? – is elected. But perhaps our discussions today will do for starters.'*

'Just one thing,' Craig intervened. *'Don't forget about my old friend Mickey Selkirk. Selkirk Global is planning a major expansion in Russia. I think he has his eyes on Pravda and Izvestia as well as RT, Russian television!'*

'I am sure President Popov will be pleased to hear that, too,' Reznikov replied.

Zhang turned the recording off. 'There's more where that came from. Of course, we don't listen to all of it. Normally, we just store the recordings after checking electronically for key words. What we've just heard happens to be particularly interesting.'

Liu Wang-Ji stood up and put his arm round Zhang's shoulder. 'Well done, old friend. You have been tested and have not been found wanting. Don't forget to take those US-flag boxer shorts with you when you go.'

Halfway to the door, Liu Wang-Ji paused: 'That Logan Act you mentioned. That's a pretty old statute, isn't it? Dates from 1799? Is it still in force?'

'It certainly is,' Zhang replied.

Liu Wang-Ji didn't miss a trick, he thought. That was probably why Liu was President and he wasn't.

CHAPTER THIRTY-EIGHT

Galina Aslanova, head of Special Projects in the FSB's Moscow headquarters, had been required to undertake many strange assignments in the course of her career as a secret agent. She had learned how to assassinate people with undetectable poisons, how to kill them with a single blow of the hand, how to hack computers and siphon money from bank accounts. But up till now she had never been asked to impersonate a schoolgirl from Illinois.

Yuri Yasonov came to see her with less than ten days to go before the US presidential election. 'I've had a message from our people in Washington,' he said. 'They think Craig's in trouble. He's closing the gap on Mann, but not fast enough. We've got to do more.'

'What more *can* we do?' Galina asked.

As the operative with overall responsibility for Tectonic Plate, the FSB's project designed to change the whole structure of international politics, Aslanova was quite ready to do whatever was necessary to influence or subvert normal democratic processes, but on this particular occasion, with time running out, she was at a loss.

'I've been thinking about it,' Yasonov said. 'I think we have to get the FBI to reopen the enquiry into Caroline Mann's emails. I'm not criticizing you, Galina. Please don't get me wrong. At the technical level, the FBI couldn't have been more helpful. We handed them 30,000 of Caroline Mann's hacked emails, via WikiLeaks. Wilbur Brown, the FBI director, put his analysts to work as we always assumed he would. Whatever the political pressures might have

230

been on him to do nothing, he could hardly duck that one. And the analysts came up with a conclusion which was totally helpful to us.'

Yasonov paused while he consulted his papers.

'Okay, I've found it,' he continued. 'The FBI read every single email and concluded – and now I'm quoting – that "out of the fifty-two email chains determined by the owning agency to contain classified information, eight of those chains contained information that was Top Secret at the time they were sent; thirty-six chains contained secret information at the time; and eight contained confidential information, which is the lowest level of classification".'

Yasonov put the paper aside. 'So where did our scheme go wrong?' he asked. 'Confronted with the evidence, why didn't the FBI bring criminal charges? They should have. We thought they were going to. Criminal charges at this point of her campaign would have holed Caroline Mann below the waterline. But what happens? What does Wilbur Brown, the FBI director, do? He lets Caroline Mann off with a slap on the wrist. Tells her she's been a naughty girl, and "extremely careless" and please don't do it again.'

'I'm not sure where this is going.' Aslanova said.

'I'll tell you where it's going,' Yasonov replied. 'We're going to force the director of the FBI to reopen the enquiry. He may not have time actually to conclude the new enquiry before election day. That doesn't matter. It may not discover anything new anyway. But the very fact that the FBI is focussing attention yet again on those illegal Caroline Mann emails at this late stage should be enough to sink her. She'll haemorrhage votes, I promise you.'

'So how do we persuade Wilbur Brown to take another look at this?' Aslanova asked. 'Some piece of kompromat, perhaps? Something that might persuade him to change his mind?'

'We have nothing on Brown,' Yasonov said. 'He's squeaky clean. And we don't have enough time anyway to set up a kompromat scenario, even assuming Brown would fall for it, which he probably wouldn't.'

'So what do we do now?' Aslanova asked.

'I checked with President Popov this morning. He thinks it's time for Plan B. Our last best hope to swing this before it's too late.'

'Plan B!' Aslanova exclaimed. 'Don't we always say, "there is no Plan B"?'

'Well, there is this time,' Yasonov replied.

Julius Lomax, former congressman for Massachusetts's 9th Congressional District, had form. A few years earlier, he had had to resign his seat in the House because of a 'sexting' scandal but he was still addicted to this particular form of entertainment.

His wife, Sandra, one of Caroline Mann's principal aides, had left early for work. His two kids were at school, he had lost his job and he had time on his hands. Only that morning he had met up online with a schoolgirl from Champagne, Illinois, who, he felt, with a bit of help, might be ready to share some of his wilder fantasies.

He typed a brief, lewd message into his smartphone. He had an appropriate photo of himself all ready to upload.

In Moscow, 4,500 miles away from Boston, Aslanova gave a thumbs-up sign as the message pinged into her inbox. 'Bingo,' she said. 'He's hooked.'

The KSB Moscow office had very kindly supplied a variety of photos of teenage girls in their underwear, all waiting to be uploaded. Aslanova quickly selected one and pinged it back.

Markova, tough, ferocious Markova, stood behind her with her own mobile, videoing the exchange. Some of these 'sexting apps' had self-delete programmes as soon as the exchange ended, so you had to take care to make real-time recordings.

'We need to fire him up a bit,' Markova said. 'Send him a boob shot. Here, what about that one? She's young and pert and pretty. I wouldn't mind her myself. I wonder where they found her?'

Seconds later, Lomax fired back. '*Great! Loved it. What's the weather like in Champagne? It's pretty cloudy here in Boston.*'

Aslanova didn't answer that one immediately. 'Could be a trap,' she whispered. 'He may be checking that I really am in Illinois.'

She Googled: 'What's the weather in Illinois today?'

'*Actually, it's unseasonably warm here today,*' she typed. '*With highs in the upper seventies.*'

Markova punched her: 'For Christ's sake, don't send that. You're meant to be under fourteen. Talk like a teenager, not like the weatherman!'

'*The weather here's great*', Aslanova tried again. '*You may think this photo's great too.*'

Within seconds the former congressman sent what he considered to be his finest literary effort so far: '*I can't help thinking about your pretty little pussy.*'

Later that morning, Aslanova phoned Yasonov.

'I think we've got what we need,' she said.

'Attagirl!' Yasonov replied.

Less than two hours later, the *Selkirk Clarion*, America's biggest-selling national newspaper, published both online and in print a series of messages sent by former congressman Julius Lomax to an underage girl in Champagne, Illinois, although fortunately they kept this as a one-sided conversation with words suggestively blanked out.

Within an hour, the FBI succeeded in obtaining a court order permitting it to seize and examine Lomax's mobile and laptop as well.

In seeking the warrant, the FBI indicated it would not only be looking for illegal activity involving the grooming and exploitation of a minor for sexual purposes. It also asked the permission of the court to undertake a complete forensic analysis and review of the files on Lomax's laptop.

The FBI argued that such a review 'will also allow the FBI to determine if there is any evidence of computer intrusions into the subject laptop, and to determine if classified information was accessed by unauthorized users or transferred to any other unauthorized systems'.

CHAPTER THIRTY-NINE

Harry Stokes, foreign secretary, called his political adviser, a bright and bubbly young man called Owen Griffiths, into his grand office overlooking St James's Park for an urgent discussion.

'There have been some developments in the "Golden Shower" affair,' he said. 'MI5 have somehow managed to depixelate the tape, whatever that means, and they report that Ronald Craig is not, absolutely not, the man on the bed. The original report which gave rise to the "Golden Shower" scenario seems to have been written by a former MI6 officer, Martin Silver, under contract to the Democratic National Committee. They wanted him to dig up some dirt on Ron Craig. Now they are asking me as the minister responsible for MI6, as well as the Foreign Office, to make it clear that we totally repudiate any suggestion Ron Craig is one of the *dramatis personae* in the famous "Golden Shower" event.'

Stokes got up from his desk and strode across to the window. It was late October and the evening was drawing in.

'Basically, Owen, I think this is a lose-lose situation,' he continued. 'If we go public and exonerate Craig, Caroline Mann's people will complain we are playing politics. They will protest that we are behaving exactly like the Russians, interfering with the US presidential election by coming out with such a very pro-Craig bit of information just days before the vote. But if we don't say anything, then Craig's people will yell blue murder. The "Golden Shower" rumour has already hurt their candidate. We can be sure Craig won't put the prime minister at the top of his visitors' list if he's elected next week.'

As a SPAD – Special Political Adviser – Griffiths was free from the normal bureaucratic hang-ups. 'I think there's some wriggle room here, Foreign Secretary. My advice would be to put nothing in writing. Why don't you have a quiet word with Warren Fletcher, the American ambassador? You'll be meeting him at London Zoo tomorrow when the Duke of Edinburgh opens the new tiger enclosure. That way we won't be making any public statement, but we can always claim that we passed on sensitive information in a timely and appropriate way. What Fletcher does with this particular piece of news is his problem, not ours.'

'Great stuff, Owen. I know why we pay you.'

Next morning, a select group of invitees, including Foreign Secretary Harry Stokes, American ambassador Warren Fletcher, Gennadiy Tikhonov, the Russian ambassador to the Court of St James's, and the world-renowned conservationist and broadcaster, Thomas Pulborough, gathered in front of London Zoo's spectacular new Tiger Territory. The Duke of Edinburgh, former president of the World Wildlife Fund, made a brief but powerful plea for more national and international action to save threatened tigers and all endangered species.

'The situation of the tiger is getting worse all over the world,' he said. 'The Bali, Caspian and Javan subspecies are already extinct. The Sumatran tiger, which you see here today – two adults and three splendid cubs – is critically endangered.'

The duke pointed to the animals in the enclosure. The zoo had done a tremendous job of recreating a pocket of Indonesian rainforest in the heart of London. While the parents lazed in the late October sunshine, the cubs explored their newly enlarged and improved home, climbing up into the trees and splashing in the lake.

'The Bengal tiger appears to be holding its own and the population of the Siberian or Amur tiger is actually increasing.'

The duke paused. As always, he had been well-briefed. 'I am delighted to see that we have Ambassador Tikhonov among the guests here this morning. I hope he will pass on to Moscow the pleasure we all feel at the progress being made in Russia today, as far as the Siberian tiger is concerned. But this is no time for complacency.'

After the speeches were over, and the brilliant new tiger territory had been officially inaugurated, guests were invited to a reception in the splendid new Thomas Pulborough Pavilion to mark the occasion.

Stokes buttonholed the US ambassador.

Fletcher had been four years in London already. He and his wife entertained on a grand scale in Winfield House, their splendid official residence in Regent's Park, barely a butterfly hop from the zoo.

'Isn't the duke amazing?' Fletcher said. 'Ninety-five years old, if he's a day, and still going strong. Wasn't it great when the tiger cubs came right up behind him as he was speaking? If they hadn't put that glass screen in the way, the tigers could have had a right royal lunch!' Then Fletcher turned serious: 'Nelly and I have had such a good time here. You guys have been really great. We'll have to leave, of course, if Craig wins. A new president will always want to have his own man – or woman – in London.'

'Do you think he will win?' Stokes asked.

Fletcher waited for a man with a plate of canapés to pass, then he said, 'Between you and me, there's a lot of dirty pool going on in this election. The release of those emails has hurt Caroline Mann badly. The Mann campaign is putting a lot of pressure on the FBI Director, Wilbur Brown, to show a bit more even-handedness. Now you guys could help there. You could help a lot. Your man, Martin Silver, reported that Craig featured in that "Golden Shower" tape. If you could come out with a statement saying there is strong and credible evidence that Ronald Craig was indeed implicated, then that could really swing things in Caroline Mann's favour.'

It was as close to a direct plea for assistance as the ambassador could get without being overtly partisan. In a way, Stokes felt sorry to have to disappoint him. The Fletchers had been fun. They had transformed the atmosphere at Winfield House. Pop stars had sung there. Jazz concerts had been staged there. Prince Charles and the Duchess of Cornwall, as well as the young royals, had popped in on a regular basis. But the day Craig was elected president would be the day the Fletchers received their marching orders.

'Oh dear,' Stokes said. 'We couldn't support that kind of statement. Apart from the fact that we don't get involved in other people's elections – officially, at least – all the "strong and credible evidence" – to use your words – we have, indicates that Ronald Craig was absolutely *not* the man on the bed in the Kempinski. On the contrary, we think the culprit's a fellow from the FSB St Petersburg, called Fyodor Stephanov. Your people ought to check that out before you finger Ronald Craig.'

Fletcher drained his glass. He checked his watch. 'I'm going to scoot,' he said. 'We had word last night that Wilbur Brown plans to make a statement this morning. I need to contact him. Can I name you personally as the origin of this information? He'll have to decide what to do with it.'

Stokes shook his head. 'Best not. We're still trying to keep our hands clean on this one.'

'What about calling you a "very reliable source"?'

'I'll settle for that.'

Just as Stokes was preparing to leave, he noticed Tikhonov standing by himself with a glass of champagne in his hand. In the months since he became foreign secretary, Stokes had been at least twice to social events at the ambassador's residence in Kensington Palace Gardens and had returned the hospitality in one of the

Foreign Office's own glittering reception rooms, the Council Chamber of the Old India Office.

Tikhonov was a large, cheerful man. He waved his glass as Stokes approached. 'Hello, foreign secretary, what a wonderful occasion! Next time President Popov will bring a lovely Amur tiger-cub as a present for your marvellous zoo.'

'Fantastic! Room for lots more tigers here!' Stokes waved his arm at the large, leafy enclosure.

The two men shook hands warmly. Officially Britain was still taking a tough line on sanctions, but Stokes didn't see why that should prevent him from having cordial personal relations with one of Russia's top diplomats.

The two men stood together for a moment watching the cubs playing.

'I see you were talking to our good friend Warren Fletcher,' Tikhonov said. 'I am sure we will all be sorry to see him go. I imagine Mr Craig has already picked his successor.'

'What makes you so sure Craig is going to win the election?' Stokes asked.

'Some little bird told me.' Tikhonov smiled.

CHAPTER FORTY

Wilbur Brown, director of the FBI, had the television on in the corner of his office.

Gina Paulson, Vixen TV's star presenter, was asking her nation-wide audience: 'Will Caroline Mann lose the election because the FBI has decided to make a further investigation into the way she handled her emails?

'Back in July,' Paulson continued, 'the FBI undertook a major investigation of the way Caroline Mann used a personal email server to handle top-secret and confidential messages. After examining some 30,000 messages, FBI analysts concluded that a large number of top-secret and confidential messages from and to several departments of government, including the State Department, had indeed been handled on Mann's private email server. But instead of pursuing criminal charges, Wilbur Brown, the director of the FBI, let Mrs Mann off with a rap on the knuckles but not much else. All he said was that Mann and her aides had been – and I quote – "extremely careless" – but not criminal with their email practices. But he also told Congress that he would reopen the investigation if – and I quote again – "relevant and substantial" information was uncovered. That now seems to be the case.

'The FBI has sought and obtained a court warrant to search a computer used both by former congressman Julius Lomax and his wife Sandra, an aide to Caroline Mann. Having received the warrant, the director of the FBI has told Congress that the FBI is indeed reopening the enquiry into Caroline Mann's emails.'

Paulson paused to allow the full weight of her next pronouncement to have the effect she intended. 'Today Caroline Mann's ratings are in free fall.'

Brown switched to another channel. It had become increasingly plain in the course of this election campaign that Vixen TV, the crown jewel in Mickey Selkirk's global media empire, had long since cast aside any pretence of impartiality. It was totally dedicated to promoting Ronald C. Craig as the next president of the United States. How much money, Brown, wondered, had changed hands? What promises had been made? The truth would come out in the end, he supposed. The FCC would get its act together and ask questions. Or maybe it wouldn't. Maybe it would be abolished or neutered by the incoming administration and Selkirk Global would take an ever bigger share of the market.

On CBS, Eric Longhurst, the revered anchor of *Good Morning America*, was putting another slant on the Caroline Mann email story. Brown used the remote to turn the volume up. He had known as soon as he authorized the second investigation that there would be fight back by the Mann campaign.

'A series of Democratic congressmen,' Longhurst said, 'have been taking to the air today to complain about the FBI's "blatant favouritism" in the presidential race.

'Here's congressman Bill Whitelaw, the ranking member of the House Judiciary Constitution and Civil Justice Subcommittee.'

Brown knew and respected Bill Whitelaw. He winced involuntarily at the personal nature of Whitelaw's attack.

'FBI Director Wilbur Brown's recent comments on former secretary of state, Caroline Mann, and her emails, apparently before seeing any evidence, and against the advice of the Justice Department, according to press reports, and even, some have suggested, in violation of the Hatch Act, make it clear that for the good of the FBI and the Justice Department, he should resign immediately.'

Longhurst chipped in for the benefit of viewers who might not be familiar with the finer details of the US Constitution:

'The Hatch Act limits the political activity of federal employees, for instance barring them from seeking public office or influence to interfere with or affect the result of an election'.

Whitelaw was followed almost immediately by Larry Kinder, outgoing Senate minority leader, who also called for Brown's resignation, comparing Brown to the FBI's notorious founder, J. Edgar Hoover.

Like Whitelaw, Kinder didn't mince his words. 'The director of the FBI's actions in recent months,' he thundered, 'has demonstrated a disturbing double standard for the treatment of sensitive information, with what appears to be a clear intent to aid one political party over another.'

Finally, Longhurst took back the mic.

'The FBI's action in reopening the email enquiry,' he said, 'less than two weeks before the presidential election, has stunned former and current law enforcement officials and rocked Caroline Mann's campaign, which appeared to be coasting to victory. The Bureau's director, Wilbur Brown, said in a memo to FBI employees that he felt obligated to update lawmakers after testifying under oath – back in July – that the investigation into Mann's private email server was complete. And he feared that word of the newly discovered emails – found in the course of a separate investigation into former US congressman Julius Lomax – would leak to the media and suggest a cover-up.'

Brown turned the TV off. He had known, when he had authorized that second investigation, that he might be stirring up a hornet's nest. But he hadn't realized just how much damage this might do to Caroline Mann's prospects of winning the election.

What an amazing coincidence, he thought, that the story about that sex-obsessed idiot from Boston had appeared in Mickey Selkirk's *Daily Clarion* precisely when it did. The timing, from the Craig campaign's point of view, could not have been more perfect.

His mobile pinged. A Google alert had just come in. 'Craig jumps into lead in two out of three national polls.'

And then a text message came on his personal number, caller ID withheld: 'Hope you can live with yourself after what you've done, you ***t!'

As Brown stood there, his secretary came in with an envelope.

'Here's an eyes-only for you, Director,' she said. 'Couriered overnight from London.'

Brown opened the envelope. It was a handwritten note from ambassador Fletcher:

> '*Dear Wilbur, I have heard from a totally reliable source that RC is not, repeat not, in any way connected with "Golden Shower" scenario. I am writing this by hand to avoid the possibility of adding yet another juicy email to the WikiLeaks treasury. I am sure you will know what action to take.*
> *Very best wishes, Warren Fletcher.*'

As Brown returned to his desk, a wave of relief came over him. Over the months, that 'Golden Shower' rumour had proved remarkably persistent. He had faced accusations, sometimes not too polite, from Caroline Mann's people that he was sitting on the file for reasons of his own. Only that morning congressman Terry Harman had called on him to set up an enquiry.

'If the FBI can reopen the file on Caroline Mann,' Harman had challenged, 'why can't they investigate the possibly illegal behaviour of Ronald Craig? Who knows whether minors were involved in the "Golden Shower" scene?'

Brown passed a hand over his forehead. Slime and innuendo. That's what politics boiled down to nowadays. Was there any depth they wouldn't sink to?

What a narrow escape, he thought. If Fletcher's note had not arrived in the nick of time, he might have succumbed to the mounting pressure and announced the 'Golden Shower' enquiry that people like Harman were calling for. And that might have allowed Caroline Mann to pull ahead again in the tightly fought race.

In the end, Brown decided to do nothing. In view of Fletcher's letter, he felt confident that announcing an enquiry into the 'Golden Shower' episode would be totally unjustified. But he also saw no need to announce that the Republican presidential candidate was not involved in the shenanigans in the Hotel Kempinski. Caroline Mann was cross enough with him as it was. If he came out now with a statement exonerating Craig, that would only add fuel to the flames.

He folded Fletcher's letter and put it in his wallet.

CHAPTER FORTY-ONE

Harriet Marshall sat at a corner table in the Metropole Hotel's Chaliapin Bar waiting for Yuri Yasonov to arrive.

Because this was a very special occasion – a US election-night party – the hotel management had erected a huge television screen which contrasted incongruously with the bar's famous art nouveau fittings and decor.

On the TV, Simon Henley, leader of the United Kingdom Independence Party, was holding forth from New York.

Strange, wasn't it, Marshall thought, how Henley had been shunted aside after the Brexit vote in Britain? Whatever you thought about UKIP and Henley, they had certainly played a part in the Leave campaign's stupendous victory in the Referendum. And after the coup – for what was it except a coup? – Henley hadn't even been offered a knighthood. No wonder he was over there in the US most of the time, cosying up to the Craig campaign team and even to Craig himself, if his frequent tweets were to be believed.

She listened more closely to what Henley was saying.

'Do you know? It feels just like Brexit day to me.' Henley beamed at the camera, holding a pint of Budweiser in his hand.

'All the smart money, all of the commentators, all of the foreign-exchange dealers, the bookmakers, they all think that Caroline Mann is going to do it.

'Well, I'm not sure they're right. Yes, Ronald Craig has got to win these swing states – he's got to win Pennsylvania, Ohio and Florida.

There's a mountain to climb. I get that, and yet I have a feeling the world could be in for a very big shock tomorrow morning.'

Marshall was so absorbed in Henley's victory-for-Craig predictions that she didn't notice Yasonov's arrival until he tapped her lightly on the shoulder.

'Sorry I'm late,' he said. 'The president called me. If things continue to look good for Craig, Popov wants to celebrate at his dacha. Says he's got some special guests, too. We should give it an hour or two while the results come in, then head on over.'

'Am I invited?' Marshall asked.

'What do you think?' Yasonov replied. 'You were one of the lynchpins.'

While Ronald Craig's tally of votes mounted and state after state declared for him, rather than for Caroline Mann, the two old friends and lovers sat in the Chaliapin Bar enjoying the moment.

'You know, Harriet, I fancied you even at Oxford, when you were still a man.'

'And do you continue to fancy me, now that I'm a woman?' Marshall fluttered her eyelashes.

'More than ever,' Yasonov replied.

Yasonov fetched himself a drink at the bar. When he came back, he said, 'I'm sorry if the police gave you a hard time when they picked you up after that Oxford Union debate.'

'Nothing like school,' said Harriet Marshall. 'I think they knew I was gay even then. They hunted in packs.'

Yasonov put his arm round her. 'Poor darling. Anyway, they had nothing on you. That's why they let you go. You, personally, had no idea what was going to happen that night. Barnard was never going to be hurt anyway. It just had to look like a serious attempt on his life by the Remainers. The only thing to suffer any damage was that bust of Gladstone. Serves him right. Dirty old hypocrite. He used to wander round the East End at night rescuing fallen women. Or so he said. He wouldn't get away with it nowadays.'

Marshall gave Yasonov a long, lingering kiss. Their affair had really begun when she went to Moscow after leaving Oxford. She came to the Russian capital as Harriet, not Howard. The transformation had been achieved a few months earlier in Bogota, Colombia, the world centre for plastic surgery, including sex-change operations. When Yasonov had got over the shock, he welcomed her with open arms.

'No need to tell anyone about the operation,' Marshall had said, when they met for a drink in Jean-Jacques, a short walk from the Old Arbat.

'Why should I?' Yasonov had replied.

Later that night they took a taxi out to the presidential dacha. By then it was clear that Roland C. Craig was home and dry. He would indeed be the 45th president of the United States.

President Popov had summoned all the key players in Operation Tectonic Plate. Along with Yasonov and Aslanova, Popov had invited Markova, the FSB's enforcer, and her all-female SWAT team, to join him at the presidential dacha.

Popov raised his glass and made a little speech.

'It gives me great pleasure to introduce Martine Le Grand, the next president of France,' he began. 'Martine is on an unofficial visit. She is travelling incognito!'

Like any practised orator, Popov knew when to pause.

'It's a bit like Peter the Great,' he said. 'Peter travelled incognito when he visited Europe. Called himself "Peter Mikhailov". Of course Peter the Great was over two metres tall, so he was quite easy to recognize. Martine Le Grand may not be as tall as Peter the Great, but already she is a figure of international stature. Martine, it is a great pleasure to have you with us today. Be assured we will give you all the help we can, including,' and here he paused again to make sure they got the joke, 'that large, no-interest bank loan you're looking for to help you fund your campaign!'

Popov's audience laughed and clapped. What a man Popov was, they thought. Where would he stop? At this moment, the whole world seemed to be his oyster.

Popov handed the microphone to the blonde lady, with strong, handsome features, who stood next to him on the stand.

'Yes, this is an extraordinary day, isn't it?' Le Grand began, sensing the mood. 'First Britain, then the United States. Will the dominoes keep falling? Will France be next? Who can say? But one thing I do know: nothing is more powerful than the will of the people. Even if we don't succeed this time round, our time will certainly come soon.'

After a while, she passed the microphone back to Popov.

'I have a few more people to thank,' Popov said. 'First, my good friend Galina Aslanova and her wonderful team, who are so brilliantly executing Operation Tectonic Plate. Please step forward, Galina, to receive the Hero of the Russian Federation medal.'

Popov kissed Aslanova gallantly on both cheeks as she came forward to receive the award. 'You're looking wonderful!' he whispered.

When Aslanova had resumed her place, Popov continued. 'I would also like to thank Harriet Marshall, without whose help I can honestly say we would not have achieved that splendid victory in Britain. It gives me great pleasure to bestow on Harriet Marshall the Order of St Catherine the Great.'

Marshall blushed as she stepped toward. 'Thank you so much, Mr President. This is indeed a great honour.'

Yasonov led the clapping, the others joining in enthusiastically.

They all knew how much of the success of the Brexit campaign in Britain had been due to the tireless activity and attention to detail of Marshall.

Finally, Popov turned to the last of his specially invited guests. 'Please step forward, sir,' he called.

From the back of the room a tall, broad-shouldered figure with a shock of blond hair made his way to the stage, with a slow ponderous gait. For half a second, Marshall thought: 'This is absurd. How can president-elect Ronald Craig be here when at this very moment he is giving his victory speech in New York?'

'Fyodor Stephanov Molotovsky,' Popov said. 'Please remove your wig!'

Stephanov bowed low, and as he did so he swept the distinctive hairpiece from his head.

Popov gave Stephanov a huge bear hug.

'Fyodor Stephanov and I go back a long way,' he said. 'We were in Dresden together that evening in December 1989, when the crowds came to sack the KGB office. We fought them off, didn't we? Now Stephanov has performed an even greater service to the state. Without hesitation or deviation he has exposed himself in the line of duty! So it gives me great pleasure to award him the FSB's specially created Golden Shower Medal.'

The Kremlin goldsmiths had excelled themselves. One side of the golden medal depicted Titian's famous image of *Danaë Receiving The Golden Rain*. The other side of the medal was inscribed simply: 'For Services Rendered.'

As he pinned the medal to Stephanov's uniform (it hung from a pentagonal mount covered by an overlapping scarlet ribbon), Popov continued, 'And I hereby promote this gallant officer to the rank of full colonel.'

As the applause died down, Popov noticed Markova and her SWAT team looking more than a little disgruntled.

'Come up here, Lyudmila Markova Sokolovna,' he urged, 'and

please bring your team, too. I believe our good friend, Fyodor Stephanov, has something to give you.'

FSB Colonel Fyodor Stephanov Molotovsky drew himself up to his full height.

'Dear ladies,' he said, 'I bear you no grudge. You were doing your job; I was doing mine. No hard feelings. I'd just like to give you something you overlooked that day you trashed my office and beat me up.'

Stephanov still had the hairpiece in his hand. Once again, he bowed low, and then handed it over to Markova.

Wild applause. The vodka continued to flow.

Markova stood there, holding the hairpiece. 'Where the hell were you hiding it?' she asked.

'In the fridge, at home,' Stephanov said. 'If you had looked there behind the pickles, you would have found the US-flag boxers as well!'

Moments later, the president entered the dacha's press room, where the journalists were waiting. Holding a glass of champagne in his hand, and conscious that the eyes of the world were upon him, Popov made a solemn and statesmanlike speech.

'A few hours ago, presidential elections finished in the United States of America. We have been following this event with attention and I would like to congratulate the American people on the exemplary conduct of their electoral process. I would also like to congratulate Mr Ronald Craig on his victory. We have heard his electoral programme when he was still a candidate. He spoke about resuming and restoring relations between Russia and the United States. We are ready to play our part in this, and to do everything in our power to return Russia–America relations to a stable development track. This would serve the wellbeing of both the Russian and the American people. And it would have a positive effect on the general climate of global affairs, taking into account the special responsibility of Russia and the US to sustain global responsibility and security.'

Christine Amadore, CNN's dashing, raven-haired star reporter, anchoring CNN's all-night coverage of Russia's reactions to the unfolding events, was the first to ask a question.

'You just congratulated the US on the exemplary conduct of their electoral process, Mr President. Do you really believe that?'

'Yes, indeed,' Popov replied solemnly. 'Elections must always be free and fair.'

CHAPTER FORTY-TWO

Spring comes late in Moscow. There were still piles of slushy snow on the streets that morning in April 2017, when President Popov summoned Yuri Yasonov and Galina Aslanova to his private den in the Kremlin to hear their latest reports on Operation Tectonic Plate.

'Let's look at Europe first,' he said. 'Yuri, please give us your summary of events to date.'

'I'd say we are totally on track, Mr President,' Yasonov replied. 'Britain's new prime minister, Mabel Killick, wasn't a Leaver during the Referendum campaign. She wasn't very active as a Remainer either. She kept her powder dry. Then, when David Cole, the former justice minister, stabbed Harry Stokes in the back before committing *hara-kiri* himself, Mrs Killick seized her opportunity. She threw her hat in the ring and was elected by the Conservative Party as their new leader. That meant she became prime minister, too, since the British Constitution doesn't require the prime minister to be actually elected by the people before taking on the job.'

Popov was puzzled. 'I thought Britain was the "cradle of democracy".'

'Basically not!' Yasonov explained. 'In the old days, Conservative Party leaders would emerge from smoke-filled rooms. They do better nowadays. Actually, no one in the end stood against Mrs Killick, so she didn't have to fight an election of any kind.'

'As prime minister,' Yasonov continued, 'Mabel Killick has been an out-and-out Brexiteer. We couldn't have asked for more.'

Popov nodded. 'Wasn't there a bad moment when that wild woman – what was her name?– managed to get the UK Supreme Court to rule that if the Brexit campaign had been about "taking back sovereignty" then at the very least the UK government should consult Parliament before making the formal application to Leave?'

Yasonov laughed. 'Tina Moller – what a brilliant woman! She had the Supreme Court eating out of her hand. Mrs Killick caved in and agreed to a parliamentary vote. What else could she do once the Supreme Court had ruled? Luckily, the British Parliament is a bit like our Duma. They'll do what they're told if you slap them around a bit. They call it the "whipping system".'

'In the good old days we had the *knout*,' Popov mused. 'So two years from now Britain's out of the EU?'

'Exactly,' Yasonov replied. '29 March 2019 is Brexit Day. Article 50 has been triggered. It's a non-recallable missile.'

'What about the rest of Europe? How are we doing?' Popov asked.

'The Dutch result was a bit disappointing. Our man, Geert Donkers, did well, but not well enough. We have high hopes in France, though. Martine Le Grand is bound to make it through to the run-off in the presidential election. Too early to say what's going to happen in Germany. That's the big one, of course, from our point of view.'

Popov turned to Aslanova.

'What about the US, Galina? Why isn't President Craig playing the game?' he asked. 'I thought we had a clear understanding with Craig. Lay off Assad. That's what we told him. And what does he do? He fires off sixty Tomahawk missiles. Why did we push so hard to get Craig elected, if he's going to kick us in the teeth at the first opportunity? It's a pity, isn't it, that the "Golden Shower" tape turned out to be fake? We could have used that now.'

Of course, Aslanova knew that Popov was joking. By now she had learned to read the telltale signs: the slight twitch in the left eyebrow, the faintest hint of a smile in the upper lip. But his remark about the 'Golden Shower' tape got her thinking nonetheless.

Back in her office in the FSB's Lubyanka building, she summoned Markova.

'There's something fishy, Lyudmila,' she began. 'When you and your team were beating up Fyodor Stephanov that day in St Petersburg, looking for the "Golden Shower" video, why didn't Stephanov cry foul? Why didn't he say he was an old mucker of Popov's, going way back?'

'Maybe he didn't want the president to know he had been free-lancing,' Markova replied. 'As a matter of fact, Popov still doesn't know that Stephanov was freelancing, does he? Of course, the FSB has been happy to claim the credit, happy to see Stephanov given the Golden Shower Award and elevated to the rank of full colonel. It reflects well on all of us, but still I think there's something that doesn't smell right.'

'I'm not sure I understand.' Markova was quite adept at the heavy stuff, but she sometimes found it difficult to follow her more intel-lectual colleagues when they started talking about zero-sum games and so forth.

Aslanova opened her desk drawer and brought out the Craig wig that Stephanov had been wearing at the election night party in Popov's presidential dacha.

'If Stephanov was freelancing, where did he get this?' she asked. 'I don't think he could have got it in Russia. I've had it examined by wig-makers here in Moscow. This is a very high-quality hairpiece. It's made out of real human hair, expertly crafted and totally realis-tic, as we saw when Stephanov was wearing it that night at the dacha. Here, watch this.'

She flipped open the lid of her laptop and pressed a button. 'This is Craig talking at a black-tie dinner the evening before his inaugu-ration in January, just a few weeks ago!'

On the screen before them they saw the unmistakable figure of the soon-to-be-inaugurated president of the United States. He was standing on the stage in evening dress, microphone in hand, radiating confidence.

'Some of you have been wondering about my hair,' Craig told the crowd. *'Well, just take a look. If it rains tomorrow, my hair won't turn a hair, if you follow me. It's all my own!'*

As the clip came to an end, Aslanova passed the hairpiece to Markova.

'Just think about the timing, Lyudmila, of that Kempinski scenario. Imagine the sequence of events. Stephanov is in his office when he gets word that Barnard is on his way back to the hotel after that dinner in the Winter Palace in St Petersburg. He has the US-flag boxer shorts and the Craig hairpiece with him. The cameras are already set up in the room. But still Stephanov has to move quickly. He has to get to the hotel, then up to the room, get the wig and the underpants on, so as to be primed and ready for action when the girls arrive. He has outside help, Lyudmila. I'm sure of it.'

'What on earth do you mean?'

'Just bear with me,' Aslanova said.

She picked up a paper from her desk. 'Did you read Ambassador Tikhonov's report of his morning at London Zoo? Tikhonov obviously had our new Earwig phone in his pocket, the one that can pick up even whispered conversation fifty yards away. Actually, he wasn't fifty yards away, I believe. More like twenty. They were all looking at the tigers in the new enclosure.'

On the podcast, they heard Harry Stokes' unmistakable voice:

'Apart from the fact that we don't get involved in other people's elections – officially, at least – all the "strong and credible evidence"– to use your words – we have indicates that Ronald Craig was absolutely not the man on the bed in the Kempinski. On the contrary, we think the culprit's a fellow

from the FSB St Petersburg office, called Fyodor Stephanov. Your people ought to check that out before you finger Ronald Craig.'

Galina switched the recording off. 'Doesn't that surprise you?' she asked. 'When we sent them the tapes, we simply wanted them to confirm that the man on the bed wasn't Craig. But they go one further and actually recognize our old friend Fyodor Stephanov. How did they do that?'

'Well, maybe they've got his face on file,' Markova replied. 'They could have ID'd him through a facial recognition system.'

'Of course they could,' Aslanova agreed. 'Particularly if Fyodor Stephanov is already working for MI6! I feel convinced the Brits helped Stephanov set this one up. The hairpiece probably came in via the diplomatic bag.'

She held the wig up. The fluffy, blond hair positively glowed in the sunshine that flooded Galina's office. 'See how beautiful it is!'

She Googled 'best wig-makers in London'. Less than a millisecond later the answer flew back. 'Archibalds of Bond Street have been making high-quality wigs for more than four centuries. Satisfied clients include King George II and the Lord Chief Justice.'

Another thought struck her. 'And where did he get the boxer shorts? Did MI6 buy those in Bond Street, too, or did they send off to New York for them? I wonder what happened to those shorts. I bet Stephanov's still got them.'

'If he has, we'll find them.' Markova felt suddenly cheerful. She rather fancied having another go at Stephanov. The team wouldn't let him off so easily this time.

CHAPTER FORTY-THREE

It was one of those delicate diplomatic compromises. Harry Stokes, the UK's foreign secretary, had cancelled his visit to Moscow at short notice. Officially, Britain's position was that it was sick and tired of the way the Russians were supporting President Assad's ghastly regime in Syria. The Americans had launched their Tomahawk missiles after Assad's chemical gas attack in Khan Sheikhoun. The least the UK could do was cancel the scheduled bilateral talks. Or at least postpone them.

Unofficially, of course, the government decided that some contacts should be maintained at ministerial level. It wasn't just a question of not being seen as 'America's poodle'. There was more to it than that. Brexit had not been won by the Brexiteers alone. Debts one day might have to be repaid. President Craig might feel he could turn on a dime. Befriend Russia one moment, revile them the next. But Craig had options that were not open to Britain.

Killick rang Barnard at home on Palm Sunday. The Wilshire countryside was at its most glorious. Barnard's Ministerial Red Boxes were stacked unopened on the kitchen dresser.

'I'm so sorry,' Melissa said. 'He's out with Jemima again.'

Later that day, Barnard rang the PM back.

'I've arranged a little trip for you and Melissa,' Killick said. 'I want you to go to St Petersburg – but on holiday this time. You've earned it. Drive across the border into Finland. Fly back from Helsinki. Perfect time of year. So much to see. Also, apart from the holiday aspect, we want the Russians to know that even though we're officially cross with them, life goes on, if you see what I mean.'

'Yes, Prime Minister,' Barnard said. Would anyone ever say that to him, he wondered? He shuddered. What an idea!

Next day, he met Mark Cooper, head of MI6, at Whites in St James's. They sat in two leather armchairs in the far corner of the library.

'The PM would have liked to join us,' Cooper began, 'but I'm afraid women are not allowed here. Except the Queen. We made an exception for the Queen once at the time of the Jubilee celebrations. We invited her to dinner and she very sportingly accepted. But the PM sends her best. She hopes you have a successful trip.'

'You'd better fill me in,' Barnard said.

'I supposed you've realized by now,' Cooper continued, 'that Jeremy Hartley was always a Leaver, not a Remainer. Did you read what he said in Kiev the other day: how he's been a Eurosceptic since birth or even before? Or, if you like, think back to that speech he made to the Conservative Party Conference in 2005, when the party first elected him. That was the speech of a Leaver if ever there was one. Hartley wanted to get Britain out of the EU and with the Referendum he found a way to do it. But a lot of people helped him. I was one of them.'

'Are you sure you want me to hear this?' Barnard asked.

'Quite sure. You've an important job to do for us.'

'Us? You mean MI6, SIS, the firm or whatever you call yourselves nowadays?'

A white-coated waiter stopped by to offer them more champagne but Cooper waved him away.

'That's exactly what I do mean. There's nothing in the rule book that says I can't recruit the chancellor of the exchequer, and that's what I'm proposing to do. Strictly speaking you should be PV'd – positively vetted – but there's no time for that. Odd, isn't it, that civil servants are PV'd, but politicians who – in theory at least – wield so much more power and influence are let through on the nod? Where was I?'

'In some fantasy land of your own,' Barnard wanted to answer. Instead he said, 'You're probably going to tell me you've known Hartley all your life, or at least since you were in the Bullingdon together at Oxford.'

'All of that's true,' Cooper admitted. 'But that wasn't the only reason I helped him. I helped him because I thought he was right about us leaving the EU and I could see a way to make it happen. *You were the way!*

'That whole Kempinski scenario, the Brexit dossier and so on – Hartley and I dreamed all that up as a way of luring you out into the open. The Leave campaign needed a Leader, and, by Jove, did we get one! But the problem now is that Catfish has been blown.'

'Catfish?'

'Our codename for Fyodor Stephanov, the man on the bed in the Kempinski. He worked with Popov years ago in Dresden, in former East Germany, when Popov was head of the KGB office there. Catfish is one of MI6's assets in St Petersburg and he has turned in a lot of good stuff. But now his life is in danger.'

'If Catfish has been "blown", don't you need to extricate him? How are you going to do that?'

'That's where you come in,' Cooper replied. 'We're relying on you. We'll give you a full briefing later today, but basically you'll bung Stephanov in the boot of your car and drive him across the border into Finland.'

'I've never met the man,' Barnard protested. 'Why should I risk my life and Melissa's?'

'He has risked his,' Cooper replied icily. 'Without him, Brexit might never have happened.'

'So you're appealing to my patriotic spirit?'

'You should have some fun, too. The ambassador's sending his

Rolls Royce down from Moscow. Then you'll leg it for the border. Top speed 150mph. Nought to sixty in less than five seconds.'

'We'll need a big boot.'

'Plenty of room in the Phantom's boot, I can assure you,' Cooper told him.

CHAPTER FORTY-FOUR

Edward and Melissa Barnard arrived in St Petersburg, ostensibly in vacation mode, although Melissa had taken a lot of persuading that she wanted to go, leaving quite a dent on several credit cards on the Thursday before Easter. That same evening, Barnard hosted a small reception for well-heeled Russian businessmen, and their blingy wives, who seemed mainly interested in finding out the chancellor of the exchequer's views on the London property market in a Brexit situation.

Barnard wisely refused to be drawn in. 'The price of property may go up or down. In London, it has a tendency to go up. But in percentage terms price rises are often higher in the north of England than they are in London. A lot of Chinese money is flowing north.'

His audience did not seem to be very interested in what the Chinese were doing north of Watford. They seemed to prefer Mayfair or Belgravia.

The Barnards spent the Friday sightseeing. Melissa, who had never been to St Petersburg before, was fascinated by the imperial tombs in the Cathedral of Sts Peter and Paul. She stood in front of the marble memorial marking the much-delayed burial of Czar Nicholas II and his family in St Catherine's chapel.

'Shameful, wasn't it,' she commented, 'how our own Royal Family refused to give them asylum? And King George V was a first cousin of Tsar Nicholas II, too. They could have made more of an effort. Still, we're going to be making an effort, aren't we?'

Barnard shot her a warning look. Even cathedrals had ears.

That evening, Martha Goodchild, Britain's new ambassador to Russia and Sir Andrew Boles' successor, arrived at the Kempinski in time to have dinner with the Barnards in the Bellevue Brasserie, with its panoramic view over the city.

Goodchild, one of the Foreign Office's high-flyers, talked them through the menu.

'I was the British consul in St Petersburg, ages ago. Used to eat here often. Top-class food, though a touch on the heavy side.'

Goodchild was a touch on the heavy side herself. Over coffee and pastries, she went through the details:

'My driver will come round to the front of the hotel at nine tomorrow morning. You can't miss him. Tall, burly fellow. Serves as my bodyguard, too. The car's still the same one Sir Andrew had, a silver-grey Rolls Royce Phantom with CD plates bearing the designation UK-1. Mind you, if we lose Scotland and Northern Ireland, we'll be Former-UK. I'm not sure FUK-1 would look so good.'

The Barnards enjoyed the joke. A bit of humour always helped relieve the tension, Barnard thought.

'How are you getting back to Moscow?' Barnard asked.

'I'll fly back tomorrow. Keep an eye on things from there.'

'What about Catfish?' Barnard murmured.

'Officially,' Goodchild said, 'you're making a detour at lunchtime to visit the site of the proposed new transnational biosphere reserve linking the Russian and Finnish parts of Karelia. Just enjoy the scenery. And remember, the car's almost certainly bugged.'

If the Kempinski Hotel porters were surprised at how little luggage the Barnards had brought with them for their two night stay in St Petersburg, they gave no sign of it.

Jim Connally, the embassy driver, supervised the stacking of the two small cases. 'Room for plenty more, if you want to do some last-minute shopping,' he said.

They made good time in spite of the poor condition of the road. Heeding the ambassador's warning, the Barnards limited their conversation to the banal or innocuous.

'These transnational biosphere reserves are an important development,' Barnard said. 'At the beginning of World War II, the Finns fought the Russians almost to a standstill in this part of the world. Now the Russians and the Finns together are going to set up a joint nature park. That's progress.'

'It certainly is,' Melissa agreed. She caught the driver's eye in the rear-view mirror. Was *he* employed by MI6 as well, she wondered?

Connally winked, as though he read her mind. Yes, he bloody well was one of 'them', and proud of it. He checked his satnav. Pretty soon, they would have to turn off the highway onto a local road, then onto a track through the forest where Catfish was meant to be waiting. He had memorized the GPS coordinates and he double-checked to make sure he had entered them correctly.

Stephanov had driven his old Lada deep into the undergrowth. He had changed out of his FSB uniform into civilian clothes. A small backpack, a toothbrush and a passport was all he needed to start a new life, though he was confident that he could always count on a little help from his 'friends'. And his girlfriend, Natasha, was already in Helsinki, waiting for him.

The huge silver-grey Rolls Royce nosed its way down the track. Connally had the boot open, almost as soon as the car came to a stop.

'Hop in,' he said.

Even though Stephanov was a large man himself, there was plenty of room in the boot.

Connally eased the vehicle back onto the track. His finger hovered over the walnut-finish console. 'Anyone want some music? "Karelia Suite"?' he enquired.

President Popov stretched out bare-chested on the grass in front of the dacha, enjoying the spring sunshine. This was as close to heaven as he was likely to get. Born and bred in St Petersburg, Karelia was his second home. As a student at St Petersburg University, he had led scientific expeditions into the forest, studying the wildlife and, occasionally, shooting a deer for the pot. For the last twenty years, he had owned this little dacha among the trees, not far from the Finland–Russia border. Indeed, the fact that Popov was a seasonal visitor and even had a little place there, had done much to ensure that plans for the transnational biosphere reserve didn't get bogged down in bureaucratic detail.

Popov insisted on his privacy during the rare occasions he managed to get away from Moscow to spend time in his beloved Karelia. Though the local police were aware of his presence, they were under strict instructions not to disturb him. Almost always, he dispensed with his bodyguard, driving his own off-road vehicle: the UAZ-469 or Patriot Jeep.

Popov was not the only person enjoying the scenery that day. Aslanova had flown down from Moscow with him in his private jet. They had landed at Vyborg, an old once-Swedish town with a magnificent castle, which stood barely twenty miles from the Finnish border. They had picked up the UAZ at the airport and driven along the dirt roads to the dacha.

Aslanova was inside the dacha, unpacking their lunch, so Popov heard the sound of the Rolls first. Not that it made much sound. Rolls Royce engineers prided themselves on their ability to reduce engine noise to a low hum, if that.

'Good heavens!' Popov got to his feet. His hand went instinctively to his belt. But his weapon was in the pocket of his leather jacket and the jacket was in the car. So he stepped out into the clearing.

'Mr President! What a surprise!' Barnard recovered quickly. 'I heard somewhere that you had a little place out in the forest in Karelia, but I never imagined we would drive right past your door on our way to visit your brilliant Karelia Nature Reserve.'

'Mr Barnard, how good to see you again! As I recall, the last time was when we had dinner in Khabarovsk. You've been promoted since then, I hear. Congratulations! And is this Mrs Barnard?'

Popov, still bare-chested, bowed and gallantly touched his lips to Melissa's outstretched hand.

'May I present Galina Aslanova?' Popov continued. 'I don't think you have met before. Galina was not with us when we were looking for the Amur tigers. That was some trip, wasn't it?'

Barnard introduced Connally to the president. 'That's quite a car, you have there,' Popov said. He gazed admiringly at the classic lines of the Rolls Royce Phantom.

'You don't do so badly yourself,' Connally replied. 'On the right terrain, that UAZ would probably give us a run for our money.'

Of course they stayed for lunch. Spoke about this and that. Barnard hadn't had a specific briefing before he left. Back in Whitehall, no one imagined he would be having a one-to-one meeting with the president of the Russian Federation in a forest clearing a stone's throw from the Finnish border. But he improvised as best as he could.

They talked about recent events. How could they not? Popov said that, as far as he knew, there was no proof that President Bashar al-Assad had been behind the chemical attack in Syria and what a pity it was that the opportunity of building bridges between Russia and the West was being thrown away.

With his mouth full of pickle, Barnard did his best to stick to the party line. Officially, Britain was all for ratcheting up the sanctions. But there was a strange disconnect between the increasing hoarse language now being used on both sides of the Atlantic and the idyllic pastoral setting in which they now found themselves A few months ago, it had all looked so hopeful.

He decided to strike an upbeat note.

'Congratulations on the Karelia transnational biosphere reserve,' Barnard said. 'That's a magnificent achievement.'

Aslanova agreed. 'When we all come to look at the president's achievements, this Karelia reserve will rate very highly. And we must thank the Finns, too.'

'Amazing people,' Popov conceded. 'A handful of their fighters held up the whole Russian Army for months. On our side, heads rolled, I can tell you.'

Popov had a sudden mischievous idea. 'Remember that time when I raced you to Khabarovsk? You were in Jack Varese's Gulfstream 550; I was flying my Ilyushin Il-96.'

'Of course, I remember. How could I ever forget it?'

'Let's have another race now,' Popov said. 'All the way to the border. Perhaps Mrs Barnard would like to come with me. Galina can go with you. She knows the way by the back roads in case you get lost. Actually, I've had another thought. I'll drive the Rolls. I've always wanted to drive a Rolls Royce Phantom VI. Maybe you'd like to take the UAZ. First one to the border post wins?'

'OMG!' thought Barnard. You could hardly make it up. The president of the Russian Federation was about to drive off in the British ambassador's Rolls Royce to the Finnish border without realizing that he had one of his own FSB agents crammed in the boot, heading for freedom!

Connally asked the obvious question. 'So Galina's going to come with us in the UAZ to make sure we find the way. That's great. But who's going to drive, sir?'

Barnard thought back to all those years he had driven his Land Rover over the Wiltshire Hills. He had had some pretty good scrapes in his time.

'I'll have a go,' he said quietly. 'You might have to show me the gears.'

It wasn't so much a question of engine capacity, though the Rolls-Royce's 6.75-litre engine certainly outgunned the UAZ's 2.5-litre engine. Given the terrain, there was never a moment when the Phantom could go flat out. No, what distinguished Popov's driving from Barnard's was the sheer determination the Russian President showed to gain and hold the lead.

'God knows what the ambassador's going to say when I bring the car back to her,' Connally said as he watched the Rolls accelerate away from them, hurling itself over ruts, potholes and fallen branches.

'Has Popov been a rally driver too, Galina?' Barnard asked, doing his damnedest to keep up.

'He's done everything,' Aslanova shouted. 'Try a shortcut here. We can run through the bog. The president won't risk it with the Rolls. Too heavy.'

'So you know this part of the world as well as the president, do you?' Connally asked.

'This isn't the first time I've stayed at the dacha,' Aslanova replied.

Connally pressed her. Too good an opportunity to miss. Personal details were often the most important. She might be a good lead to cultivate for the future. Rumour had it she was going to step up a rank soon in the FSB, so getting close to Aslanova would be a real coup.'

'Are you in a relationship with the president then?' Connally asked.

'What does it look like?' Aslanova laughed. 'But I won't be much longer if Popov loses today, I can tell you. The president doesn't like losing.'

Of course, Popov won. He was already at the border post, standing next to the Rolls with Melissa by his side, when Barnard drove up in the UAZ-469.

Popov beamed. 'Great car, your Rolls Royce! Fantastic race! Mrs Barnard was tremendous. We were bouncing all over the place but she hung on in there. Hate to think what it would be like for someone in the boot!'

The Russian border guards saluted. 'Good afternoon, Mr President.'

Popov mopped the sweat from his brow. 'No formalities, please. These are high-level guests of the Russian Federation. Rolls Royce. CD plates. Whatever.'

They shook hands all round. The president, no longer shirtless, once again kissed Melissa's hand.

Aslanova winked at Barnard. 'All's well that ends well.'

Then she gave him big hug. 'Come back soon,' she said.

The Finnish border guards, tipped off in advance by MI6, waved the Rolls Royce and its cargo through.

Once they were safely on the Finnish side of the border, Barnard got out of the car, followed by his wife. He walked round to the boot. As he did so, Connally pressed the button to raise the lid.

Moments later, a pale and sweating Stephanov staggered out. 'Never been bounced around so much in my life,' he said. 'Not since that evening in the Kempinski anyway!'

They had less than a hundred miles to travel from the border to Helsinki. Stephanov sat up front, next to the driver. The Barnards sat in the back.

The road ran along the coast. 'It's motorway all the way now,' Connally said. 'We take the E18, then join up with the E75 outside Helsinki. You'll be okay to talk if I put some music on. Shall we stick to Sibelius? We had the "Karelia Suite" already. What about "Finlandia"? You can't beat "Finlandia", can you?'

The Rolls Royce Phantom had a brilliant sound system. Since the car retailed at over £300,000, you'd expect a pretty good sound system, thought Barnard. What he didn't expect was to hear Ronald Craig's distinctive voice: *'Are you telling me, General,'* the president was saying, *'that at this moment in time we don't actually know whether President Assad was responsible for gassing those poor innocent kids or not? You're the National Security Adviser. If you don't know, who the hell does?'*

Then they heard the sound of a toilet flushing, and another voice, deeper than the president's but with a southern twang: *'Hang on a moment, sir. I'll be right out.'*

Oh my God, Barnard thought. They're still bugging the president. This is Popov's way of letting us know.

'Shall I turn it off, sir?' Connally asked.

'No, let's hear a bit more,' Barnard replied. 'They must have picked this up last week, when Liu Wang-Ji, the Chinese president, was making a state visit to the Florida White House as they call it: Hasta La Vista. They had to interrupt their dinner, as I understand it, so that the president could go into a huddle with his advisers. Looks like they met in the loo. That's got to be the national security adviser, General Ian Wright.'

'What I mean, sir,' they heard Wright say, against the sound of running water, *'is that it's quite possible that ISIS or Daish or whatever was responsible for the chemical attack, rather than Assad.'*

'Then why the hell am I about to authorize a Tomahawk strike on a Syrian Government Air Base?'

'People will expect you to do something, sir. Provided it's an appropriate and proportionate response, of course.'

Then they heard Craig say, *'Those little kids! Goddammit, I can't stop thinking about them.'*

That evening, while Connally took Stephanov off to the British Embassy in Helsinki for the first debriefing of many, the Barnards had a quiet dinner on the waterfront.

Barnard raised his glass. *'Hyvä terveys!'* he said.

'What does that mean?' Melissa asked.

'It means "good health" in Finnish. Years ago I had a Finnish girlfriend.'

He looked at his wife fondly. They were growing old together. That was how things were meant to be.

'You did brilliantly today, darling,' he said. 'I guess Popov knew we were planning to visit the Karelia transnational biosphere reserve. It was on the schedule. That was our cover for the detour into the forest in case anyone asked. Popov just seized the opportunity for some back-channel diplomacy. Did you talk to him?'

'Of course I talked to him. He's a human being, isn't he, not some kind of ogre?'

'I mean when he was driving. That was tricky terrain.'

'I don't think Popov had any problems,' Melissa said. 'Most of the time he was driving one-handed.'

'What was he doing with his other hand?'

'Had it on my knee. Just for reassurance, of course.'

CHAPTER FORTY-FIVE

Both Wilbur Brown, director of the FBI, and Bud Hollingsworth, director of the CIA, had made time in their busy schedules to respond to the US attorney general's urgent request.

'This came in the post today,' Dirk Goddard, the former Senator for Mississippi explained. 'Brown-paper envelope. Posted in Washington D.C. yesterday.'

They sat round a table in Goddard's office to listen to the tape.

'*Okay guys,*' they heard Craig say. '*This is what we're offering if I'm elected president. Number one, the US is going to drop the current sanctions against Russia, as regards Crimea and the Ukraine. We would hope that NATO will follow us in this, but even if they don't, we will act unilaterally.*

'*Number two: if I'm elected president, the United States will not challenge the deployment by Russia of the ground-based, nuclear-capable 9M729 missiles, even though possession of these missiles is a violation of the terms of the INF . . . Bert, what the hell does INF stand for?*

'*INF means the Intermediate-Range Nuclear Forces Treaty, Ron.*'

'I guess that's Bert Rumbold,' Brown commented. 'Sounds like he's still on six packs a day.'

'*Thanks, Bert,*' they heard Craig say. '*We understand the 9M729s have a range of 620 to 3240 miles. Apparently they hit Syria from the Caspian the other day. So if we agree that their use is compatible with the INF, then Russia can legally hit every capital in Europe. More to the point, perhaps, Russia will be able to blast the living daylights out of every city in China.*

'*Let's take China's build-up in the South China seas. I believe the United States must be ready to go to war with China over these illegal bases. But it would be better still if Russia and the US could take a coordinated approach. We can say to China "Pull back from the Spratlys or the Russians will whack Chengdu or Xian or wherever their 9M729 missiles can reach."* '

'Now we're going to hear the Russian ambassador to Washington, Georgiy Reznikov,' Goddard said.

They listened right to the end of the tape, until they reached Reznikov's damning conclusion.

'*Thank you, gentlemen. This has been a most productive meeting. I can assure you that President Popov will be pleased. In view of what I have heard today I am authorized to tell you that between now and Election Day we will make sure that our cache of emails from the Democratic National Committee, including those from Caroline Mann, the Democratic presidential candidate, is deployed to the fullest possible extent. We further undertake to offer Craig Shipping and Craig Oil the most favourable terms possible as far as their operations in the Russian Arctic are concerned.*'

There was a pause. Then they heard Reznikov say, '*Of course we will, I hope, have further conversations, many further conversations when Ron – may I call you Ron? – is elected. But perhaps our discussions today will do for starters.*'

There was one last intervention from Craig, the presidential candidate. '*Don't forget about my old friend Mickey Selkirk. Selkirk Global is planning a major expansion in Russia. I think he has his eyes on Pravda and Izvestia as well as RT, Russian television!*'

Goddard switched the tape off. 'So my first questions, gentlemen, are: did this conversation really happen and is this an accurate recording?'

He looked at them expectantly. They were the experts; he wasn't.

Hollingsworth raised his hand. 'Hold on a moment, Dirk. Let's assume for a moment this isn't a fake. It's a real recording of a real conversation. What would you say the implications are?'

The attorney general answered without a moment's hesitation. 'Totally massive. Lethal actually.'

'Lethal to whom?' Brown asked.

'To President Craig, of course,' Goddard replied. 'People have tried to argue the contrary, but in my view – and I'm attorney general – there's no presidential immunity for crimes committed before taking office.'

'You're talking about violations of the Logan Act?' Brown said.

'You bet I am,' the attorney general replied. He pulled down a thick, brown volume from a shelf. The page was already marked.

'Listen to this,' he said.

'*Any citizen of the United States, wherever he may be, who, without authority of the United States, directly or indirectly commences or carries on any correspondence or intercourse with any foreign government or any officer or agent thereof, with intent to influence the measures or conduct of any foreign government or of any officer or agent thereof, in relation to any disputes or controversies with the United States, or to defeat the measures of the United States, shall be fined under this title or imprisoned not more than three years, or both.*'

'Now, I'm a supporter of the president,' Goddard continued. 'He appointed me to the high office, which I now hold. But when I took up my job, I solemnly swore to uphold the law and constitution of the United States. So help me God. What we've just heard is a clear violation of the Logan Act.'

'Nobody's ever been prosecuted under the Logan Act, not for the last two hundred years or more,' Hollingsworth said.

'They darn well should have been,' Goddard countered. 'Do you remember, back in 2007, when then-House speaker Lucy Wainwright went to Syria to negotiate with President Bashar al-Assad? Or 2015, when another House speaker, David Draper, invited Israeli Prime Minister Ariel Moses to address Congress without President Matlock's permission? I would have used the Logan Act then, if I'd been attorney general. But that's chickenfeed besides the deal that Craig was trying to set up with the Russians.'

There was a long pause as the two very senior officials tried to digest the full implications of what the attorney general was saying.

Brown shook his head. 'You're a lawyer, Dirk. If you based your case on the evidence of that tape, you'd lose. The president would set the pack on you. They'd ask you where you got the tape. Did the Russians send it to you as their way of signalling that the honeymoon is over? Or if the Chinese sent it, which is another possibility, did they manage to bug the Russian Embassy? The government's lawyers would query its authenticity every which way. They'd argue that it was in any case inadmissible because it must have resulted from an unauthorized surveillance operation, so the court would have to ignore it.'

There was another long pause. Goddard, an honest man, looked truly crestfallen. He had always believed that Washington was indeed a "shining city on a hill" and, if what Brown said was right, he was going to lose the chance to prove it.

'Shall we tell him the good news, Wilbur?' Hollingsworth asked. 'Will you go first? Or shall I?'

'You go first, Wilbur.'

Hollingsworth took out a pen and doodled some stick-figures on the yellow legal pad in front of him.

'Let's take first things first. In my view, the conversation we just heard actually happened and this is an accurate recording. I can say this with total confidence.'

'You mean it rings true?' Goddard asked.

'I mean more than that. I mean it *is* true. We have exactly the same recording ourselves.'

The attorney general looked stunned. 'You're not telling me, after all these denials, you actually bugged Ronald Craig, after all?'

Hollingsworth sighed. 'It's a bit more complicated than that.'

He pushed the pad aside.

'Let me explain,' he continued. 'You may not be familiar, Dirk, with the executive order that President Brandon Matlock signed on 18 May 2016. President Brandon was worried that Ronald Craig's personal security could have been compromised. I've still got the text on my iPhone. Only half a dozen copies of that executive order were ever produced and I was one of the recipients.

'Let me read it out:

'*Whereas it appears to be possible if not probable that Ronald C. Craig may unwittingly have been the target of an unauthorized attack by a hypodermic dart or some other intervention while visiting the Russian Far East . . .*

'*Whereas it is necessary through a clinical examination to establish whether such an attack or intervention has indeed taken place, and to take all appropriate measures . . .*

'*Whereas the implications for national security of the said event need to be fully evaluated . . .*

'*Now therefore: I, President of the United States, have decided and determined that the said Ronald C. Craig should be immediately brought by federal marshals to the Walter Reed Medical Center, Bethesda, Maryland, and that the said federal marshals are authorized to use all necessary means, including force, towards that end. Signed: Brandon Matlock, 44th President of the United States, 18 May 2016.*'

'To cut a long story short,' Hollingsworth went on, 'as soon as that executive order was issued, Craig was picked up in Florida, whisked up to the Walter Reed Medical Center in Maryland and subjected to a clinical examination as specified. We didn't, as a matter of fact, find any evidence of a Russian bug, though we believe that such a bug may still be in place, but not where we were looking.'

'So?' Goddard was looking for some light at the end of the tunnel.

'I want to make it clear,' the Director of the CIA explained, 'that Wilbur and I were determined to act strictly in accordance with the law. The issue here is quite simple. I'll read that paragraph again:

'Whereas it is necessary through a clinical examination to establish whether such an attack or intervention has indeed taken place, and to take all appropriate measures . . ."

'The crucial phrase, of course, is that we had the president's explicit authorization by means of an executive order not just to ensure that Craig was submitted to a clinical examination but to *"take all appropriate measures."'*

'I still don't see how that helps us get the tape we just listened to into evidence before a court,' the attorney general said.

'Oh ye of little faith,' Hollingsworth sighed. 'Wilbur and I have heard every word of that conversation before. We have listened to it a dozen times, if we've listened to it once. How did we do that? Well, while looking for the Russian bug, we planted a bug of our own in Ronald Craig's posterior. I can tell you that our recording of that fateful conversation repeats word for word, phrase for phrase, the text we heard earlier.

'The vital point is that while the tape you just played us would not be admitted in evidence, our own tape, properly sworn and notarized, undoubtedly will be *since it was authorized under a specific presidential executive order.'*

'Mah, oh mah!' The former senator's Mississippi drawl was working overtime. 'You two ole boys really have got it all worked out.'

Goddard rose to his feet. What was he going to do? He had surely come to a fork in the road. Which path should he take? How did that poem go? *The one less travelled by?*

'I'll let you know my decision,' he said.

A last thought occurred to him. 'So basically you're telling me that the 45th president of the United States is at this very moment walking around with three bugs implanted on his person, like a goddamn pincushion? The Russians put one on him, though not where we originally thought. We've put one on him, on his backside if I understand correctly.'

'The left buttock actually,' Brown said.

'And where is the Chinese bug?'

'We don't know for sure. Probably the right buttock, but that's just a guess.'

'You mean he's literally talking through his ass?' the attorney general asked. 'How long will they go on transmitting, these bugs? 'Till the next election?'

'Negative,' Brown replied. 'All these systems use solar radiation. Subcutaneous insertion, which is what we have here, means that they have to rely on the initial battery charge without any recharge being possible. Realistically I would say that all three bugs must be approaching the end of their useful life.'

'Let's be grateful for small mercies,' Goddard said.

With Southern courtesy, the attorney general escorted them to his private elevator. 'Thank you, gentlemen, very much for stopping by today. I'll be in touch.'

On the way down, Brown asked: 'Would a criminal conviction under the Logan Act lead to impeachment? Impeachment, as we know from experience, can be a long process and is seldom successful. You have to have a majority vote in the House and a two-thirds vote in the Senate.'

'A criminal conviction would be enough to force him to step down,' Hollingsworth replied. 'But I'm sure there would be a lot of people, Goddard included, who would be ready to launch a formal impeachment process if the president looked as though he wanted to cling to office.'

'What does all this make us, Bud?' Brown asked. 'Co-conspirators?'

'Patriots. It makes us patriots,' Hollingsworth countered. 'That wasn't one of his aides, or potential Cabinet nominees, trying to do a shady deal with the Russians, a deal with immense geopolitical implications. That was the man himself. Negotiating with a foreign power with no authority to do so. If ever there was a time to invoke the Logan Act, this is that time. The man crossed a red line, Wilbur. That's all there is to it.'

'What if Craig knew all along he was being bugged?' Brown asked. 'Knew we planted one on him ourselves, quite apart from any devices the Russians or the Chinese might have succeeded in installing. He might be testing our loyalty. He really might. And then we would look stupid.'

Hollingsworth laughed. 'You're getting carried away by your imagination.'

There was a lengthy pause as they each thought about what had just been said.

Then the two men looked at each other. They weren't laughing any more.

'The President could terminate us overnight,' Hollingsworth said.

'Overnight?' Brown countered. 'You must be joking! He'd fire us without notice or warning of any kind. We'd probably see it on the news first.'

The Director of the FBI shuddered. Deep down, he knew he'd probably handed the election to Ronald Craig, back in the fall of 2016 when, with just days to go, he reopened the inquiry into Caroline Mann's emails. But that fact by itself wouldn't necessarily save him. Not with a man as ruthless as Craig. How did the old saying go? No good deed goes unpunished!

CHAPTER FORTY-SIX

After all the excitement of that mad dash to Helsinki, Melissa Barnard decided to have a quiet weekend with her daughter, Fiona, and her partner, Michael.

They lived in a whitewashed fisherman's house set above the harbour in a small village called Goleen on the south-west coast of Ireland. On the Saturday they went to the pub for lunch.

It was a bright, sunny day, warm enough to eat outside. They were sitting there, at the table, while the seagulls swooped overhead, when a motor-boat came round the headland and made for the quay.

They recognized Jack Varese, of course. The whole world could recognize Jack Varese. The young woman with him, Melissa realized, was Rosie Craig.

Melissa rose. 'Good heavens!' she exclaimed. 'Can I introduce myself? I'm Melissa Barnard, Edward Barnard's wife. This is my daughter, Fiona, and this is her partner, Michael Kennedy. What are you two doing here?'

'The same as you, I imagine.' Jack smiled. 'Looking for a quiet weekend before World War III breaks out. Rosie's father's just been firing missiles at Syria, he's thinking about bombing North Korea and we're all wondering whether the Russians or the Chinese will retaliate. How's Edward? I haven't seen him since he got bitten by a spider in Australia. Has he recovered? Do you mind if we join you?'

'Things were getting pretty hot in Washington,' Rosie explained as they sat there in the sun. 'Quite apart from the geopolitics, I'm in the middle of a turf war with Bert Rumbold, so I said to Jack, "Let's get the hell out of here". We just flew over in Jack's plane and parked it at Shannon. We're staying at a hotel down the coast. They suggested we pop up here for lunch. Lent us the boat, so here we are!'

What a charming young woman she was, Melissa thought. Yet there was an inner steel there, too, by all accounts. Before coming to Washington, she had run a multi-billion dollar retail empire, and you needed more than a pretty face to do that.

Rosie was fascinated to learn about Michael's work.

'I grew up here,' Michael explained. 'Went to Trinity, Dublin, and then worked as an international maritime lawyer in London before coming back to Ireland.' He waved his hand at the little harbour. 'With the internet, you can work anywhere nowadays. This is heaven on earth. Mind you, I travel a lot. I'm going to be in Yellowknife next week. We're trying to push through some new international rules to protect the Arctic. It's a free-for-all at the moment and as the Arctic opens up with global warming, it's going to get worse.'

Michael couldn't have found a better audience.

'I've a personal stake in this,' he told them. 'Back in 1979, my father died in the Whiddy Island disaster, not far from here. An oil-tanker caught fire and exploded. He was on it. I was a kid at the time. Better rules could have prevented that accident. Forty years on, we still haven't got the standards we need.'

Jack chipped in. 'Watch this space,' he said. 'Rosie's going to win her battle back in Washington and a lot of the things you care about are going to happen.'

'My father will listen to me.' Rosie replied. 'I know that. But there are other ways of getting to him, too.'

With that cryptic message, the golden couple jumped into their boat and chuntered back up the coast.

'Pity Rosie didn't run for office instead of her dad,' Michael said. He was clearly smitten. They all were.

Melissa followed through on Michael's line of thought.

'Maybe she *will* run for office one day,' she speculated. 'If the US president for some reason has to stand down, doesn't the vice-president succeed? That would leave a vacancy. Rosie could step in there as vice-president, then next time round she could stand in her own right. Finally, a woman president!'

'But why would the president step down?' Fiona asked. 'He's only just been elected.'

CHAPTER FORTY-SEVEN

Mabel Killick was sitting in her study in Number 10 Downing Street with her two closest aides, Mortimer and Percy. They had moved with her from the Home Office when she succeeded Hartley as PM in the aftermath of the Referendum. What an extraordinary turn of events that had been, she reflected. First, David Boles, the justice minister, ruthlessly assassinates his fellow Leave campaigner, Harry Stokes. Then he plunges the dagger into his own breast, leaving Andromeda Ledbury as the only possible rival. Well, Mickey Selkirk soon did for Andromeda Ledbury, the PM reflected. Maybe Ledbury had been too trusting. She had confided some of her most personal thoughts to that clever-clever duo, Molly and Tanya, from *Selkirk News*, only to see those thoughts splashed across the front page next day!

'Bad luck, Andromeda,' she thought. Best keep your gob shut. But good luck, too, since Ledbury's withdrawal from the race meant she, Mabel Killick, veteran home secretary, was the last one standing when the music stopped.

Good old Mickey Selkirk, she thought, setting those two young newshounds on Ledbury like that. Hand on heart, she hadn't had much to do with Selkirk before the Referendum. She hadn't had much to do with the Leave campaign at all. She had been a Remainer then, a 'shy' Remainer as they called it. She hadn't played a big part in the campaign. But she was an out-and-Out Brexiteer now. Last October, when she had only been prime minister for a few weeks,

281

she had told the Conservative Party Conference in Birmingham that 'Brexit means Brexit' and, by golly, was she going to deliver.

'Quite soon it will be a year since we moved in here,' she said to Mortimer and Percy. 'We ought to have a celebration when the time comes.'

'I'll put the champagne in the fridge,' Mortimer said. He would be even more handsome, Killick thought, without that great black beard.

The two aides glanced at each other. The PM obviously had something on her mind.

In the good old days, you could fiddle around finding the cigarette packet and a match or a lighter, then take a reflective puff or two, before coming to the point. But now they had banned smoking in offices and that applied to Number 10 as well. So Killick took the plunge without faffing around on the diving-board.

'Remember that COBRA meeting I chaired?' she began. 'The one I set up to discuss the so-called Referendum dossier Edward Barnard brought back from Russia?'

The two aides nodded.

'Of course we remember, Prime Minister,' Mortimer said. He glanced at his colleague. 'As a matter of fact, Holly and I have sometimes wondered whatever happened to the enquiry you set up. I imagine Dame Jane Porter, the head of MI5, reported to you but we weren't invited to that meeting, as I recall.'

There was a hint of reproof in Mortimer's voice as though he felt disappointed, if not actually wounded, to have been excluded for such a key encounter.

'You can't be everywhere, Giles,' the PM said sharply. 'Though I know you think you ought to be. But you're right,' she continued, 'Dame Jane did report to me. She said that the documents in the dossier were authentic. The narrative they portrayed was what actually happened: the run-up to the PM's Bloomberg speech, the PM's manuscript additions to the manifesto, late in the day, indicating his personal commitment to the Referendum. Those were all genuine, verifiable documents.'

'What about the cash for policy aspect?' Percy asked. 'I remember there was stuff in the dossier about huge cash transfers into Conservative Party funds in exchange for the Referendum commitment. Ten or twelve million pounds, as I recall. Were those documents genuine, too? That was lethal, surely?'

Killick kicked her shoes off (why did the press have such a fixation with her shoes?) and tucked her long, shapely legs beneath her on the sofa.

'Please don't imagine I wasn't aware of the implications,' she said. 'But remember the timing, too. We were days away from one of the most important votes in this country's history.'

'Prime Minister, I think you should be very careful about how you handle this one. You could lay yourself open to all kinds of accusations.' If Mortimer sounded portentous, he meant to. 'From what you have just said, it sounds as though you were complicit in covering up a crime, or at the very least in failing to report your suspicions.'

Killick sighed.

'I had it out with Jeremy Hartley the day after the vote,' she said. 'He had gone out into Downing Street that morning to announce to all the journalists that he had lost and that he was going to step down. But as you recall, he was pretty vague about the timing. It sounded as though he wanted to stay on at least until the party conference in October. So I said to myself: "This won't do. This won't do at all". I asked to see him urgently at No. 10. Remember, I knew about the Referendum dossier, but the PM didn't know I knew. We met privately in this very room. I told him that the experts were convinced that every single document in the dossier was genuine, and that included the additions in his own handwriting to the draft of his Bloomberg speech, back in January 2013, when he wrote: "That is why I am in favour of a referendum".'

'What about the money?' Mortimer asked. 'What did he say about the money?'

'I told him we hadn't been able to trace the £10 million or £12 million paid by persons unknown in exchange for this referendum commitment. We suspected it came from Russia but we couldn't be sure. But the fact we couldn't trace it didn't mean the transaction never occurred. We were confident the Crown Prosecution Service would take the same view.'

'Oh my God!' Percy exclaimed. 'That must have been some meeting. There's Hartley trying to adjust to the most humiliating defeat in his political career and you're sitting there, threatening to put him behind bars. What did he say? Did he make a clean breast of it?'

'On the contrary, he insisted he never asked anyone for money and no money was ever paid,' she said. 'The record of those financial exchanges was a crucial part of the Referendum dossier, but they were faked, in the sense that even though the correspondence bore his signature, no money ever changed hands.'

For the next few minutes, Killick explained to her two aides Jeremy Harley's motivation, as far as she understood it: how at heart he had always been a Leaver, how he needed to persuade Edward Barnard to lead the Leave campaign, and how the dossier was a crucial part of that.

'As I say, Hartley strenuously denied receiving any money for the Conservative Party,' Killick continued, 'but he undoubtedly passed the dossier to the Russians so that they in turn could give it to Barnard. A brilliant move, actually, in terms of human psychology. Hartley read his man perfectly and recruited him without Barnard ever realizing what was happening. If Hartley hadn't gone into politics, he could have joined MI6.'

'Not too late, I imagine,' Mortimer said. 'I hear he's looking for a job.'

They all laughed. 'Let's have some champagne now, anyway,' the PM said.

Percy's eye fell on the PM's copy of the Brexit dossier. 'I'm not sure you ought still to have that, Prime Minister. That's a numbered copy. We all turned our copies in after that COBRA meeting. That's the instruction you gave us at the time.'

Percy put out a hand to pick up the file. 'Please leave it, Holly. I think I'll take it home tonight and store it in my scarf drawer. Might come in handy one day.'

There was mischievous look in the PM's eye which Percy had never noticed before.

'Imagine our negotiations with our EU partners go terribly wrong,' the prime minister speculated, 'and we don't get the deal we're hoping for. Imagine that we face the prospect of being confronted by tariff and non-tariff barriers on all sides and at every turn. Imagine that the City of London is going into meltdown as key firms shift to Brussels, Frankfurt or Paris with all the implications that has for the tax base. Imagine that the United Kingdom itself looks like going down the drain because the Scots prefer to stay in Europe and maybe Northern Ireland prefers to throw its lot in with the south, rather than face all the turmoil a new hard border between Northern Ireland and Eire would create.'

Her two aides nodded their heads in unison. 'Yes, Prime Minister, we are imagining all that.'

'Well, then?' the PM challenged, 'what would we do?'

Mortimer fell back on the standard response, beloved of politicians throughout the ages.

'Well, obviously, we're not going to answer hypothetical questions.'

'Oh, come now, Giles,' the PM reprimanded him. 'You're not on *University Challenge*. Do you need a few minutes to think about it? Shall I go and put the kettle on?'

The PM's sarcasm was palpable.

Mortimer was beginning to see what the prime minister was getting at.

'What you're saying, Prime Minister, is that it's possible this whole Brexit business may be a total cock-up and there really isn't any good option out there for us, there are no broad sunlit uplands waiting for us, and if that situation does arise, say eighteen months from now, we may just conceivably want to reconsider our decision to leave the European Union.'

Killick nodded. 'Something along those lines, perhaps.'

Mortimer shook his head. 'But that won't work, Prime Minister, I can assure you. Parliament will never vote to withdraw our application to leave the European Union without a mandate, without the clear instruction of the people, and that would mean a second Referendum. And you've already ruled out a second Referendum. Categorically.'

Killick was not to be deterred.

'Just imagine,' she said, 'that the Electoral Commission had sight of that Brexit dossier. Over in the United States half a dozen committees of enquiry are looking into possible interference with the electoral process in the run-up to last year's presidential election. If the Americans can raise all these issues, then why can't we? I am sure the Electoral Commission, once fully apprised of the situation, would feel it had to look into the conduct of last year's Referendum, and then who knows what might happen? Or what about some brilliantly enterprising individual, like Tina Moller, for instance, who won such a victory in the Supreme Court last year over Article 50? Damn nuisance, from our point of view. But you have to hand it to her – she had us running for cover. Imagine the situation if the redoubtable Tina Moller gets hold of that Referendum dossier and goes back to the Supreme Court to ask them to declare the first Referendum null and void.

'Which way do you think the Supreme Court would rule? Don't you think they might order, not a second Referendum, but a *re-run* of the first? I'd put money on it.'

The two aides were gobsmacked. They had long admired Killick's nifty footwork, with or without the kitten heels. But this was something else again.

Percy raised the obvious objection. 'But how on earth would the Electoral Commission or some Tina-Moller figure ever get to hear about the existence of the dossier? After all, there's only one copy left in circulation and you're taking it home with you, to hide in your scarf drawer.'

'How would Tina Moller ever get to hear about the Referendum dossier?' the PM mused. 'Well, I suppose someone would have to tell her. Or else there could be a break-in at my home. We'd have to make sure the police weren't on duty. We do have break-ins, you know, from time to time, even in leafy Surrey.'

As her aides made ready to leave, Killick asked Percy to stay behind for a second.

'My scarves are in the chest of drawers in the dressing room,' she said. 'Third drawer down.'

Percy made a note on her pad. 'Scarves. Third drawer down.'

CHAPTER FORTY-EIGHT

It wasn't President Igor Popov's first visit to Australia. He had been to Sydney in 2005 and Brisbane in 2014. But that had been official G20 business. They might have kicked Russia out of the G8, but they could hardly expel her from the G20.

But this visit, in the early summer of 2017 (late autumn 'down under'), was different. Popov was on holiday. He flew into Kununurra in Western Australia in the presidential plane, the sleek, dark Ilyushin Il-96, with Galina Aslanova in the co-pilot's seat.

'I've sacked Pavel Golov. Useless fuck,' Popov had told her on their way south. 'Golov couldn't see what was going on in St Petersburg. It wasn't just our good friend Fyodor Stephanov. The FSB office there was rotten through and through. As the new director of the FSB, you'll have to clear things up there. That will be one of your first priorities. Still, a few days' break won't hurt either of us.'

Mickey Selkirk had sent a helicopter to Kununurra airport.

When Popov and Aslanova landed at the Lazy-T ranch thirty minutes later, both Mickey and Melanie Selkirk came out to the helipad to meet them. The Selkirks had invited plenty of distinguished guests to the Lazy-T ranch in their time, but it wasn't every day they entertained the president of the Russian Federation.

'Please don't keep calling me "Mr President",' Popov insisted, as they sat down to dinner that evening beneath the stars. 'I'm here as a private citizen. We're on holiday.'

He leant forward to sniff the aroma of the fine, red wine the Selkirks were serving that night.

'What is it?' he asked.

'It's a Grange Hermitage, 1952, the year you were born. Penfold's vineyard, just outside Adelaide. One of the oldest wineries in the country. Your good health!' Selkirk raised his glass.

He had really pushed the boat out that evening. If you were lucky enough to find one, a 1952 Grange Hermitage would cost you at auction around AUS$16,000, that was about US$14,500. But, hell, Selkirk thought, better hung for a sheep than a lamb.

He drained his glass.

'Igor,' he began, taking Popov at his word, 'I can't tell you how glad Melanie and I are to welcome you and Galina to our humble home. We've only got a million acres here at Lazy-T and I know that's nothing when you consider the size of your vast country. But still it's a real privilege to have you both here as our guests. Tomorrow we are going to do some mustering. Can you fly an R22?'

'I can fly anything!' Popov said.

He, too, drained his glass. Selkirk's Chinese manservant, Ching Ze-Gong, refilled it. At this rate, he reckoned, he'd have to open a second bottle even before the main course had been served. Selkirk must really want something from this guy, he thought. He made sure he kept as close to the table as he could.

Selkirk, he noticed, had been a bit cool since his return from New York to the Lazy-T ranch.

'I gather the police paid you a visit while I was gone,' his boss had said. 'Anything I need to know?'

'Just checking papers, sir,' Ching had replied. 'All in order. Illegal immigrants – big problem now.'

'You can say that again,' Selkirk said. 'Ron Craig's building a wall to keep them out. Like the Great Wall of China. You guys thought of it first, didn't you?'

Truth to tell, both Ching and Fung had been alarmed by that visit from the constabulary. It was clear the authorities were looking for something, but whatever it was they didn't find it.

Since then, things had settled down nicely. He was still filing his reports to Hu Wong-Fu, the owner of the Kimberley Asian Cuisine restaurant in Kununurra. There might be something to report on tonight, he thought.

Ching was right about that.

'We've got elections next year,' Popov said, as Ching served the dessert. 'I'm thinking about whether to stand again for president of the Russian Federation. Maybe the time has come to make way for a younger man. I've been around a long time.'

'Oh, come on! Born in 1952. You're just a stripling!' Selkirk protested.

The old man was suddenly serious.

'The reason I invited you down here this weekend, Igor,' he said, 'is because I've got a proposition to put to you. I don't want to influence your decision about your political future. That's entirely your business, but if you *did* decide to step down at or even before the end of your current term of office, I would like you to consider taking over from me as president of Selkirk Global. With you as the leader and inspiration, Selkirk Global will span the world. I hope you will think about it, at least.'

Popov had already thought about it, of course. As soon as he had received Selkirk's invitation, he had guessed what the old man had in mind. The Russian economy nowadays was about the same size as California's. Being president of Russia wasn't really such a big deal.

To run Selkirk Global, with a whole world still to conquer, that was something else again. He could take over the BBC for starters.

'Yes, I'll definitely think about it,' President Popov said.

*   *   *

Next day, while Selkirk, game as ever, took his guests on a five-mile hike up the rugged Kimberley Gorge, with the Pentecost River cascading through the rocks, Popov reported for duty at the helipad.

Jim Jackson, the pilot on duty that morning, was already waiting for him. Two R22s were parked side-by-side, ready to go.

Jim pointed to the nearest machine. 'This one's yours,' he said. 'Jack Varese flew it when he was here. The left skid's a bit bent. He was using the skids to herd the cattle. But it's quite safe.'

Popov gazed admiringly at the little R22 helicopter. 'I've herded reindeer in Siberia with one of these,' he said. 'Piece of cake.'

The mustering went well. Popov had seldom enjoyed himself more. He nipped in and out of the trees, turning the cattle this way and that, until he had massed a bunch and they really started to move, throwing up clouds of dust.

'This is the life,' Popov thought. If he took up Selkirk's offer of the top job at Selkirk Global, maybe he'd move the headquarters back to Australia from New York. That would be one in the eye for the Yanks. And the Aussies would love it.

They brought upwards of a thousand head to the holding area, and were going back for more, when Jim received a message on the RT.

'The old man has slipped on some rocks five miles up the gorge,' he told Popov. 'Hurt his leg. He can't walk. We'll have to pick him up. Could be tricky. The gorge is steep and narrow and there can be a hell of a wind. Depends where he is, but in some places you've only got a few feet clearance on either side, so you've got to keep dead centre otherwise you're done for.'

They took off together, flying about 1,000 feet above ground level. Below them they could see the gorge and the foaming river.

'There they are!' Jim caught sight of Selkirk's party far below, waving hats and handkerchiefs.

'Why don't you hover here?' Jim said. 'Call into base and tell them what's happening. I'll go down. Looks pretty tight but I think I'll make it.'

'No, I'll go,' Popov said.

Before Jim could countermand him, Popov dropped into the sheer chasm. Jim was bloody right, he thought. There were, literally, only inches to spare at either side and the wind was totally unpredictable. Blowing a blast one minute, and then dropping completely. If the rotor blade clipped the rocks, that would be it. Kaput. Finito. Game over.

Sweating with concentration, Popov landed by a rock pool. He left the rotors turning.

'Room for one,' he shouted. 'The rest will have to hike back.'

Selkirk tried to put some weight on his leg, but couldn't manage it, so they manhandled him on board.

'Thanks, Igor!' he shouted above the noise of the engine. 'You've saved my bacon.'

Getting out of the gorge was as hard as getting in. Popov gritted his teeth, hand on the joy-stick, eyes gauging the distance between the heli's blades and the jagged rock face.

'Great piece of flying,' Jim congratulated him over the RT as Popov's little heli finally emerged from the deep chasm, like Venus rising from the waves.

That evening, they switched to Margaret River wines. 'Western Australia's finest,' Selkirk assured his guests.

Melanie tactfully took Aslanova for a post-prandial coffee by the pool.

'Can't tell you how grateful I am, old boy,' Selkirk said, when the two men were alone.

He kneaded his bandaged knee. 'I'm not sure how I would have gotten out of there. That's a rugged climb at the best of times, even with two sound legs to walk on. How you managed not to smash into the sides of that gorge, I will never know.'

Selkirk paused. He thought about his father, that great man – yes, that great Australian – who had first sown the seeds of the Selkirk empire. Of course he could pass the whole thing on to his own kids, but did they really have what it took? Selkirk Global had the chance to make a quantum leap into the future. Igor Popov was the man to make that future happen.

'Did you think about what I said last night?' Selkirk asked.

Popov took his time. Historians would later describe the moment as one of the most important moments in his life. The moment of decision. So much would turn on it.

'It's a very interesting proposition, Mickey,' he said. 'Very interesting indeed. And very timely, too.'

He pointed to the big TV screen above the bar.

'Look at that!' he exclaimed. 'I do believe the British prime minister is about to call a general election in the UK, three years ahead of time.'

'Good heavens!' Selkirk exclaimed. 'Hasn't she already got a mandate?'

'Hardly a working majority,' Popov said. 'Just listen to her speech.'

'You've seen it already? You know what she's going to say?'

Popov laughed. 'Come on, Mickey! What kind of a show do you think I'm running?'

The two men took their drinks inside to watch the British prime minister, standing on the pavement outside Number 10 Downing Street, at that very moment about to make the most important announcement of her career.

There was obviously a bit of a wind in London that morning. The prime minister's hair from time to time blew across her forehead but she brushed it back.

'*I have just chaired a meeting of the Cabinet,*' the prime minister began, '*where we agreed that the government should call a general election, to be held on 8 June.*

'I want to explain the reasons for that decision. What will happen next, and the choice facing the British people when you come to vote in this election.

'Last summer, after the country voted to leave the European Union, Britain needed certainty, stability and strong leadership, and since I became prime minister the government has delivered precisely that.

'Britain is leaving the European Union and there can be no turning back.'

Selkirk noticed that Popov had been following a script on his mobile phone all the time the PM was speaking.

Popov nodded, evidently pleased that there were no departures from the CHECK ON DELIVERY text he had in front of him.

Killick was coming to the end:

'The Liberal Democrats have said they want to grind the business of government to a standstill.

'The Scottish National Party says they will vote against the legislation that formally repeals Britain's membership of the European Union.

'And unelected members of the House of Lords have vowed to fight us every step of the way.

'Our opponents believe that because the government's majority is so small, our resolve will weaken and that they can force us to change course.

'They are wrong.

'They underestimate our determination to get the job done and I am not prepared to let them endanger the security of millions of working people across the country.

'Because what they are doing jeopardises the work we must do to prepare for Brexit at home, and it weakens the government's negotiating position in Europe.

'That is why I am calling for a general election on 8 June.'

When the PM had finished, Popov put his phone away, smiling with satisfaction. 'Word perfect. Couldn't have put it better myself,' he said.

Popov was in a reflective mood. 'We may have thought Brexit was in the bag last June, Mickey, but we still needed to nail it. And that's what Mabel Killick has done today. Of course, I will give her all the help she needs. I expect you will, too.'

Ching was puzzled. His instructions had been very clear. 'If Popov refuses Selkirk's offer, use spider. If he accepts offer, leave spider in box.'

Oh dear, Ching thought, what should he do? The instructions might have been precise, but the problem was he couldn't work out what answer Popov was actually giving in response to Selkirk's intriguing proposal.

When Selkirk had offered him the job of president and CEO of Selkirk Global, Popov had just said, 'Interesting. Very interesting indeed.'

But what did that mean? Did it mean 'yes', or did it mean 'no'?

Ching took the little wooden box from the crate in the storeroom and shook it gently. Yes, the spider was still there. Just as well they had given him two, he thought.

CHAPTER FORTY-NINE

Killick was pleased by the slant the media put on her decision to call an election. 'Strong and stable PM seeks personal mandate!' The *Daily News* thundered. The *London Echo* printed a full-page photo of the PM with the caption '*The New Iron Lady!*' The *Selkirk Press* went to town, offering unsubtle suggestions about the priorities she should pursue, apart from clinching Brexit. 'Slash foreign aid' and 'Scrap environmental burdens' being two of the most prominent.

Fred Malkin, as Conservative Party chairman, had been one of the very small group of people who knew in advance about Killick's decision to call for a general election. He and his team would have a crucial job over the next few weeks before the vote on 8 June.

The day after her Downing Street announcement, Killick visited Conservative Party headquarters in Matthew Parker Street, Westminster, to rally the troops.

Ushered into a first-floor canteen by Malkin, she told a cheering crowd of party workers, 'We can't take victory for granted. The leader of the opposition – what's his name? – anyway, that miserable little worm – may dredge up some support somewhere. It will be our job to force him back into the gutter where he belongs.'

Later, she had a quiet word with Malkin in his office.

'I know I took most people by surprise, Fred,' she said, 'calling the election when I did. That must have thrown out your financial calculations. How is the party off for funds? Do we have enough money to fight the election? I'm told that the Labour election war-chest is pretty full with all the new members they pulled in last year, and the same goes for the Lib Dems. How are *we* going to find the money? Apparently we need an extra £10 million at least just to get to the starting line.'

Malkin pulled a face. 'Well, I agree. We hadn't been planning on a 2017 election. We were going to build up a fighting fund for 2020, three years from now, when – under the Fixed Term Parliament Act – the election should have been called.'

'So what are we going to do? Put out a special appeal?' Killick asked.

'I'm not sure that is going to work, Prime Minister,' Malkin replied. 'There are a lot of people out there who don't seem to be as keen on having this election as you are. They seem to think they've had enough elections to be getting on with. I'm not sure how we are going to raise the funds.'

Killick hadn't studied the Referendum dossier for nothing. She well remembered the message that Jeremy Hartley's office had sent to Malkin when they were discussing how much the onservative Party would need to be paid if the prime minister promised to call a Referendum on Europe:

'*PM is prepared to settle for latest proposal, so we will aim to include appropriate reference in Bloomberg speech. Our friends are talking in terms of 10, possibly 12 M.*'

'What about the funds President Popov is alleged to have sent the Conservative Party?' Killick asked.

Malkin sighed. 'Let's be clear about this. As far as Jeremy Hartley was concerned, the exchanges he and I had about possible "cash for policy" donations to Conservative Party funds were totally ficti-tious. We included those exchanges in the Referendum dossier as part of the wider strategy of getting Edward Barnard on board as the chairman of the Leave campaign.'

'Okay, I accept that Jeremy Hartley is totally in the clear,' Killick replied, 'but what about *you*, Fred, in your role as party chairman? You didn't by any chance spot an opportunity to do a bit of freelance fund-raising for the Conservative Party? Set money aside for a rainy day? Like an early election, perhaps?'

'Good heavens, Prime Minister!' Malkin exclaimed. 'How could you suggest such a thing?'

CHAPTER FIFTY

Friday, 9 June 2017, 3:00A.M. Moscow time.

Igor Popov, president of the Russian Federation, and Galina Aslanova, newly appointed Director of the FSB, sat side by side on the sofa watching television in the den of the president's dacha outside Moscow. Though it was well after midnight, neither had the slightest intention of going to bed. The news that night was simply too riveting.

Over in London, Nancy Ginsberg was assessing the results of the UK general election where the polls had closed just hours earlier.

'Though all the votes have not yet been counted, Prime Minister Mabel Killick's election gamble looks to have backfired,' she said. 'It seems clear that the Conservatives' hope of a landslide victory, or even a substantially increased majority, have evaporated, leaving the party scrabbling to hold on to power. Though the Conservatives are set to emerge as the largest party, the UK is heading for a hung parliament with no single party having an overall majority.'

'What does she mean by "hung parliament?"' Popov asked. 'Who are they going to hang?'

'They'll probably want to hang Mrs Killick,' Aslanova said. 'They may not do it straight away, but sooner or later the knives will come out.'

'And will Miles Pomfrey, the Labour leader, take over? He seems to have done much better than expected,' Popov asked.

'Not necessarily,' Aslanova replied. 'There may have to be

another election later in the year, but for the time being it looks as though Mrs Killick will try to cling on to power.'

Popov poured himself another glass of Glenmorangie. 'You know, Galina, I rather like what I'm hearing. Of course, I would have preferred Mrs Killick to win. Achieving Brexit was one of the main goals of Operation Tectonic Plate, as we know, and she was very determined to do it. But there are different ways of skinning a cat.'

He walked across the room and took down one of the hunting rifles from the rack on the wall. Raising the rifle to his shoulder, he took aim at the priceless Gobelin tapestry, which hung over the hearth. He pulled the trigger and loosed off an imaginary round.

'The exit wound often causes the most damage, doesn't it? Last night's election results in Britain, as I understand them, will help us ensure that the Brexit process does indeed cause the maximum possible damage. Remainers, like Tom Milbourne, the former chancellor of the exchequer, will be encouraged by last night's ambiguous election results to put a spoke in the Brexit wheel whenever they can. That is fine by me. The chaos and confusion will last for months, if not for years, and it will not be limited to Britain. Europe will be thrown into turmoil, too.'

While Popov had been speaking, Aslanova's mood had sensibly lightened. She had been worried that Popov would be angry that his crucial Brexit scheme had, momentarily at least, been thrown into doubt. But the reverse seemed to be the case.

'Do we have any preferred candidates as possible successors to Mabel Killick?' Popov mused. 'What about our friend Edward Barnard? He's a safe pair of hands, surely. Much cleverer than he lets on. I think he knew right from the start I never darted that tiger. Or what about Harry Stokes? That would be fun!'

Popov pointed the remote at the TV to switch channels.

If 8 June had been a big day in Britain, with its startling general election, it had been a big day in the United States, too.

The huge TV on the oak table beside the fire showed Jack Varese addressing a rally in Pittsburgh, with Eddie Turner, Pittsburgh's Mayor, standing next to him.

'President Craig,' Jack's voice boomed across the crowd, 'has just pulled out of the vital Paris Agreement on Global Warming. He says he was elected to represent the people of Pittsburgh, not Paris. But Eddie here tells me the people of Pittsburgh want to stick to the Global Warming Treaty, not torpedo it. Is that right, Eddie?'

When the Mayor shouted, 'Darn right!' the crowd erupted in approval.

'Well, we're going to impeach him, aren't we, for endangering the planet?' Jack shouted.

The crowd erupted again. 'Lock him up! Lock him up!'

'That won't make any difference,' Popov commented as he watched the screen. 'Craig's not going to listen to Jack Varese or Eddie Turner.'

'What about Rosie Craig? Won't he listen to his daughter?' Aslanova said.

Popov shook his head. 'There's too much at stake. Craig wants an ice-free Arctic as much as we do.'

While Jack worked up a head of steam sufficient to drive a small turbine, Popov switched channels again.

CBS's Eric Longhurst was commenting on developments, not in Pittsburgh, but in Washington. 'At a hearing that riveted Washington and millions across America, FBI Director Wilbur Brown branded President Craig a liar. He said he believed he had been sacked because of the FBI's investigation into Moscow's meddling in last year's presidential election. Brown's explosive testimony lasted over three hours.'

Popov turned the TV off. 'Pah! Fake News! God, how I hate it!' he exclaimed. 'They'll be writing Fake Books next!'

CHAPTER FIFTY-ONE

The large Amur tiger lazed in the sun on the banks of the Ussuri River. From time to time he raised his head and licked his balls. Just to check they were still there. They hadn't seen much action recently. Female tigers on the Chinese side of the frontier seemed to be few and far between. He looked upstream, then he looked downstream, then – to be sure – he looked upstream again. The coast seemed to be clear.

The tiger got to his feet, sticking his hindquarters into the air first, then pushing up on his front paws. He ambled down to the river and sniffed at the water. At this time of year, the flow in the Ussuri was sluggish, but still it was cool and refreshing. He would enjoy the swim. And there would be more females, too, on the Russian side. That was obvious. It wasn't just the grass that was greener the other side of the river.

Later that day, Jang Ling-Go, director of Forestry and Wildlife in China's Heilongjiang Province, received a message from one of the rangers. 'Amur tiger seen crossing Ussuri into Russia at 11A.M. today. This is visual sighting, but please check with GPS, too.'

Jang Ling-Go switched on the bio-monitoring tracking system.

Within seconds he had picked up the slow-moving pulsing blip that denoted the Amur tiger 127's progress as it left the river and headed back into the immense birch forest of Russia's Far East.

The steady pace of the moving dot indicated that this was a tiger with a very clear idea of where he wanted to go.

CAST OF CHARACTERS

UNITED STATES OF AMERICA

Ronald C. Craig: *Republican Presidential candidate and later US President*

Brandon Matlock: *US President (outgoing)*

Caroline Mann: *Democratic Presidential candidate*

Rosie Craig: *Ronald Craig's daughter*

Malvina Craig: *Ronald Craig's wife*

Dirk Goddard: *Former Senator for Mississippi; later Attorney General*

Bert Rumbold: *Ronald Craig's Campaign Director*

Bud Hollingsworth: *Director of the CIA*

Wilbur Brown: *Director of the FBI*

John Hulley: *CIA boffin*

Jo Silcock: *Attorney General*

General Ian Wright: *National Security Adviser*

Julius Lomax: *Former US Congressman*

Sandra Lomax: *Wife of of Julius Lomax, aide to Caroline Mann*

Gina Paulson: *Vixen TV*

Eric Longhurst: *CBS*

Bill Whitelaw: *Congressman*

Larry Kinder: *Senator*

Pedro Gonzales: *Federal Marshal in Florida*

Jimmy Redmond: *Ditto*

Elmore Singer: *Senator and vice-presidential candidate*

Georgiy Reznikov: *Russian Ambassador in Washington*

Jack Varese: *Movie star*

Terry Caruthers: *Co-pilot of Varese's plane*

Terry Harman: *Congressman*
Eddie Turner: *Mayor of Pittsburgh*

RUSSIA

Igor Popov: *Russian President*
Fyodor Stephanov: *FSB St Petersburg*
Ivan: *Head Ranger in Siberia*
Yuri Yasonov: *Chief aide to Russian President*
Galina Aslanova: *Head of Special Projects, FSB, Moscow*
Pavel Golov: *Aslanova's boss, Director at FSB, Moscow*
Lyudmila Markova: *FSB, Moscow*
Christine Amadore: *CNN, Moscow*
Ling and Kong: *Two Chinese agents in St Petersburg*
Sir Andrew Boles: *UK Ambassador in Moscow*
Julia Boles: *Ambassador Boles's wife*
Martha Goodchild: *Boles's successor as UK Ambassador in Moscow*
Jim Connally: *Embassy driver in Moscow*
Sergei: *Driver of car in Siberia*

GERMANY

Helga Brun: *Chancellor*
Ursula Hauptman: *Chancellor's main aide*
Thomas Hartkopf: *State Secretary at German Ministry of the Interior*
Dr Otto Friedrich: *German Minister of the Interior*

CHINA

Liu Wang-Ji: *President*
Jang Ling-Go: *Director of Forestry and Wildlife, Heilongjiang Province*
Shao Wei-Lu: *His assistant*
Zhang Fu-Sheng: *Minister of State Security (MSS)*
Li Xiao-Tong: *MSS Counter-Intelligence*
Professor Wong: *Archaeologist (in Xian)*
Professor Gung Ho-Min: *in Khabarovsk Hospital*
Wang Tao-Yu: *Chinese Premier*

Deng Biao-Su: *MSS analyst*

UNITED KINGDOM

Edward Barnard: *MP, Secretary of State for the Environment (DEFRA) and later Chairman of the Leave Campaign, still later Chancellor of the Exchequer*

Joyce Dugdale: *Barnard's P/A at DEFRA*

Jeremy Hartley: *MP, Prime Minister at start of book*

Mabel Killick: *MP, Home Secretary, Prime Minister at end of book*

Melissa Barnard: *Edward Barnard's wife*

Dame Jane Porter: *Head of MI5*

Mark Cooper: *Head of MI6*

James Armitage: *Deputy Head of MI6*

Shirley Wilson: *Head of MI6 China desk*

Roger Wales: *Head of MI6 Russia desk*

Giles Mortimer: *Killick's joint-chief aide*

Holly Percy: *Killick's other joint-chief aide*

Tom Milbourne: *MP, Chancellor of the Exchequer at beginning of book*

Sir Oliver Holmes: *Metropolitan Police Commissioner*

Cornelia Gosford: *Deputy Police Commissioner*

Harriet Marshall: *Director of the Leave Campaign*

Christine Meadows: *Harriet Marshall's partner*

Harry Stokes: *MP, former Mayor of London, later Foreign Secretary*

Owen Griffiths: *Stokes' aide*

Joshan Gupta: *Employee of MI5*

Jill Hepworth: *Employee of MI6*

Lillian Peters: *Employee of FCO*

Jack Kellaway: *MP, former Minister for Social Affairs*

David Cole: *MP, Justice Minister*

Andromeda Ledbury: *MP, Leave leader*

Miles Pomfrey: *MP, leader of the Opposition*

Fred Malkin: *Conservative Party Chairman*

Monica Fall: *MP for Blyth*

George Wiley: *Editor of the* Sun *newspaper*

Louise Hitchcock: *BBC journalist/broadcaster*
Arthur Pemberton: *President of the Oxford Union*
Lord Middlebank of Upper Twaddle: *Conservative Grandee*
Jerry Goodman: *Security aide for Edward Barnard*
Mnogo Abewa: *MI5 interrogator*
Noel Garnett: *Veteran BBC journalist*
Thomas Pulborough: *Conservationist*
HRH Prince Philip, Duke of Edinburgh
Simon Henley: *Leader of UKIP (United Kingdom Independence Party)*
Nancy Ginsberg: *BBC political correspondent*
Warren Fletcher: *US Ambassador in London*
Gennadiy Tikhonov: *Russian Ambassador in London*
Nikolai Nabokov: *First Secretary at Russian Trade Mission, London*
Geraldine Watson: *MP for Milton Keynes*
Fenella Gibson: *MP, new Justice Minister*
Sam Berryman: *MP, Department for Exiting the EU*
Mohammed Abbas: *Employee of MI5*
Martin Silver: *Former MI6 officer*
Tina Moller: *Challenged Brexit referendum in Supreme Court*

AUSTRALIA

Mickey Selkirk: *Head of Selkirk Global media empire*
Melanie Selkirk: *Mickey Selkirk's wife*
Ching Ze-Gong & Mrs Fung: *couple who work for Selkirk at Lazy-T ranch*
Hu Wong-Fu: *Owner of Chinese restaurant in Kununurra*
Jim Jackson: *Cattleman and helicopter pilot at Lazy-T ranch*
Dr Phillips: *Doctor at Kununurra Hospital*
Professor Cohen: *Consultant at the Kununurra Hospital*
Professor Irwin Jones: *Australian Toxicologist*

IRELAND

Fiona Barnard: *Daughter of Edward and Melissa Barnard*
Michael Kennedy: *Fiona's partner*

BRUSSELS/BELGIUM

Michael O'Rourke: *President of European Commission*
Mary Burns: *O'Rourke's Chef de Cabinet*
Arne Jacobsen: *Danish Prime Minister*
Eloise Pomade: *Senior Official in EU Council Secretariat*
Lazlo Ferenczy: *Prime Minister of Hungary*
Jacques Petit: *President of France*
Martine Le Grand: *French Presidential candidate*
Otto von Wiensdorf: *German Ambassador to EU in Brussels*
Sir Luke Threadgold: *UK Permanent Representative to EU*

TURKEY

Ahmet Ergun: *President*
Nuray Ergun: *His wife*
General Aslan Bolat: *Turkish Army*

KEY INSTITUTIONS AND AGENCIES

CIA: *US Central Intelligence Agency*
FBI: *US Federal Bureau of Investigation*
FCC: *US Federal Communications Commission*
FCO: *UK Foreign and Commonwealth Office*
FSB: *Successor agency to KGB*
KGB: *Main security agency for Soviet Union*
MI5: *UK Counter-intelligence agency*
MI6: *UK's Secret Intelligence Service*
MSS: *China's Ministry of State Security*

KEY ANIMALS

Amur tiger: *crosses border into China*
Helga: *tiger cub presented by President Popov to Berlin Zoo*
Jemima: *Edward Barnard's bay mare*
Sydney funnel-web spider: *Atrax robustus, bites Edward Barnard at Lazy-T ranch*

ABOUT THE AUTHOR

STANLEY JOHNSON is a former MEP, environmental campaigner, journalist and author of twenty-five books, including ten thrillers, one of which, *The Commissioner*, was made into a feature film starring John Hurt. Stanley won the Newdigate Prize for Poetry and has awards from Greenpeace and the RSPCA. He recently received the RSPB Medal as well as WWF's Leader of the Living Planet Award, both awarded for services to conservation. He is an Ambassador for the United Nations Convention on Migratory Species and Hon. President of the Gorilla Organization.

In the run-up to the EU Referendum in 2016, he founded and co-chaired Environmentalists for Europe. Stanley Johnson recently starred in ITV's *I'm a Celebrity... Get Me Out of Here!* and is taking part in the second reality series of *The Real Marigold Hotel*. He was one of the first presenters of More 4's *The Last Word*, and has appeared on *Have I Got News For You*, *The One Show*, *Pointless* and *The Fake News Programme*.